THE GROTESQUERIE

A Horror Anthology by Women Writers

Compiled and edited by Gerri R. Gray

A HellBound Books Publishing LLC Book
Houston TX

A HellBound Books LLC
Publication

www.hellboundbookspublishing.com

Printed in the United States of America

PREFACE

The witching hour rapidly approaches. Dead leaves, the color of dried blood, crunch beneath your feet as you hurry through the dark and desolate cemetery, uncertain of what lurks in the shadows... and not really sure you want to find out. The night wind moans like a banshee presaging someone's death, and the far-off baying of a hound sends a cold chill along your spine.

Strange figures begin to move ghost-like among the decaying tombstones, and your heart begins to pound as your instinctive fear of the unknown mounts within you. Your breathing increases. Your palms grow clammy. Your skin crawls as you sense eyes watching you.

But whose... or what?

Suddenly, to your dread, your ears pick up the sound of footsteps, growing louder and louder as an unseen horror creeps closer. Paralyzed by fear, you find yourself unable to run... unable to cry for help. Trapped like the proverbial fly in a spider's web, you're completely helpless.

And then, from the shadows around you they emerge—the Graveyard Girls—to share with you nearly thirty nightmarish tales spun from the darkest threads of their imaginations. Take hold of their icy hands and they'll transport you to realm where the most diabolical of supernatural forces lurk and unspeakable terrors lie in wait.

Go forth now and read the spine-chilling stories birthed by this sinister sisterhood—if you're not faint of heart, that is. You'll find some of the darkest things this side of Hell waiting for you within the pages of this anthology: unspeakable things that dwell beneath the floorboards and behind the wallpaper, demonic concertos, and a dive adventure fraught with horrifying consequences are but a few examples of the things that lie ahead. You'll be served a dessert with a deadly bite, and put on a quick weight-loss diet that's simply to die for. You'll meet a young woman who makes a gruesome discovery after mysterious strangers begin to appear in her home, a handsome vampire with a voracious appetite, and a man who regrets his decision to offer a stranger a ride. You'll visit a doll shop whose inventory includes the stuff nightmares are made of. In the realm of *The Graveyard Girls*, you will not only attend a blood-soaked family reunion, you will encounter a less-than-charming prince with an axe to grind, little girls that are sugar and spice and everything not nice, a murderous high-tech stalker, and many other personifications of evil.

Some of these tales will leave you with goose bumps.

Some will surely make you shiver.

And some will haunt you forever.

On a final note, for anyone who might be of the opinion that horror is strictly the domain of men, we graveyard girls are here to change your way of thinking—and to make you sleep with the lights on.

Un-pleasant dreams.

— G.R.G.

—

"It is women who love horror. Gloat over it. Feed on it. Are nourished by it.

Shudder and cling and cry out, and come back for more."— *Bela Lugosi*

Contents

THE GRAVEYARD GIRLS

ETERNALLY YOURS
Written by Xtina Marie

I lay here stretched out on your grave
Begging for the end
There's no hope for me at all
I can't even pretend

Why did you leave me all alone, I scream
As the tears roll down my face
What can I do now?
You- I can't replace

Sweat begins to sting my eyes
As my fingers rake the dirt
And I claw at the ground
Welcoming the hurt

I spit curses at a God
That I've come to despise
And I'll no longer pray forgiveness

To what I can't see with my own eyes
Warm blood stains my white skirt
Self-inflicted wounds- I guess
A small smile forms on my lips
As I take pleasure in the mess

What once was pretty inside me
Has turned my heart pitch black
And I scream again my sorrows
Begging you'll come back

But the skies are turning dark now
The cold winds drawing near
And I bid the demon closer
That I've not sense enough to fear

My throat burns as I plead
The demon take me home
Because I know you hate it
That you left me alone

He strokes my cheek in silence
Moves in for a kiss
And I close my eyes submitting
As the ground below me starts to hiss

The demon leaps from beside me in terror
And I chuckle at his whine
My lover's hand shoots from the earth
And he says, "She's forever mine."

Contributor's bio:
Xtina Marie is an avid horror and fiction genre reader, who became a blogger; who became a published

poet; who became an editor; who now is a podcaster, and an aspiring novelist—and why not? People love her words.

Her first book of poetry, *Dark Musings,* has received outstanding reviews in addition to being nominated for a Bram Stoker Award for poetry. It is likely she was born to this calling. Writing elaborate twisted tales, to entertain her classmates in middle school, would later lead Xtina to use her poetry as a private emotional outlet in adult life—words she was hesitant to share publicly—but the more she shared, the more accolades her writing received.

Light Musings: The Expanded Edition is ready for publication early in 2018. Later in the year, Xtina's dark poetry fans will be treated to some of her darkest work ever in her third book, tentatively titled: *Darkest Sunlight*. Her first romance erotica novel is well under way but has taken a back seat to an ever-increasing number of commitments.

DEAD LINES
Written by M. W. Brown

A harsh click penetrated the silence of the room. The metallic double-click of a handgun was a familiar sound to Esther. The quieter first snap as the slide drew back and the second louder crack as it popped back into place.

It told Esther two things about her intruder: First, the owner of the gun would not kill her straight away, otherwise the gun would have already been cocked and she would already be dead. He, or she, wanted her to know who he was. It gave Esther negotiation time.

The second thing it told her was he was a professional. She knew every creak of the house. She knew where to walk to avoid detection. The intruder must have mapped out the groaning floorboards when she had been out. He wanted to surprise her. He wanted to scare her.

Now in her sixties, with silver-streaked hair, Esther used ageism to her advantage, lulling those who didn't know her with a calm, grandmotherly aura. Those who knew her, including her family, called her 'The Polar Bear.' She appeared soft and cuddly, but possessed the cold viciousness of a merciless predator.

Esther put down her pencil and inched her hands above her head.

"Please…" she said, gulping deliberately, "don't hurt me."

"I know who you are, Mrs. Jones. You can stop the fragile old lady act."

Esther lowered her hands and straightened her body. Calmly, she swiveled round in her chair to face the gunman. On her sofa, lounged a man dressed in black. Black shoes, trousers, shirt and cap were all designed to blend into the background. He rested a Ruger .22 on his thigh, but Esther noted his finger on the trigger and the barrel pointing in her direction. Dark eyes stared at her from an unfamiliar face. He was neither ugly nor handsome, but possessed a face that would not stand out in a crowd, not to the average person anyway. But Esther had not spent her life around average people. She had grown up around characters that made their own laws and followed paths far from normal life. In her world, violence and death could be ordered as easily as a takeaway. Murderers, psychopaths and madmen were her companions. She saw the icy sharpness in his eyes. She saw the harsh lines creeping from the corners of his piercing eyes and thin lips. She saw ruthlessness slithering from him as easily as a hawk spots a snake in the undergrowth.

"And what should I call you?" she asked, matching his icy stare. "Or are you going to say something predictable like your name is not important or I don't need to know?"

He responded with a slight smile. "It doesn't matter

who I am."

Esther would have laughed at his obvious reply, but something about his smile made her guts twist with an icy ripple and all humor fled the room. "Why not?"

"Because I am here in a purely professional capacity."

Despite the frequent threats against her, and a couple of clumsy attempts to kill her, an unexpected chill prickled her neck. Regretting sending everyone away for the evening, she did a roll call of the weapons in her house. Esther's reputation and the company she kept meant that weapons were not an absolute necessity for her. However, she realized the world contained plenty of crazies out there who were oblivious to common sense, and sought revenge or glory, so she kept a knife in a hidden pocket in her handbag, and a tiny razor blade was discretely incorporated into the pendent she usually wore. The bag sat on the kitchen table and, after the bath she had taken an hour earlier, the necklace hung uselessly on the handle of the bathroom cabinet.

"And what profession is that? Carpet salesman? Estate agent?" She flashed her eyes at him and added, "Assassin?"

"You are a perceptive woman, Mrs. Jones." He leaned back in the chair, crossing his legs, but keeping the gun aimed at her.

"Who sent you?"

He scrutinized her face but remained silent.

"Is it a secret?"

"No."

"So, who wants me dead?"

"I would think that's quite a substantial list. Is there anyone who knows you or knows of you that doesn't want you dead?"

Esther laughed, but the sound was hollow to her ears.

"I have a loyal following and a loyal family."

The assassin leaned forward, fixing her with his dark eyes. "You demand loyalty. That is quite different. Who, out of all your people, do you think wouldn't stab you in the back if they knew they would get away with it, if they knew it would be completely undetectable?"

"Nothing is completely undetectable. There is always a trail—money, motive, opportunity. Someone always slips up. Someone is always ready to blab."

"That is if anyone would care to investigate. The authorities would have a weeklong street party to celebrate your demise and then carry out a half-hearted investigation. Those you control would sigh blissfully at being free."

"My family would care," Esther replied, a defensive shrill crept into her voice. She took a deep breath. "My family love me and I love them. Each of us would die to protect the others—" The words caught in her throat. Now the prospect of her own death was uncomfortably close; would she die for them, for anyone?

"They would die to protect the family name and reputation. But would they care if you were gone?"

Esther's blood raced around her body like a turbo-charged snowplow, spewing an icy blast of frozen snow and fear to every cell. She couldn't bear to ask the question, but there was no way she couldn't. "Is it someone in my family?"

He leaned back, and an infuriating smile appeared on his face.

Esther thumped the armrests with her fists. "God damn it, does someone in my family want me dead?"

The assassin waved his gun at her. "Calm down, Mrs. Jones. I heard that you were cool, always in control, never stressed. Psychopath was even mentioned an alarmingly large number of times. Please don't disappoint me, Polar Bear."

Esther slumped back. A dull ache shimmied through her shoulders, down her back and settled in her hips.

"Don't get me wrong. I've long been an admirer of yours." He stood up and walked over to the fireplace. All the time, the gun barrel pointed at her like an ominous compass with Esther's name replacing north. "I know that to be the most feared name in the criminal underworld you must demand loyalty from everyone. You must be ruthless. You must teach harsh lessons and punish disrespect with a sentence tenfold worse than the crime. If you don't, those pesky little minions will be eager to jump all over your throne."

He straightened the clock on the mantelpiece, carefully lining it up so it was parallel with the edge of the shelf and gave her a sympathetic smile. "I know what it's like. It can be quite exhausting and sometimes it takes great courage to know when to step aside."

Esther's brow crinkled. Could she know the assassin? He spoke as if he ran his own organization. Perhaps she knew who he was; any information could be valuable.

"If you are going to kill me, you could at least do me the courtesy of telling me your name."

"I've already told you, my name does—"

"Doesn't matter. Yes, I know. Well, I shall just have to name you myself." She looked her assassin up and down. He was no longer mister average, designed to blend in with the crowd. Standing before her was the unruffled and black-hearted angel of death. "Mr. Death. Yes, I think that will be a suitable name, unless you care to correct me?"

"Mr. Death will do just fine." A flicker of amusement lit up his face for a moment. "I knew this would be an interesting assignment. These things are usually done quickly, but I thought, I hoped, an encounter with the infamous Polar Bear would be interesting. It can get very boring, very… samey."

"I'm so glad I could break the monotony for you," Esther said, sarcasm oozed from each syllable.

Her eyes darted about the room, jumping from the brass lamp on the side table to the crystal decanter on the dresser and to the wine glass on the desk. If she could distract him for a while, she was certain she could disarm him, or kill him. There were plenty of potential weapons. She certainly wasn't ready to die, not tonight and not by the uninspiring hands of a contract killer. When she left this world, it would be on her terms. The story of her life and death would become legend. It would be passed down to future generations in hushed voices filled with awe.

"If you won't tell me who, at least tell me how much. I will double it."

Mr. Death sighed. "The one drawback of engaging with clients—the predictable bartering."

"Well, you are a businessman after all. How much?"

"A contract is a contract. I am honor bound to fulfill it—and you couldn't pay anyway."

Esther raised her eyebrows. "A hitman with scruples. Try me."

He stared over her head and frowned; his gun arm slowly lowered to his side. Esther held her breath; perhaps he was contemplating a deal. She quietly released the air from her lungs so not to disturb him and calculated the time it would take to smash her glass, take four steps towards him and thrust the shards into his neck.

His piercing eyes flicked back to her.

"I shouldn't really disclose the confidential details, but it's quite amusing."

"Oh?" She forced a smile onto her lips.

"The contract is an unusual one. In return for your death, the client will pay with his life."

A cold chill spiked its way up Esther's spine and filled her brain, along with a myriad of questions. Someone was prepared to die just to see her dead? How would Mr. Death benefit with someone else's death?

"So, you see, if you double the price, I would have to kill you twice or him twice. I'm not sure which." He chuckled. "An interesting concept, but even I can see that's a bit pointless."

"What do you get out of it? Someone you need dead, dies. You could kill him anyway. I can give you actual money. Cold hard cash."

He sighed. "If only it were that simple."

"Cash is simple."

He pursed his lips. "I have no beef with the client, but his death would be beneficial. He has little money and came to me because I deal with the more unusual requests. I must say, he really wants you dead."

"Who is it?"

Mr. Death rolled his eyes. "I'm becoming bored of your questions, Mrs. Jones. I think I shall conclude my business now. Things to do, people to see, you know."

He raised the gun.

Esther's gut tensed and, instead of butterflies, a swarm of angry wasps erupted in her stomach. She gulped painfully. Was this it? She wasn't ready to go. She thought of her brothers and their children. Would they mourn her or miss her? Was the traitor in her closest circle? It couldn't be. Mr. Death said he was poor. Her family was financially comfortable. She made sure of that. Did they love her? She wasn't sure, but she valued their loyalty.

"Any final words?"

"I have no regrets, but…"

She had lived her life the only way she knew how. It was the way she was raised. Be tough or die. Her eyes fell on the stack of paper on her desk and an overwhelming surge of sadness engulfed her. She hadn't realized how important the project was to her. The looming vacuum of leaving her work unfinished sucked the strength from her body. She hadn't known how powerful the need was until the possibility of never being able to finish it had slipped into her living room.

This was her regret. Tears prickled in the corner of her eyes and she blinked the unfamiliar sensation away.

Esther took a short breath, straightened her body and looked Mr. Death straight in the eyes.

"There is perhaps one thing you could help me with, before you carry out your assignment."

"Yes?" He raised one eyebrow, inquisitively.

"Before I die, I would like to finish writing my novel. I'm on the final chapter and I can't leave it unfinished. It has become a bit of an obsession with me. I need to finish it."

"I never took you for a writer, Mrs. Jones."

Esther clasped her trembling hands together and forced a shrug. "It's something I've always wanted to do. Life has its way of taking over and before you know it, the years have passed and you haven't done the one thing you dreamed of doing."

"Not really, but then I've never been much of a dreamer."

"Well, this is something I have to finish. I could leave it as a parting gift. Think of it as my last request.'

"I don't usually grant last requests, but I must admit I am a little intrigued. What's it about? I can't imagine you've written a romcom," he chuckled. The sound made the hairs spring to attention on Esther's arms.

"No, that's not really my thing," Esther said and

pushed a smile onto her face. "It's the story of a woman who is born into a life of crime and how she becomes the most respected and feared gangster of all time despite her sex."

"A biography then?"

"I'm flattered you think that's what I am. It is based on my life, but with a little artistic license thrown in. Now I have the perfect ending. A visit from Mr. Death."

"What's it called?"

"Criminal World."

He nodded approvingly. "I've always thought that I should write a book. I have some interesting tales to tell."

I bet you do, Esther thought.

"But I guess no one would want to read it."

Esther was taken aback for a moment. Did he expect her to stroke his ego? Silence hung in the air.

She sighed inwardly and then spoke. "I'm sure they would. I know I would."

"Hmm. Maybe." He stared off into the distance and then shook his head slightly. "How long will you take? Don't think that you can delay things until someone turns up to help you."

"Two hours tops, maybe three. No one will be here until morning. And you will get to be in the story—the enigmatic Mr. Death."

Mr. Death lowered his gun. "Congratulations, Mrs. Jones. You have piqued my interest. I'll let you finish your chapter. Let me read some of what you have written so far."

Esther nodded. The glacial tingling on the back of her neck subsided. She now had either enough time to formulate a plan or at least finish her book. If she died tonight, so be it. But now she could complete her story. She couldn't die with that one regret. A gaping black hole had opened inside her and only writing 'The End' would fill the emptiness. She fidgeted uncomfortably.

"It's only a rough draft." Esther reached for her laptop.

"Slowly, Mrs. Jones."

"Ha. You think I might email someone for help? Post a message on Facebook?"

"Who knows? Just slide it over here." Mr. Death sat back on the sofa and tapped the floor, like an owner summoning his pet.

Esther pushed her laptop over. He rested it on his lap and opened it up, still holding this gun.

"What's the password?"

"Gavreel."

Mr. Death smiled as he typed. "Ah, the angel of peace. An interesting choice. Why that name?"

Esther frowned. "I don't know. I guess I saw the name somewhere. It stuck in my head."

He chuckled. "I like it. Mr. Death and the Angel of Peace. Perhaps you should make that your new title."

Esther shrugged.

"You'll find the file on my desktop."

"I see it. Do you need this to write?"

"No. I usually write the first draft on paper and edit it as I type it up."

Mr. Death nodded in her direction. "Okay. Get to it and I'll read it on here. Just remember my gun will be on you at all times. You make one move from that chair and I will shoot you. No questions. No final requests. No final chapter."

"I understand." Esther turned to her desk and stuck her pencil in the automatic pencil sharpener. Its buzzing filled the quiet room. She was used to playing classical music while she worked but guessed she could forgo it this time.

She grabbed a sheet of paper and wrote 'Chapter' at the top, paused because she couldn't remember if it should be eighteen or nineteen, and then added 'The Final' in front.

Her pencil hovered above the page. Her stomach flipped over and back. She realized this was the first time someone else would read her words.

"You know, I haven't shown it to anyone else?"

"Quit stalling and get writing."

Esther sighed and wrote the first line:

A harsh click penetrated the silence of the room.

* * *

Esther pushed her pencil into the sharpener and looked over at the clock. She was shocked to see that an hour and a half had already passed since they had last spoken. The room had been silent except for the scratching of her pencil on the paper, the clicking of the mouse by Mr. Death and the frequent whir of the automatic sharpener.

"How are you getting on, Mrs. Jones?"

"Good."

"I'm surprised at how much you are writing, considering the circumstances."

Esther laughed hollowly. "It's amazing how an impending deadline sharpens the mind. What about you? What do you think?"

"Hmm…" The leather sofa creaked and Esther turned in her chair. Mr. Death was walking over to the fireplace. "You use 'that' way too much and the chapter on your family history is a bit dry, but otherwise it's a good story, so far."

"Do you think I should leave the background bits out?"

"Oh no. It's interesting and boy do you have one fucked up family. I mean, two centuries of bitches, murderers and psychopaths is some back-story. Just make it a bit more entertaining, maybe some humor."

"I can see that. But I don't think I've the time to change it, do you?"

Mr. Death chuckled. "That shows how much I'm enjoying it. I almost forgot why I was here… almost."

Esther shivered and looked back at her pages. The carbon scribbles blurred and merged into dark trails on the paper. She blinked them back into focus. "Can I carry on?"

He nodded and returned to his seat.

* * *

Esther sharpened her pencil and wrote 'The End' in crisp, large letters. She let out a tired sigh and stretched her arms forward on the desk, releasing the tension in her muscles.

She stole a quick glance over her shoulder and felt a small pang of pride. Mr. Death stared at the screen. Its faint glow gave his skin an eerie luminosity. He was completely still, except for his eyes. They darted rapidly back and forth, across the screen. He was engrossed.

She glanced to her left. The kitchen door was eight feet away. Numbness had crept into her legs, but could she make it across the room before Mr. Death realized what was happening?

"I may be enjoying your book, Mrs. Jones, but I'm still aware of your every move," he said without looking up. "I'm nearly finished."

Esther settled back, lined up her pencils, and stared at the pages on her desk. A dizzy relief spread through her head. She had finished her story. Whatever followed, the book was complete. Her desire, her need, had been fulfilled.

She wasn't afraid to die now. She had stared at death many times in her life. The one that had shaken her the most had been averted by a stranger. She had been on the way to the hospital to see a friend, and, in her rush, had hurried across the road without looking, straight into the path of a bright red double-decker bus. The terrified look on the driver's face was still etched in her brain. A rush of stale, warm air hit her body and she froze. If the stranger hadn't pushed her out the way... The man helped her up and then collapsed on the bench. His hands trembled as he ran them through his hair. The poor soul had been just as shaken as Esther. She shook as she dusted herself off and went to thank him, but he had vanished. Perhaps he had recognized her. She promised herself if she ever saw him again, he was due a substantial reward: Money for a life. Some people saved lives. Some people took lives away.

In the silence, her mind turned again to who would dare to take a contract out on her. She wondered what sort of person would give up their own life just to see her dead. Revenge was understandable, but not at such a cost.

Mr. Death's voice pierced the silence.

"It's riveting. Are you finished?"

Esther nodded. "It's done."

The sofa creaked, and light footsteps crossed the room. A shadow fell over the desk. Esther tensed and curled her fingers around her pencils.

"You want to see how it ends?"

She spun round in her chair with the speed and ferocity of a bear. Mr. Death opened his mouth, but before a word could leave it, Esther thrust the sharpened pencils deep into his neck. The hard points pierced his skin like skewers into Plasticine. For a moment, no one moved. They were both frozen in a macabre tableau of contradiction: a frail, elderly woman with viciousness etched into every wrinkle on her face, and a strong, calm man with a slightly puzzled expression.

Time unfroze. His forehead crinkled in confusion and Esther yanked the makeshift weapon out of his neck. Blood spurted out, showering her in warm, sticky streams. His gun dropped from his hand as he grabbed the jagged wound. Esther struck again. The pencils drove mercilessly into the back of his hand with a sickening crack. Mr. Death let out a gurgled gasp and crumpled to the floor.

With his hands clawing at his neck, he writhed like a snake. Esther pushed herself back in her chair, watching the dark pool of blood spread around him. With a final shudder, the assassin's hands thudded to the floor. His dead, empty eyes stared blankly at Esther.

She turned back to her desk and removed a tissue from her pocket. With a sigh, she wiped her face and dabbed at the blood-splattered pages. A metallic smell of blood wafted around her and she crinkled her nose. Billy would have to come and clear the mess up before it left a permanent stain on the floor, but at least her final chapter was still readable.

A polite cough from behind Esther made her jump. She sprung to her feet and spun round. The breath caught in her throat and her tissue dropped to the floor, turning crimson as it soaked up the blood of her victim. It was her turn to wear the confused expression. Her eyes blinked rapidly, not believing what she saw.

Mr. Death stood before her, straightening out the creases in his sleeves. His neck was clean and smooth. No wound, hole or mark blemished his skin. He took a step backwards, away from the pool of congealing blood and raised one eyebrow.

"Now, that wasn't a very nice thing to do, was it, Mrs. Jones? But then I shouldn't have expected anything less from you."

Esther opened her mouth, but nothing came out. Numbness spread through her body and she grabbed the back of the chair for support.

"I was thinking that it might be fun if you meet my client. I'm sure you're curious about who took the contract out on you… and a few other things." He chuckled. "Let's call him, shall we?"

Esther dropped into her chair. Lost for words, not in control and confused, all unfamiliar sensations to her, she could only gawp at the impossible figure.

"Oh Gavreel, Gavreel. Come out, come out wherever you are," Mr. Death said, theatrically.

Why is he calling out my password? Esther didn't think it was possible for her to be any more confused. She had to be dreaming.

A young man stepped through the doorway. He wore a tatty, faded, white t-shirt and ripped jeans. Dark smudges sagged below his tired eyes and his skin was a pale, sickly gray. He managed to look old and young at the same time.

Esther frowned. His face was familiar, but she could not place him.

"Esther, meet Gavreel. The one who wants you dead. The one who will die to see it happen. Esther, meet your guardian angel."

"I—I don't understand." Esther could feel her sanity breaking. *This is not possible.*

"I think you should be the one to explain it to her," Mr. Death said, looking at Gavreel.

"It's true." Gavreel shuffled further into the room. His eyes drifted to the bloodstain on the floor. He shuddered and shifted his gaze to his scuffed trainers. "I am your guardian angel—your family's guardian angel. Since 1663, I have protected your family. Your great-great-great, I don't know how many greats, grandfather was a good man. He was honest, selfless, kind, and died saving the lives of twelve children, trapped in a burning school. We asked him what his reward should be and all he wanted was for his family to be safe, to be protected from danger. And not just his family—all his descendants—right to the end of the line. I was assigned the task. I became your family guardian angel." Gavreel sighed, and kept his eyes down, never once looking at Esther.

Mr. Death picked up his gun and chuckled. "This would've livened up the back-story in your book."

"It was a good assignment at first. I watched over everyone and had little to do—diverting a runaway horse, pushing someone out the way of a falling tree branch. One particularly hard Christmas, I even got to play Santa Claus. But then the family started to go bad. Small things at first—lying, shoplifting. Then, bigger crimes: Blackmail, robbery and," Gavreel choked on the next word, "murder."

"It's—I mean it can't be—I don't believe—" Esther's voice trembled as she spoke. Her calmness and control melted from her body.

"Unfortunately, it's true. And I have to protect your family until the last one dies. No matter what they do. It has been *written*."

Mr. Death rolled his eyes. "You and all your rules. See what crazy shit it causes."

"They've changed the rules now. But this was one of the old contracts," Gavreel said defensively.

"And you got stuck with this lot."

Gavreel nodded and dropped onto the sofa. He buried

his head in his hands. "I can't do it anymore. Protecting these monsters goes against everything good that I believe."

"But isn't all life valuable, according to him?" Mr. Death pointed his thumb up to the ceiling.

Gavreel looked at Mr. Death. His eyes glistened. "I'm so tired. Too tired."

Esther sat in silence watching the unbelievable exchange. Her body tingled, and she felt light-headed. It was as if she was watching other people act out a chapter in a book.

Her guardian angel ran his hands through his hair and Esther gasped. It was the stranger who had saved her life. It was the same movement. The same shape. The same sad face. Gavreel had saved her that day.

"So that's why you contacted me." Mr. Death turned away from Gavreel and towards Esther. "You see, I work for... the other side. I deal with the contracts. When you hear of someone selling their soul to the devil, it's me who deals with it. I usually deal with the admin side of things, but occasionally I get out and take on the more interesting cases.

"Poor Gavreel has no way out of this. You see, guardian angels can't die or welch on a contract, but I can take their souls. Angel souls are a boost to our power and always fun to play with," he added with a grin.

A flood of icy tremors rippled through Esther's body. She shook her head. "This can't be happening."

"Oh, it is. You'll believe it soon enough. Time's a-ticking." He pointed the gun at her head.

"No!" Gavreel screamed and sprung to his feet.

"Too late. It's time to settle up." Mr. Death clicked his fingers and Gavreel vanished.

He turned his attention back to Esther.

"See you soon, Mrs. Jones."
Death grinned and pulled the trigger.

THE END

Contributor's bio:

M.W. Brown likes to sneak away and travel to planet Bowie to write horror, supernatural thrillers and anything dark that pops into the imagination en route. Ziggy, Aladdin and the Thin White Duke supply copious amounts of coffee while keeping the mood suitably twisted. While on planet earth, she wanders around in the middle of the UK and, when not working, can be found people watching and searching for the elusive 'normal person' to study and dissect. For further information and details on other publications, please visit: http://www.mwbrown.co.uk

DEMONS OPUS
Written by Rebecca Kolodziej

*H*ollow chords, deep as a wise man's soul. Powerful and courageous. Weak and melancholy.

It's strange, isn't it, how a sheet of music can mock one's soul. Those chords, just as a man's life reach their zenith then fall into baritone despair to finally fade.

Those gentle tinklings of happy memories will stay with a man until he draws his last breath. The deep, mournful twangs will continue to pierce the heart until it can bleed no more.

For you see, music is powerful thing, an incredible thing. It is the key to life. And the symphony of death.

Music is the funeral march that wanders the cobble streets. Music, is the cries of a grieving widow as she whispers her final farewell to her deceased betrothed. Music is the sound of a dying man's heart fading away. Thump thump. Twice at first, thump thump. Twice again. Then slower, thump....thump, the final chord is struck and the dead man's song ceases to play.

This is what the note had read from my late friend. I, Maurice Van Hern, am a constructor of music, composer of emotions. I am a man of music, the piano being my chosen profession. They say of some musicians that when they play a piece of music that it sounds beautifully haunting but they never really question if the music itself could ever be haunted.

I know, I would have laughed too and I often did. For how could a piece of music be haunted?

I suppose one would call me a skeptic when it came to the abnormal and unnatural; I am, myself, a rather terse man. I have known many acquaintances who have insisted that they have experienced the paranormal. Most cases I have heard of have insisted upon communicating with loved ones beyond the grave, most whom communicate via a séance accompanied by a batty old woman who projects forth the so-called messages from beyond our realm.

I even attended one, once, and laughed my way out of it the entire time I sat there.

When I entered the grand stage, my eyes were focused on the glossy, black piano that awaited my presence. The auditorium roared with praise as I had entered the stage, their clapping becoming music to my ears. Ironic, isn't it?

Their all-time favorite was to hear me perform the dark and broody masterpiece composed by the late Ludwig van Beethoven. He had been a good friend. I was devastated when he passed. The musical world lost a great talent the day my old friend left us. However, it seemed the rumors of Ludwig's madness were true.

The day I received news of his passing, I was at home in old London, sitting at my piano as I wrote a piece of music that I was preparing to use at my next show. I never got to complete that piece, however, as I received an unexpected visitor who claimed to be a mutual acquaintance of Ludwig's. I found this strange, as Ludwig was a solitary man. He never interacted with the outside world. He was too engrossed with his music.

This man, who claimed to have known my old friend for a very long time, said that if anything should happen to him, I should become the new owner of this strange piece of music that Ludwig had been working on, but had died before completing. I found this notion very strange, for even though I knew the late Beethoven; he never really seemed the type to entrust a man with a piece of material that he had not yet completed.

"I don't understand," I postulated. "Why would Ludwig entrust me with such a personal piece? Surely it should now be placed in the archives at the British Library?"

The burly man, who had delivered this anomaly to my doorstep, simply nodded his head in a slow, precise manner. "Indeed, sir, you are right," he interjected. "But the old madman clearly stated in his will that if anything should happen to him, that this particular sheet should be handed down to you immediately after death."

"Preposterous!" I exclaimed exasperatedly. "I knew the man; he would never do such a thing. He was very secretive with his music; therefore, I cannot take this from you. Take it away. Take it to the archives or, better yet, bury it with him."

But, of course, that never happened.

"I'm afraid I cannot leave here until this is in your hands," the burly man addressed, calmly. He was very persistent. He left without saying another word, but it was his eyes that spoke volumes to me. There was an air about him that I could not fail to brush aside. He left the thin, brown parchment on the table near the door with his back facing me. He turned to face me once more, his hand resting gently on the brass doorknob. I will never forget the strange look that flashed in that man's eyes. There was something hidden behind his gaze that exuded a strange unease.

The parchment sat, untouched, on my dresser for a few days. I often tried to overlook the envelope, not wanting any part in Ludwig's madness. However, it was on one night in particular that I felt a compelling urge to open up the letter and read what the old fool had written me in his last remaining moments of lunacy.

Situated at my piano, my mind wandered as my fingers caressed the keys effortlessly. A small gas lamp sat atop the grand piano, basking my face in the warm glow it emitted. I delighted at the sound of the deep booming bass the final chord resonated around the parlor. I sat still for a moment, rejoicing in the vibrations the piano sent rising up my hands, when the brown parchment fell from its perch and onto the floor.

Inasmuch as a week it had sat there, untouched, never moving from that exact location, only now to fall to the ground as if pushed by a gentle wind. As if expecting to see a window open, my eyes began to contemplate a reasonable source for the sudden breeze, only to find nothing. Not even the gas lamp flickered. There was simply no breeze blowing through the house.

Believing that I was tired and that my mind was just too weary to comprehend reality in that moment, I opted to retire to my chambers and rest for the night. However, upon my approach to the fallen parchment, I became aware that I could not just simply return it back to its rightful place atop the dresser. Indeed, it came with me to my chambers, furthermore perching it on the vanity near the window in plain sight.

It was on this night that I was awoken by the most bewitching sound echoing from the piano parlor. I whirled out of bed instantly, my ears attuned to this strange phenomenon. At first, perhaps, I tried reasoning that the maid had risen from her chambers early and had taken it upon herself to play at my piano, but I knew the girl had more common sense than that.

My eyes were greeted by darkness and a queer chill filled the air. Already could I feel the predawn chill cutting into my flesh as my body left the warm sanctuary of my bed. Slipping my feet into the velvet slippers that lay tucked safely beneath the bed, I rose to my feet, searching the room for a light. Certain that I had placed the gas lamp on the vanity next to the parchment before I had slipped into bed, its sudden absence now bewildered me.

The melody evoked a peaceful state of mind, gentle at first before falling into a darker tone, sympathetic almost. The sound was alluring, transfixing, hypnotizing, and I knew I had to follow it, curiosity burning within my heart.

But, at first, a nagging interest in the unopened parchment took over me.

I reached through the darkness, my fingertips brushing against the brisk night. Blindly, my hands scoured the vanity for the envelope that I had set there only hours earlier, only to now find that it was no longer where it had been seated. Something within me spurred me forwards and out of my room in my own brief moment of madness. My mind began to conjure complicated scenarios: a burglar, a drunkard—but never had my mind entertained the possibility of something more unnatural than the living.

The hypnotic melody grew louder as I grew closer to the music parlor, my heart quickening with each strike of the chord. The door to the parlor was half closed, just as I had left it, and no light shone through the small crack. I stood at the doorframe, breathing rapidly as my eyes desperately tried to spy the source of the sound, only to find obscurity and fear resting bitterly upon my tongue.

"Hello!" I called out, shakily, anxiety constricting my vocal chords so that I sounded like a choking frog. At once, the music ceased forthwith in a rather unsettling and jarring manner. For a drawn-out moment, I stood with my face pressed, peering through the crack of the door, breathing hard as my hot breath mingled around me. "I know someone is there! Speak now and you may leave my premises unscathed. Refuse, and you will be escorted off my property by a man of the law!"

But the threats fell only on deaf ears. I was my met by a stony silence.

Without warning, something shifted behind the door that I was peering through. At first, I thought my eyes to have deceived me before I saw the swirling mist pooling around the piano. Incipiently brooding over the mystifying haze, I was not prepared for the horror that peeped back at me through the crack in the door.

I glimpsed a face of ashen gray, its pallid flesh bilious and diseased. Only briefly did I foresee the ghastly pockmarked features as well as the entity's elongated face gawking back at me through the crack in the door. Its mouth seemed to open its shrinking lips, revealing a cavernous, black void that was to be its mouth. A distressing shriek vibrated up the throat of the being, shrill and penetrating. Just as the mouth was nothing but a hole, its eyes, too, resembled two sunken recesses, scaled crust thick with canker and putrescence.

Withdrawing at once, the figure there and then dematerialized as soon as my breath expelled my lungs at the sight of it. Tumbling backwards, my head impacted with the wall behind me, rendering me just about unconscious, but even through my hazed delirium, my ears still made out the sounds of sharp, incessant fingers banging their agitated nails over fragile keys, forcing the piano to screech out of pitch before an abrupt silence.

Thrice the clock chimed before the coming of the dawn awakened me from my trepidation, and thrice I blinked exasperated into the blackness. The flush of morning broke through the heavy drapes, bright and resplendent, blinding me momentarily, although waking my senses completely.

"Sir, is everything alright? You look pale as the morning light!"

I cannot say how long I was perpetually focused in the parlor or that I heard the maid of the house approach me; I must have been so unsettled that even the walls of reality gave me a turn. Spinning on my heel, my eyes glowering into the innocent maid's face, I replied to her with chagrin.

"All's well! That is all you need to know!"

Leaving her with every intention of making her feel small, my actions were out of distress and I found myself pitying the girl, but I had no time to ponder over her questions. My mind was fixated on one thing only: the hideous specter from my parlor doorway.

"You're losing your mind, old man," I scoffed at my behavior. "You are simply overtired and overworked. All you need is a good night's sleep." But then I remembered the parchment envelope and how it had not been where I had left it. "Foolishness!" I scolded myself. "Nonsense, bloody ghosts? Pull yourself together man!" But even then as I uttered those words, I found my feet trudging back down the stairs towards the parlor.

What I had expected to see, I did not know. In my mind, I needed some sort of validation as to what had caused such a sickness. Somehow, I was convinced that the parchment wasn't sitting on the piano, that it was still in my room and that I had imagined the entire thing; yet, by the time I had convinced myself otherwise, I was already staring at the brown envelope sitting in the music stand.

A sudden rage consumed me in that moment, an animosity so belligerent, so menacing, that my actions resembled those of a madman's. Jaunting towards the piano, I viciously snatched the envelope from its stand and thrust the pages into the crackling fire burning in the hearth.

From behind me there came a sharp exhale. Turning my eyes to the young maid, she was eying me with a horrified expression upon witnessing such an irrational outburst.

"Sir, the parchment!" she proclaimed, rushing towards the hearthside to rescue the burning pages.

"Leave it!" I bellowed, frustrated and weary. "Let them burn! I told the man I wanted no part in Ludwig's madness! Let the damned pages burn, along with his legacy. I want no part of it."

I left her kneeling in front of the fireplace, bewildered, as I turned my back, ready now to return to my chambers. Climbing the staircase, my limbs hanging heavy against my side, my body felt as if I were hauling rolls of lead. A great fatigue consumed my aching form. Deprived and hallucinating, I put the night's events down to a rather overactive mind. But, for the coming morning that was to follow, no man could have been ready.

I awoke with a new found lightheartedness. A great sense of relief washed over me and I awoke feeling refreshed and well slept. The fire had been stoked upon entering the piano parlor, the dying embers still breathing tiny puffs of smoke. Expecting to find the parchment nothing but a burnt pile of ashes, you can imagine how astounded I became immediately upon seeing the brown envelope sitting unmarred, unburnt, and in perfect state of affairs atop the dying cinders. Never have I known cowardice until that moment. I knew there should be nothing left. My eyes saw the white-hot fury in which the flames burnt. They had been hot enough to melt metal, yet a simple thing such as paper remained uncharted.

There is no other reason other than inquisitiveness that compelled me to remove the pages. For something to remain untouched and in perfect condition was thought provoking, and my curious mind desired to behold the magic that kept those pages from burning.

Gingerly removing the pages from their ashy entombment, my composer eyes saw that the music written was rather pedestrian.

Nearly drowsing in an almost volcanic bath that evening, I reveled in the complacency the hot water provided for nagging ache in my bones. Reclining, I inhaled the steam and relaxed for the first time since that begotten envelope appeared on my desk. What ailing lunacy had let Ludwig turn that envelope to my door? Perhaps it was just my mind, indigestion at best. A forward-thinking man has no time to place in spooks and specters. The scent of French lavender caressed my senses, and I let my body revert to my usual bath time hobby. I tinkled at the keys of a piano that existed in my mind, finding that my best work always began in the bath. I raised my hands to play my phantom piano and slowly let my fingers descend.

There was an awful calamity of drongs and clangs the

moment I began, from the study downstairs.

Maddening, infuriating, these words fell far too short of what I felt in that moment, upon hearing my beloved abused so brutally.

I shot up, sloshing hot water over the black and white tiled floor. Reaching for my robe, I marched into the hallway; as I proceeded into the hall, I could hear the ferocity with which the keys were smashed cruelly against their will. Usually, that beautiful muse sang for me; now she screamed. Cocooned in nothing but a bathrobe, I fumed along the hallway, full of piss and vinegar, intent on thrashing whomever it was who was playing my piano without my permission and with such cruel abandon at this hour.

With haste, I threw open the heavy oaken doors to the study, only to stiffen where I stood. The instrument I knew to weigh more than what three men could lift comfortably, hovered inches above my chamber floor, my playing stool occupied by none other than that terrifying hatchet-faced specter.

I could barely tear my vision from this spectacle; the thing's lithe, twisted form was dressed in a tattered and decayed pianist's suit, ragged sails billowing in its ghastly wind. Its hair, a wild shock of shoulder-length, wind-blown static, flailing side-to-side as it enjoyed its own hellish cacophony. Its face still harbored the pallid ashen gray of decay, just as it had appeared before.

The room became anarchy and darkness, shelves rocking viciously back and forth, spewing heavy books forth to the floor in a beaten pile. The intensity of this madness tied inexplicably to the ghoul's own. The French windows exploded open as a wild gust of wind tore through the velvet drapes, forcing the glass to shatter and the door to slam shut. Suddenly, the chilling bone-like fingers of dread crept on needle-like feet up my spine.

The thing was still sitting at the levitating instrument, seemingly engrossed in every sonorous note. Taking not a breath lest I give away my presence, I began a snail's pace creep towards the unlit fire and the mantle above, whereabouts hung my father's old saber. Every step was long and desperately methodical; every slow creak of floorboards could signal my demise. There, just beyond my hopeless grasp, lay my only hope at salvation. The music intensified higher, taking my heartbeat to dangerous excitement.

The feel of cold steel felt like a lover's embrace; slowly I lowered the sword and, as silently as I could, unsheathed the blade. My only indication that I was yet to be seen was the continued draconian sonata still in play.

"Leave me, demon!" I bellowed, confident in the strength of muscle and tempered steel; I pirouetted about in a wild haymaker swing, all power and no finesse. There was a satisfying crunch as the blade bit into mummified flesh; I spun to inspect the damage.

It sat, in dead silence, blade embedded in its neck. I took this reprieve of noise to find my victory. Then the shriveled husk began to shudder in random jerks and twitches. I watched in dismay as an impulse crept up its cracking spine, culminating in the shoulders.

A sickening snap, like the sudden stop of a neck in a hangman's drop.

A berserk crescendo screeched forth from the piano as its head snapped backwards, cackling maniacally as it eyeballed me from above, mummified eyes staring down at me with a dried up century-old grin stretched across its crumbling features. The sickening sound of glass being heel-trodden onto cobbles filled the air as the torso twisted around to meet its disfigured body, legs still facing, the keys of the piano still playing without the aid of the devil's hands.

Confidence deflated the moment the being twitched its gangly limbs towards me, outstretched arms hovering in mid air, as an insidious cackle escaped its granular lips. Fear paralyzed me, momentarily, before spurring my legs into action. I tore from the room, my hands scratching against cold oak as my body collided with the doors. Behind me, the sounds of a maniacal creature gibbering and whooping emerged in the background, leaving me ill with trepidation.

I turned to eye the creature, only to find it thrashing wildly behind me in the same awkward position that it had been sitting in at the piano. Its twisted limbs had the appearance of a scuttling spider; so crude did the apparition allude. Its ashen features pierced the blackness, its ghastly appearance, slack-jaw rattling loosely as its vile body juddered along the tiled floor.

Fleetingly, my feet moved across those tiles in hopes to turn a sharp corner, when my body came crashing to a grinding halt, my head colliding with the floor. I relied only on the peripheral vision in that moment, fluorescent white lights flashing in my mind like a camera as the spider-like entity scurried across the floor towards me. The last thing my mind processed before my eyes could take the strain no more was the slack-jawed grin impending.

I awoke to a symphony of panic piercing my ears. The first thing to greet me was the cold kiss of the ceramic tiles that I lay upon. A small pool of blood swirled upon the obsidian glittering in the morning light, my head pounded as if that same light was piercing my head and burning inside my skull. A heavy unease bubbled in the pit of my stomach as disorientation and concussion spun my vision. Each fiber of my tired frame ached and I yearned for my bed. Flashes of the previous night sparked in my mind's eye, forcing my eyes to twitch as the intensity of the pain grew.

"Sir...Master Van Hern?"

I could hear the urgency in the tone of the voice that spoke to me. Rising slowly to my knees, looking around the room, I saw a panic-stricken boy staring down at me, concern flooding his young features.

"Are you alright? Do you need a doctor? I can run back to the theatre and tell them that you're too hurt to play tonight!"

The thought sent me ungainly upwards, rising to my feet. I would have no such thing happen! I had worked too hard and for too long to let this setback end me. Swaying and clutching my robe, failing gracefully at finding any kind of composure, I eyed the young errand boy carefully before giving him my answer.

"No, Gods no. It's a minor bump I can assure you," I lied. "I am well and will be at the theatre at eight o'clock on the dot!"

"Yes sir." The boy turned to run back.

"Wait! Wait, William, correct?" I proffered.

"Billy, sir."

"I need two things of you: first, take my sheet music from the parlor; it's in the envelope." I sluggishly lurched to my jacket hanging on the door, finding some loose coins. "Take this and stop by the chemist; I need something to dull the pain. You can keep any change, Fair?"

"Yes, sir. I'll be quick as I can." And with that, he tore away from me.

I spent the rest of the day trying to make myself presentable and testing that my functions were still adequate. A few hiccups and migraines later, I felt confident to perform. So I washed the blood from my hair and put on my best suit and headed for the door.

At around half past seven, I began a beleaguered stroll to the theatre; for once my cane was bracing me upright and not just for fashion. The dizziness had left with mercurial speed once the fresh, crisp air caressed my scalp. The streetlights cast golden slivers onto the wet cobbles; my shoes rang out a distinct clip-clop as I walked along this empty street.

Suddenly, to my left, I caught sight of that face of terror. Recoiling and tripping over my own feet, I landed hard on my lower back on the street. Grasping my cane like a weapon, I scrambled to my feet and readied myself to be finished off by this bastard, but not without a fight. I found myself face-to-face with no ghoul or apparition, simply a well-cleaned window and my own dour reflection.

Upon arriving at the theatre, I found Mr. Tallow fretting and pacing; he didn't even speak, simply directing my attention to the clock. I was late by a few minutes. With no reply other than my shame, I made haste to the stage. The gathered crowd hushed from their quiet chatter as I approached the piano; there were hundreds of them. No small amount of pressure fell on me.

"Ladies and gentlemen, my apologies for my lateness." Their eyes focused now, and true silence fell. "No excuses then, I promised you all a new piece, and here it is."

I sat in silence at the grand black piano, its ivory keys greeting me like the broad smile of a cherished friend. My sheet music lay on top, still in the envelope. I reached out and withdrew my music.

Alas, this was not my music. That God damned demon song had followed me, here and now at the hour of my potential magnum opus. I looked back to the audience; I lived well, but even my pockets could not reimburse this many people.

Biting my lip and wincing with anticipation, I gave in. This was all I had; I was not intent on disappointing.

I struck the first note and suddenly my apprehension left me; this was my skill. My deft hands began their intricate dance across the ivories, fingers scattering quick and precise to where they needed to be. The song that I had avoided and decried for days suddenly came alive to me; it was a simple song, but the tempo was irregular and prone to catching you off guard.

It was longing. You could hear it in every stroke of hammer on string; this was music of sadness. Each pluck of high note set against the dark and demure tune was a tear from the eye of a forlorn and lost beauty, striking the hearts of all who heard. This was not the dreadful, maddening din of that blighted phantom. I looked up for the first time in this dreaded performance; I expected the rows to be hardly populated by now, what with this music being so far removed from my own. But far from that; there appeared to be more people arrived, and every single one had the gentile glint of tears in their eyes. Each one was leaning forward in their seat, visibly showing the emotion of sorrow. I had spent my last two days in denial of genius.

Turning back, I barely caught the music. Suddenly it took a more ominous tone, like the quiet tendrils of rage spreading through a broken heart. I could feel it too, welling inside my own chest. I felt personally wronged and viciously vengeant, as though I was the subject of this sonata. I could feel the tension in my hands and chest; my fingers began to crook as though they were wrapping around some bastard's throat. This rage was growing, unfulfilled, festering. It was rotting me from the inside out; I was filling with hot coursing fire that flushed my face and made my body itch.

My vengeance was creeping at my mind, undone, driving me to madness. This powerful song was growing dangerously fast; I couldn't tear my eyes away for fear of missing a note.

I turned the page; desperation sunk in; there was a second part. I had not checked; there needed to be another piano and player. I started to panic; it slicked on my hot rage and I began to lose focus on all but the page. The world around me was abyss, forgiving the paper on my piano. I pulled in every ounce of my reserves, determined to play two parts. I felt as though my fingers were to tear free of their constraining flesh, as I performed nothing shy of a miracle.

Faster and faster and faster, ever increasing in tempo and desperation. Fragments of a memory of pain, a single thought played to increase eternity. Rage undone, vengeance unavenged and desires suppressed. Clawing and scrapping and shredding, no rest or respite.

No peace, no rest.

Let the bloody chill winds howl and whistle; they should find no more peace than me. Let the lights go out as my own have surely done. Let there be purpose for this grating at my mind.

I barely noticed myself beginning to cackle madly.

After endless hours, it seemed I reached the finale; it was a glorious release of the building feeling in the sonata. I felt as though I had been reborn. Standing up, I felt the chill air on my sweat-covered body; this had been an ungodly task. I turned, eyes down and bowed. There was nothing, not even crickets. I could not blame them. This was not what they had come for.

Raising my head to see the final nail in the coffin of my career, I witnessed the silence and its cause.

In every chair in every row, and spilling down the aisles, were bodies—torn and shredded, bleeding from anywhere soft enough for a finger or umbrella or cane to penetrate. Stabbed and smashed corpses, all undeniably dead. They had torn each other apart; some held makeshift weapons; some held clumps of bloody hair, and most held a gruesome part of someone else.

I began to walk amongst them. Skinless knuckles, fingernails thick with gore or ripped from their cuticles. These were common sights, much like the bruised and ruptured flesh and torn clothes.

But, by far the worst, the most harrowing thing—it wasn't the carnal depravity of the violence, nor the seeming unity of the insanity—the worst thing of all was a shared feature across all the dead:

It was that grin…

That same, gaunt, tight, distended rictus...

That demon smile from my study, at my piano…

On every single face.

THE END

HONG
Written by Anya Lee

I always fixated on my hand whenever I outstretched it towards the sky. I could capture the slip of star-dotted night between my palms and fingertips as I wiggled them. It looked as if the sky consisted of wet, haphazard brush strokes, dripping down between these concrete spaces, painting Chinatown with a smoky hue of vivid purples and blacks. My face wrinkled in delight each time I felt like I was grabbing it, and even though I was freezing out here, I was well occupied. It was my mom's birthday dinner, and I had just worn the dress she had picked out for me. I forgot to pair it with a coat, but who really wore coats? I was at peace with my shivering.

Well… until the windows above my little snow-covered playground began to rattle and slam open.

"Victoria?"

The voice was upset and nasal; I knew who it was. I looked up, pushing back my fringed bangs.

"Victoria! Get up here now! Put on a coat! You're

going to get it if your grandmother sees you!"

Red lipstick, a dyed brown updo, hoop earrings and deep red, v-neck shirt covering poorly adhered implants were all signatures of my Aunt Eileen, who was simply someone who ran more hot than cold—probably a hereditary thing. Her tone indicated that more was going wrong upstairs than the high-fire cooking. Her on-again/off-again cheating, white boyfriend, Greg, was entirely absent—a place he liked to stay when he was lying to Eileen. It was sad, but I wouldn't like being around her either since I had never heard her do anything but scream. I chuckled lightly at the thought of her screaming at him constantly, little airy breaths escaping my lips as I fixated on how much I was laughing, while staring at her. Eileen's eyes expanded after some light sniffling, and a telltale look of disappointment and annoyance melted her tackily painted face.

She most definitely knew I was high. The entire alleyway was lit up, the smell of whatever it was I had gotten from that Cuban boy at school was definitely strong, and was so thick in this alley, all you had to do was basically breathe to smell it. Hopefully, she would inhale deeper and catch a contact. I laughed again, imagining her high.

Eileen's lips pursed and her eyes, which were accumulating a fair share of smudged eyeliner, narrowed. She drew her neck back in the most melodramatic way she could muster.

"Get inside," she snapped at me, slamming the window shut after drawing the shutters.

So, I shrugged. I dropped the blunt in my other hand and let it die down in the snow. Whatever I had gotten was mostly smelly stems and seeds, so it wasn't a huge waste. I pranced about, walking to the front of the building near the busy sidewalk. One of my neighbors was exiting the building, and stared me down—because, of course, he would. The pervert looked directly at my chest, which, typical of most fourteen-year-olds, was already developing—but not nearly enough for him, or anyone else, to carry a conception that I was somehow older. I was already taller than most fully-grown Asian women in town, and that seemed to be enough for men to assume I was older. Unfortunately, I was just a mutant at 5'8.

I brushed past him and he smelled just like Indian curry, somewhere between pungent and appetizing (a judgment I should've reserved, considering I often reeked of weed) and walked up a few flights of stairs. The stairs felt like they were going on forever, as they usually did, but tonight they felt especially heavy. My chest did, too; maybe being stressed gave you bigger tits. I didn't want to be anywhere near my family this evening. My mother had to have everything perfect on her birthday, and my grandmother being there didn't make it better.

But that's not what I was concerned with. My father would be there. Drug dealer. General scoundrel. He provided for us, but that wasn't enough for me. I had honestly, really hated him. I lamented this a little as I rose up the steps, furrowing my brows in disgust. I felt sick to my stomach, knowing he would be here soon. I was dazed, but I certainly wasn't calm.

The hatred I felt definitely went past the typical bounds of father-daughter antagonism. No, I definitely hated that man. I really, really did.

I took a quick left, facing the door. Before I could even open it, my Aunt Lisa opened the door. She glared, apparently tasked with retrieving me. She was larger than Eileen, and was the older sister. She had pretty much spent her entire life scolding Eileen, obviously upset that her younger sister was a "big hoe." Comparatively, Lisa was modest, wore very little makeup, and her hair was neat in a short black pixie. She worked as a biochemist, and as a result was very professional looking, wearing a wool cardigan and button up—still saving herself for marriage, probably.

"Victoria, hurry up and get inside! It's freezing out there. Have you lost your mind?"

I lowered my head and brushed past her as she berated me in her usual condescending tone. She always felt like she needed to judge everyone else since she was the only one who escaped the midst of the family restaurant that called my name.

The chatter of the women in my grandma's living room filled up both the apartment and my head, and the aroma of *char siu bao* pork and something smoky Eileen had likely burnt filled my nostrils, reminding me I was sufficiently hungry. But before that...

I rushed into my room and closed the door, grabbing a small spray bottle from my desk to eliminate the scent that I brought into the house. I doused myself in it, and fixed my hair. Growing up with a somewhat incorrectly vain aunt made me more superficial than anything, but the environment of critique weighed heavily. I wasn't mousy; I had good skin and my *own* long hair, as black as it could possibly be. I was definitely attractive, but it was so burdensome. I know I wouldn't deal with catcalls, or... well, anything if I didn't look this way. I wouldn't have to deal with *him* either. I sat on my bed and gazed at my thighs for a long time. Pale. Thin. Womanly.

I think I hated being a woman more than I hated being attractive. If I were ugly, or even if I was a boy, I wouldn't have to deal with this bullshit. It would only go downhill from here, I bet. I knew. I would end up washed up like Eileen, with someone who didn't love me, waiting tables and making excuses as to why he wasn't coming home. I'd, at least, be a better man than that, with some encouragement. My thoughts were interrupted by a small tap at my door, followed by a coo.

"Toria…?"

My mother's voice was sweet. I had clearly done something. Or she wanted something.

"Yes, Mama?"

Before she could respond, my father opened the closed door. I wanted to show my discontent on my face, but instead I smiled. She couldn't know, and even if she did, I didn't want her to take a guess at it. He moved past her, and placed his hand on my shoulder while sitting down on my bed—uninvited, of course. Eileen pulled my mother away, chattering in sharp Cantonese. My mother knew I didn't care to deal with my father; so, of course, it was sensitive, and I would've preferred she stayed there.

"You should go to Mr. Gam, and bring him some food," he immediately ordered me around.

"Why? I'm not delivering anything."

My tone was sharp, and my father tightened his grip on my shoulder. Because, when she wasn't there and I disagreed, he'd hurt me. I didn't budge, and looked away.

"You'll go to Mr. Gam's."

He had pimped me out again. That was the nature of what he had been doing. He released my shoulder and pushed it tightly. His tone was flat and he stood and left the room. I frowned, gasping for air. I hated this. I hated him. How could he do this to me, his own flesh? Did he raise me just to sell me to men? If I didn't look this way, I'm sure this wouldn't happen, and we could have a normal relationship.

I hated my body and blamed it. I rustled my hair and my face turned red. I grabbed my head and held it low, trying to fight back tears. If only! I took a deep breath, and rose from my bed, ripping my red hoodie from my bedpost. I lifted up the hood over my face, and shoved my hands in my pocket, walking to the living room, where my grandmother smiled sweetly at me, completely oblivious.

She thought I was just running an errand to one of my father's "partners."

She thought her son-in-law was a good man, and she was oblivious. He helped bring business into the restaurant, but not the kind you'd want. I hugged her and took a plastic bag from her, where boxes of food were kept, heat radiating from it. I smiled back at her, and walked out the door, ignoring the chatter from the living room as Eileen ran into the hallway to call her boyfriend.

Down the stairs I went, my high almost completely gone—if it was even there at all. Down the street. It wasn't a far walk to Mr. Gam's apartment building. It smelled like someone was frying something on the entry floor, and as I took the stairs, I felt my heart sink with each flight. Closer, without even thinking about it, I did this. It was my only option, I had guessed. As much as I hated it, as much as my own body disgusted me, they disgusted me even more. It seemed I was eager to run to do what my father ordered. I had imagined he owed Gam a debt or three. I knocked on the door, the reek of cigarettes coming from the inside.

Mr. Gam didn't open the door; a white man did. I narrowed my eyes. "Is Mr. Gam here?" He smelled like liquor. It was disgusting.

I was so utterly disgusted.

The door opened wider, Gam and another man revealing themselves. Gam spoke. "Yeah. Your dad owes me again, y'know. But not just me." He pointed to the white man, who grabbed me by the hand. I dropped the *char siu*, pork and vegetables spilling all over the apartment floor. I tried to pull away, but the man was stronger than me. I was thrown onto the sofa, and the door was closed.

I hated it. I was so disgusted. I felt unclean, like every inch of my body was something to be hated. Because of my body, because of this hair, this face, I was lesser. Because I had this body, I was vulnerable. I had aspired to be a wolf at one time. Feral and strong. You didn't screw with a wolf. They were violent. Fearsome. Even the female ones. Any wolf could rip your throat out. My vision was hazy and I had blacked out several times, the image of a ceiling burned into my vision because it was all I could look at. I'd rather look at anything other than their sweaty, putrid forms. Each one of them, human trash. Garbage. You threw out garbage; yet, everywhere, people like this were allowed to live, and do this. Why was it fair?

If I were an animal, I would've killed them on the spot. Ripped them into pieces so I couldn't be touched. If I were a wolf, I was sure I wouldn't hate my body. I leaned against the wall, my hoodie being tossed to me.

"Get out already," one of them said.

"Maybe the bitch liked it?"

I could hear them mocking me. Wasn't this enough? Didn't they have feelings?

I guess if you repeatedly fucked people over, including their children, feelings weren't necessary. I bet animals didn't have feelings, either.

I gathered myself up, and my clothes, and swiftly left, my face red, eyes welling with tears. I stalled in the doorway of the building itself, attempting to collect myself, to catch my breath. My vision was hazy with tears and I could hardly see, wiping away at my eyes with the ends of my sleeves. And when they had cleared, I spotted it. A vendor had left his stall set up, which was essentially asking to be mugged. But something glimmered. It called to me, pulling my body towards it with the kind of warmth I had felt only from my mother. I found something so powerful there, hanging by a white string. It looked vengeful, like a perfect mirror—a reflection of myself.

I had found a wolf mask, growling and fearsome. It looked real to me, the way the wax seemed to form natural wrinkles in its snout, detailing resembling real bristles of fur and the way the fangs looked to be real bone. It was much more realistic than the other masks hanging. It seemed special, like it was just for me. Like it was I, and I was it. I snatched it up and strapped it onto my face, peering through the eyeholes. I was focused. My haze had lifted with intent.

I staggered up the stairs of the apartment building, looking to the wall. A fire axe lingered in a box on the wall, the glass already cracked. Or maybe I had broken it, but it was dead silent. Everything was hazy. Darkness pulsing all around me, the building felt like it was trapping me, sucking the air out of my body and filling it with fire. I lifted my red hood over my head, pulling it snug and zipping my jacket up.

I tightly clutched the axe, removing it from where it waited for me, and found myself at the familiar pork stench of Gam's doorway. I knocked twice, holding my finger over the eyehole.

"You forget something?" I heard as the door clicked, opening. As soon as I had someone, anyone, in my sights, I swung the axe in my hand, like a natural instinct; it had become an extension of my arm. The thick cleaver ripped into Gam's associate's head, cleanly, dropping him to his knees. There was a pop that came from his head; his eyes bulged out; his face turned purple, as well; and air escaped my mouth in a whimper.

Perhaps, it was a snarl. I don't think wolves whimpered.

I kicked him down with the strength that my body had lacked earlier, possibly due to my new hunger; which, at the moment, was to rip them all to shreds. Each action rang through my body like explosives, heat rising and falling through my body.

Gam screamed, and his white friend turned towards a gun on a table, locking onto it as my eyes did. I trotted—maybe leapt—to the nearby table and I swung the axe overhead, bringing it down atop the gun to meet his greedy, fat fingers, crushing each bulbous finger, and severing his digits down to the bone. I withdrew the axe before he could do anything other than wail at me, the smugness of his face over mine replaced with terror. I swung into his neck, pressing down into his chest. I turned to face Gam, who had already made his way out the door.

He had slipped over the pork, tumbling down the stairwell, smashing his face onto the linoleum of the hallway. The lights flickered, and nobody cared to step outside. Each step down the stairs seemed to fill me with more fire. I snarled, trying my best to resemble a feral wolf. The grip on my axe was tight, but I couldn't kill him like this. For months, my father had been selling me to him. A weapon was impersonal. I was going to taste his skin as he had tasted mine. I twisted the axe, focusing on the flat side, and smacked him across the face, smashing into his lips and teeth as he tried to scramble away. The pallid flesh of his lips split, blood burst from his wide mouth like a popped bubble, and the bottom row of his teeth bent inward. I cornered him in the stairwell. I dropped my axe, and crouched onto him, peeling back my mask, which I was sure had molded my face into an image of itself. I *was* a wolf, and excited about it! I opened my mouth, hoping I had gained fangs and strength. I released the fire that had built up inside of me as I felt it rush to my head, and I buried my face in his neck, digging into his flesh with my teeth. It was warm and wet; the hunks of flesh I was ripping out and spitting to the floor accumulated quickly. The taste was savory, sweet. It made my mouth and mind feel hotter than hell. I quickly found myself blacking out, surrendering myself to the heat haze building in my body as I made my last feeble attempts to devour Mr. Gam, grinding my teeth between the sinews of his throat, and pulling, snapping. Darkness overtook me quicker than anger had.

When I came to, I found myself in my room once again, resting on my bed. It was dark and quiet in the apartment, no longer smelling of food. I had been changed, but had the sickest taste in my mouth: the lingering remnants of copper. Had I been dreaming? Sitting at my vanity table, I stuck out my tongue and checked to see if I had bitten it. It was then that I spotted it: Staring back at me was the very satisfied face of a wolf mask, lacking the former dimension it once had. It was cheap plastic with cartoon details, and when I rose to examine it, I felt sick. Bits of flesh and blood were stuck to the underside, staining the hollows brown. Fighting my nausea, I pressed it to my face, rubbing it across the contours of my jaw and cheek. I was more beautiful there, in the moonlight that peered through my window, than I had ever been in my life.

THE END

Contributor's bio:

Anya Lee resides in Louisville, Kentucky, and in addition to consistently being frenzied at all times due to an existential complex, this is her first publication! Attempting to blend her anxious woes with extreme physical discontent, Anya utilizes

body horror and dysmorphic imagery to convey herself in her writing. When she isn't a walking advertisement for treating your children for ADHD, she can be found abusing her Amazon prime subscription or watching Japanese b-horror (and yes, these hobbies do overlap.)

THE CORAL DEMON
Written by Barbara Jacobson

Emma and I squirmed on the bench of the fifty-foot dive boat as Dave, the handsome divemaster, told us the story about the coral demon.

"After several bloodied bodies of dead scuba divers washed up on the shores of the Riviera Maya a few years ago, the police started an investigation. Only five divers out of the hundred or so questioned claimed they had seen a copse of purple brain coral that was shaped like a man. After close examination, the coral man turned into a horrifying beast that resembled some sort of demon—you know, fangs, claws, pointed ears—the whole shebang! Most of the victims were never seen again."

Dave ran his fingers through his thick blond hair as he watched the twelve divers express their shock and terror, or laughter. I turned to my eighteen-year-old daughter, Emma, and pleaded, "Let's not make this dive. We'll stay on the boat."

"No, Mom!" Emma cried. "I want to have some fun on this damn vacation!"

"Okay," I surrendered.

I guess it didn't count that I had taken her to various Mayan ruins, horseback riding on the beach, ziplining over the jungle, and two other dive adventures during our two-week vacation. However, this was the first time I was allowed to see her in ten years. While her father had reared her, I had been living a wild life of booze, drugs and men. My life was a blur of fast and hard times until I crash-landed in a rehab or mental institution. Therefore, I deserved to be mistreated by my daughter.

Dave went on, "I trust none of you are faint of heart." His eyes stopped on me. I shook my head.

"Are you two redheads sure?" He asked and winked at me. I smiled, but he had already looked away.

He addressed the group, "Be sure to have your marine GPS with you. Remember, this is a drift dive. You could get pulled away by a powerful current, and we'll have to come and find you. The boat will be anchored far ahead of you; so don't come back to this location. Enjoy your dive."

He smiled and made eye contact with me one more time. A giggle escaped my lips. I turned and looked at Emma. She was glaring at me.

"Aren't you a little old for that behavior?" she asked.

"No. I don't think that thirty-five is old."

"Oh, that's right, Mom. Teaching yoga keeps you young."

Actually, I was quite proud of that. It was the first job I was able to keep for over a year. It helped keep me sober and balanced.

There was no more time for cat fighting. All the divers had left their benches and began slipping into their gear. Instead of suiting up with me, Emma took off through the crowd in the middle of the boat and found another diver to check her equipment. Then, she pulled on her mask and stepped off the back of the boat into the water. I started to push through the throng of divers when I felt myself being pulled back. I turned and saw Dave smiling at me.

"My daughter took off without me," I said with a tremor in my voice.

"She'll be all right," Dave said as he fastened my buoyancy vest. "It's you that concerns me. You look too nervous to safely dive."

"No, I'm fine. I have over a dozen years of diving experience."

"But," he started. "I assume you can never have enough experience as a mother – especially a young mother."

"We planned to stay together during the entire dive. She's bent on finding the coral demon by herself. She might get lost."

He nodded and took my hand. "I'll be your dive buddy and help you find her."

"I'd appreciate that."

After we were suited up and stood on the back of the boat ramp, we slipped our fins and masks on. Dave and I left the boat together. The moment I hit the water, my body relaxed.

The water was pleasant and in the upper eighties, and the Caribbean was gentle that day. The color of the water was a beautiful aqua blue, and it was so clear I could see the bottom, which was about thirty feet down. The sun shined on the sea like sparkling crystals.

I used my deflator hose to release air from my buoyancy vest to control my descent to the bottom. Dave grabbed my hand right away so that we wouldn't get separated as we were pulled into the drift current.

For now, the current was mild.

We drifted slowly enough to see the coral on the bottom, strange shapes reaching up. Suddenly, the bottom fell away and we found ourselves in deep water. As the bottom grew darker, the wall of coral bristled with color. There were clusters of yellow tube sponges, and purple brain coral. Glistening white angelfish darted in and out of purple sea fans, orange stars, and green cactus coral. I resisted the urge to reach out and touch the fragile finger coral, or any coral that could break off and die.

With my hand affixed to Dave's, we moved in unison. I closed my eyes for a moment and allowed myself to feel the sensation of flying. For a few minutes, I forgot about Emma's resentment toward me. I forgot about my dark past—in and out of rehabs and brutal relationships, existing in a stagnant pool of drunken or drug-induced highs and sober lows of self-loathing. I dreamed of a meaningful future that included sobriety and motherhood. I needed to prove to Emma that I really loved her and that I was sorry for being a bad mother to her for eighteen years.

Without warning, Dave yanked my arm and spun me around. Startled, I swallowed a gulp of seawater. I began choking more water into my lungs. Eventually, I controlled myself and coughed into my regulator until the water cleared.

I saw what he wanted me to see: Emma floating lifelessly. Her long red hair hovered around her pale face, and her arms were stretched out before her. Her regulator floated two feet away from her mouth. We rushed to her and forced her regulator back into her mouth. We started our ascent. Emma spat out her mouthpiece and coughed. We filled our buoyancy vests to keep our heads above water. In the middle of the

Caribbean Sea, the three of us held onto each other. Ahead of the drifting current, a few dive boats were within our sight.

"We could wave our arms and send a distress signal to one of the boats," Dave suggested.

"No!" Emma shouted. "I saw him – the coral demon. He looks like my boyfriend."

"We didn't see anything," I said. "But we did see you unconscious in the water."

"He's on the wall!" Emma went on.

"I would have seen something," Dave insisted.

"What the hell is *he* doing here, Mom?" Emma growled through her teeth.

"He was helping me find you!"

"Oh," Emma said accusingly. "Is that what he's doing here? Are you sure you two weren't making it somewhere and just lost track of time?"

"Emma, please stop this attitude!" I begged.

"No, it's him or me. I'm going back down. What are you going to do, Mom?"

She pulled away from us and descended back into the sea, leaving a trail of bubbles behind her.

"I must go after her," I told Dave. "And alone! This is my last chance to be a real mother to her."

Ignoring the rising sea swells growing around me, I went after Emma. I didn't look back.

As soon as I descended to twenty feet, I saw Emma swimming close to the wall, about thirty feet ahead of me. I wrestled against the powerful drift until I was about to lose my strength and just let go. Then, I saw Emma disappear into a wall of yellow tube sponges.

Infused with more power than I thought I had, I swam to the place where I thought I saw Emma vanish. I reached for the rocks on the wall to help move my body along, but all I got were handfuls of beautiful, fragile coral. It was Emma or the coral. I pressed on and pulled myself along, grabbing and destroying precious coral that took forever to grow.

Soon, I came across a dark hole in the wall, which was surrounded by more yellow sponges. The hole grew to the diameter of six feet—the mouth of a cave. Then, quickly, it shrunk to the size of the mouth of a man... with white teeth. As the seconds evaporated, the mouth stretched into a smile surrounded by a handsome face. Amazingly, the face resembled Dave's: hazy blue eyes, a straight nose, prominent chin and blond hair that floated around his face. His arms were muscular and hairy. The chest and legs were made of purple brain coral. From his belly slithered a long black sea snake.

For a moment, I thought I was experiencing nitrogen narcosis, or the martini effect. I checked my depth gauge and I was at a safe twenty-five feet. What I was seeing was real. It had to be the coral demon!

I thought about Emma. She must have seen the coral demon before I did. What happened to her? I started to pound my fists on Dave's face and hellish body. In a matter of seconds, Dave's mouth stretched into a large hole. The coral demon became part of the wall again. The transformation left a wide opening—about six feet wide. I had to go in no matter how scared I was. The coral demon had Emma. He lurked in the darkness and waited for me.

The cave looked dark and treacherous. I reminded myself that this cave was really a cenote. I had dived a few cenotes and they were beautiful and mystical, with an aura of danger. The Mayans had used the cenotes as a portal to pray to their gods. They had also used cenotes for human sacrifice.

Actually, cenotes were freshwater pools and caverns that had formed by the collapse of porous limestone bedrock. All tunnels led to the surface—fifty feet or fifty miles away. With that in mind, I entered the cenote.

Quickly, I was surrounded by darkness. I wished I had brought a light source with me, but I hadn't planned to search any cenotes. To control my movement, I stayed to the right side of the cenote and allowed my hand to guide me along the surface of the wall, which was jagged and slimy. In less than two minutes something bit my finger. I grabbed my hand and felt the bite mark on the on the tip of my finger. I rubbed my finger and steadied myself. There was no time to worry about a tiny bite.

A dozen feet in, the passage narrowed to about four feet in diameter. Ten feet ahead of me, the wall tapered to about three feet.

Damn, I would have to remove my buoyancy vest and my tank in order to fit through that small tunnel. I had to be very careful not to yank the regulator from my mouth. I knew I was getting low on air, but I didn't bother to check my gauge because nothing would stop me from getting to Emma.

I removed my tank and vest and pushed them through the opening. I climbed in slowly. Inching my body along, I managed to advance several feet. Soon there was a turn in the tunnel and I was screwed.

I had to find a way to climb up the tight passageway. I kicked my fins off and braced myself for pain. Because it was summer, I hadn't worn a wetsuit over my bathing suit, and the water had softened my skin; which meant I would cut easily by the sharp edges.

I found footing on a smooth bulge on a rock. While reaching for a rock to grab above me, I balanced the bottom of my tank on my shoulder. I found a protrusion on the wall and used my fingers to pull myself up. I tore off a fingernail and tried to ignore the flash of pain.

Pushing with my feet, I pulled with my good fingers for a few feet. The space got smaller.

I let air out of my lungs and wriggled up and backwards onto a tight ridge. When I breathed in, the wall got tight. I started to freak out and hyperventilate. I struggled to slow my breathing down. I filled my mind with an image of Emma and began to breathe deeply and slowly for five or six minutes.

It worked.

Calmer now, I shimmied, inch by inch, backwards. The rock was so close it knocked my mask off, and scraped my arms, hips and knees. *Breathe deep and slow*, I told myself. Finally, I moved a couple of feet and found myself in a sitting position. I pushed my feet very hard and felt something snap in my foot. I screamed and got a mouthful of water. I tried to control myself and coughed into my regulator until I stopped choking and expelled all the excess water.

To get my emotions intact, I gave myself a few minutes before I proceeded.

Regardless that my right foot was swelling up, I used my left foot to push myself upward. It was getting difficult to breathe. My air was low. I pushed, pulled and squirmed until I moved enough to get into a vertical position. Feeling terrified that I was going to lose my air gave me a burst of energy, and I pushed and pulled wildly.

I moved at least ten feet. I could breathe again. Ascending ten feet caused the compressed air in my tank to expand and enable me to breathe fully. Kicking another ten feet with one foot, I freed myself and swam upward until I surfaced in the water. I found myself in the cavern part of the cenote... with fresh air to breathe.

At the cenote opening, sunrays filtered through waterfalls. I looked for the hummingbirds, butterflies and tropical fish that I remembered. Instead, I saw snakes, roaches, pus-colored frogs, and huge spiders that hung in clusters from the ceiling. Up above, long brown tree roots dangled like the entrails of giants.

I looked for Emma and called out to her.

Nothing.

Then I heard her scream from a distance. I swam to the dark tunnel from which her voice had come from.

"Emma!" I yelled.

Her screaming reached a hysterical pitch. "Mom!"

"I'm coming!"

Shortly, I caught sight of her. She was up against a wall. Her hands and feet were tied with vines. I swam toward her.

The coral demon stepped in front of her. He was even more monster-like than before.

The creature didn't have Dave's features anymore. Now, he had a skull-shaped head, wild bloodshot eyes, a hole for a nose, large pointed ears, black lips, yellow fangs and a brain coral scalp. The rest of his body was also covered in purple brain coral. He had long filthy claws, and he had a long black sea snake that lived in his belly.

He walked through the water toward me. At least seven feet tall, he hovered over me.

"She's mine," he growled. His breath was hot and putrid.

I tried not to gag. "No!" I screamed. Take me instead!"

"No!" Emma cried and banged her head against the wall.

Without another word, he grabbed me and pushed me up against the wall. I felt his claws slice into my arms and back. He bit my face and neck. His sea snake started to chew its way through my bathing suit. The pain was excruciating. The last thing I remembered was Emma's screams.

When I came to, I was in a hospital bed. A doctor smiled down at me. "So, you've come out of your coma."

"Where's Emma?" I asked.

"When you are stronger you can visit her."

"Where is my daughter?" I demanded an answer.

The doctor informed me that I had been in a coma for two weeks. I also learned that Emma was in a mental health facility because she was under the delusion that some sort of sea monster had mutilated me. And here I was without a scratch.

The day before I left the hospital, Dave came to visit me.

"Are you the coral demon?" I asked.

He said "no" and handed me a check for $25,000. "Here, you will need this more than me. It was you and your daughter, or my wife."

"You bastard! So, you think you can pay me off for what Emma and I went through? You can keep your money."

He turned and walked away. Before he left the room, he said, "Keep it, you'll need it."

He had spoken the truth.

One year later, I was back in Florida and unable to work because I had a three-month-old baby with special needs. I had named him David.

When he had been born, the doctor wouldn't show him to me until they had explained that my son was born with strange birthmarks all over his body and face. He was covered in purple brain coral. And, he had claws for hands.

For the first time since I was home, Emma came to visit little David and me.

"I thought you might need me," Emma said. "I don't think you can do this alone."

THE END

Contributor's bio:

I've been writing for over twenty years and this is my first short story to appear in an anthology. In "The Coral Demon," I wrote about a sport I love—scuba diving. Over the years I've written non-fiction articles, poetry, humor, short fiction and screen treatments. My writing has appeared in a number of literary publications, including: *The Poet*, *Golden Isis*, *Jean's Journal*, and others. I am also a contributor to the book, *A Witch's Halloween* by Gerina Dunwich (Provenance Press, 2007.) I am currently working on a novel—a thriller, of course! In addition to writing, I love to paint, mostly watercolors. I reside in the Chicago area.

OF BLACK BUTTERFLIES SHE DREAMT
Written by Gerri R. Gray

Whiter than calla lilies, the soft satin of Marie's gown billowed like clouds around her; the whispering jasmine breeze from the window caressed her flaxen hair like a secret lover, and of black butterflies she dreamt.

In slow motion, she glided across a sun-drenched meadow, her naked feet barely touching the ground. Arriving at a hilltop, she laid her body down upon a blanket of dewy grass blades and nodding wildflowers; the azure-blue canopy of sky above flooded her eyes with its expanse. And then, within her field of vision, there arrived a butterfly with majestic wings the color of midnight. It circled her in its dance of silent grace before it lit down upon her forehead. And then there came another black butterfly, which circled her as the other one had done, and then landed on her hand. Soon, there were more—dozens, hundreds, thousands. The winged insects covered every inch of her body and face, pinning her helplessly to the ground, obscuring the azure-blue from her eyes. Parting her lips to scream, her mouth became an open invitation, and scores of butterflies fluttered into it until no space remained, silencing her, choking her. In the back of her mind, she heard, like water droplets echoing in a dark cave, the choppy voice of the punk-haired Chinese woman from her psychiatrist's waiting room. "Black butterflies," the stranger explained in a whisper, "are the harbingers of death. Very bad omen." Marie's ivory flesh suddenly felt pricked as if by millions of tiny needles. She could feel a million tiny droplets of her blood being siphoned into a million tiny proboscises, simultaneously. She came to realize, with ultimate horror, that the black butterflies were slowly devouring her alive.

Marie awoke with a start. Her heart was rapidly beating; her face was dampened by sweat turned cold by the night breeze from the open window. She instinctively reached across the bed, groping in the darkness to procure the comforting warmth of her husband's body; however, cold and empty space next to her was all she could feel.

She spoke his name, softly, almost inaudibly, "Cliff. Where are you? Cliff."

She waited, swathed in shadows, for his familiar voice to emerge from out of the darkness and whisper to her, "I'm here, Marie. You needn't be afraid. I'll never ever leave you." Minutes passed, slowly at first, then grew agonizingly long. The darkness of the bedroom remained voiceless. Marie felt alone, abandoned. She then recalled the dream, her mind's eye playing and replaying the scenes, mercilessly. The disembodied words of the Chinese woman haunted her memory like a ghost unable to rest in its grave.

Shuffling noises, accompanied by several thumps and

creaks, sounded from across the room. Marie turned her head in the direction from which they emanated. She was unable to make out who, or what, was moving about in the darkness.

"Cliff?" she called out in a slightly louder voice than before. "I need you."

The door to the master bath creaked part way open and brightness spilled out into the bedroom and into Marie's eyes, causing her to squint until she adjusted to the light. From the bed, she was afforded a partial view inside the adjoining bathroom. To her ultimate horror, the white tiled walls surrounding the bathtub, as well as the tub itself, were splattered with copious amounts of blood. A tall, longhaired man, whose face she was unable to recognize, hummed softly to himself as he diligently wiped up the red splashes and drips with one of the embroidered face towels, which he periodically rinsed and wrung out in the sink.

Oh dear God, Marie thought. *He's murdered Cliff!*

Sickened by the prospect that her husband was dead, and fearing for her own life, she gingerly slipped from the bed, crept across the bedroom in a stealthy manner, and quietly hid herself inside the closet, keeping a constant watch through the slanted louvers on the door. Her heartbeat pounded like a bass drum in her ears as adrenaline pumped through her body like liquid fire.

Time stood still, suspended in fear. Marie's mind floated with a heightened sense of awareness. And then, from out of a realm of obscurity, there came the sensation of fingers, frigid like dead meat, curling around her wrist. A chill sliced through her like a blade on a quest for blood, and she struggled to stifle the scream that was pushing its way up her throat and into her mouth. The unseen fingers closed around her wrist all the tighter, dominating the warmth of her flesh with their horrible lifeless cold, crushing her to the bone. Marie shut her eyes and winced with pain.

You aren't real, she denounced, inside her head. *Go away. You don't belong here.*

The fingers withdrew to the shadows. The pain ceased. The warmth returned. Marie re-opened her eyes and resumed her vigil. The minutes multiplied.

Upon completion of his gruesome task, the man with the long hair switched off the bathroom light, and a veil of blackness once again fell over the bedroom. He paused for a moment or two, as if listening for any stirrings of life; Marie tried not to breathe, fearful he would hear her. He let out a cough and then exited the room; Marie allowed her breath to creep back into her lungs. She waited and listened, and when the diminishing footsteps could no longer be heard, she emerged from her sheltering space and crept through the lampblack darkness, careful not to make a sound. She located the bedside table and the telephone that was perched atop it. She picked up the receiver and dialed 911.

"The number you are trying to reach is no longer in service," the recorded voice of a woman stated. It was cold, monotonal, almost scolding. "Please hang up and try your call again." There was a click, followed by a succession of loud, rapid beeping sounds. Marie followed the recording's instructions, only to again reach a disconnected number. She hung up, stunned. Her panic level was increasing by the second.

The house was heavy with a deathly stillness and filled with shadows as Marie cautiously made her way along the empty hallway and down the stairs to the kitchen, where she armed herself with the chef's knife she kept in a cutlery drawer. Creeping on tiptoes, she proceeded from the kitchen into the dining room, and then into the living room. From atop the painted mantel of the fireplace, eyes stared at her from framed family photographs.

Oh, how she yearned for the power to will her body into the sanctuary of those smiling images, forever frozen in time. In a photograph, she would remain safe, always blissful. She would never again know pain or fear or sorrow. Dreams of black butterflies would never be able to find her. She sighed with sadness at the impossibility. Words that she once read in a book, in a time long ago and far away, floated into her head like wispy midsummer clouds. *Photographs can steal your soul.*

The spell of her wandering mind was abruptly shattered by the sound of a car's engine starting up. She followed the sound, like a moth to a flame. She slowly cracked open the door leading to the attached garage and peered inside, unprepared for the sight of what was waiting for her.

The trunk of Cliff's car was open, and the tall, longhaired man who had scrubbed the blood from the master bath was loading black plastic trash bags into it. From the bottom corner of one of the bags, there came a scarlet seepage of blood that left a heart-shaped puddle on the concrete floor of the garage.

Marie cringed as she watched, and realized. *Oh, dear God! Cliff's body parts are inside those bags!* Her lips trembled. Her legs felt weak, as if any moment she might collapse. A sick feeling gnawed at her stomach like a rat and she fought hard to overcome the urge to vomit.

Tighter and tighter, her fingers squeezed around the handle of the knife, as an animalistic desire to kill surged through her body. She imagined plunging its stainless steel blade deep into the killer's back, cracking bones, slicing through muscle, severing arteries, and puncturing vital organs. The mental images filled her with glee. She hungered to avenge Cliff's murder and the unspeakable acts done to his lifeless body. She took in a deep breath and advised herself to act with patience, to strike only when the opportunity afforded itself to her. The timing of the kill had to be just right. Nothing less than perfection would do.

The door on the driver's side of the car swung open, and to Marie's relief, her husband, who was very much alive, emerged. Tears of joy instantly welled up in her eyes, and the urge to run to Cliff for comfort twisted her stomach into knots. She felt compelled to scream out her undying love to him, and she ached for him to hold her and make her nightmare vanish. And then her eyes shifted to the bloodstained shirt he was wearing, and her blood turned to ice in her veins. He strolled to the rear of the vehicle and helped the other man load the rest of the bags into the trunk.

The longhaired man glanced over at him and chuckled. "You'd better change that shirt before we go, just in case." His voice, which bore a trace of a California surfer accent, was friendly sounding and had a youthful quality to it. It wasn't at all like the voice of a monster that Marie had expected.

"Don't worry, Jason," Cliff reassured. "I will."

The man, who Marie now knew was named Jason, gave Cliff a wink. He tossed another black bag into the trunk. "You know, Cliff, I never thought you were really serious about carrying out our plan. I know we talked about it for almost two years, but I never believed this night would actually become a reality."

"Well, it's a little late to start having second thoughts."

"I'm not," Jason replied, shaking his head, gently.

"And there's no regrets either," he added. The corners of his mouth curled up into a smile. "Hey, haven't I always been your ride-or-die buddy? I'm with you all the way on this, Cliff. You know I'd do anything for you. Anything just to be with you."

The two men embraced in the way that lovers entwine around each other. And as their lips met in a tender kiss, the seam of one of the overstuffed trash bags split open and out rolled a decapitated head. Its face was gruesomely contorted, and, despite the dark coagulated blood that matted its hair and clung to most of its face like a mask of gore, Marie was able to make out the features. It was a face that she instantly recognized. It was hers.

This isn't real. This isn't real, Marie chanted to herself, hoping the nightmarish scene in the garage would retreat into the shadows like the hand in the closet. But, to her dismay, it remained steadfast in its horror.

She slowly shut the door to the garage. In a daze, she staggered into the living room, vertigo spinning its web around her like a spider. The stench of car exhaust, plastic bags and death continued to assault her nostrils. Reality disconnected itself from her, and all pain and fear and sorrow crystallized into a numbness that reminded her of the unchanging faces in the picture frames. She returned to the kitchen and placed the knife upon the gray granite countertop. She would no longer be in need of it.

Floating in a haze, she managed to make her way back up to her bedroom. She once again picked up the receiver of the phone; this time she dialed her psychiatrist's number. After what seemed like a million rings, the answering service picked up.

"Please," Marie begged, "let me speak to Doctor

Wexler. This is Marie Gravelle. I must talk to the doctor. Please! This is an urgent matter!"

"Hello?" A hint of irritation crept into the switchboard operator's voice. "I said, 'you've reached the answering service for Doctor Wexler.' Is there anybody on the line?"

"This is Marie Gravelle!" Marie shouted into the phone. "I need to talk to the doctor right away! Something horrible is happening to me again! Can you hear me? This is an emergency! A matter of life and death!"

"Hello? Is anyone there?"

Before another word could erupt from Marie's paling lips, there came the sound of a click, followed by a dial tone that buzzed in her ear like the eerie drone of a bee in flight. In slow motion, she returned the receiver to its cradle, a sinking feeling overcoming her. Staring blankly, she turned away from the phone and her feet carried her, zombie-like, into the master bath, where the stinging smell of chlorine bleach still lingered in the air.

She reached for the medicine chest containing her pills, but froze. She expected to hear herself scream, and knew that she should have, but silence gripped her vocal chords. Her mind struggled to make sense of what was happening. Ever so gently, she placed the palm of her right hand against the mirrored door of the medicine chest. She could feel it, cool and solid; it was really there, and not a dream. What choice did she have but to accept the inevitable? She had gazed into the glass, but no reflection of her had gazed back. The only thing the mirror showed was the white tiled wall behind her. Marie's mind slowly filled with clouds.

She stumbled back to the bedroom, without her pills, and lay down upon the bed to stare up at the ceiling. She didn't know what else to do. Soon, she found herself surrounded by dewy grass blades and nodding wildflowers. Above her, the white ceiling became a sky of azure-blue. She felt Cliff's body lying next to her; his breath danced inside her ear, warm like the whispering jasmine breeze. Slowly, he opened the front of her satin gown, whiter than calla lilies, and gently caressed her naked breasts. His fingertips circled her rose-colored nipples, and Marie shut her eyes. *I'd do anything for you. Anything just to be with you.*

Something warm and sticky glazed her bosom. With her eyes still shut, she imagined it to be honey, golden like the tresses of her hair, sweet like the taste left upon her lips after a tender kiss. Not wanting to, she opened her eyes and gazed down at her breasts. They were smeared with bloodied handprints, as was her gown. She turned her head to look at Cliff, but he was no longer next to her. She was alone in the sun-drenched meadow, except for the single black butterfly perched above her heart.

THE END

Contributor's bio:

Gerri R. Gray is a poet with a dark soul, and the author of the bizarre adventure novel, *The Amnesia Girl* (HellBound Books, 2017) and *Gray Skies of Dismal Dreams* (HellBound Books, 2018). Her writing has appeared in numerous literary journals and anthologies, including *Beautiful Tragedies; Demons, Devils & Denizens of Hell 2;* and *Deadman's Tome Cthulhu Christmas Special.* She has also contributed to the book, *Ghost Hunting the Mohawk Valley* by Lynda Lee Macken (Black Cat Press, 2012). She is currently working on a second bizarro novel. Among her passions are cemetery photography, paranormal investigating, and watching reruns of *Dark Shadows*. She is originally from the Chicago area, and currently lives in a haunted mansion in Upstate New York.

Links:

For more information, please visit Gerri's website at:
http://gerrigray.webs.com.
Follow her on Facebook at:
https://www.facebook.com/AuthorGerriGray.
Goodreads:
https://www.goodreads.com/author/show/17311761.Gerri_R_Gray
Amazon author page:
https://www.amazon.com/author/gerri_r_gray

AFTER THE SCREAMING STOPPED
Written by Christina Bergling

The screaming stopped. The screaming finally stopped.

Once the baby cries lost their razor edges and wilted into coos, a heavy silence swelled up and swallowed the house. I could feel the quiet in the way the air was different. It no longer prickled with the jagged decibels of my daughter's screams; it smoothed out, becoming only swirls of my muted breaths and her noiseless snores.

A paralysis crept over me at the coveted lack of sound. My daughter lay flat on her back, barely taking up any of the crib mattress, her arms and legs still tucked into her body. My hands hovered above her; one finger left lingering on her chest to assure her that I had not abandoned her.

I retracted my hands slowly, painstakingly to not disrupt the air around her, and I stood trapped beside her crib. The floorboards all around me were a minefield of betrayal. One false step would start the screaming again, would mean I would have to hold her angry, tiny body longer as I failed to put her to sleep.

I tried not to breathe, taking long exaggerated steps like an old cartoon character. My foot depressed the wood floor carefully, hesitating my weight and listening. One silent step gave me confidence, and I moved to the next, faster. Then to the next.

Creeeeaaaaak!

The sound echoed through the nursery. Then I heard the tiny gasp. Abigail turned her head, and her tiny eyeballs surfaced. Without a thought, I dropped to the floor, crouching out of sight.

I squatted painfully and awkwardly like a horrendous statue, wavering on my ankles that still swelled from my last month of pregnancy until I heard sleep weight her breathing again. Then I scurried silently over the floor and pulled the door to its frame behind me.

As the door settled on its hinges, I finally released a full, relieved breath. My lungs emptied, and my ribs collapsed around them. I threatened to tumble into a pile of my bones right there at the nursery threshold. The miniature victory was a rush that made me feel heavy. With each step away from the closed nursery door, the paralysis climbed up my limbs.

Every cell in my body begged for sleep, beckoned to capitalize on the precious seconds when Abigail did not demand from me. I knew I should sleep. *Sleep when the baby sleeps.* But in the same cells, I could feel the stack of unwashed dishes, the mountains of unfolded laundry, and the overflowing DVR queue—so many things to do in this already shrinking window of opportunity.

I dragged my bones down the stairs, hips popping and back knotting, as I fought the weight heaping on my eyelids. Each blink became longer, more seductive. My limbs felt heavy as the pressure built on my forehead. I could actually hear the wispy voice wafting up from the couch cushions, pleading me to indulge.

Yet, simultaneously, I felt an itching sort of excitement under my skin, a kind of reserved freedom. I could take a bath or take a nap or clean the kitchen or put away the laundry or read a book or watch a show. I could do anything within these walls, and that possibility fluttered beneath my exhaustion.

The house itself seemed to relax around me, releasing all the agitation from hours of relentless screams. I could hear it sigh into the silence. And in that breath of quiet, I heard it for the first time—a low, barely audible growl that seemed to ripple under the floorboards in a wave towards the nursery. I thought I heard it. I almost stopped, then shook my head, softly, and kept moving.

I stood at the foot of the stairs, rolling my hands softly over one another, doubtful and hesitant. I wanted to do everything; I wanted to do nothing. My mind whirred as my body threatened to fall over. Abigail had not slept over four hours since birth. I could feel my mind struggling to form thoughts, patterns that I could assemble into a decision.

A break. I could take a break first. Even with the grime of three unshowered days on my skin and unwashed yoga pants on my legs, I deserved a break.

Shuffling into the kitchen, I measured my footfalls. I heeded the tender pull and tug of my moving muscles under my stretched and sagging skin. Already, I felt my breasts filling on my chest, stockpiling more milk.

I wanted wine. I could feel the desire on my tongue. I craved the sedative pressure on my forehead as the alcohol unfurled along my veins. I settled for chocolate, allowing my fingertips to trace the wrapper in anticipation as I lowered myself to the couch cushions.

My body piled on top of itself loosely, a wobbling

stack of squishy pockets and distended skin. Soft, alien, and hollow. I shifted uncomfortably in myself, trying to find an angle that was comfortable against the tug of my stitches but did not feel disgusting.

I tried not to feel the awful crawling sensation at my own skin, the way I wanted to burst from this unrecognizable form. I tried to repeat to myself all the affirmations. *Breastfeeding makes the weight drop off. Look how beautiful the baby is.* Yet, *bowl full of jelly* just repeated in my brain, a phrase entangled in the frayed edges of my unraveling insecurity. Though Santa himself was probably tauter than my sad, deflated state.

I shook my head and tore into the chocolate. I let the flavor spread over my tongue and the blissful feeling sink into my nerves. The raging of my mind waned.

Abigail's shriek shattered the silence.

My body seized at the sound. All the freedom vanished from around me as obligation swelled into its place. I felt the oppressive drag on every muscle. I wanted to melt into the couch, but her cry pierced the air again, and the chocolate taste went sour in my mouth.

I felt heavier and sorer, heaving myself back up the stairs; careless now of the squeaky boards announcing my inflated weight. I clung to the railing, pathetically, as Abigail's cries only grew angrier from behind the door.

"It's okay, baby girl," I cooed, hoping the sound of my voice would temper her panic. "I'm here. I'm right here."

As I pushed her door open, in the space between her screams, I thought I heard the impossibly low rumble again somewhere below us. I could almost feel it in my toes. Then Abigail's cry sent shock waves over my senses again.

Abigail's fragile, new skin was already bright pink. I reached down into the crib, pushing shushing breaths from my lips, and wrapped my hands around her small ribcage. I pressed my fingertips into the back of her head to support her neck as I gathered her to my chest.

At contact with my skin, Abigail's crying changed. I felt the flush run over me too, the way we felt more connected sharing body heat, the way my mind turned to focus on her touch, the way we were simply together. For a moment, the touch calmed her; then the cries began to climb again. She clumsily mashed her face against me.

Hungry. Hungry again. Always hungry. Always wanting. Always wanting from me.

I sighed, forgetting myself, and eased us down into the rocking chair beside her crib. Grabbing the U-shaped pillow and tucking it against my bulging midsection, I balanced Abigail in front of me, holding her steady with one hand as I dug my breast out with the other.

When Abigail latched on, I felt the rip at my nipple followed by a dull ache of contraction deep under my squishy layers. The pain tugged me back toward myself, causing me to lament the discomfort and the confinement in the chair as Abigail nursed. Then, as the milk let down and the warm relaxation followed, I felt a surge of affection replace it.

I gazed down at Abigail's tiny face as it undulated through suckling. Her eyes had immediately fallen shut again. I could have mistaken her for sleep-nursing, yet I knew better. I could tell from the force of her mouth that she was still committed. If I were to retract myself, the screaming would start again.

Abigail's body steadily grew heavier in my lap, her lips less vigorous. I was trapped in that dreaded limbo between feeding and sleep. If I moved too quickly, the sedation would be ruptured. My skin began to itch beneath her. My legs twitched for movement. Time slowed to a crawl between each of her long, baby snores.

In that heavy stillness, I heard it again. I felt it. I was sure this time. The sound grumbled along and below the quiet, around it. Not a shake like a tremor, not a movement of the house or the earth. It had life to it. Like breathing. The fear tugged my hair follicles on end. The arching sensation of each pore crept down my back and up over my scalp. It possessed me in an instinctual way, the same way Abigail's cries could blank my mind and overtake my reactions.

I had stopped breathing at some point, feeling my heartbeat thudding in my head in the echo of that sound. Then it was gone. So completely gone that the air managed to sound hollow and empty. The void made me think I had never heard it at all, yet my heart continued to bang a warning on my ribcage.

I strained to hear it again, trying to stretch my eardrums out by focusing. I slowed my breathing, yet only the ticking of the clock downstairs and the thumping of my heart rose out of the quiet.

There was no sound.

Slowly, the contraction on the surface of my skin released. The muscles beneath began to relax to their doughy drape from my skeleton. My breaths filled to complete volume.

I looked down to Abigail. Her bottom lip fell fat and ajar as her mouth curved into a lazy O shape. It struck me, as it had in so many instances since they placed her bloody little body on my chest in the delivery room, how alarmingly gorgeous she was. The shape and composition of her perfect, miniature face frozen in sleep conjured such a flood in my chest that I thought my heart would break. From frustration to fear to euphoric love, I thought the roller coaster might snap my neck.

She was asleep. I could feel it. I slid my arm beneath her, gathering her small body up from the pillow. With my other hand, I discarded the pillow from my lap silently beside the rocking chair. I flexed my stretched, torn, and unpracticed muscles hard to heave us upward in the smoothest motion possible, holding my breath until I finally unfolded myself upright.

I limped my way cautiously across the floorboards, dodging the squeaky ones that had already crossed me. I pressed my hipbones into the railing of the crib and very gradually began to lower myself down around it. I kept my arms in the same position against my chest. I brought my entire upper body along for her descent to the mattress.

Finally, I got her to the crisp sheets with tiny cupcakes printed on them. She had scarcely spent enough time on them to flatten the wrinkles. For two breaths, I hung there immobile, still clutching her as the railing of the crib jabbed into my wounded midsection. Then I kept my chest pressed against her as I snuck my arms away.

Despite the increase of the whine in my abdomen, my breasts remained glued to the tiny rise and fall of Abigail's chest. Eventually, I slipped my hand between us and left it lingering on her chest as I stood. My back whimpered; my flabby stomach cramped; my neck kinked. The pain points cried in symphony as I cringed silently and kept my hand planted on my baby.

I could see Abigail's face contort before the sound started. Her cheeks went bright red. Her mouth twisted as her tongue arched in preparation. Her tiny limbs went rigid and began to quake.

Then the screaming started again.

The disappointment crashed down over me. I thought

I could hear the impact itself, but it was more another quiet snarl beneath my feet. Yet my fear, any reaction to whatever that noise was, was overwhelmed and beaten back by the burning failure in Abigail's cries.

"No no no no no," I hissed to myself.

I did not want to hold her again. I did not want to touch her. I did not want to still be in this room now that the walls seemed to be closing in on me with each cry. My entire body throbbed in an uncomfortable rhythm and sensation. I wanted to scream louder than her and run hysterically from the entire house.

Instead, I fought the resistance in my bones and reached gently for my baby. My body cringed around my raging desire to flee. I allowed it to vent through the grimace I knew she would not see or understand. My skin squirmed away from the feeling of her touch. I bit down hard on my own lip and let that painful spike distract me from wanting to pitch her back into her crib.

"Please stop. Please stop. Please stop," I repeated, more to myself.

Abigail responded by screaming louder.

I cringed as I pressed her tiny head back against my shoulder. Abigail resisted me in blind rage, fighting my comfort while demanding my attention. She did not want me to put her down. She did not want me to hold her. She did not want to sleep. She did not want to be awake. She did not want to eat.

She wanted nothing. She wanted everything.

The defeat burned over my brain, the fire tingling and spreading down my extremities, making them itch to drop her. I just wanted her off of me, but the sound of her cries in my ears made my body frantic to ease them. Without a thought, my muscles moved through the soothing patterns, troubleshooting on instinct.

Nothing worked. My emotions began to collide and

crescendo. The frustration, the exhaustion, the sadness, the inadequacy fed off each other in ravenous and cannibalistic bites, growing louder and more competitive.

When the sound rippled below the floor again, I almost dismissed it as the raging sensation on my nerves and the desperate muddling of my brain. I could scarcely form thoughts the way each baby scream scrambled my mind and caused my impulses to flare over reason.

Her cries continued in a relentless chain, muted by her age and the infantile size of her lungs, yet they thundered on my nervous system. They blanked out the world. Until I felt it. The sound, that low growl, boomed loud below us, and the reverberations stole my attention long enough for me to acknowledge it was real.

The rumble started at the floor in the distance outside the room. Then the sound moved like a wave towards us, rattling as if the floorboards themselves were rising and falling above it. When the growl reached the nursery, it climbed up into the walls enough to make the pictures vibrate in their frames.

My maternal torment dropped away. The tangled and twisted fog in my brain instantly evaporated, replaced by the clear, rigid, and icy focus of fear. Abigail cried with stubborn commitment against my chest, but I barely heard her. I heard only the fading echo of that terrible grumble below the floor.

We did not have earthquakes. When I snatched a glance outside, the sky was a painfully clear blue, and the sun burned brightly in afternoon heat. We did not have a dog. What was growling in my house? What was snarling so loud that it could shake my walls?

"Shhh, baby, shhhhh!" I hushed Abigail aggressively.

I needed to hear it again. I needed to identify it.

"Abigail, please," I begged.

Abigail did not listen. She continued to cry unrelenting just the same. I could not stand here and hold her. I had heard it. Something was out there. I had to go see. I had to protect her, even as she wailed until my ears threatened to fall off.

Abigail bucked against my hands and managed to fume an even deeper red as I gently lowered her into the crib. The louder she screamed at me, the more restless and approaching the growling sounded. She was agitating it, angering it. I could see the sense of betrayal on her miniature face. She raged blindly at me for abandoning her.

"I'm sorry, baby," I said over her screams. "Mommy will be right back. I'll be right back. Baby, hush. Right back."

I continued spitting soothing phrases as I darted from the nursery and pulled the door closed behind me.

The hallway seemed cavernous now alone. As the door mumbled against the frame, the house rolling out in front of me fell eerily quiet. Only Abigail's relentless, never-ending stream of cries, a steady rhythm that crashed like the tide in my head, ripping back on my nerves at each ebb. Yet I knew I had heard the sound. I knew it had been moving toward the nursery. I knew it was in the house. The echo quivered on my bones.

I padded a careful path down the hallway, my fingertips trailing along the warbled texture of the wall. With each baby cry from behind the door, my uterus contracted and attempted to drag me back to her. Physical discomfort climbed my cells at forsaking my biological obligation. I continued slinking over the floorboards just the same.

An unnerving quiet clutched the house, luring me deeper. The air seemed utterly immobile, without even the normal dance of the dust particles in the light. It felt like that pregnant breath before a scream.

I am crazy, I thought to myself. Abigail continued to holler with enviable resolve. The sound drew me back to my reality, a place where a child could cry for unfathomable hours without ever tiring enough to sleep. *You're just tired*, I soothed myself, hoping my ragged heartbeat would temper in my chest. *You're just hearing things because you're so tired. Because Abigail won't sleep. Because she just keeps crying.*

And she just kept crying. I sighed, defeated, and then turned to go back to the tiny cell with dancing elephants on the wall.

The growl returned even louder. The sound clapped through the house like thunder. It consumed the structure, causing the windows to quiver in the frames and the pictures to sway on the walls. I wobbled as the floor seemed to ripple beneath me, ripple back toward the nursery. Moving toward my baby.

We don't have earthquakes here. Earthquakes don't crawl along the floor.

I moved to sprint back to Abigail, but my distended muscles failed to contract in the forgotten patterns. They dangled from my pelvis, flabby and useless even now. Another tremendous rumble shook my balance. I could hear glass shattering on the floor behind me. The floorboards arched up to collide with my palms before I even noticed I had fallen.

My heart throbbed through my eyeballs, making my head ache. My fingers scratched clumsily against the hardwood, willing me up from the floor. Another sound bellowed, shaking beneath me before climbing the stairs toward my child.

I felt paralyzed. Why could I not get up? Why could I not get to her? I needed to get to my baby. The panic seized my chest and made me feel even more restrained and inept. My emotions skittered around my brain in useless arrangements, setting fires in my head.

The growls rose and fell, moved up and down, like breaks for an inhale. It sounded alive. The movement alarmed me, the purpose it seemed to embody. I had managed to scramble to my feet, yet my palms still lingered on the ground. Somehow, I could not find the balance or the core strength to pull myself upright. I crawled in an awkward, gangling movement until I got my fingertips to the first stair.

Unbelievably, the snarl grew louder, booming in the hallway between Abigail and me. The volume nearly stole my breath. Then the thick, heavy, smooth sound of the growl shattered, fracturing into abrasive edges. When I managed to raise my quivering eyes, I saw the floor splinter in front of me.

I felt my jaw drop to the limit of my skin as a shower of wood dusted over me. I could hear the toothpick-sized pieces tinkling against the walls. I clawed up the stairs, arching myself up painfully to peer into the fissure. Something was moving beneath the fractured floorboards.

With another deafening crack, coupled with a rumbling howl, and another wave of splinters, something thick and fleshy slammed itself up through the hallway floor. The large mass wriggled through the crack, moving in fluid undulations. The shape grew in girth as it slithered up the wall. It climbed until it began to fold over itself at the gravity. As it writhed, I expected to see circular cups on the underside, like a tentacle, yet instead, there were barbs. White points protruded from the thick, gray flesh.

I lost the capacity for thought. I lost the capacity to process what was happening in front of me.

Somewhere in the distance, on the peripheral of this

nightmare, I could hear Abigail still screaming. She was hysterical now. She probably had cried herself to vomit, a puddle of half-digested milk beside her on the crib mattress. I had to get to her. I had to save her from this thing. It did not have to make sense. I did not have to understand what was between us; I just needed to get to her.

I found my body again. The limb wavered in front of me like seaweed until I placed my foot on the next step. Then, as if hearing me, it went rigid and spun its spikes towards me. Some part of me, deep and buried beneath my motherly drive, wanted to run, wanted to turn around and flee this broken house to safety. Yet the flash was so fleeting that I did not even twitch in that direction. I took another firm and resolute step toward the nursery.

The arm reacted to me again. The meaty flesh slammed against the edge of the hole closest to me, barbs quivering at the impact. They looked so sharp and appeared to be dripping. The entire length seemed coated in some viscous liquid. I lunged forward with pre-pregnancy power and agility. The creature struck like a python. I felt one large barb dig into my arm. As I recoiled, the spike remained imbedded into my flesh. I could feel the blood pouring out from the wound, making the hardwood beneath my bare feet slippery. My own screams joined in concert with my child's.

I clutched my wound and slid down the wall, horrified to take the long, smooth spike with me. When I glanced up feverishly, I could see the void where it had danced on the skin of the tentacle. I cowered on the stairs with the blood spurting from my forearm and stared dumbstruck at the appendage consuming my hallway.

My fingers hesitated around the barb. I could still feel the sharp edge piercing into my skin as it shifted with my movements. I vaguely remembered some first aid canon of always leaving the impaled object in the wound, but I needed this sticker out of me. What if it was poisonous? There was a massive tentacle splitting my hallway—anything was possible.

I tried not to think. I tried not to feel the slimy, slick texture of the spike as I thrust my hand around it and plucked it reluctantly from my flesh. The sharp edge carved a line of protest down my palm. I tossed it away from me, and it clashed with the wall in a sickening splat.

The blood was everywhere. It geysered from my forearm, poured from my palm. I left a roadmap between every movement in the blood trail spilling around me. Clumsily, I tugged the thin sweatshirt over my head, leaving my body exposed in the nursing tank that clung to my rolls like sausage skin. I wrapped the sleeves around my wounds and pulled my arms in opposing directions until the pain exploded in stars across my vision.

Abigail continued to wail. My uterus again contracted violently at the sound, punished me for being so inept, so neglectful.

"I'm coming, baby," I managed to holler over the growl and continued splintering of wood. "I'm right here, baby girl. Mommy's coming."

The thing reacted to my voice. The edges and ridges of the form stiffened. It menaced tall in the air, arching directly out of its hole, then slammed forward toward me. The spikes quivered as it collided with the ragged edge of the hardwood, and the growl deepened, once again making the walls tremble.

I covered my ears at the piercing intensity of the sound, burying my face in the sweatshirt slung between my leaking wounds. Even as the grumble deafened me, I could hear Abigail's screams penetrating the air, assaulting my ears, begging me.

"I'm coming, baby," I whispered, now to myself. "Mommy's coming."

I felt my maternal instincts course through my veins, overriding my other programming. I heard only Abigail. I pictured her squalling on her thin pink sheet. I envisioned her red, wrinkled face as it shrieked for me. The imperative drove down the fear welling up around my brain on all sides. It sedated my heartbeat into a purposeful rhythm and numbed the pain centers that sent garbled and panicked messages along my nerves.

Abigail let out an inhuman cry that rivaled the mewling of the creature. In response, the tentacle whirled around, spiraling in the chasm in my floor, and turned its spikes toward the nursery. In horror, I watched the tip of the grotesque appendage jab at Abigail's door.

I did not think. I slung the sweatshirt from my arms, hearing it splatter on the floor. I sucked in a desperate breath and held it tight as I leaped from the ragged edge of the floorboards and onto the beast. The skin was tough and rippled and disgustingly warm.

My skin contracted as my face skidded down the texture.

The slimy coating sent me sliding rapidly toward the origin of this dreadful arm. I flailed around the shape and latched on to the burs on its front. I noted the spikes were shredding my hands as I clung to them, but no pain signal interrupted my thoughts. My purpose, my Abigail transfixed my brain, and I grabbed sharp edge after slicing spike, climbing up the back of the tentacle.

As the tip of the appendage slammed through the frail white door of the nursery, I released my grip and dove, tumbling into the room ahead of it in a pile of blood and slime. The tentacle waggled menacingly in the door, inching its way deeper into the nursery. I scrambled to my feet and yanked myself up by the edge of the crib.

Abigail lay just as I had left her, screaming just as I had left her. I reached down and drew her to me, smearing blood over her white pajamas and already reddened skin. My touch did nothing to soothe her. She continued to shriek as if I had never returned to her.

"Shhh, baby, shhhh." The tears spilled onto my cheeks now. A flood of desperate and defeated tears fled my eyes and dribbled down onto her crying form. "I got you, baby. It's okay."

The growling rose again, booming from the hallway. The tentacle flailed frantically against the confined space, twitched and pulled to shove itself closer and get its barbs into us.

I held Abigail close to my chest, wrapping my bloody arms around her protectively. I slammed my back into the far wall and slid down to cower behind her changing table dresser. The sobs now shook my body, and the two of us cried to together, huddled in the corner.

I closed my eyes tight and brought my face down to Abigail's. I could hear the doorframe begin to splinter and the drywall start to fracture. I felt the tip of the tentacle discover us. It wormed aggressively between my arms. I felt it slither around Abigail. I screamed and clutched tight to her tiny body.

"It's okay, Abigail," I whispered. "It's okay, baby. I got you," I cried.

Then the house fell completely silent.

The key turning in the lock echoed down the hall, a crashing, scraping sound that drown out the world. As the front deadbolt rolled from the frame, the house froze. I looked around me with wide, unbelieving eyes. Abigail's small body sprawled motionless across my lap. The floorboards beneath us had mended back together, stitching flat and unflawed. The blood from my arm and hands had vanished. The cuts disappeared, though I still felt their gape on my nerves. The monstrous tentacles no longer clutched Abigail; it was my own two hands I found wound around her neck.

The monster was me.

The front door squeaked open, but the screaming had stopped. The screaming had finally stopped.

THE END

Contributor's bio:

Christina Bergling is a Colorado-bred author who has always been drawn to horror. She has published two novellas (*Savages* and *The Waning*), one novel (*The Rest Will Come*), and has been featured in multiple horror anthologies (*Collected Christmas Horror Shorts*, *Collected Easter Horror Shorts*, *Collected Halloween Horror Shorts*, *Demonic Wildlife, 100 Word Horrors, Collected Christmas Horror Shorts 2.*) She is the mother of two young children and lives with her family in Colorado Springs. She spends her non-writing time running, doing yoga and barre, belly dancing, taking pictures, and traveling.

Links:
https://christinabergling.com
https://www.facebook.com/chrstnabergling
https://www.twitter.com/ChrstnaBergling
https.chrstnaberglingfierypen.wordpress.com
https://www.goodreads.com/author/show/11032481.
Christina_Bergling
https://www.pinterest.com/chrstnabergling
https://www.instagram.com/fierypen/
https://www.amazon.com/author/christinabergling

BEAUTIFUL DREAM
Written by Julia Benally

*T*he body of a woman was discovered earlier today near the Rim in northeast Arizona. Authorities are asking that residents stay in their homes. They believe that it may be the same suspect who killed Lillian Billings in Payson last month.

Tierney rubbed her delicate chin. "I hope Mitch will be safe coming home."

"Tierney," a husky female voice snipped from the kitchen, "get away from that TV. I need more flour."

The small woman jumped. Who was here? The stranger sounded as if she knew Tierney. Poking her head into the kitchen, she beheld a rough woman kneading dough on the plastic fold-up table. Leaves and pine needles hung in her tangled black hair like bugs in a spider web.

"Um…" Tierney rubbed the collar of her white shirt between a thumb and forefinger. "Wh-who are you?"

The woman stared at the ceiling, as if supplicating for

help. "Janice." She glared at Tierney. "Now get me the flour!"

Tierney's shoulders inched forward. "O-okay." She hefted the flour onto the table. Goodness, the strange woman was too bossy for Tierney's taste. Hopefully Janice didn't have too many demands; Tierney wasn't sure if she could carry them all out. It seemed wrong not to obey Janice. What would Mitch say about this? He wouldn't be home for another hour.

Janice grabbed a handful of dough. "I didn't think it would be this sticky." She dumped it onto a wooden cutting board. "But of course, only *I* think it's sticky. As soon as I stop believing it's sticky, it won't be anymore."

Tierney sat on a red stool. "Um…s-sorry, but what are you talking about?"

Janice punched the dough. "Beliefs! It's what you believe!"

"But it's still sticky. Sh-shouldn't you add more flour?"

"That's what you believe."

Tierney decided she had better change the subject. What could she talk about, though? Her dark blue eyes scanned Janice's filthy form. It wasn't just leaves in tangled hair, but Janice's clothes were also torn and stained. Dust stuck to Janice's ashen arms.

"You're a mess," said Tierney, realizing she had sounded too bold. "D-did you even wash your hands b-before you started?" Did she sound too critical?

Janice coughed into the dough. "Of course I washed my hands." A crunchy brown leaf flitted to the linoleum floor and landed on a faded pink flower. "Nobody will get sick from me. Do you know how I know? Because I believe it to be so!"

"I-I don't think…" Tierney stuck her fingers in her

mouth.

"That's why you'll get sick. You believe it. Everybody who believes it will get sick." Janice flipped the dough over, *squelch!* "Ms. Hennesy doesn't believe it. She won't get sick."

Tierney yanked her collar. "Ms. Hennesy?" Did Janice think Tierney knew her?

Janice tossed hair out of her face. "Ask her. She's at the door."

No sooner had she said it than *rap-rap-rap!*

Tierney screamed. "H-how did you…"

Janice stared at the ceiling for help again. "Get the door!" This tiny woman was enough to drive a lunatic insane.

"I-I…okay." Tierney scrambled off the stool and opened the door. A tall stately woman in a dark blue suit stood on the porch. Her blonde hair was done up in a French bun. Leaves and pine needles stuck in the golden strands.

"Oh!" Tierney could hardly believe it. Janice was right. How did she know?

"I'm Ms. Hennesy," said the woman. "I'm here to see Janice." She pushed into the small house and marched to the kitchen. "Janice, who is that girl?"

"Tierney." Janice sounded annoyed.

"Has she been here long?"

"She was here first."

"That means she's the one ruining this disgraceful place." Tierney peeped into the kitchen as Ms. Hennesy draped her suit coat on a chair. "Tierney, wash the dishes." She didn't even look at Tierney. "Why don't you take care of your house?" Removing her white heels, she lounged in a chair.

Tierney gripped the wall. Ms. Hennesy was bossier than Janice! What was she to do? If only Mitch were home!

"But…I…"

"None of your excuses. This is your house." Ms. Hennesy indicated the sink with a long glossy nail. "Take care of it. Were you not here first? What kind of an impression are you making?"

Heat ran up Tierney's neck and reddened her cheeks. "Oh…o-okay. I d-didn't expect—I mean."

Janice pounded her fist on the table. "Now, Tierney!"

Tierney fluttered to the sink. If this was her house, then surely she had to make peace in it! What could she say to Ms. Hennesy to settle her down? What did they have in common? She glanced at Janice, who turned the stove on. Good, she wasn't glaring back at her. It was awful when Janice glared. Daggers could leap from those glittering black eyes. Janice had eyes like the panther Tierney had seen at the zoo last summer.

"M-Ms. Hennesy," said Tierney, "Janice sneezed in the dough b-before you came. She said you didn't believe that you would get sick. Why?"

Ms. Hennesy groaned in exasperation. "Janice, please?"

Janice began rolling the dough into balls. "How many times do I have to tell you, it's what you believe, not what you see. I might not even be here. Ms. Hennesy might not be here. Are *you* even here? Did I really sneeze in the dough? We may be a dream, for all you know. Therefore, you won't get sick. Nothing can get sick from nothing."

Ms. Hennesy smoothed her skirt. "I didn't see it, therefore it isn't true."

"You see?" said Janice. "It only really happened if we all saw it."

"Therefore, whatever you say is a lie," said Ms. Hennesy.

Tierney grabbed her head. "You're confusing me!"

"Dearie, you have the I.Q. of a homunculus." Ms. Hennesy shined her nails on her blouse. "Imagine that!"

Bam-bam-bam!

"That'll be Chloe," said Janice.

Tierney dropped the dishes in the sink. Greasy water drenched her front. "Wh-who's Chloe?"

"Go find out."

Tierney fled from the kitchen. What an awful day. How many more people were coming? Hopefully this new person was nicer. It didn't seem like Ms. Hennesy and Janice knew anyone nice, though.

The woman's head was shaved and her clothes were missing, although there were no signs of sexual assault on her body.

"Tierney!" Janice shrieked. "I told you to turn it off!"

Bam-bam-bam! Bam-bam-bam!

"Haven't you got the door yet?" Something crashed in the kitchen.

Tierney squeaked and opened the door. A teenage girl in a mini-skirt and silk shirt popped a blue bubble in her mouth. She twirled a string of sky blue hair on her finger. Four thick pigtails stuck out of her head. More hair veiled her eyes and cupped her pointed chin. Leaves and dirt peppered her frame.

"Um…" Tierney twisted her collar. "W-what can I do for you?"

The girl rolled her purple eyes. "What can you do for me?" She laughed. "Get out of my way and let me in the house." She shoved past Tierney, swinging her hips. "What's up, Janice? Hey, Ms. Hennesy."

"Hi, Chloe," said Janice, "how are you?"

"Hello, dear," said Ms. Hennesy.

"I finally got it on with David," said Chloe.

Janice cooed. "Was it good?"

Tierney skulked back into the kitchen. Chloe had taken her stool. The girl didn't smell very good. Tierney made a mental note to wipe the stool down later. She returned to the sink. More dishes had accumulated in the water since she had gone to answer the door. She had never detested washing dishes so much. If only everyone would leave!

"What's the matter, Tierney, never heard a conversation like this before?"

Tierney turned from the sink. Had someone addressed her? Chloe was glaring at her.

"I'm s-sorry," said Tierney, "I wasn't listening."

"Just like Tierney." Chloe rolled her eyes. "Always off in her own world, doesn't know what's going on."

Tierney gripped the wet spot on her shirt. "I-I know what's going on." She glanced at Janice and Ms. Hennesy. This was an opportunity to show them that she wasn't so airheaded. "D-did you hear about the murders?"

Ms. Hennesy groaned. "You mean what's been blaring on the TV this last half hour?"

Janice slapped out a tortilla. "I told you to turn that stupid thing off twice now! You think we want it to exist?"

Tierney grew desperate. "But it *does* exist. The murders *did* happen!"

"Is there any such thing as truth?" said Janice.

Chloe rolled her eyes so far back that it was a wonder that they came back down. "Listen, *Tierney.*"

Tap-tap!

"Abby's here," said Janice. "The door, Tierney. Turn the TV off this time." She slapped the tortilla in the pan.

Tierney scuttled by Chloe, who stared at her as if she had never seen anything so weird.

"That girl gets on my nerves," Janice said before

Tierney had completely left the room. "What's the matter with her?"

Chloe popped a bubble in response.

"Mitch," said Ms. Hennesy, "always wanted a clinging, helpless, stupid creature."

Tierney's heart seized up. They knew her husband? Were these awful people his friends? She couldn't believe such a thing. Mitch was the sweetest man that had ever lived. How could she confront them about it? Oh dear, where was Mitch? She glanced at the clock. Only thirty minutes had passed!

Switching off the television, she opened the door. A five-year-old girl stood on the porch. Leaves filled her windswept brown locks. Her cheeks were rosy from cold and running. Smiling, Tierney rested her hands on her knees.

"Hello, what are you doing here? Don't you know it's dangerous? There's a suspect running around."

The girl scowled. "I don't want to talk to you! Where's Janice?"

Tierney stepped back like the girl was toxic. "Sh-she's in the kitchen."

"Move!" The girl stomped on her foot and ran inside. Her voice took on a playful note. "Hi, everyone!"

"Hi, Abby!" they cried, as if she were so cute.

Tierney stared at the floor. This was horrible! How could she make these creatures leave? They might rise up and beat her to a pulp! She gazed at her thin little hands. Abby's wrists were thicker than hers. She had the lurking suspicion that Abby could hurt her. Only thirty seconds had gone by since the child had come. It felt like hours!

"You must be strong, Tierney," she whispered to herself. "You still have dishes to do. You will do them!" She forced her feet back to the kitchen.

Abby thrust a finger at her. "I don't like her."

"Nobody does." Chloe sniggered. "She's just washing dishes. Don't pay attention to her."

Amazingly, nobody did. Ms. Hennesy fried meat and beans in a pan. Tierney didn't like that combination, but it diverted the tall woman's attention. Chloe sliced up lettuce and tomatoes. Tierney wished that she would bring out the cheese and hot sauce, but said nothing; it would call attention to herself. If only Janice had thrown out the dough! Tierney bit her tongue. Janice would just go on with that madness about existence. It gave her the creeps.

"Tierney is so sweet," said Chloe.

Had Tierney heard correctly? She turned to Chloe, who smiled. How did this happen? Had Tierney's perseverance paid off?

"Thank you, Chloe," said Tierney.

Chloe rose to her feet. "I bet if she got cut, sugar would come out." She turned the knife in her hand. Light winked on the mirror surface.

The blood rushed from Tierney's cheeks. "What?" She pressed against the sink. "Oh, Chloe, please don't!"

Seizing Tierney's fragile arm, Chloe slashed it with the knife. Tierney screamed. Blood spattered the pale pink flowers on the floor. Red rivulets seeped into Tierney's white shirt. Pale bone peeped through the parted skin. Tierney slid to the floor, clutching her arm.

Chloe chortled. "Her arm feels like it's made out of cartilage." Hopping on the stool, she continued chopping lettuce. Dark blood bathed the crispy leaves.

Abby cackled. "That was funny! Do it again!"

Janice tossed a hot tortilla onto a pile of others. "What are you crying about now, Tierney?"

"She cut my arm," Tierney sobbed. "It hurts!"

"I saw nothing, so nothing happened. You're lying

again."

"There's blood on the floor! Look at my arm!" Tierney could feel hysterics rising to her throat.

"Who's to say there's blood?" Janice slapped out another tortilla. "We all see it differently. Chloe sees sugar and Abby sees a joke. You can see it as blood if you want, but since you don't exist, there is no blood." She dropped the tortilla in the pan. "Whatever you say is a lie. Nothing can say truth if there is nothing. Set the table."

What could Tierney do? They were so much bigger than her, so much surer of themselves. Perhaps there was no blood. As she set the table, trails of blood dripped across the plastic surface. They seeped into the grainy pattern and spread, scarlet snowflakes on white snow. Red smeared the clean glass plates.

"I don't want this plate," said Abby. "I want the blue plate with the bird on it."

Tierney bit her lip. "How did you know I have a plate like that?" She recalled that Ms. Hennesy and Janice knew Mitch. Was he seeing them? The thought entered her head before she could stop it. She suddenly felt lightheaded.

Chloe rolled her eyes. "Give her the plate already!"

"Oh!" Tierney scuttled to the cupboard and yanked the plate out. The edge clanged against the side of the cupboard. The smooth glass slipped out of her hand, but she caught it with her knees. Janice stared at the ceiling. Tierney carefully kept her eyes off the other three.

"I want pop," said Abby.

"I don't have pop," said Tierney.

The girl kicked the table. "Yes, you do! It's in the cupboard!"

Ms. Hennesy shook her head. "How could you lie to a child like that? You better get the soda out and give her some."

"Hurry up," Janice snipped.

Tierney almost slipped on her own blood as she obeyed. Blood dripped into Abby's cup as she poured Sprite into it. As if the blood were nothing more than the sugar that Chloe believed it was, Abby drank it down with the Sprite. Tierney stared at her. Was Janice right? Was there no blood? But the pain still throbbed in her sliced arm. It was a wonder she could still use it.

Janice tossed a tortilla on each plate. "Sit down."

Tierney sat. "Um, c-can I ask you something?"

Chloe spat her gum onto the floor. "Now what?"

"Um…I'm sorry, but…" That gum was awful! "Why are you a-all here?"

"For dinner, stupid! Hurry up and eat, I'm hungry!"

Ms. Hennesy glared at Tierney. "Take the first bite, and don't be slow about it."

Tierney gazed at the brown spots on the tortilla. A dried leaf had been cooked into the bread. *She can't make anyone sick. She can't make anyone sick.* She made her burrito and bit.

The others followed suit.

"Didn't I tell you, you wouldn't get sick," said Janice.

"Janice tells the truth," said Chloe.

Tierney would have burst into tears on the spot, but gravel crunched outside as a car pulled in. Mitch! She knocked the table with her hip as she lunged into the living room. She yanked the door open.

"Oh, Mitch, you're finally here!"

Mitch smiled. "Hello, my love." He kissed her on the cheek. "How was your day? You look like a mess. Did the kitchen blow up?" He chuckled and kissed her again. "It smells good in here. What did you make?"

Tierney clung to his blue shirt. "M-Mitch, there are

some people here. It's been awful. I don't even know if I exist anymore!"

Mitch laughed. "You don't exist? Are you my dream?" He caressed her cheek. "What a beautiful dream you make. I don't want to wake up."

"Oh, please, Mitch, make them go away."

He kissed her on the mouth. "Okay, I'll make them leave." He walked into the kitchen. "What have you been doing, Tierney?" His voice had taken on a note of alarm.

Tierney scuttled into the kitchen. Four dolls sat at the table before the remains of four burritos. The baby doll looked like it had been picked out of the dumpster. The other dolls had been hand-stitched. The ones in the mini-skirt and blue suit had button eyes. The other doll was made of corncobs. It had no face. Hair cascaded from each doll's head. Dark blood trails congealed in the flour-covered floor.

Tierney clapped her hands to her cheeks. "What is this?"

"Are you crazy?" said Mitch in a low voice.

Tierney began to palpitate. "Th-they're playing a trick. That's n-not them!" She ran through the house. "Janice, Ms. Hennesy, Chloe, Abby!" Where *were* they? Screaming, she sank to her knees.

"Stop it, Tierney!" Mitch pulled her up and shook her. "I don't know what you're trying to do, but enough!"

"They were here, they were!" Janice's words reverberated through her head. Were they really there? Did Tierney exist? What was real and what was not?

"Tierney!" Mitch's voice rattled her head and she looked into his face. A measure of tranquility returned to her.

"Am I your dream, Mitch?"

He touched her face. "You are." He kissed her again. "Now clean up that mess. Make something for dinner. Everything will be okay." He went to the bedroom to remove his work clothes and shoes.

Tierney cleaned up the kitchen, although she couldn't do anything about the blood dripping from her arm. She gazed at each doll as she picked them up.

"They were so horrid to me." She flung them into the wall behind the trashcan. Bits of their clothing and hair fluttered to the floor. Tomorrow, she would figure out what to do with the dolls. This was such an awful trick to play on her, though. Not only had those four eaten everything, they had made her look insane. Had they been planning this? Why target her?

The TV switched on with the six o'clock news.

"The body of a child was found in the forest between Pinetop and Hondah a few hours ago. Abigail Carter was five years old and playing in her backyard, when she suddenly disappeared two weeks ago. Like the other victims, she had been stripped and shaved. Witnesses say they spotted a Caucasian man in a blue polo shirt and khaki cargo pants heading towards Hondah. He wore a fishing hat low over his face. The police have blocked the roads and are conducting a manhunt..."

Luckily, Janice had made extra bread. She just had to make meat and cut fresh vegetables. As she dropped ground beef into the pan, her blood sizzled on the dark surface. It vanished into the red slop. As long as fresh blood didn't fall in after the ground beef cooked, it would be all right. By the time the news finished, dinner was ready.

"Mitch, come eat."

The TV silenced. Mitch walked in, surveying the kitchen for anything out of place. Everything seemed to his satisfaction. Smiling, he sat at the table and Tierney served him. He bit into the burritos with relish.

"You're the best cook, my love," he said. "Now tell me about these people who were tormenting you today."

For the next hour Tierney went off on a tirade. She tried to stay as honest as possible, but sometimes it was hard. Her dear husband listened intently. His face never changed, though his air grew graver as she went on. Finally, she concluded with, "Chloe cut my arm! That's why there's blood all over the place!"

Mitch's brows knit. "Honey, let me fix that." Dropping his burrito as if it meant nothing, he dug in the drawers for a needle and thread. He returned to her with the precious items and threaded the needle.

"Don't worry, my love." He set her arm on the table. "It'll hurt a little bit, but you'll feel much better."

"I know it, Mitch. As long as you're here, I know it."

He pricked her tender flesh and pulled the needle through. Tierney whimpered and looked away. The sharp end of the needle hurt worse than Chloe's butcher knife. Slowly, the two flaps of raw skin closed. Neat stitches kept the blood inside. Knotting the thread, Mitch broke it off with his teeth. He kissed her gory arm.

"All better."

"Thank you."

"Now, to bed." Lifting her up, he carried her to the bedroom. "Remember how I carried you on our wedding night?"

Tierney rested her head against his muscled shoulder. "I do, Mitch, oh I do. I could never forget. You're as gentle now as you were then."

Lying down, he folded Tierney in his arms. "I miss my beautiful dream all day." His lips rested on her temple.

The small woman closed her eyes. "It was so awful. They made me wonder things that nobody should wonder."

"It's all over now, my love," said Mitch. "Don't think of it. I'm here for you."

"I'm glad you are. I'm so, so glad. I love you so much."

Mitch kissed her head. "And I love you, my beautiful dream."

* * *

Morning light crept through a crack in the curtain. Tierney opened one eye. It traveled up Mitch's powerful arm draped across her middle, and rested on his face. He was so stalwart and steady. She breathed in the strong cologne he always wore. This imbued her with life. She couldn't live without him. Not until yesterday had she realized that she could love him even more than she did.

Movement caught her eye by the bedroom door. Had Janice and her fiends returned? Tierney's heart seized up, a scream on her lips. A woman with golden brown hair stared at them. Her hair was the exact shade of Tierney's.

"What is going on here?" the woman cried.

Mitch jerked awake. "What are you doing in here?" He threw a protective arm across Tierney.

The woman's face contorted. "What are *you* doing?"

"What's it look like?" his voice challenged.

"What's that supposed to mean?" The woman thrust her finger down the hall. "Why are there dolls sitting around your table?"

"They're n-not sitting around the table," Tierney said. How did Janice and the others get inside?

The woman's eyes landed on Tierney. "Is that real hair?" Her voice was barely audible.

Fearful tears stung Tierney's eyes. "What's going

on?"

Mitch seized Tierney's hand. "Be quiet!"

"Are you *talking* to it?" The woman backed up.

"I'm not an 'it,'" said Tierney, hands shaking. "How did you get in? Who are you?"

"'It?'" Mitch's voice shuddered. "She's my wife!"

Covering her mouth, the woman sped down the hallway. Mitch tore after her. Their steps thundered into the living room. The woman screamed. Something crashed and Mitch cursed. Tierney had never heard him use such language.

"Mitch!" She stumbled into the living room. One of the lamps lay on the floor. The front door was wide open. Her trembling legs gave out beneath her. "Mitch! Mitch!" She pressed her face to the soft carpet, heart hammering against her chest. A car roared from the drive. Had Mitch been hurt? Screams retched from her throat. He was dead! He was dead!

Suddenly, Mitch's strong hands grasped her arms. "My darling, why are you crying?"

"Mitch!" Tierney gripped him around the neck. "I thought...I...Wh-who was that? What's going on?" Her voice sounded small and childish. "You're s-scaring me!" Janice and her minions wouldn't approve.

Mitch paled. "Nobody, love." He cupped her face in his hands. "Please, I couldn't stand if you were afraid of me. I'm so sorry!"

"Sh-she knew you...she acted l-like you were..." Tierney swallowed and forced herself to say it. "She acted like you were cheating on her w-with me."

"No, no!" Mitch crushed Tierney against him as if she would vanish. "She's crazy. Nothing can come between you and me." He covered her face in kisses. "I love you more than anything! She's my sister, Lisa."

"Y-you're not with...her?"

He shook her by the shoulders like a rag doll. "No! How could you say that? It's me and you, always, no one else! I promised you that a long time ago, and you know I never break my promises." He caressed her hair. "I think you better take a bath. You'll feel better when you come out."

Tierney gripped his wrists in shaking hands. "The whole world is falling down."

"Not while I'm here."

"P-promise?"

"Promise." He smiled in that calming way of his. "I'll make breakfast, but first, your bath."

Tierney kissed the palm of his hand. "I'm so happy you're here."

Carrying her into the bathroom, he filled the tub and placed her in it, with all her clothes on. "I'll come back when breakfast is ready." He went out.

Dishes clanged in the kitchen. The aroma of bacon wafted into the bathroom. Tierney breathed it in. Bacon was a comforting smell, but not today. Something strange was going on. Janice's words haunted her. Try as she might, she couldn't banish them from her head.

To her utter shock, Chloe marched inside. "Little Tierney is getting the special treatment?" She leaned against the wall. "Mitch took off my clothes before he put me in the tub last night."

Tierney's heart seized up. "What?"

"He put my clothes through the washer." She scoffed. "He just threw you in."

"W-what were you doing with Mitch?"

Chloe popped a blue bubble. "Wouldn't you like to know!" She sauntered out.

Panic seized Tierney's breast. Now she knew how Lisa had gotten into the house. Chloe had let her in! Somehow Chloe had hidden in the house. Did Mitch know? It couldn't be!

Scrambling from the water, she stumbled into the kitchen. "Mitch, what were you doing with Chloe?"

Her husband turned from the sizzling pan. "What are you doing out?"

"Chloe said you were with her l-last night. I thought *I* was your beautiful d-dream." Tierney burst into tears.

"I don't know who Chloe is!"

Tierney clawed at her face. "You promised, you promised!"

Mitch dropped the spatula. "Shut up with the hysteria!" He slapped her cheek, and then his face contorted. "Oh, my love, I'm sorry!"

"No!" Tierney rushed out the back door and into the woods. Mitch's agonized wail followed her, but she couldn't turn around. She ran until her legs gave out under her. She crashed into the pine needles. Thorns slid into her flesh. The stitches on her arm snapped. Knitting flesh ripped apart and fresh blood oozed to the ground.

How could Mitch do this to her? How many women was he seeing? She would have to leave him. Pain, worse than the red spot on her cheek, seared her heart. How could she leave him? But she had to! Burrowing her face in her arms, she screeched into the earth. Betrayed! Betrayed! Betrayed!

The storm of her emotions ravaged her aching heart until the sun reached its zenith. Now she lay like a limp doll on the forest floor, golden brown hair splayed around her like sunbeams. The cold ground had soaked in her tears and blood.

Something snapped in the forest. Stealthy movement crunched on dead pine needles. Lifting her head, she came face to face with two intense eyes, eyes like the panther she had seen at the zoo last summer.

It bit into her face. Teeth sank through her cheeks and

eyes. Tierney shrieked, but blood flooded her throat. It squeezed from her flesh. Claws raked into her torso. Guts spilled through cracking bone shards. Slabs of the back of her head flapped free, hair dangling and dripping blood. The earth soaked it in. The cougar's snarls drowned out her weak cries.

"NO!" Mitch screamed. A gunshot shook the air. The cougar tore into the forest. Mitch stumbled beside Tierney with a strangled cry. "No, no, no!" He fell over her mangled body. His heavy cologne couldn't dispel the stench of carnage.

"Mitch," Tierney choked out.

He gasped. "You're still alive!" Lifting her into his arms, he sprinted back to the small house. Tierney stared at the trees. Their gnarled branches dragged across the blue sky. Suddenly, the kitchen ceiling cut them off. They had already reached the small house.

Laying Tierney on the kitchen table, Mitch rushed to the drawer for the thread and needle. "Don't die on me, my love!"

As he threaded the needle, a breeze whistled in from the living room. Tierney managed to turn her head as Mitch spun around. Lisa stood in the kitchen doorway, a rifle pointed at him. Panic seized Tierney all over again. She struggled to move, but her body wouldn't respond.

"What are you doing?" Mitch asked.

Lisa's eyes turned to slits. "You killed my sister." She went livid. "You chopped off her hair and stuck it on that doll!" She pulled the trigger. A bloody hole opened in Mitch's stomach. He hit the floor. Blood and guts poured through his fingers. Tierney couldn't hear her own scream.

Lisa sped to her side, snatched her off the table by what was left of her arm.

"Please, please," Tierney cried.

Lisa ripped the golden brown hair from Tierney's scalp. Fresh pain coursed through the mangled woman's frame. Mitch could only stare as Lisa piled paper high on the table.

"You made dolls out of the women you murdered!" Lisa threw Tierney on top of the pile.

"Please, no," he whispered. "My beautiful dream."

Lisa glared at him. "Monster. Baby killer!" She set the pile ablaze.

"Mitch!" Tierney screamed. The flames caught her torn hands and ate away the cotton dress. Rushing over her hairless scalp, it raged inside her broken head. She stared at Mitch's agonized face until the fire melted her blue-embroidered eyes.

THE END

Contributor's bio:

Lurking in the forests of Arizona, I'm a wild Native with a taste for writing horrific things—unless something bizarre happens and I pop out a romance. I've been published in lovely anthologies like, *The Haunted Traveler*, *A Shadow of Autumn Halloween Anthology*, and *Grey Wolfe Publishing's Legends: Passion Pages*. My works have also been featured in wonderful magazines such as, *Liquid Imagination*, *Wagon Magazine*, *Sanitarium Magazine*, and *Scarlet Leaf Review*. I also have a couple of freaky tales read aloud to music in *The Wicked Library Podcast*. I'm so thrilled to announce that my first novel, *Pariahs*, will be coming out in November! When not writing, I love reading, wandering the mountains with my trusty nunchucks Harley Quinn at my side, playing the piano, and killing zombies.

Links:

For news on upcoming works and more, subscribe to my blog at http://sparrowincarnate.blogspot.com/

https://twitter.com/SparrowCove/

https://www.facebook.com/SparrowCove/

https://www.amazon.com/Julia-Benally/e/B017C8WCJO

https://www.goodreads.com/author/show/6950221.Julia_Benally

https://www.linkedin.com/in/julia-benally-0b439a10b

IN THE NAME OF THE PEOPLE!
Written by Olga Werby

"In the Name of the People! Brighter! Bigger! More brutal!" My director continued to urge me on. The video production for the horror story about devil worship and child sacrifice was already dripping with gore. I tried to stuff as much ghastliness as I could in every frame, but my boss wanted more. This particular story was written by SienaBlue, our best poet, just presently awarded the highest honor of the realm. She was away now, getting therapy rehabilitation after completing the script for our production. With luck, she might be able to return to be a fully-functioning member of our society, but the way these things go...

"Are you listening to me?" The director, RoseBerger, was standing directly next to me, screaming into my ears. I figured he was already dozed with anti-psychotics. I took mine every morning. "We don't have much time, MauveRo. I want this thing done before the crew falls to pieces."

"Yes, sir." RoseBerger had a good point. This was my third production and probably my last. Most of my people were either second production red veterans or first-time greens. I had the most experience, and I could tell our time was running out. We've already had to let a few people go—two cameramen fell apart in the middle of a shoot yesterday, and I was told that the makeup crew was staving off vomiting spells only by injecting themselves every hour. That couldn't go. We had to finish shooting today. I saluted my boss and returned to the set. He ran to hide in his office trailer with probably a tranquilizer for company. He was such a wuss. But I didn't judge. It could... no, *would* be all of us at some point. But before then, I had work to do.

We had several actors dissecting and dismembering animatronic babies, and the set designers smeared the walls with slow-dripping ruby goo. The sun was high in the sky, adding high contrast to every action shot. I motioned for the brights to get turned on and indicated for the camera to keep rolling. No point in wasting a single moment—we can always use the extra footage for some future production. I was a believer in reuse and recycle strategy—just keep layering one horror on top of another. If one dead baby was good, then dozens dismembered children were even better.

After four days of shooting, the ground was smashed into a pulp by crew and actors and slippery with special effects residues. I had to be careful to keep my balance and not slip in the mock; I didn't think my nervous system could handle a fall. I twirled a nice happy pill in my pocket for courage, just in case. But if I did lose my footing, I hoped the camera crew was smart enough to catch the drama. I had dozens of cameras rolling from every angle. It was my invention to dress all of the film production participants in costumes, in addition to the actors. That way, we had free extras any time we needed them. And if accidents happened, like they tended to towards the end of any shoot, we would have that on film as well. Layers of horror—my specialty.

One of the bigger dolls broke apart loudly, and the demon-dressed actor jumped.

"Looking good, looking good!" I screamed, encouraging my people. Sounds, of course, didn't matter. We sent out the whole thing as visuals only. So exaggerated reactions really helped sell the narrative.

"Bigger! Brighter! More brutal!" I called. And people leaped and waved their arms in the air. Some were pulling on their faces, real gore mixing in with the fake. A few fell to the ground, convulsing. It was a great performance... unless it wasn't. But we had doctors standing by. "Awesome! Great job!" I kept screaming as more and more actors attacked the poupées with axes, hammers, and saws. I saw an eyeball flying past my head. "Good, good," I encouraged just as I raised my arm to protect my own eyes from other projectiles.

I noticed during my first *In the Name of the People!* production that people get into horror, embody it in a way that other genres just never truly get under their skins. Something clicks, and the brain goes wild. And as hard as it was to get people into that head space, it was even harder to get them out. It took over a year for me to let go after my first completed film. I had nightmares. Daymares, too. I saw walls of the sanitarium, where they locked us up, ooze with body parts. I knew it wasn't true, but my brain saw it anyway. They gave me fifty-fifty that I would be able to go back to filming. Yet here I was, my third production. But everyone was different. I've known guys that never made it out of their padded cells. Me? I'd never see my family again. But that's okay. I was making the world safe. That's my job. *In the*

Name of the People!

I've pushed myself to refocus on the here and now. The little side trips into my own psyche were getting more common, and I lost time more and more often. "In the Name of the People!" I shouted at the top of my lungs, and people growled around me, deep in the blood rapture. The lucky ones won't remember any of this.

The horror was reaching the fever pitch. The medics, dressed in sensory deprivation suits, removed several of my cameramen on stretchers. The cameras continued to roll.

Something collided into me, and I was knocked off my feet, face into the dirt and synthetic gelatin and ground-up doll parts. That was the last that I remembered.

* * *

"MauveRo?" I heard the voice of SienaBlue. I tried to smile, but my facial muscles weren't obeying me yet. Anti-convulsant, I guessed. I found that it took longer for my smaller muscle groups to come back online after the injection, even after my legs and arms were able to move freely.

"Give him time," said RoseBerger.

"No, I'm back," I struggled to say. It came out as gibberish of course. Soft music was gurgling in the background; glowing pastel-colored lights softened the atmospherics of my hospital room.

"You did it," SienaBlue said and gently brushed my face. It felt good... after the first discordant touch. Watching her arms helped translate the experience from something to endure to a positive sensation.

"It's too soon," RoseBerger said and pulled SienaBlue's arm away from me. I was grateful. There was only so much I was ready to take. "Your production is a masterpiece. It's the best *In the Name of the People!* film ever made. You will be commended. When you are ready, of course," he hurried to add, as my face must have scrunched in horror of leaving the safety of my hospital bed.

"It was put together and transmitted into space last night," SienaBlue said. "It will be used at least ten more times in the future—more than any other transmission. The senior planetary consul believes your work will protect our home world for decades to come. You are the hero of the people, MauveRo. The universe will see the transmission of your film and will tremble in fear of our people's ferocity, will shudder at the horror you were able to conjure up. You bought us years of peace. You can choose any life option from here on."

I smiled. I wrestled control over my facial expressions and smiled. I knew what I wanted: a peaceful end to terror. No more waking to nonexistent horror, to fictitious violence, to imaginary savagery, to dreadful panic, to disgust, to shock, to endless anxiety. I wanted a peaceful end, having accomplished my mission of creating horror stories outrageous enough to scare away the aliens who wanted to come and take our beautiful planet, our tranquil way of life, from us.

The drug made a funny bubbling noise in my veins. And then it was over.

THE END

Contributor's bio:

Olga Werby, Ed.D., has a Doctorate from U.C. Berkeley with a focus on designing online learning experiences. She has a Master's degree from U.C.

Berkeley in Education of Math, Science, and Technology. She has been creating computer-based projects since 1981 with organizations such as NASA (where she worked on the Pioneer Venus project), Addison-Wesley, and the Princeton Review. Olga has a B.A. degree in Mathematics and Astrophysics from Columbia University. She became an accidental science fiction indie writer about a decade ago, with her first book, *Suddenly Paris*, which was based on then fairly novel idea of virtual universes. Her next story, *The FATOFF Conspiracy*, was a horror story about fat, government bureaucracy, and body image. She writes about characters that rarely get represented in science fiction stories—homeless kids, refugees, handicapped, autistic individuals—the social underdogs of our world. Her stories are based in real science, which is admittedly stretched to the very limit of possible. She has published six books before 2017's end and had two more in the oven. Her short fiction has been featured in *Alien Dimensions Magazine*, *600 second saga*, *The Carmen Online Theater Group's Chronicles of Terror*, with many more stories freely available on her blog, Interfaces.com.

Links:
http://www.interfaces.com/blog/
https://www.amazon.com/Olga-Werby/e/B002WKLH5I/
https://www.goodreads.com/author/show/4056895.Olga_Werby
http://Pipsqueak.com

SHE BELONGS TO THE SEA
Written by Kelly Glover

This protruding piece of land was the northernmost tip of the island, sticking out like a tongue teasing the sea. The sand in this area was rarely graced with footprints, aside from the gulls and various shorebirds that found themselves foraging here. This was especially true during the off-season. The end of the Franklin Shores State Park was about six miles to the south and any campers or visitors stayed farther in that direction, closer to the bathrooms and civilization.

It was a brisk, late afternoon in February. The sea was relatively calm and the ocean spray was cold enough to elicit a shiver if it reached a face. These were the conditions that Rita Casaldi loved to run in the most, so it was no surprise that she was out there on that particular day. She belonged to the sea, worshiped it. She was a Cancer, so it was only natural she felt drawn to the ocean.

Rita had spent all twenty-nine years of her life living

on the island. Her parents moved out West to Arizona to retire, and most of her friends had moved away throughout the years. She was a bit of a recluse and her social anxiety kept her away from much human interaction. It wasn't that she disliked people; she just preferred to observe rather than engage with those around her. Rita had always been an active body. She played for the high school basketball team all four years, until she tore her ACL during her senior year, requiring reconstructive surgery. The ever-present reminder of this procedure was a lovely three-inch scar that looked like a pale earthworm. She also swam competitively every summer from the age of seven until she aged out. She loved the feeling of being in the water, hearing the spectators cheering with each breath she took. The adrenaline that racing provided kept her competing and she found herself getting depressed after she was no longer able to do so. This general malaise coupled with a messy breakup with a cheating boyfriend led her to try her feet at running.

Initially, she started out stomping the beach with angry steps and Eminem in her earbuds, screaming about Kim. The angrier the music, the better. Every day her pace would quicken until one day she found herself running. Her feet took off on their own and she and her mind tagged along behind. It wasn't long before she realized what people meant by having a runner's high. It was as if each step she took released a heavy stone from her shoulders, and she simply couldn't get enough of that feeling. The music she listened to while she ran began to soften. Now she was more of a Missy Elliot and L.L. Cool J kind of girl, and she retired from her career as a homicidal hate rap lip-syncer.

Rita had always had a figure that matched her athletic prowess. She was just under six feet tall with long, lean legs that accentuated her already flawless physique. The bright side to running away from all your problems is that fat just falls off of your ass. In fact, if you run too much, you need to incorporate some squats into the routine so you don't lose too much of the booty. It's ironic how the same boys in middle school that taunt a girl for having a big butt will inevitably drool all over said butt several years down the road. That is what high school reunions are for, after all: showing those boys what they missed out on. Rita didn't feel the need to revisit her high school years last summer at their tenth reunion. She was quite certain no one had missed her.

That evening around dusk, Rita threw on her favorite purple running shoes with the hot pink laces and headed out for a chilly run—the kind of run that stings your cheeks and instantly reddens your nose. She proceeded along the same route she was so familiar with.

Her blonde hair was tucked messily under her baseball cap—the same cap that kept all those thoughts inside that wild head of hers. She cut through the side streets, saying 'hello' to all the dogs that barked as she went by. She lived just a few blocks away from the park.

She closed in on the last house before the undeveloped area began. It was a monster three-story beauty that stayed vacant nine months out of the year. *It must be so nice*, she thought, *to have that much expendable dough that you don't even have to bother with renting it out.* Rita often wondered what kind of conversations and thoughts were had behind those huge glass windows facing the sea. *Were the owners of this property happier than those that will never see that kind of money in their lifetimes? Or, do they have the same problems, just gold laced?* She knew once she got past this point that she was completely alone with her thoughts.

She liked to pretend she was the last person on Earth, that this was her own little deserted island—just she and the expansive beauty of nature. She ran on, sucking in the salty air and blowing out the stress of the day with each exhalation and step. The pounding rhythm was soothing, almost hypnotic. She was lost in her familiar trance when, in the distance, she saw what looked to be a person sitting on the beach.

Each step she took brought a better view of the out-of-place person. It had long brunette hair, so most likely it was a female. Whoever it was came prepared for some time in the cold because they were sitting and bundled up in layers of colorful blankets. From a distance, it looked like a fallen rainbow. Rita found herself thinking about what brought this person out here this cold evening. She laughed to herself as she thought that this person must have been thinking the same of her. *What idiot runs on the beach in the final hours of daylight when it's cold enough to see your breath and frost your tits?* Clearly she wasn't the only glutton for punishment on this particular day.

She had almost reached this person, and as expected, Rita's social anxiety tapped her on the shoulder. She felt her heart flutter, perhaps a bit stronger than usual. She had become very observant of her many neuroses over the years. She was highly in tune with her body and she knew that a couple of deep breaths would usually get her grounded again when she started to float away in her anxiety bubble. There was nothing to worry about here. She has been on this route hundreds, if not thousands, of times over the years. This was her home. There was just a visitor today, that's all.

Her shoulder-length bronze hair rustled gently in the breeze. She was ethereal. That word just popped into Rita's head—*ethereal*. She was the definition. The sun glistened off of her golden highlights. The woman looked up and made eye contact with Rita. Her instant smile revealed teeth as white as the sun bleached seashells scattered through the sand.

Rita couldn't help but return her grin with a genuine one of her own. Normally, she would have made a point to keep her eyes down as to not invite any type of interaction. She had been trying to stop being so reclusive and this smile was a small step.

For the past couple of months, Rita had been making an effort to step out of her comfort zones. It could be as simple as choosing a new gas station at which to fill up or eating lunch by herself in a crowded restaurant. She was determined to not let her anxiety and phobic tendencies control her life any longer. When the woman gestured for Rita to join her, her instant gut reaction was to politely say 'no' and be on her way. That is what the old Rita would have done, but she was the new Rita—unafraid, bold, and confident… or at least that's what she pretended to be. She stopped her jogging and walked over to the woman. She made it a point to introduce herself first.

"Hi! I'm Rita. What's your name?"

"Sirena," said the woman in a mellifluous voice.

She had the most intense set of green eyes Rita had ever seen. It was hard to look away. Her skin was a pale shade of alabaster and her lips had a natural crimson hue, thanks to the cold temperature that evening. "It's nice to meet you Rita. I thought I was the only one crazy enough to be out here today in the cold," she said with a smile.

"Haha, nope! I love running in the cold. It keeps my heart warm, if that makes any sense. That probably sounds weird." There went her anxiety again; she doubted herself and her worth.

"That doesn't sound weird at all. It's rather poetic, actually."

Rita felt her cheeks flush as they always did when too much attention was paid to her.

"Now, I'll run the risk of sounding weird, but I have to compliment you on your gorgeous legs! Running has served them very well. You looked so lovely running, like a gazelle with those long beautiful strides. Forgive me if I am being too forward, but I like to point out other people's beauty to them. It is very difficult to see yourself as others do, so if I encounter beauty, I acknowledge it."

This only made Rita's cheeks burn brighter as she humbly thanked her. "Well, I could say the same about you. You are strikingly beautiful, in the most natural sort of way. I haven't seen your legs, but I am sure they are just as lovely as the rest of you."

Sirena looked down at the pile of blankets surrounding her. "If only that was true," she said, the cheeriness of her voice all but gone.

A stiff wind blew and the blankets rustled. For a brief instant, the waning sun caught the reflection of something glittering amid the flapping blankets. A piece of jewelry perhaps? Rita didn't think much of it, but she sensed sadness coming from her new acquaintance. Was it something she said? She was always saying things to turn people off. She shouldn't have stopped; she should have just kept running and ignored this person that she now upset.

"Is everything okay?" inquired Rita, genuinely concerned for Sirena's state of mind.

"Have you ever wanted something so bad, so very bad, and the only way to get it was to hurt someone else? When does one person's desire outweigh another's? Who is to say what's beautiful anyway?

What I find visually appealing, you may find repulsive, and vice versa. Beauty is in the eye of the beholder and the hand of the giver." Sirena cast a vacant stare at the sea and an awkward pause followed. It was awkward to Rita, anyway. She decided she should try and make a quick exit.

"Well, I think you are a very beautiful person. It was nice stumbling upon you. It's not often I meet anyone on my run. In fact, I dare say this is a first. There is no one ever out here. I need to get going. I have two dogs at home that surely need their potty break by now. Do you have any pets? They are a lot of work; I assume that is what it's like to have a kid. Someone needing something from you at every second." Rita felt herself nervously babbling—another anxiety response. She had enough of being confident today. She had to get the hell out of there; she could feel the panic attack banging on the door to her brain. She looked at Sirena, staring vacantly at the sea. "It was lovely to meet you. I won't take up any more of your meditative time out here."

Rita stood up to leave and make her hasty getaway. She saw the flash of the tail, right before it hit her. She found herself taking a face dive into the sand. She felt wet blood pooling around her on the sand. She tried to stand up, but that was hard to do with no legs. She turned over to see Sirena removing her badly deteriorating tail. It smelled as rotten as it looked. Rita never knew mermaid tails were detachable.

"Yes, these will do just fine! I knew when I saw them run that they were the legs for me. Perfect, except for that scar on the knee, but beggars can't be choosers, right?" Sirena jammed her new legs onto the stump where her tail used to lay. They attached to two bony protrusions from her torso. It reminded Rita of Mr. Potato head. "I'm so sorry we had to meet this way. You will be immortal now! People will come from miles around to gawk at your dead body. Beautiful forever!" Sirena took the decrepit tail, still shiny with disease, and put it on Rita's bloody stump of a body. "Now! See how lovely! The world has been waiting for a mermaid. It may as well be you."

As the final pints of blood left her body, Rita watched as her legs carried away the most beautiful creature she had ever seen. Right before she closed her eyes for the final time, Rita looked at her new appendage. She always knew she belonged to the sea.

THE END

Contributor's bio:

Kelly Glover is a thirtysomething-year-old single mother who grew up and resides in Greensboro, North Carolina. She is the supreme leader of three kids, two cats, and one failed marriage. She spent a good portion of her life working in the restaurant industry, where she learned much more about human nature than food preparation. Life has taught her to find humor in the darkness, and from that humor bursts the light. Cliché could be her middle name, but she prefers Louise. She can be found at SerenitySavage on Facebook, and her blog is: SerenitySavage.Blogspot.com.

RE-AWAKENING
Written by Lee Franklin

Kelly could feel the pleasure of blood pumping through her body as the pavement peeled away under feet, the burn in her lungs, the pounding of her heart, the early morning sun kissing her face. A blur of black and gold fur, snarling snapping teeth, an old man—was it Santa Claus? No, it was terror in a white, bushy beard.

A punch of icy water to the stomach woke Kelly with a grunt. She tried to open her eyes, but the brilliant white lights blinded her. Kelly tried to scream, but the water had ripped the breath from her and it came out as a rasping, panting, gurgle. Just as it started to feel warm, the water stopped. She heard a chuckle before the clunk of a fire hose head hit the floor.

Kelly's shaking rattled her chains, and her teeth chattered so hard in her head that she thought they were going to break. The whole side of her face felt on fire and her leg throbbed like it had been backed with hot smoldering coals. The sterile, icy surgical spotlights blinded Kelly from seeing anything other than the polished concrete floor, but the details were in the cries of agony, pitiful sobs of hopelessness, and that horrible fetid smell of blood. The sweet-sour taste of fear overwhelmed her and told her everything she needed to know.

"Hey, Dad. It looks like your lady friend is finally awake."

Kelly smelt the rancid breath of a smoker, thick with bourbon. Rough, calloused fingers tilted up her chin to look her in the eye. His eyes were blue, bright with excitement and lust. He licked his lips, hungrily, with yellow spittle built-up in the corner creases of his lips.

"She's a beauty, Dad. Pity you messed her face up some. That's okay. I'm not too fussy. Besides, I like them a little raw. I still might warm her up for you." He smiled with yellow teeth.

It was only when Kelly felt his hands on her, she realized she was naked. Never had she felt so completely vulnerable. Kelly's scream came out as a rasping whimper; her terror remained locked up inside. The man grinned as he pushed his fingers deep into her vagina. Instinctively, Kelly felt her legs clamp shut, bucking and swinging, trying to reject his blunt stubby fingers.

"Oh, not a virgin?" he crooned. "That's okay, babe. There is always your sweet little asshole, or maybe we just cut you a new one," he added before reaching down to bite her nipple.

Kelly's stomach heaved at the thought of his touch; scouring herself in a steaming hot shower would not remove his touch or obliterate the sense of helplessness. There was something dark and diseased in his touch, different than the drunken, groping creeps in the pubs and bars that she could silence with a slap to the face or a knee to the groin. Kelly screamed at him to stop, her voice soft and raspy, the pain bringing tears to her eyes. He bit hard and pulled away, holding the tender flesh between his teeth as though he wanted to tear it off.

Suddenly, his head jerked to the right and he released his bite with a yelp.

"Get out of it, you little bastard. She's mine first. You can have what is left," Santa growled as he smacked the man around the head. "You got yours. Leave me have fun with mine."

"Aw, c'mon Dad. I've almost finished with mine," he whined as he gestured across the room. Santa looked over to where he was pointing, and Kelly saw a spark of pleasure in those black pools.

"I know you like little boys. You can have a go if I can. Oh, and look," the other man said as he stalked over to the other side of the room.

Straining to look in that direction, Kelly saw what initially looked to be a young woman. She realized it was a young man whose eyes were wide open, like in surprise, but glazed. Kelly couldn't see the stitches that held his eyes open.

The other man spun him around. Deep cuts under his arms that looked like fish gills bled slowly. "Dazza gave me some leftover bits from his woman's butt cheeks, and look, I gave him little boobs," he laughed, squeezing them between his hands "Isn't it great?" He laughed excitedly, full of pride as he grabbed the breasts and ground his hips against the young man's bloodied buttocks.

Santa laughed. "You're a funny bastard, I'll give you that. Is he still alive?"

"I think so. He's still warm at least," the other man answered.

Kelly started whimpering as gorge rose in her throat. The sickness was beyond belief—a darkness she had never allowed to permeate her somewhat sheltered existence. In between her large wracking sobs, she looked at the young man, in horror, and begged, "Please, you don't have to do this. Please don't hurt me." If they could do that to someone so young, what would they do to her?

Santa looked at her, intently, and held her jaw between his hands, forcefully.

"You see, Kelly. I've been waiting and watching you for a long time now. I have fantasized about you. What does your fear smell like? Taste like? How can I bring you ultimate pain? Will you scream? Will you beg? Will you fight? Oh, I hope you do. Remember this?" He showed her a baton that was just over a foot long with one-inch reversed barbs around the end.

She remembered the dark, cramped space of the boot, the bright light and those black eyes demanding she get out. The agony that had exploded from her leg as he impaled it deep into her thigh came back to life because of the memory. Kelly looked down at her thigh and saw the mangled flesh, as if a bear had clawed her at her. *The phone, yes.* She remembered she had hit the emergency speed dial. *The police could be here any minute.*

Santa saw the flash of hope in her eyes.

"You were thinking about this? Silly me, I forget you kids always carry phones on you these days. Good thing I had to get something else from the boot or we could have had more company than I'd care to." He chuckled as he showed her the phone on a nearby table.

Kelly let her face show hopelessness, but silently prayed. It was not a typical phone—rather an emergency beacon type device, a GPS-tracked panic button. Most mobiles were too cumbersome to carry when running, but her dad had always told her that the world was full of psychos, so she always ran with it, never thinking something like this would ever happen to her. Now it was the only hope she had left.

"Now, don't look so miserable, girl. We are going to have so much fun together. You inspire things in this old man. You bring me to life." He chuckled, rubbing his hardened crotch against her. "We all enjoy different things. Look!"

He swung her around. Her manacled wrists, like her ankles, were attached to a pivotal, metal D shackle so she could be spun to face any direction he chose. The room was only slightly smaller than a basketball court, and the walls appeared to be polished concrete like the floor. There was only one door, which she vaguely remembered stumbling through earlier. It was steel and double-padlocked. There was no way out—even if she wasn't chained, hand and foot.

"See, there in the corner is Kevin. Very straightforward, not too much fun, that old fart."

Kelly could not see that far past the lights and was relieved. She knew a Kevin. Kevin was her dad's name, and she didn't want to hear that name again—not in this place. Kevin, her dad, was a man of great big warm hugs and a big, deep belly laugh.

Turning her face farther around to face the middle of the shiny room, she saw a man vigorously working a carving a knife through what looked like a huge hunk of meat. Before she could close her eyes, she realized it was a man's leg, thick with hair and layered with muscle.

"That, over there, is Trevor, our resident butcher, who keeps our families in meat for a good part of the year and has an exclusive market on tender flesh like yours," Santa explained as Trevor cut a measured chunk and threw it into one of the several buckets around him.

Kelly spat out the bile that hit the back of her throat. *What kind of sick fucks were these people?* she wondered as she alternated between retching and trying to cry.

"Did you know adrenalin makes meat more tender to eat? I'm not really into eating it. I mean Shirley loves it. You remember Shirley, my beautiful girl."

Looking down to where he pointed, Kelly saw the German shepherd that had knocked her over at the park. The dog lay there, licking at a clump of long, black-brown hair, with blood staining the fur around her lips. Looking closer, Kelly's stomach dropped as she recognized a small diamond drop earring—it was hers, a gift from her boyfriend. The hair wasn't brown; it was blonde, thick with clotted blood, and a patch of flesh. Kelly screamed.

Santa smiled and turned around, rescuing the clump of hair from the dog. Showing it to Kelly, who started sobbing, he said, quite simply, "You shouldn't have moved. I sliced off half your face with my hatchet, silly bitch. I had to clean you up a bit. I'm not as good as some skinners, but not a bad job if I do say so myself. I gave you something for the pain because I didn't want you to miss any of the fun I have planned. Besides, we couldn't have this big flap of skin getting in our way. Oh well, nothing wasted. Shirley will enjoy it."

Santa nonchalantly threw Kelly's clump of bloodied hair and scalp back to the dog, which launched onto it like prize.

"I have a reputation for supplying the tenderest of meats. In fact, my meat is so sweet, so tender. A body like yours, mmm, will go for a good price on the international market, and will keep me financially stable for a year."

He bit hard, tearing the skin on her collarbone. Kelly jerked away, shrieking in agony. Fat teardrops, like candle wax, ran down her face, and snot ran out of her nose. He ran his fingers over the raw flesh and muscle where Kelly's cheek had been. She desperately tried to move out of his way. To hold her still, he dug his thumb in hard.

Kelly slipped into the darkness and escaped as the shock subsided and the pain exploded on the side of her face. It was in this place she found her five-year-old self—big green eyes, face and hands sticky with lollies and fairy floss, a satin pink party dress and matching plastic shoes. It was just after her birthday party; all her friends had just gone home. Kelly felt her younger self take her hands with those sticky little fingers and lead her around the garden. She started to feel panic prickle up and down her spine. She didn't want little Kelly to go down the side of the house. She couldn't remember why, but her panic exploded in her chest and she jerked back into consciousness.

A burst of intense pain shot through the cleft of her buttocks and snapped Kelly awake. She jerked on the chains so violently she thought she would rip her wrists off. Her body went into spasms, twitching uncontrollably as her bladder involuntarily released. She heard a loud laugh and then she felt Santa breathing in her ear.

"Wait till I put my cock up your ass." He brought his arms around in front to show her the electric cattle prod.

Kelly's whole body still jittered and spasmed with the after effects. Her bowels relaxed, pinched and then puckered, cyclically, threatening an explosion of fecal matter. Her legs hung, uselessly, causing the handcuffs to dig deep into the flesh on her slender wrists.

"Don't go napping again. I don't want you to miss

this," he snarled, his breath smelling like a pissing trough at a pub. "Here is José, an old friend of mine." He spun her on her chains to face the other corner of the room.

José was a tall, weedy man in his fifties, who looked like an IT teacher from school. In front of him lay an old woman with her hands and feet nailed onto a large wooden crucifix. She had a ring of barbed wire biting into her head, and she was alternating between mumbling prayers and swearing curses at José. The Latino-looking man noticed his new audience watching, and smiled and waved at Santa.

"Meet my psychotic bitch of a mother. Today she is going to dance with the devil and spend eternity in hell," José announced, triumphantly, pointing with glee at the woman on the crucifix.

Santa continued to explain, waving the cattle prod dangerously close to Kelly's face, as he whispered in her ear like a lover, "José has Mummy issues, and religious issues, and he has been refining his techniques especially for today's lunch date with his mum." He added, with genuine excitement, "This the best bit, he has been starving these rats so much that they have started eating each other."

José placed a cage of hissing and shrieking rats on the woman's abdomen. He slid out the bottom panel and then sat back in satisfaction as the rats escalated their fighting to a feeding frenzy. As they tore into the woman's stomach, her screams filled the room. Kelly couldn't tear herself away, hating herself as she was held in fascination at the depravity around her, a tickle of something familiar settling in her stomach.

As the old woman's screams died away, Santa turned Kelly again. This time, she saw a woman, spread-eagled, dead and completely devoid of skin. Walking around the body, with his hands intimately caressing its flesh, a seemingly handsome man intensively examined the corpse.

"That's Darren. He is Kevin's son, a surgeon, one of those types that give the women big tits and stuff. But here he is the best, most careful, damned skinner I've ever met—can almost take it off in one piece now. He seems to enjoy catching up with his old girlfriends and boyfriends. It's the wriggling and squirming when he gets started that makes it tricky. But this is how he likes to fuck them—raw, dead, but still warm."

Kelly lost a heartbeat as she recognized this man prowling around the woman. It was *her* Darren—her brother Darren.

"Darren!" she shouted. It came out a little more than a croak. Santa noticed the recognition in her eyes and tried to shut her up quickly with a cuff to the head, but her second shout caught the young man's attention. The young man stabbed his knife deep into the body of the woman, and walked quickly in long great strides over to Kelly. He lifted Kelly's chin and pushed the hair back off her face. His eyes narrowed and turned to stone and a look of distaste crossed his face. The expression on his face made Santa go pale.

"What the fuck is going on here, Nick? That is my little sister, you sick fuck!" he shouted, wrapping Kelly in a sheet. "Dad! Get over here! Nick's gone and got Kelly! Give me the keys, you fucking muppet. You know families are out of bounds. Goddamn it, Nick. You get family photos every year so you know who not to hunt. What a fucking mess!" Darren stormed at Santa.

"I didn't know it was your goddamn sister," Santa spluttered as he quickly found the right key.

"What the hell is going on over here?" Kevin roared as Darren quickly wrapped Kelly in a sheet, holding her close.

"Oh my God, what the hell is my daughter doing here, Nick?" he shouted, as Santa tried to back away.

Kelly was completely confused. She didn't know if she should feel relief at being rescued, or terror that her father and her brother were involved in something like this. Darren carried her away to one of the gurneys as she watched her father grab Santa and lock him in the chains where she had once stood. Her dad looked at her in despair and shame. He had tried to protect her from this, this sickness that ravaged his family. She was his princess, and now?

Kelly's mind reeled to make sense of everything, but all she could hear was her dad raging in the background, "What the fuck have you done, Nick? My girl is not a part of this. Oh God, what does she think of me? You bastard." Kelly felt a quiet satisfaction when she heard Nick scream. The group gathered around Nick and Kevin. This had never happened before. There were rules in place to stop this from happening and Nick had either gotten lazy, sloppy, or both. It wasn't acceptable.

Kelly felt the bite of the needle, and heard her brother whisper in her ear, "It's okay, little Sis. We'll get this sorted. You have a little sleep."

There was little Kelly, once again, pulling on her fingers, anxious, desperate, pleading for Kelly to follow her. She followed the little girl in the pink party dress, which was now stained with grass, her little plastic shoes discarded on the lawn. Kelly looked and found little Kelly leading her around the side of the house. No, no, no, she didn't want to go there. She didn't want little Kelly to see, but little Kelly had already seen.

Around the corner, next to Snowball's rabbit hutch, was Darren. Darren looked angry. He was always angry since Kelly was born. Always jealous of his daddy's new precious little angel that seemed to get everything she wanted.

Darren had owned a pet guinea pig before—before he covered it in hairspray and then set it alight with his dad's BBQ lighter. His dad never said anything, but promised him that, one day soon, he would get another pet. Kelly was not his idea of another pet, and when his parents proudly brought her home, cooing and crooning all over her, he ran outside and caught the neighbor's cat, Fatty. His dad didn't say anything when Darren came home covered in scratches and blood. Kevin dug a hole and then spent the next two weeks helping the neighbors look for their beloved Fatty. Soon after that, Kevin took his son camping. They always brought back 'bush tucker' for the family to enjoy.

So, there was Darren with Kelly's Snowball. His bottom lipped pushed out in concentration as he leant over the rabbit. Snowball was still alive and Kelly felt the little girl's relief and joy.

Kelly woke up, bleary eyed, praying the whole thing was a nightmare. The cold metal of the gurney and the burning pain in the side of her face told her differently. Sitting up quickly, she felt sickly dizzy, the taste of copper in the back of her mouth and a pounding headache. She heard voices arguing vehemently and excitedly, but everything sounded like echoes and she couldn't wrap her mind around the words. Still, she felt safe for the first time in what felt like a lifetime. They wouldn't hurt her, would they? She knew too much, but they wouldn't hurt her. Kelly heard a murmur of agreement, and then, just as quickly, Darren was by her side.

"Hey Sis, how are you feeling?" he asked, looking intently into Kelly's eyes. Her head was foggy and her tongue felt thick in her mouth.

"I'm okay, I think. I want to go home, I just want to go home," she mumbled, looking at her brother beseechingly.

"Good. I understand that, but," he answered, taking her hand, "you know this is a tricky situation, but we have come up with a solution. It's simple. You know too much, but everything must make so much more sense now." He looked sincerely sorrowful.

"Where is Dad?" Kelly asked feebly, looking over her brother's shoulder for him. She couldn't take this all in; it was too much. Her whole childhood, her life, had been a shopfront to a sick and depraved family. Did her mother know? Was her mother a part of this? Sunday family roast was just some kind of sick joke. How could she have not known? Did she not want to know? Was it all as simple as that? The hunting trips, the deeply private relationship between her brother and father, which, for the most part, appeared competitive in nature…

"Dad, he's really struggling with the situation, you know, with you being here. He's ashamed. He doesn't want you looking at him like he is a monster. He's outside waiting for you, but he can't face you yet," Darren explained. "Anyway, we all agree it's clear that Nick broke the rules and needs to be punished." Darren said remorsefully. But in his eyes Kelly saw a glint of excitement.

Kelly and Darren had never been close; he had always inexplicably disliked her and pushed her away. But now he was all Kelly had.

"The others have agreed. If you kill Nick, you can walk out of here, as one of us. If you can't do it, well…" he paused. "I will, I mean Dad and I will make sure it is a quick death, no fun and games."

Kelly retched, her stomach searching for something

else to purge, as her body started heaving in shuddering sobs. She couldn't wrap her mind around it; it was a sick game, surely. Kelly started to babble in protest. Darren took her hand firmly and placed a cold metal handle of a knife in it and squeezed her fingers firmly around it. He looked deeply into her eyes; she never realized how beautiful his blue eyes were when they looked so intense. Kelly thought she saw a predatory gleam flicker within their steel blue depths, but everything felt blurry and bright, far away, yet so close.

"No, Kelly. We all agreed this is the only way."

Kelly weighed the cold steel in her hands. It didn't feel like a knife. Its weight was unbearable as she watched the knife tremble with her hand. "Dad, what does Dad say? I want to talk to Dad," Kelly begged Darren, trying to fight through the fog in her mind from the sedation.

"This was Dad's idea, Kelly. These men won't let you go home innocent. They have families to lose as well. You'll be setting an example, Kelly. These guys play their games, but we know families are out of bounds. Nick fucked up badly and now he needs to pay the price."

Kelly sobbed. Everything was just so overwhelming. She just wanted to go home.

"I would love to do it for you, Sis, but it's got to be you. That's the only agreement we could get. Dad is just devastated about this. He can't even face you. Just do this man, stab at him like he is a piece of meat. We've covered his face so you don't have to look. We know it's hard for your first one. Please, Kelly, do it for me, for Dad, for Mum. We just want you home, safe again. But these men, they are scared and the whole group can implode—families too. We don't want Mum to get involved," Darren pleaded desperately.

Kelly nodded her head, numbly with some relief. Mum was not involved in any of this. She still had a home. Kelly just wanted to go home. She wanted it over with. Standing up with wobbly legs and leaning on Darren for support, she asked, "Where is Dad? Is he over there?"

"Yes, he is Kelly. He can't bring himself to watch you. But trust me, Dad is out there," Darren soothed, his voice notably tightening as he held her steady. Kelly imagined that he was just as nervous as she was. Kelly just nodded, meekly. She barely had the strength to stand up, let alone walk, and she had no idea how she was going to be able to hurt, let alone kill, anyone. Everything appeared hazy and blurry in front of her eyes. Walking towards the chain area where she was before, the white lights blinded her and the icy cold concrete floors burned through her bare feet. The tension was almost a feverish excitement, yet Kelly was numb.

She could sense the terror of the person in front of her, wriggling in his constraints and mumbling into his canvas head cover. Kelly could feel the weight of their expectation as they, the depraved, watched her walk towards him, holding onto Darren's arm for support. She felt Darren wrap her hand in his and squeeze her fist tightly against the handle of the blade. The blade extended almost a foot long in itself, more of a short sword than a knife. It had a serrated edge that glinted cruelly in the white surgical lights.

"Now, what you're going to do is just stab him in the middle near his belly button and push the knife upwards. It should kill him very quickly and with little pain," he whispered, encouragingly, into Kelly's ear.

She did not see his eyes shining bright with excitement. Gasping and sobbing, she could barely see the man in front of her, as Darren thrust her hand and

143

knife forward. Kelly heard a mumbled scream as she felt the knife hit and grind against bone.

"Dammit!" Darren swore. "You missed. Now quickly stab him again!" he shouted urgently in her ear.

Kelly did not see the large grin spread on his face as the bright red blood splashed across his face like a ribbon. Blindly, Kelly plunged backwards and forwards almost sawing into the body with the blade. After feeling so numb and helpless, she felt so alive. She felt so powerful.

The thought momentarily paused her in mid-thrust. Powerful, like she was high and untouchable, a knot of recognition starting to unfurl in her belly. After feeling so helpless and feeble, surely any action would make her feel a semblance of control. The blood was warm on her arms and hands and she could taste its saltiness as it splattered across her mouth. Eventually, she noticed the entrails oozing out of the slashes in his belly like a snake come to life. The stink of blood and bodily fluids permeated the air, making the gorge rise in her throat.

The blood had now stopped pounding in her ears. Kelly could hear the mumbled moans and screams, and she felt excited by the revenge she exacted. It was a small justice for those before her. It didn't take long until the noises stopped and the body stopped its twitching and jerking.

Out of breath and with sheer exhaustion, she leant against Darren. She looked at her hands in horror and relief as blood and tissue covered them like gloves. A few large cuts peeled open on her palms where her hands had slipped onto the blade. Expecting to feel rage and disappointment in herself, grief even, she felt nothing. She had done it. Kelly was a killer and all she could feel was relief and joy that it was all over with. The fact that it was so enthusiastic was simply due to a terror-spiked adrenalin rush, she told herself.

"Well done little Sis, well done." Darren patted her back tenderly. "You can go home now. But just one last thing," he added, turning her to face the corpse.

Someone reached forward and removed the hood. Instead of Santa, there was her father, his lips sewn together and torn through by the thread when he had tried to shout out, blood bubbling out of his nose, and an expression of terror on his face. Kelly roared in terror and was about to run to him when Darren grabbed her by the waist.

Rage and grief ripped through Kelly as she snatched the baton off the nearby table. She swung it viciously at her brother's so very handsome face. She would never forgive him for this betrayal, for tricking her so hideously. Darren cried out in shock and pain. Kelly lost her balance and fell heavily to the floor, tearing her brother's face into shreds. Howling in pain, he flew towards her on the floor

"I'll get you, you fucking bitch," he slurred as his lips flapped loosely against his jaw.

Kelly found strength—he bled too.

"Why, why are you doing this, Darren? You said I could go home. Why, why? Why did you make me kill Dad?" Kelly asked as she tried to crawl away from him, her hands covered in blood, slipping on the polished concrete. The other men huddled around, watching in fascinated delight at this domestic drama being played out in front of them.

"Because, you little bitch, I hated that bastard. He turned me into this. You were always the perfect one; I was just 'the sick bastard, the worst of him,' he would tell me." He slurred as he kicked at her jaw with his leg, missing it by millimeters.

Kelly continued to back away, but ran out of room.

Crying out as she tried to pull herself up on the metal countertop next to her, somebody kicked her in the torn flesh of her leg, sending waves of colors across her vision as the leg gave way. Grunting in pain and frustration, her brother leant down and pulled her onto her knees by her hair and held her face close to his. Kelly could see the tears that raked through and tore his cheek into little strips of flesh. She could see the bone of his jaw as a mix of spittle and blood hit her in the face while he hissed in her face.

"Hey, this is fun, you know, little Sis. My perfect little sister, look at you. Hey, imagine Dad's face when he heard you grunting like a pig as you stuck that knife fist-deep into him. You're almost a natural. But no, Dad said you were nothing like us. We were the sick ones; you were his perfect princess. But we know the truth now, as I knew the truth then." He laughed softly, heaving Kelly by what remained of her hair into standing.

Kelly shrieked in agony, flashes of red and white dancing before her eyes. Darren laughed. It sounded like a gasping wheeze as it whistled through the flayed skin of his mouth. As Darren was pulling her onto her feet, Kelly desperately tried to swing the baton at him again, but he was too fast this time and caught her arm in mid-swing. Grinning, he twisted her elbow until he heard the loud pop as it dislocated. Kelly gasped in pain and then cried in hopelessness as the baton dropped from her hand.

Darren kicked the baton away. Signaling for the keys and help, he chained her up, back to back with her dad, and pulled out a knife that was small like a scalpel. "Did you know," he began, ignoring her pleas. "Did you know that your daddy used to make me wear little dresses and play with your dolls, then he would make me his little girl? He wanted you so bad, but kept you his precious angel. He never believed me when I told him. Dad always blamed me. It should have been you too!" Darren shouted in her face before slashing the scalpel across her face in anger, narrowly missing her eye. Kelly barely registered the cut; so sharp and quick was the movement.

"I knew what you were capable of and you proved it to me and Dad today. So easy to convince you to do it, and that's because deep down... you wanted to."

Kelly looked at her brother. "Please Darren, don't do this. I'm your sister," she begged through her tears, as she tasted the fresh blood on her lips.

Darren's eyes were like granite as he slid the blade from her armpit up to her elbow in one swift motion. He groaned in pleasure.

"Oh, you are definitely my sister. But don't worry," he whispered, "I'm not a sick fuck like some of these men. I won't fuck my own sister. That's a line I won't even cross."

Kelly whimpered as the burn lit up under her arm.

"But Rory here," Darren gestured to the first man Kelly had seen with the young child. "And let's not forget your good buddy, Nick," Darren continued.

Kelly whimpered in anguish to see Nick alive and well, albeit with a few slashes across his face, but grinning from ear to ear. Nick had lost his prize, but he was alive and still enjoying every minute. He stood just inside the spotlight, already stripped naked, watching and enjoying the show, licking his lips as he was tugging on his cock that was poking out hungrily underneath his paunchy belly

"They'll fuck you good and proper, while I find out if you are sexier without this. Most women are," Darren murmured whilst he slowly peeled off a piece of skin from under Kelly's arm.

Kelly held on for as long as she could, locking everything they did to her far away in a part of her mind. Eventually, she welcomed the darkness. She didn't hear the police sirens approaching the barn. She didn't hear the men and her brother escape through a hidden trapdoor. She didn't feel the ambulance crews fighting to keep her mutilated body alive.

Little Kelly looked closer at what her brother was doing and watched in fascination when she saw him peeling the foot off her bunny, Snowball, shrieking in pain. "Let me have a turn or I'll scream and tell Daddy. Give me a turn now!" Kelly stamped her foot and began to wail.

"Shut up!" Darren shouted at her. "Shut up or I'll take his eye out," he threatened.

The little girl in the party dress just screamed louder. She was curious as to what Snowball's eyeball would look like. Would he still be alive?

The boy lost his temper and swiftly poked out the rabbit's little red eye and held it up to his sister. Kelly grinned; it looked so funny, and the little squealing sounds were almost musical. Kelly suddenly heard her father coming and pretended to scream in horror and faint. Little Kelly felt satisfaction when she heard her daddy throw Darren into the wall and march him off, whimpering, to the woodshed. Little Kelly rolled over and began examining Snowball, still twitching on the little board he had been tied to.

Giggling, she copied her brother and poked out Snowball's other eye. Daddy never believed Darren, but today had been close, too close, and she would have to stop for a little while. Darren had already copped the blame for the neighbor's kitten. Kelly smiled as she remembered how cute it looked, as its eyes grew larger and larger, its little pink tongue sliding out of its mouth as it desperately tried to suck air into its little lungs. Then, there was Mum's goldfish, so funny flipping and flopping about on the floor, their little mouths gulping at nothing. Darren frantically trying to rescue them and put them back into the tank. Mum finding him with his hand in the tank and several floating fish. She had screamed in terror and anger, and again Darren was taken to the woodshed with Dad. But seeing her mum's terror and disgust had stopped Kelly, until Snowball. She didn't want to be looked at like that.

But now on the abyss of death, Kelly's eyes were open wide; a blood lust had been re-awakened. A hidden and forgotten depravity unfurled in Kelly's chest. Now the hunters would become the hunted.

THE END

Contributor's bio:

After ten years in the Australian Army, Lee Franklin has been a personal trainer, a Logistics Officer, and the mother of three boys. Recently moved from Western Australia to the Yorkshire Wolds in the United Kingdom, she is now focused on her writing career in the horror and historical fiction genres. Lee's Berserker-Green Hell novella is due to be released this spring by Hellbound publications. Lee Franklin is also a committee member of the Rydale Book Festival, focusing on their inaugural Horror theme in October 2018.

TO BE A PREDATOR
Written by Linda M. Crate

Beneath the softly singing lyric of midnight moon, a pale faced man with dark hair and yellow eyes swiftly walked in the darkness far quicker than it seemed the eyes should allow. He was tall and thin with long eyelashes that any woman would dream of having for herself, mostly...

The architecture of his handsome face was high cheekbones, crimson lips, and a disarming smile of teeth that were whiter than the moon. They glittered like stars in his mouth, though his words were a galaxy of lies to potential victims. He housed planets within, but none of them were able to be lived in by any man or woman of mankind. Even his own shunned him sometimes because he was a silver-tongued devil who knew not any fire of compassion or wave of love for anyone. He was lone, haughty, and proud. Even his own children steered clear of him because he was very draconian.

He never let any wrong go unpunished. His anger

was wilder than the winds and waters of hurricane and burned hotter than any star. His mercy was brittle as stale old bread, and he forgave more slowly than the sun or moon.

He was good at holding grudges and believed in an eye for an eye. He felt the world was already blinded because they didn't see the things they ought. They only looked with their vision; they didn't truly see. They felt nothing, they said nothing of worth, and they were nothing. They were just living people whose souls and hearts were already dead, cast in the mold of an apathetic society that embraced conformity and rigid rules.

He missed the defiance and rage of people who fought for things that mattered. Everyone either seemed to care about all the wrong things or didn't care at all. It was very frustrating to deal with victims who seemed to think they were invincible and entitled to life simply because they were born.

This was dull to him. He liked a battle of the wills when he chose his victims, but so few of them were worth chasing. He usually killed them quickly to spare himself the disappointment of hearing their voices.

So few people interested him anymore—even among his own race. Since the murder of his wife, he had no interest in life, but he continued living. He was haunting as a ghost with a bit more bite.

The vampire snorted at that mundane thought.

He had to live, though, because he didn't think the gift of immortality should be graced upon the shoulders of just anyone. That was something the beast inside him and he could agree upon. They didn't always agree on much. The beast wasn't particularly concerned with the stupidity of the victims or if they were perfectly boring—it only cared about being fed. He thought that was rather barbaric. Wasn't he more than just this beast within, screaming for the secret sin of the consumption of the blood of another?

Some vampires insisted on only harming animals, but he thought they were far more innocent than these humans. Not to mention their blood didn't taste so sweet to him.

His favorite shade of blood was that from the faeries, but faeries were altogether tricky to capture. They were magical, fierce creatures and they weren't easily deceived. They were a lot more work than they were sometimes worth in the end.

Unlike some of his kind, he couldn't be satisfied with the blood of only one victim. He wished his thirst was that easily slaked. It wouldn't cause so much irritation and annoyance if it were.

It would solve his problems before they began, but life couldn't be so simple for him.

Even when he was born, life decided to give him a cruel brush. Who decided to name their son Humphrey, after all? It was an ugly name that people always mocked or tripped over. Or they would make insipid jokes about "humping" or ask whom his 'Rey' was. It was more than a little annoying to be perfectly honest, and very immature and vexing. They found themselves delightfully creative and clever, of course, but he thought they were taking a dead horse and beating it any time he heard those sorts of jokes.

He cursed his parents to oblivion for giving him such a name. How could they have been so cruel?

Humphrey often would go by his middle name Edward and his surname Rothschild. Sir Edward Rothschild had a better ring to it than his natural name, and everyone who knew him knew it were wiser to go by the name he preferred rather than his natural name.

The vampire scowled as the city lights pressed nearer. The lights had always hurt his eyes even when he had been human hundreds of years ago. He was not one of the few that were born a vampire, so even with his title, the pureblooded ones always judged him unfairly. It was all nauseating to him. Why should he have to grovel or apologize for who and what he was?

He was who he was without apology—even if his existence meant the flight of life for some. He smirked. It wasn't as if they didn't deserve it. Either they were bullies, cowards, or impudent fools that thought death would never knock on their doors. Sometimes they were all three.

The vampire glanced over his shoulder as he felt a familiar shadow cross over his path. It was a vampire named Audrina. She went by Aud, and was one of the ancient ones who had never liked him. The feeling was mutual. He knew only reason for her to be here now, and he would not be the one to fall. He felt her presence behind him, and without looking threw flames behind them. He heard her screams, but paid them no attention. They were meaningless to him. It wouldn't stop him from destroying her. When he looked behind him he saw her ashes and made haste to scatter them so she could not return again.

"I guess I'm not a filthy little vampire witch now, am I? My skills in my human life make disposing of you ancient ones easy work. Perhaps, you should've never crossed me, Audrina. But as you have, you are no more."

Humphrey crushed her fangs in his palms after examining them several moments. Her teeth were rather small, he thought, for an ancient one. The fangs were rather shorter than he had anticipated. After all, when he had killed her brother his teeth were at least thrice this size. Then again the vampiric males did seem to have longer teeth than the females in most cases. This wasn't always the case.

Shrugging, Humphrey continued walking to the city. His thirst wasn't going to go away even if he had gotten revenge on one of his enemies. The fire did nothing to him when cast his way. After all, he knew magic and could destroy the flames before they got anywhere near him.

He could sense the presence of another elder. "How many elders does it take to down a miscreant like me?"

"Why did you kill Aud?"

"Don't be stupid, Edward. You know I had to. Just as I'll get rid of you." Humphrey used his flames again, a bored look across his handsome face. "You're all the same assuming your oldness and your wisdom will protect you from someone like me, but in the end it's your prejudice that kills you." With that he scattered the ashes of the second elder and crushed his fangs, as well.

He cast flames behind him to destroy the other thirteen that followed him in the darkness thinking that they cast no footprint. He was ravenous and his hunger made him more sadistic. A part of him thought that he should draw out and prolong their pain, but he also knew that he had to take care of them swiftly because the elders did have an advantage on him when it came to strength. However, his flames quickly took that away from them. Crushing the collective thirteen fangs and scattering the ashes so those he disposed of couldn't return, Humphrey whirled around to find yet another elder.

Fifteen wasn't enough? Now a sixteenth member of the elders had to have found him? There were only twenty. If they weren't careful none of them would be left.

The eyes of Dimira were lovely. They were lavender, which was very rare a sight, indeed. Humphrey smirked, but her pretty little face wasn't enough to save her. He sprang before she registered him and bit deeply into her flesh. Drinking the elder's blood, he was surprised when memories and dreams that were not his own came to him. There was power in the blood, as that silly song his mother made him sing at church had said. Sweet power, but they weren't wielding their power responsibly and, therefore, he would make them pay for it! Handsomely, he might add, with their lives.

Dimira shoved him away. "Enough, you little brat. Do you think you're a match for me?"

She was strong, but he could tell that he had drank enough of her blood to slow her down and inhibit her movements which was what he had intended on doing because she had been the fastest and the strongest of the elders. He then threw his flames towards her, and found she burned the slowest.

Her silver hair mocked him from the flames until they were consumed, but her lavender eyes scorched with a heat his fires never could. He scattered her ashes and smashed her fangs, which were the longest of any of the elders. She was the oldest of the vampires, after all. Her bloodline was said to go back so far as to attach to that of the father of all vampires. Though, he did not know if that were true.

He could probably examine the memories and dreams that she had given him, but perhaps when he had more time and patience. With the blood of the elder running through his veins, he felt as if he would never die. Perhaps, it was their blood that was their undoing, he thought. Perhaps, the assurance that they had been around for centuries longer than other vampires gave them a false lull of security.

The witch nodded to himself. Aye, that made sense. But as they would soon know, their age would not spare them from his death. He would make them see the folly of their ways.

He knew that the coven would probably seek to hunt him down and destroy him since he had killed sixteen elders in one night, but for the moment, he did not care nor concern himself with that.

His thirst, like always, hungered onward.

Humphrey was a threat to both his own kind and humans alike. Let them chase him to the ends of the earth. He would adapt and survive killing them with his fires until even their own bones wouldn't recognize them in the afterlife.

"Ashes, ashes, you all fall down," Humphrey cackled, taking out the last four of the elders who thought they had stealthily followed him. The only one that had taken him by surprise was Dimira, the dark skinned beauty with her haunting lavender eyes.

The rest weren't clever enough to evade his detection. They relied too much on old ways and old thinking, which was outdated in this day and age. The vampire made sure to scatter the ashes of the last four.

The ancients were now gone.

Humphrey had freed the world of their existence. He ought to win some sort of prize for that, he thought.

The coven, of course, would probably be divided. He would have both allies and enemies, but in the end, he freed everyone to do what they wanted, and so many of them had complained to him of feeling enslaved by the elders whilst his life had been among the realm of the living.

But he could not remember her now. If he did, he would incapacitate himself and make himself an easy villain for the humans to kill. That he would never allow to happen. He was the killer and they were the prey, and he would never endure the opposite becoming truth.

As he entered the city, Humphrey noticed the brightness of the lights was less agitating than before. He thought he had Dimira's blood to thank for that. She was one of the elders that could walk in the light of the sun and not be burned. He hadn't yet achieved that feat although he was told that one day he could.

Though, it would probably require more centuries than he was willing to wait. He just wouldn't take the chance until it was no longer an option of him to hide in the shadows should that day come.

He watched the swaying of the human women's hips as they sashayed down the street, the strong and masculine walk of the strongest men, the tinier figures of children laughing and running in the dark beneath the smile of stars. There were small figures of little women and men that often tried to avoid what they observed as the stronger of their species.

He was tall and imposing himself, which often meant that they would stray far from him, but in the darkest of alleyways was always some unwitting victim that was ready to lay down their life for him.

Today, he felt as if he could kill a thousand of them and it still wouldn't be enough, but that was probably the razor's edge of his punishment for drinking the blood of an elder. Surely, it wouldn't have to be a literal thousand? If so, this city was damned and cursed; that was for certain.

Humphrey's gaze fell upon a woman who was walking with a man. The woman looked young with thick curly blonde hair that fell upon her bare shoulders. She was wearing a tank top and shorts so short that her backside wasn't even covered.

He tutted softly beneath his breath. Some women had

no class. He missed the olden days where women would cover up and still betray the loveliness of their figures. Not that there weren't any women like that today, he thought, but it seemed they were marginally smaller than the number of women that behaved in that manner when he was but a mortal witch.

The man was muscular-looking with a pair of shorts and a tank top, and a rather goofy looking ball cap that was pulled down over a head of tousled light brown curls.

They turned into the alleyway without taking any notice of him. They were arguing about something, he noticed, as he watched them.

"So why was she commenting on all your posts then?"

"She's a friend, you stupid bint!"

"Oh, that's a real nice thing to call you girlfriend," she snapped back, arms folded.

"Baby, come on, I'm sorry. All right? I'm sorry."

"Not as sorry as you will be," Humphrey breathed.

"Who said that?"

"Oh God! You have to protect me!"

"Don't worry, baby, no one will hurt us. It's just some wise guy that I will pummel into the ground," the man insisted.

"I'm scared."

"Baby, it'll be fine. Come on and show your face, wise guy."

"As you wish."

Humphrey stood in the pale light provided by a dingy streetlamp. He was taller than this man by several feet, his yellow eyes glistened like topazes; he made sure his fangs were visible.

"He's not even human!" the woman screamed, taking off and running.

"Oh, baby, they're fake," the man said. He stormed over to Humphrey and tugged on his fangs as if willing them to come out of the vampire's mouth.

Humphrey smirked wider, slapping the human away from his mouth. "Now that I've got your attention, it's time to die." The man crumpled away as his blood left his body drop by drop. Humphrey dropped his body like it was nothing more than a bag of garbage before he leisurely followed after the woman.

He noted that she was slowing down. At first, she was throwing down trashcans and anything she came across to impede his progression in getting to her, but she was out of breath and trying to replenish some strength before running away.

Unfortunately for her, he had centuries of practice in dodging obstacles from the many victims he had taken into the arms of death. He wondered why death hadn't given him a greeting card for the holidays yet. He certainly deserved one, he thought, with a toothy grin.

He let the false lull and sense of security wash over her. Humphrey was like a cat in that he liked to play with his food. What fun was it to let the kill come swiftly and kindly like a prayer?

Nay, it was fun toying with little mortals as if they were mice before his mighty cat paws. Ready to snuff their lives out like the brief candles they were.

He slowly stepped from the shadows after her as she walked. He could see how frantic she was, whirling around herself, wondering where he was. He stealthily climbed on the side of the building, using a windowsill to launch him to a low hanging roof before he sensed what direction she was going in. He quickly got to the end of the alleyway before she could turn out of it.

The look of horror on her face when she saw him waiting for her was priceless.

"No!" she protested.

"I'm sorry, did you think I was going to let you live?" he sneered.

"Stay away from me," she insisted, taking out a lighter from her pocket.

He laughed at the small flame that it procured. Did she really think that was enough to stop the likes of him? He used magic to put out the flame before uttering a spell beneath his breath in a malicious tone of voice. The lighter came flying into his palms and he set a trash can on fire behind him before using his other foot to knock it over.

"So which is it, darling? Me, or the fire?"

"I'd choose the fire a thousand times before I'd choose you, but you forgot. I don't have to go that way. How would I escape you, if I did? You idiot."

"I thought I already proved I can outrun you, so tell me how am I the stupid one again?"

There were few things that Humphrey could forgive. Being called a fool wasn't one of them. He chased after the girl, allowing her to turn down an earlier path in the alleyway.

Too late she discovered it was a one-way street.

She turned backward to look into his smirking face, which apparently woke some fire in her because she broke the window of an abandoned building and crawled through it.

Humphrey chuckled. Well, perhaps, this would be a fun night, after all. Seemed some humans still had some fire within their bones. Good. Because most of his prey bored and chored him. It was good to know that some of them would still give him a purpose to be a predator.

He allowed her to get a healthy head start into the building before he calmly climbed into the window after her. He was amused that she thought any number of obstacles was going to stop him.

She came at him from a corner of the room with such speed that he was actually impressed. She was wielding a crowbar. If she had connected with his face, it could have done quite a bit of damage to his fangs.

However, Humphrey easily dodged this assault with his heightened senses and faster movements than those of a human. He had hated the vampire who had turned him when she had changed him many moons ago, but he had found satisfaction as a vampire since. He would thank her should she have still been in the realm of the living, but she had been killed in the flames of a human seeking vengeance. She had been like those idiot elders who had relied too much on their age and supposed acquired wisdom.

Sometimes the student superseded the master.

He grabbed the crowbar and hit the woman in the chest with it so hard that she fell to the floor with a clatter, but not hard enough to break any bones because that wouldn't make this chase any fun.

She looked at him with something like loathing as she stood to her feet.

Humphrey had to admit that this one was entertaining. She had a stronger will to live than most of his victims. Most crumbled before him like the spider that knew it would be smashed. They squirmed and flailed their appendages until they were no more.

It made him hate her a little less than some of his other victims.

"Leave me alone!" she shouted, lifting a fire extinguisher off the floor. She shot it at him, but Humphrey merely shrugged, allowing its contents to hit him.

"Not likely," he whispered in her ear, coming at her from behind when she was still fixated on the sight of the mess the extinguisher had made. He bit deeply into her throat, reveling in the woman's screams until she was no more.

He turned, kicking overgrown rats of his way, hissing back at them when they dared to cross his path. The vampire thought this chase had been rather entertaining, but his thirst still wasn't completely slaked. The beast was a greedy bastard, he thought, darkly.

How much blood did it take to sate a monster?

Humphrey didn't know if he'd ever know the answer to that. The thirst came to him every night. It never went away.

Even the elders had to contend with it.

Humphrey looked up as he saw a group of people: two women and two men. His lips curled into something sinister and cruel.

First, he attacked the one man before he knew what was happening.

The second man he had a little fun with. The second man thought he could beat the vampire with his rippling muscles.

Humphrey thought the man rather brave but also very stupid for thinking he could have nearly enough strength to beat a vampire with his fists alone. He punched the man so hard in the face that he staggered backward with a bruise and a broken nose.

"You won't defeat me," he promised.

"I can try."

"It will be futile and in vain, but yes...you can try," the vampire scoffed, amber eyes dancing maliciously in the light that poured downward from another lamp in another alley.

The man let out a snarl, charging at Humphrey, who easily stepped out of the way before the vampire drained him dry, dropping him to the ground like a piece of rotten fruit, snorting when a couple of the man's teeth fell out of his mouth in the process.

He had forgotten how fragile humans were. It was both amusing and a little pathetic, if he were honest with himself.

One woman was particularly disappointing in that she just stood there screaming, a simple lamb that was all together ready for her slaughter. Perhaps it was shock because most humans convinced themselves that vampires didn't exist until a vampire proved them otherwise.

The other woman, however, ran.

Ah, he loved it when they ran. It made this all worth it. The hunt should be thrilling or it wasn't worth it at all, he thought.

She pulled out a lighter as she stood near an abandoned gas station. The flames shot out all around her.

"That's right, shrink away from the fire, vampire. You've lost," she informed him, dark eyes laughing at him louder than the hoarse one that escaped her lips.

"Have I?" Humphrey said, his voice smooth as marble. He whispered a few incantations of dark magic and put the flames out with such speed that the woman didn't realize she was completely bathed in darkness again until he was standing directly beside her.

"Oh, God!"

"God has nothing to do with me," Humphrey remarked. "Even He can't save you now; it's too late." The vampire then bent down at the woman's throat, biting deeply into the life-giving resource that pumped so freely in her veins. She fought back, punching and screaming. She even stomped on his foot at one point, but slowly she found she could fight him no longer.

Humphrey licked the blood off his lips. Ah yes, she

had been a delight, and his thirst was vanquished. At least for tonight.

THE END

Contributor's bio:

Linda M. Crate is a writer born in Pittsburgh, yet raised in the rural town of Conneautville, Pennsylvania, whose works have been published in numerous anthologies and magazines, online and in print. She is a two-time Pushcart nominee and has a Bachelors of the Arts in English Literature. She has four published chapbooks: *A Mermaid Crashing Into Dawn* (Fowlpox Press, June 2013); *Less Than A Man* (The Camel Saloon, January 2014); *If Tomorrow Never Comes* (Scars Publications, August 2016); and *My Wings Were Made To Fly* (Flutter Press, September 2017).

THE PRINCESS
Written by Vanessa Hawkins

Once upon a time in a land of knights, kings and castles, there was a girl.

That was how the stories always started. Jane, a small child with tiny wrists and thin hair, would be sat in front of her mother, before the hearth of their small farmhouse picking at the strings of her mother's embroidery. The fire cast shadows over the creaking floorboards: characters yet to be introduced, and Jane, hearing her father chop wood outside, would listen as her mother wove fairy tales as expertly as she did her old needle and thread.

"And those fair, wonderful, innocent princesses rode off into the sunset, to live happily ever after."

Sitting in her mother's shadow, reveling in her own imagination, it didn't matter to Jane that she was unlike the fair princesses from the stories. That she was an ordinary girl, bland, dull and unimportant was no matter. Stories of love were granted to girls with dreams, and of those Jane had plenty.

"I'll find love someday, right Mummy?" Her mother always nodded sagely, swatting away the flies let in through the windows and commingling over the stew pot.

"Yes, yes. Now to your tasks." Jane giggled as she always had, going to fetch the chamber pot to empty it. She had been but a girl playing about the skirts of her mother, but now at sixteen, she was still sure of the stories her mother used to tell.

Mushrooms tumbled into her rough-spun apron like severed squirrel heads. Night had settled fast as she had harvested, and Jane, picking her head up from her endeavors, glanced in the direction of the forest path just as the sun shot its final blades of light through the underbrush. She had grown up on the threshold of the city, basking in the fumes of the polluted throwaway that meandered down the Alabaster River and embraced her family's farmlands, but even the smell of the river was obstructed by the scent of pine needles and the graveyard of seasonal foliage.

"Have I wandered too far?" she thought aloud, balling her apron in a knot about her waist as she threw back her mouse-brown hair. She pursed her pinched lips, looking across the scattered trunks of flaking birch trees with gray eyes. She had a slight jaw that sat beneath a full, round nose and her chin jutted out slightly past her upper lip from when she had fallen one summer, and took a rather harsh tumble down a craggy hill.

Her mother always scolded her for being clumsy. Jane had endeavored to be more graceful, like a princess, after that. Though she was a poor, demented farmer's daughter, bound for the city brothels if the harvest failed, Jane hung onto a dream of better times, regardless.

She surveyed the forest, turning in an effort to locate the path. Jane gnawed on her lip, scratching anxiously at the rash she had acquired a few days past. All that lay behind her was the pins and needles of the evergreens, and the scent of rotting leaves from a century of growth passed.

Jane felt frightened. She didn't realize how far she had strayed from her path. Holding her mushrooms tightly in her apron so as to not lose them, she began to walk back, chewing on her bottom lip until it was raw. The red swells upon her neck had fallen a few days ago, and only the skin down the length of her throat was peeling, but Jane scratched at it anyway. Earlier this morning she had been happy, happy she hadn't received the angry carbuncles that had begun to sprout along her mother's neck. Jane had hoped, with any luck, that they would ignore her for someone more interesting.

When she heard the sound of coyotes however, yipping like laughing devils, Jane began to run. A dull and bland girl she may be, but certainly a meal enough for wild dogs.

Her skirts flapped wildly behind her, grabbing at roots and fallen branches like a traitor. Jane's thin hair swept from her shoulders in a tangled clump as she ran, and flakes of skin flecked off from her neck like snowflakes. She ran until her breathing overpowered the sound of the forest and she bent over, retching yellow bile, void of meat, into the brush. When Jane looked up, her eyes widened like ripe, white peaches.

All Jane had ever dreamed about was adventure, of love and romance and of meeting Prince Charming. She couldn't read a single letter, but her mother's words were decorated by tales of young girls being swept away by knights, or of princes coming to claim their brides. Jane had heard of castles and knights and of royalty, but never had she seen a thing like them.

Her mother was a milkmaid after all. Every Monday the tired old shrew went to the market to sell milk and whatever other things she had managed to grow in their gardens. Her father, oft times full of liquor and dementia, usually spent his days in the barns forgetting who he was. He would kill the meat-kings when they got underfoot and he mistook them for elves, and yell at the trees when they took on the guise of hellish underlings. Amid all the poor, lonely images farm life granted to a young girl, nothing—not even her mother's words—could breathe as much life into the surreal picture before her now: a hilltop sprouting a wondrous castle, like a mound of stale bread with a dollop of cream on top.

For all the sickness and filth and dead meat-kings in her life, Jane clasped the image to her breast, dropping the mushrooms to bounce about her feet.

The moon illuminated the castle, dappling the ramparts in sparse light strangled by clouds. It towered above her, greater than any mountain she had seen before. Turrets with dark red roofs, and square stone ramparts decorated the outer wall like lace. The drawbridge yawned open over a sleeping brook, and large diamond shaped windows winked back at her from above.

Jane stood up, still gasping for breath like a bunny with an arrow through its chest. The moon above swept behind a thick blanket of cloud and the stars hid beyond. Jane looked about herself, her apron covered with dirt before walking forward, dreaming.

The inner courtyard was overgrown. Weeds and groves of hemlock crawled up the castle walls among the vines and yellowed lichen. There was a large wooden statue of a horse with red flowers blooming from inside its belly. Flora meandered out from the cracked and moldering wood, and down the beast's legs. A large bush loomed close to the inner doorway. It looked to have once been an angel with majestic cedar wings, but had since grown amok and now resembled a monster.

Jane shivered from the cold. Dead leaves had caught in the hem of her dress and were dragging behind her like a rotting child. Approaching the door, she pushed on the slightly rusted handle and wasn't surprised when it folded open before her.

Dank carpets; old, moldering furniture; and dusty wooden tables filled the great hall. Jane scratched at her neck and shook her hand free from dead skin.

"Hello?" She called, but no one answered.

It was like an old music box, she thought. Inside, the castle still sung to an old tune of royalty, romance and chivalrous knights. It was dark inside but, curiously, candles and lanterns had been lit and they illuminated the way like tiny sprites.

She breathed in the stale air as she departed the main chamber into a den. Her heart was knocking in her chest, and Jane couldn't help but hope someone other than her would hear it.

"Hello?" Jane called again, her voice raspy and full of phlegm. The den was much like the entry-hall, full of dust and cobwebs, but in the center of this room was a large sofa of jade leather, unlike anything she had seen. Sitting in the center of it was a crown of gold decorated with dried and withered hemlock.

Jane blinked, taking a step forward. She had never before beheld gold. She remembered her mother telling her once that gold was sunlight spun into stone, and that only the noblest of men could ever seek to grasp it.

Taking her apron into her hands to protect her fingers

from the wilted hemlock, Jane gingerly removed the poisonous plant. She wondered if the gold would burn her, if a small farm girl could even grasp such an object of beauty. But as it slipped into her hands, cool like an axe blade in winter, Jane smiled, wondering if she was not so bland after all.

She polished the delicate crown. It was inlaid with diamonds, and one sparkling ruby in the center. The jewels reminded her of the bulb-like heads on her mother's sores. Jane was caught in a moment of awe when she endeavored to lift the golden crown atop her mousy brown locks. Visions of grandeur and a man with satin lapels floated behind her eyes. She had meant to set it on her head when a noise came from the closet.

Jane shrieked, almost dropping her treasure as she spun to regard the door. It sat off to one side of a bookshelf, and was half hidden by a fallen and ragged tapestry.

Clutching the crown to her breast like a simple child would their doll, Jane went to the door, worried that whatever was inside may try and take it from her. She opened it anyway, thoughts of magic luring her curious mind forward. When the door swung open however, her eyes threatened to consume her face.

There was a body inside, wreathed in hanging weapons. Axes, swords and bloody maces swung like old limbs around it. Its skin sagged from rot, and in sections it had sloughed off like boiled parchment. Tiny, bluebottle flies moved around the body, dressing it in shimmering sapphire. Some parts were so dense Jane had trouble seeing flesh beyond. The smell was overwhelming. It was worse than the Alabaster River.

It smelled like so many of the meat-kings her father had left to rot underfoot. It smelled like waste, like her mother's boils when Jane had been forced to kiss her goodbye. Atop its head the skin was completely degraded, and long hair fell dead around its shoulders from a section of scalp that had slid from the skull. Still tangled midst the hair were stems of dying hemlock.

Jane backed away. Her scream had caught in her throat and was as choking as a mad man's hand. The chorus of flies hissed deafeningly in her ears, a deathly serenade. Her fingernails dug into her palms, drawing blood, and in an instant she had turned, running out the den and down the entry hall towards the main courtyard.

"Who are you?"

Jane tripped when she saw the man at the entrance, falling forward and crushing her nose against the stone cobbles. Tears fell down her dirty cheeks in brown rivers, and pushing herself back she watched him as he spoke to her again, her fluttering heart still not free from the cage of her mother's fairy tales.

"Who are you?" she replied, blood and snot spurting out her nostrils. His clothes were sodden, and past him she could see out into the night and the new rain that was falling in sheets. He was wearing a loose, white tunic, opened at the throat and exposing his chest. Long, black hair fell around his thick shoulders and broad jawline. His eyes were squinted as he regarded her, his mouth pressed into a thin line beneath a rounded nose.

When he spoke, his voice was deep, like a chasm. "I am the Prince." In his hand was a woodcutter's axe, and still clinging to its edge was a bright, red splash of blood. "Are you my new Princess?"

In all the stories the Prince was handsome. He had a thick neck that broadened into a large, dark chest. Black hair spilled over his collarbone like oil. His face was square. The Prince had brown eyes that stared at her.

"Your…" she began, wiping her nose.

"My new Princess." This time, when he said it, it

wasn't formed as a question. Jane paled, pressing her palms into the cobbles to force herself to her legs. All at once her mother's stories were transforming, and the shadows she recalled dancing about the hearth as a child were finally taking their forms.

"No-no-no sir. I just got lost. I…"

He showed his teeth. He had the smile of a mad wolf.

"You have my crown." He had begun to walk towards her, the axe dragging along the ground like a dead thing. It hissed against the cobbles. "Who else would steal into my home and take it?" His dark eyes narrowed, as his voice grew dark like a devil's kiss. "Yes. Who else could you be?"

Jane took a step away, wiping the heel of her palm on her rough-spun gown. A thin grease of snot shined along the fabric. Her breath came out as ragged gasps. "I-I-I'm sorry, sir. I'll…" She looked down at the splatter of bright blood along the axe blade. "I'll just leave."

He screamed, and as the sudden burst of noise echoed along the entry-room, Jane spun on her heels, running away towards a large staircase leading up to the second floor. The carpet lining the stairway was moth-eaten and slippery from age and she tripped going up, slamming her chin on the edge as her fingernails clawed along the surface and snapped off in an ill attempt to keep her momentum.

The Prince was behind her, swinging the axe and missing along the fabric between her legs. Jane ripped herself away when he attempted to grab her and haul her back. Her bladder let go as she once again began to run up the stairs. She could feel the warm urine running between her legs to spill along the carpet and was ashamed, disappointed, despite the fear hammering in her belly.

"GO AWAY!" She shrieked, struggling to escape

him. Tears wet her cheeks as she reached the top. When she looked behind her, Jane saw him pulling the axe from the stairwell and pick up a small shred of her dress that had been torn from her gown. She coughed from the sudden exertion, looking towards the left corridor as he lifted the soiled cloth to his nose and inhaled.

The door at the end was unbarred, but when she entered, Jane was thrilled to find a brass key already in the lock. Turning it, she backed away, wiping her mouth and chin with the same hand that still held the golden crown.

"Oh delightful! A new dainty to liven up the place!"

Jane slapped a hand over her mouth before she could scream at the sudden voice. Behind her was a large, velvet curtain of dark crimson. It swept across the room on golden hooks, bisecting the large space otherwise filled with nothing.

Jane could feel her nostrils flare, blowing out stale breath over the backs of her hands.

"Don't worry, dainty one. I won't hurt you. I can help you." The voice was masculine, but high pitched and nasally. "Just open the curtain my dear so I can see you."

Jane looked back towards the door, listening for footsteps or any indication that the Prince had followed her. She felt like sobbing, betrayed. Her mother had given hope to a poor girl who hadn't any. Lowering her hands, Jane swallowed hard before stepping close to throw the curtain aside.

She shrieked, clutching at her breast, coughing up phlegm as she stumbled back and attempted to quell the involuntary noise. A long, spindly man wearing a jester's garb was drawn over a large, wooden wheel. His limbs were tied to the ends, and he was spinning very, very slowly. Atop his head he wore a three-tiered harlequin cap with rusty little bells at the end.

"Who are you?" She whispered coarsely, blinking back her tears and very aware of the wet spot running between her legs.

"Oh Dainty, I'm his court jester of course. Just been hanging around for the fun of it!" He cackled with laughter, and the bells atop his head chimed.

"Shhh! He'll hear you!" Jane looked back towards the door handle, expecting it to shudder. When it remained silent the Jester continued and Jane sniffed.

"Oh," his thin face frowned, and she noticed the white face-paint crack and peel along his forehead.

"The poor Prince. He hasn't been the same since his True Love died."

"True love?" Jane bit the inside of her cheek, realizing she had a canker sore and wincing.

"Yes!" He shook his head, causing the bells to jingle. "She died a long time ago, and a curse was set on the poor dear Prince."

Jane scratched the back of her neck nervously, biting her nails after to scrape the dead skin from beneath them. "I just want to go home." She began to cry, her face ugly and red. "I'm sorry I came. I'm so, so sorry."

"Shh shhh." The Jester cooed from atop his wooden wheel. "No need for tears, dainty one. *You* could break the curse you know. Stop the Prince and become a real Princess. It's easy! Then you could live here."

There was a faint hope in her belly, something that told her all fairy tales had their share of monsters to defeat. But princesses didn't slay monsters; they were rescued from them. "I don't want to. He's demented."

"Ah well most nobles are my dear. It's caused by inbreeding." The Jester smiled. "But if you could break the curse he would be as sweet as cured ham once more. I promise." Jane bit her lip, wiping her nose. "I bet you could do it. Yes! You have the crown after all."

Jane looked down at the crown. She had almost forgotten about it. The diamonds and ruby in the center seemed to glow like stars. They were so shiny they hurt her eyes.

"R-Really?" She felt her mother's stories crawling into her mind. Sunlight spun into stone. Only the noblest of men could seek to grasp gold, she recalled.

"I bet that's why you're here, in fact!" His bells danced from atop his cap, interrupting her thoughts. Though he was tied to the wheel, his body jerked in his restraints happily. "To wear the crown and become the new Princess!"

"But…"

"It wouldn't be hard. All we need's a kiss."

"A kiss?" She pressed her fingers to her lips. They felt scaly. She wished they didn't.

The Jester nodded, the wheel spinning so he was slowly becoming upright. "Yes. You just need to let him give you the kiss!"

"But he tried to kill me. He's a murderer!" Jane took a step back, but the Jester only guffawed, seeing hope like a mote of blood in her eyes.

"That's because you weren't wearing the crown, Dainty. Put it on your head. Come on, do it." Jane considered him uneasily. The crown was heavy in her hands, still cold. Reluctantly she complied. It sat upon her tangled locks like a golden egg nestled within a snarled nest.

"Beautiful! Pretty, pretty! A dainty doily!" The ropes held fast as the Jester jerked from mirth.

"N-Now what?" The fear in her voice was palpable.

"Now go let him give you the kiss!"

The door handle rattled. Jane jumped. The remainder of her bladder let go. She whimpered, grasping at the fabric between her legs for shame. Her eyes pled to the Jester for help, to turn her into a real princess, not this bland, dull girl smelling of piss.

"The kiss!" He said jovially. "The kiss, the kiss! He will love you, I promise!"

"But look at-"

"True love cares not, Dainty! Cares not! Save him from the curse."

The voice was low and husky as it crept from beyond the door. "My Princess?" It said. There was a scratching sound coming from the other side. Jane turned, weeping, her nose running into her mouth. There were no windows in the room, or other doors. This was the only way out.

"Come out, Princess." She clenched her skirts into a ball, moving towards the door. The crown atop her head sat perfectly in place. There was another long scratch, as though from a fingernail. Jane felt her teeth grit together. Behind her the Jester was still whispering, *the kiss the kiss* as she tore open the door, dreaming of the better things young girls deserved.

He was there, smiling down at her, his eyes immediately claiming hers. His dark skin looked warm in the dim lighting from the candles, his teeth, like chiseled pearls.

The kiss! The kiss! The kiss!

Jane looked past him into the corridor. In his hand he still held the axe, bright with blood. There was no way past him, but maybe she could finally have her Prince Charming. Maybe this was the beginning of her life of adventure and romance. The beginning of her own story, just like the ones her mother used to tell.

Jane tilted her head up towards him, her lips trembling as they sought his. Her eyes closed, and tears ran down her cheeks. The Prince kissed her, and his mouth was warm and tasted sweet.

The kiss! The kiss! The kiss!

Jane felt herself smile, exhaling out her nose as his lips traveled along hers. She could still smell the scent of the Alabaster River around her. She wished she could smell like flowers and lovely things, not the human grease that had poured from out the city.

"THE KISSSSSSSSSS!"

The Jester cackled.

" – of death."

The Prince stepped back as Jane was caught in a dream of pretty dresses, and ivory lace.

He buried the axe into her skull.

* * *

The Prince smiled as he carefully entwined hemlock through the golden barbs of her crown. She had been cleaned, disrobed and redressed to fit her new station. She looked resplendent in green brocade. He had combed her hair until it shined, and coiled silk, golden threads betwixt it to hide the large yawning cleft in her skull. She was perfect, and he had rescued her.

Jane stared at him lifelessly from the royal throne, glassy eyes still caught in a silly girl's dream. Her eyes were held open by pins cleverly stuck into her eyelids. He had hammered iron spikes into her hands to keep them from sliding away, and smeared a poultice over the rotting rash on her neck to keep her from spoiling early. Behind the Prince the Jester laughed and tumbled along the floor in cartwheels.

The kiss, the kiss, the kiss of death!
Bound to take away your Breath!
The Prince no longer loves Bereft.
Your Soul be gone but your Corpse is left!

The Jester sang, his bells jingling a tune as he somersaulted. The Prince paid him no mind, having eyes only for his True Love. He smiled lovingly at his new Princess and bent to kiss her cold, dead lips.

"I promise to love you forever." He said, eyes full of heartfelt devotion.

"Or until the bugs come in." The Jester yowled back, turning once more on his heel and flipping backwards like an imp as the sun began to crest the forest undergrowth.

THE END

Contributor's bio:

Vanessa Hawkins was born and raised in rural Canada. Her hometown in sleepy St. George, New Brunswick, afforded her a considerable amount of time to peruse her imagination. After a few short years of boredom, her creative thoughts quickly began to metamorphose into the musings of a macabre and downright weird—though charmingly social—child. A life-long lover of horror, Vanessa wrote her first story in the genre when she was only in grade five. It was titled *Mutilated* and it warranted her a trip to the school guidance counselor. A lifetime later, she continues to write about anything gruesome, terrifying, paranormal and erotic, though she has since found herself enthralled in the world of fantasy steampunk. Her first two books, *Gloryhill* and *A Sinister Portrait of Cherie Rose,* exemplify her fascination with the weird. Currently she is partying it up with her husband, Brendon, and a dog she really wants but hasn't gotten yet.

YANKEE ROSE
Written by P. Alanna Roethle

The screen door banged in the hot desert wind. *Slap, slap*. As despondent as the rest of the world, the world of this hot tin house, the quiet moaning wind that sifted dust into the cracks of her face, into the bed sheets, under the window in dust fingers to the gold-flecked white Formica kitchen counter. The sighs and slices of the old ten-piece—*well, nine-piece now*—knife set marked the counter. The missing knife still lay under the bed where she'd laid it, so quietly, remembering with a pause in her mind where it lay— how coldly and patiently it waited. She could see it now, closing her eyes, its cheap serration glinting among the dust and atop the shag green carpet, a deeper green where it hid below the bed from the scorching rays of the Mojave sun. The sun bore through the windows and the blinds to strain the color from everything, until it all matched the bone and dirt colors of the desiccated landscape.

Anton was out now. He'd torn off in the bleached old yellow Corsica, clouds of the fated dust following him, ghosts of thought waving at him as they hovered in his trail, watching to see if he would skid into the creosote, spread his brain matter among the spines of the cholla cactus.

Rose blankly stared at the rounded dirty-white walls of the trailer, picking like an addict at a frayed spot in the short jean cut-offs that bit into thick pale thighs. She tried to stay out of the sun. Mom said even Navajo get the skin cancer. Old Dezba had a large dark mole like a face that grew out of the side of her chin, with white hairs feeling the air like tentacles. Rose supposed that was skin cancer. Skin cancer might not be a terrible way to go. She could imagine it crawling from her face to her throat, inside and stealthy so you couldn't see it from the outside, from the round smoothness of her skin and face. It would start as a tiny brown spot, but it would go deep and, by the time that little line of rot reached her heart, it would be time to die. No one would know what was happening to her, no one would know until it was too late. She knew she would probably feel the pain, feel the deep angry ache as it burrowed to her heart, the cancer. She would hold her face still as stone, still as the masks *shima sani* had hung on the adobe walls of her house on the res, when she was still alive.

Rose was good at that. She was good at holding her thoughts deep behind her face, so that the twitch of errant nerves and cold blackness of her eyes were the only things that moved. Most people couldn't read anything when her stone face was on. Except for Anton. Sometimes he could tell, from across the room even, and if she was thinking about him a small cruel smile would tighten the bottom of his face, never reaching his odd brown eyes. She would feel a chill then, inside her, as if he was touching her heart with ice. It was stronger than that—his eyes could hold you, choke you, deep and oppressive as black thunderclouds that could build in minutes over the purple mountains. It was the feeling of dying, when you looked at him. Those last fluttering beats of the heart, the sigh of air as it left lungs for the last time. She shuddered deep within her still self at the thought of him, behind the soft fuzz of the weed she'd been smoking since she awoke. He never left her alone anymore, never. Here she was wasting precious time being stoned, when she could be…what? She deserved it. She deserved him.

Tick, tick, tick. That stupid clock. The supreme quiet had descended, the quiet of the afternoon when the sun was baking the land. The whitewashed sky fell in heat waves to the sun stroked earth. Rose let the weed spread her out over the house, let other tiny sounds enter her head and calm her. The sigh of the trailer as it settled, heated, and expanded. The slap of the screen door in the stiff gusts of air. The clock.

That fucking piece of shit clock!!

The noise bothered her, snapped her out of the reverie. Paranoia tinged her high. He'd be back soon—he had to be. He wasn't working today. The fear of him was growing day by day. She was mad at herself, so mad that she'd thought he was ever her friend. That she could have been so naïve, such a stupid little girl. She hadn't known any better. There had been no one to tell her. She tried to believe that.

Rose, Rose. You gotta get out of here. She couldn't move herself, couldn't think anymore. She was hiding under this new face, hiding bound and gagged in a dark place where nothing made sense.

Shima sani had told me. She knew. The words knocked against the fragile onion layers of her consciousness. She pictured her grandmother dying, her small shaky hands clasping and opening, clasping and opening as she gripped the last few seconds she had to live. Rose hadn't been there, off partying, who knows where. Getting fucked up again so she didn't have to think about anything. The old woman's last words had been for her, for Rose. She said them in Navajo, quiet and raspy, in her daughter's ear. Because it was in Navajo, Rose knew she meant it.

"Tell her, tell my Rose. Tell her no *Nakai*! Not ever." It was a strange last thing to say, a strange use of the only air left that your lungs will ever hold. "Tell her to promise me."

When Rose had gotten home the night her grandma had left the world, she'd stumbled as she entered and knocked the keys crashing from their hooks to the floor. The light came on in the living room, and she watched bleary-eyed as her mother came out of the dark from where she had been sitting, hands folded around her sanity. Small, cold hands, like her heart. "Shima's dead. She died tonight."

Rose felt a twinge under the vodka. It was a black twinge, like the lowering of clouds before a storm. Like the darkness of a mineshaft. She headed back to her room, wavering and feeling the wall. Her mother went back to sit on the couch. Over coffee the next morning, her mother told her what *shima sani* had said. She hadn't made any breakfast, and Rose was happy because the bile rose vodka-flavored to rub seductively against the back of her throat.

"No Mexicans?" Rose said softly. "That was it?"

"And to promise her, Rose. She said it because of Brenda, and because she said some spirit told her." Her mother watched her out of the corners of almond-shaped eyes, solemn but still condescending, always condescending.

Brenda was dead too. She had died a few years earlier, at the uncertain age of twenty. Her boyfriend had strangled her and hung her from a closet rod. Right now the boyfriend still lived in Arizona somewhere, safe and happy with his new wife and the baby he had started right before he let Brenda's children see how blue Mommy could turn. The social workers found out how she died when the two- and- four-year-olds acted it out with Barbie dolls. That didn't turn out to be enough evidence, and they never found her body anyway. That boyfriend had been Mexican, and now Rose's family thought the whole race was just bad juju. Rose hadn't thought much about it, besides that it sucked and was sad.

Now she knew. She knew *shima sani* had seen Anton, and seen what he would do to her granddaughter.

* * *

He had hunched over her last night, his little dick half-flaccid as he tried to put it in while she laid there, an unfeeling lump. Inside her rage grew; a hatred for him and his pathetic attempts at sex. He could only screw little girls, girls he found online like he'd done her. She was nineteen, she was lonely, and she wanted to get out of the house. Anton talked to her for months before he'd suggested they meet, and always she laughed him off.

"Whatever, perv," she said, full of confidence that he couldn't touch her. Finally out of boredom one day, and because he said he'd take her to see Ice Age and buy a bottle, she'd met him at Circle K. He never looked at her the entire time, eyes shifting away when she faced him, strange shuffling movements and nervous tics. He was ugly, she thought. His head was strange-shaped, and his eyes were too light for his skin. After that he'd started buying booze when she wanted, bringing over coke when she wanted to be high, and always never touching her. One night when he dropped her off after another movie, she ran back out to the car in only panties and her t-shirt to grab her purse that she'd drunkenly left on the holey pleather seat. That's how much she trusted that he'd never touch her.

Rose felt the rage begin to break loose inside of her, where it danced in faster and faster circles like molecules in boiling water. She moved suddenly, shoving Anton backward, his penis flopping ludicrously. He looked up, shock flashing in his pale weak eyes. Anger quickly replaced shock, replaced by something else, that suffocating thing.

"Get off of me, you piece of shit! You aren't even a man! You can't even get it up!" Rose shrieked at him, turning away from his eyes, wiping her hands across her stomach where his sweat polluted her skin. Her naked body stared at her in the cracked half mirror hanging from the back of the bedroom door. It was all pale, corpulent, except for the redness where he had kneeled and sweated on her. All of her was dead, except where he leeched on her. She turned to look at him again, to scream something.

He hunched at the end of the bed, his stringy body shaking, mumbling to himself, growling. He had his penknife in his hand, drawing it slowly across his arm where the myriad scars already there looked like the lines on the moon, the aftermath of a cataclysmic meeting of masses with no control over trajectory. The dark blood followed his knife, a trail of thought.

Rose had turned and hurried to the bathroom to lock herself in there. She spent hours painting her nails, listening to Anton's death metal rage tonelessly as she layered red polish over itself until her toes glittered like rubies. She hummed to herself, comforted by the thrum in the back of her throat, trying to dispel the darkness that blackened every corner of her thoughts like burning paper, the way the black would creep in from each side in little tongues and the crumbling ash follow. Rose had started drawing the same blood lines with that serrated knife over the inside of her arms and thighs, where nobody could see. She had never seen anyone do it until Anton. Now she knew his crazed spirit; the crazy in him was rubbing off on her. *Fa la la, fa la la,* she sang under her breath. *Fa la la la la, la la la la.* Anton said her humming drove him crazy, that she needed to keep her mouth shut. *You're already crazy, ma'ii,* she thought.

* * *

She heard the car, far down the dusty road, spinning past tall watching saguaros and the dry, sad palo verdes. Her heartbeat quickened in the dullness of her body. It was the only sign that she was afraid. She lay back against the cool tub, feeling the trickle of sweat down her spine as it ran away from her. She looked numbly down at her arm, then at the knife in her other hand. She didn't remember pulling it from the carpet under the bed. She didn't remember drawing its biting teeth across her arm, or maybe she remembered but it blurred together with the other times—his and hers. Spots of bright red blood dotted the white of the tub, of her thighs. It matched her nails, and she smiled a little to see it. The Corsica stopped in front of the door and jerked a few times before silence descended again. She heard the door slam, and his quiet shuffling steps come up the two rickety wooden steps to the door, the steps she always tripped on when she was drunk. She closed her hand tightly around the knife, and shrunk against the tub.

You crazy bastard. Don't come in here, don't talk to me.

She heard him come down the hall, heard him muttering to the spirits in his head, to the demons that possessed every waking moment. He just got worse and worse, after she moved in, telling her that loving her made him that way. With him, emptiness was the only thing she knew. A great, cavernous emptiness like a carved pumpkin, its seeds and guts spread in the dirt and its new face one with only one expression. Then it starts to rot. The inside of her mind was full of holes, rotten parts that had fallen in on themselves, that smelled like vomit. He had taken away her friends, deleted her phone, and ostracized her family.

Rose crept from the bathroom, avoiding the creaks in the floor. His back was to her, as he typed away, looking for other little girls to take advantage of. He told her he was doing black magic on them, the same black magic he'd done for some of the Oklahoma tribes—the same magic that had caused his girlfriend before her to kill herself while on the phone with him. He told her these things, and she believed him.

Her mind snapped, the elastic of a rubber band eaten by the sun—a crack! Red flashed as she leapt with the little knife gleaming in her hand, raising it high and slim and deadly. In her strained mind's eye she saw herself, poised like a warrior, strength and purpose in her arm—and his face. The stark fear as the steel entered his body, the jerk—and then nothing.

* * *

Everything was white, and she couldn't get away.

The sweat beaded on her forehead, down between her breasts, and panicked struggle only made her bonds tighter, the heat greater, stifling. Her eyes opened, and the padded walls around her shocked her with their anger, their forbidding presence.

"NO!" she screamed, flailing her arms, bucking against the bonds, panting. "No, I'm not crazy! Somebody help me!" Even through her fear she realized she needed to calm down.

Hyperventilating, she stopped thrashing, craning her neck up to look out the tiny square window. His small, cruel smile was there, framed in the reinforced glass, his watered coffee eyes gleaming in at her. His black magic worked. He was right.

THE END

Contributor's bio:

P. Alanna Roethle is a freelance technical and copy editor and writer currently based somewhere between Tucson, Arizona and Austin, Texas. She is renovating a 1970s Airstream and welcomes all assistance with wiring and plumbing. She has recently published a children's book, *The Rat Who Didn't Know He Was King*, and has a forthcoming memoir titled *Roads on Her Face.* She can be found online at roadsonherface.com

BLOOD PUDDLES
Written by J Snow

Catori strode down the vacant street in hurried, long, purposeful steps. She had one thing on her mind and hoped Kaedan had everything ready when she got home. They were due one good night. She picked up her pace.

The summer night temperature dropped several degrees in mere minutes. The howl of the winds grew loud. Catori lifted her chin, squinted at the ominous red-lined, black skies gathering overhead. The building storm seemed alive, threatening, and she couldn't shake the thought it was aware of her, watching her. Biting down on her bottom lip, she folded around herself, rubbed bare arms with cold fingers, then hunched her shoulders and increased her stride rate with tiny, offbeat skips.

Absent were the night walkers headed to or from dealers or tricks, gone were the rust-bucket hooptie-mobiles that littered this end of town most times, and with both, the packs of teenage boys in search of the elusive *two dolla' booty*.

The lack of police was most unusual. She witnessed no cruisers during either of the mandatory run-throughs, a new requirement by the city council in response to the staggering rise in missing persons reports the last couple months. Increased patrolling was a measure taken to ensure their presence was significant and noticeable to ease the minds of both locals and booty tourists alike.

Vibes of tranquility brought on by the inactivity of the street were misleading. Something was not right. Streetlights broke the silence with a steady humming, but the flickering lost rhythm and caught her eye. She stopped and stood rigid, watching, listening.

Darkness crept along the well-worn paths of the missing and settled deep into the yawning shadows. Shivers crawled upward along her spine, a ripple of goosebumps across her flesh. The tiny muscles of her eye flexed as she strained to see through the fog slipping down and settling into the crevices of the valley.

Wrapped in mist was a silhouette—a small girl in a flowing gown. Wind whipped hair the length of her frame whipped around and behind her like long, tangling tendrils. Catori blinked hard, trying to bring the shadowed face into focus, but it, instead, stretched the distance between them.

Who the hell—

Amarinas.

An unspoken answer to her unspoken question.

How—Wha—

Her breath caught in her throat, choked back her thought as the stench of decay seeped through the inky shades of moonless night. She swallowed rapid shallow gulps of thick, sticky, somewhat salty air; breathing became laborious, each inhalation harder than the last.

The presence of a spectral being was so intense Catori thought a hand had wrapped around her neck. She fought to free herself from it, but hers alone clutched the skin stretched tight across her windpipe.

"You've been toying with me far too long," a low, guttural hiss in her ear, a vibration inside her head.

A single droplet of blood hit the pavement at her feet. It splashed as the world slowed—every frame a tick of a second, the length of an echo. She watched with ever widening, dilating eyeballs as the drop spread into a dark, dense puddle.

No, Draven. Lay her down with dignity. She has suffered enough, the silhouette unspoke, a distant ringing in the silence, but the words pulsated through Catori as if a growl had risen from the depths of her bowels.

"She chose death over dignity long ago," the hiss replied.

Only the foul and wretched belong to you. She is not yours. She is ours. You may have the other. The one who crushed her spirit and has kept her captive these many years.

The girl's voice formed inside her mind, thoughts placed in proper sequence like puzzle pieces, but reflected off her flesh with a burning, prickling sensation. The effect was painful, dizzying.

Thunder cracked open the storm clouds.

Behind Catori, a footstep. She broke into a run.

Fat raindrops pounded her face, drenched her as she raced through the blackness of the windswept street. She was just shy of three blocks from home, covered the distance like lightning, but was sure half an hour had lapsed since she'd fled the blood puddle.

Survival mode triggered, she was working off blind, adrenaline-pumped panic alone, unable to rationalize her experience, movements, anything.

She burst through the door and slammed it shut behind her. Exhaling a heavy breath, she pushed herself against it, her back to the cheap, flimsy, panel-like wood that couldn't withstand the kick of a child but provided a sense of protection, a divider between her and the rest of the world with all its horrors.

Ringlets of bleached blonde hair clung to her oval face as she turned and pressed her ear to the door. Her awareness heightened, all was quiet except the tick— tick—ticking of a cheap watch and her controlled, almost-soundless, panting.

Black makeup smeared her eyes, made them look hollowed out if not for darting pupils seated in strained, protruding whites.

Too terrified to scream as she ran, her heart and lungs had tightened with every pound of her foot against concrete and every clap of thunder that peeled open the starless sky. The cool wood of the door and the lack of all but rain on the other side brought relief in the form of tears spilling down her wind-blistered cheeks. She covered her face in her hands and slid down to the floor.

Kaedan cleared his throat and tapped his faux gold Timex. Head tilted back, eyebrows high with inflated mockery, he tried to be comical looking down a crooked, blackhead encrusted nose from five too many bar fights. "What the fuck happened to you?" he teased.

His voice was a deep, soothing baritone, one that sent quivers through the cores of most women until their eyes fell on the disgusting animal that owned it: a short, greasy, three hundred pound, bloated, abscessed, tumor of a man that stunk of rotting goat cheese.

How she got so lucky to land such a man was beyond her reasoning skills.

His mouth curved downward in a soft frown though

more relaxed than fraught, he continued to survey her, a sopping heap piled at the foot of the door.

He asked again, this time with a note of annoyance, "What's got you stuck stupid, Cat?"

Catori replied with parted lips but no words. Her eyes unfocused and cast downward, she sought a believable explanation, but the harder she tried, the more the corners of her mouth curled downward and the more her bottom lip pushed up to meet it. She sat motionless, frowning, unblinking.

She broke her own silence with a quick sniffle to keep snot from dripping onto her lip—she was not a runner, the extent of her exercise routines being legs-skyward aerobics and gymnastics-worthy dismounts, and the sprint home had opened her airways wide to take in the heaving gasps of oxygen, the result being reddened, raw, flared nostrils and a running faucet of mucus.

Catori wiped away tears with the back of her hand in one quick movement, then her nose, trying to compose herself before turning to face Kaedan.

"Talk to me, Cat?"

She struggled to speak, brows upward slanting and knotted, she was holding her breath without realizing it, ears burning, throat swollen.

"The fuck, girl?" There was a hint of concern in his words; irritation overshadowed it.

Still and silent beneath the weight of fear, she was unable to put her thoughts into words, continued to stare at him trembling muteness.

"Crazy bitch," Kaedan muttered with a shake of his head. He rose from the brown vinyl sofa—yellow tufts of cushion pushed itself up through cracks of aging and switchblade slashes from his rage fits—and walked over to Catori.

He held out his hand. She gawked at it, stunned motionless a moment, then up at him, forehead furrowed, then back to his extended hand. She lifted her own, reached for his, slow and timid, watchful of his expression. He pulled his hand back with a jerk.

"Goddamnit. The *fuck* is wrong with you? The take, Cat. You get paid to lay or what?"

Understanding dawned on her. She let out her breath and slid her hand down the front of her shirt, low cut black satin torn at the shoulder, to fish out the folded stack of bills from her tattered bra. He snatched it from her hand, fanned it out for a quick count, then squeezed shut his eyes, pinched the root of his nose between them, lips tightened into a thin, pale line, and inhaled a sharp breath. He held it two counts before exhaling with a harsh and ragged quake.

In a tight, steady voice, he asked, "Anything else?"

Catori answered with a cautious shake of her head. Her listless, pewter-gray eyes turned into liquid tremors. Pupils unadjusted to the indoor lighting and cracked open a monster headache. Shaking it, moving it at all sent spikes through her brain.

"What is this? Huh? What?" he mimicked her head shake with exaggerated movements. "The fuck, Cat? No? Nothing? You didn't score even a bump?"

She responded with an unblinking stare.

"So help me, bitch. If you're holding back—"

"No. No, Kaedan. I wouldn't ever. No. I swear."

"Can you tell me," he paused for dramatic effect, "what good a whore is if she can't even score a solid bump?"

Her lip quivered.

Kaedan turned away and paced the twelve-foot length of the cramped room, head down, tensed orbs of dull green to the floor. He crumpled the bills in one hand while the other ran through thick knots of matted black curls once, again when he turned directions. Each pass of the floor's length was a rake through the hair.

Catori sat, her eyes the only thing moving. They followed him back and forth, back and forth. When his feet stopped, so did his hand. He tossed the money onto the coffee table.

"Don't move. Don't you dare fucking move," he growled.

The crumpled bills landed next to a bent-handled spoon holding a small chunk of cotton torn from an unused cigarette butt. Her eyes moved from it to the syringe, still wet with amber droplets, to a thin, cracked, leather belt. The sight of the tourniquet created a tickling at her center.

Kaedan headed down the hall toward the bedrooms. "Fuck!" he thundered and kicked open the door on the left at the end of the hall. Catori did as told though the allure of dope tugged strong at her insides. So inviting, enticing, wicked maddening.

She didn't dare disobey him, having spent many bloody, bruised, broken and fractured nights with sleepless eyes knowing death was close.

"No... I'm doing my best..." Catori heard him on the phone. "I'll have it by Friday... Yeah, Friday... I'm positive... I am! Goddamn, man, be cool and spot me... You know I'm good for—"

Catori jumped, startled by the loud slam of the phone's receiver. "Fucking cocksucker!" he hollered at whoever had been on the other side of the line once in the safety of disconnection.

All the dealers had the same phone. The thirty-year-old, beige, wall phone with the long, curly cord. They all believed the lower the technology, the harder it was to monitor by the 'feds, man.' It was their idea of safety net, Catori's idea of a weapon, one that didn't stray far from thought when home with Kaedan.

He returned to the living room and sat on the sofa. He jerked his hefty form with a violent thrash, threw his arms forward, causing Catori to flinch, and shook them with a bellow, "Ahhhhh!"

He believed he could force tension from his body through the fat, flat tips of his fingers. So long as it kept his rage in check, she didn't argue. He cracked his knuckles, and his pitted face sprung into the crazy grin of a lunatic, a broad, gap-toothed smile. It appeared genuine and warm. Odd.

"Fuck it. You only live once. He wants more money? He needs to come off more dope. Period."

"Oh, hell. You wish," she sighed then shot a wide-eyed glance at the front door, a response to the sudden but faint sound of scratching.

"You need to relax. It's just the mice," he laughed.

Kaedan held up a small baggie, eyeballed it, then Catori, and winked. It wasn't much, but it was better than nothing, and after two, miserable, sweltering days in hell without it, puss-filled veins stretched thin across the deep ache of bones, her body responded with a shudder. She salivated.

Her eyebrows stitched together, pleading. *Please don't play games. Not tonight. I need this*, she begged him with her mind, fearing to speak the words aloud because it would be the exact reason he withheld the dope. She wasn't chancing it, but she couldn't hide the desperation in her stare either.

"Oh, come on, babygirl. You deserve a treat once in awhile," he said, his voice kind, his mouth a lopsided, affectionate smile. Rare.

Her pinched face betrayed her doubt, and he replied to it. "I got you. Fuck that dude. There are plenty of other connections in the opiate seas. Let's not worry about that bullshit tonight. Let's just... saaaail."

She stood and crossed the room to sit on the couch beside him with controlled, methodical movements. He liked to punish her when she acted eager. Odd, rare, generous mood or not, she wasn't going to fuck this up.

Kaedan set the cotton on the table and tipped the bag over, tapping the stiff corner, filling the dip of the spoon with powder. He drew water, collected in a bottle cap, up into the syringe then emptied it onto the powder and stirred the mixture with the needle tip.

He lifted the spoon eye-level, flicked a lighter to life, and held it close beneath but not so close the flame kissed the metal. He moved the orange glow back and forth in a slow and fluid motion for equal heat distribution until the liquid came to a rapid bubbling. It was a thing he did without thought, frequent repetition having evolved into autopilot movements, but his lip curled inward over his bottom teeth, and his tongue traced its length, concentrating.

Catori watched, biting down on one side of her own lip, anticipation as electrical sparks shooting through her with a wave of free-falling weightlessness. It was a short lived exhilaration, then the itch and coldness crept over her.

He placed the tip of the needle into the cotton and drew the filtered honey-yellow solution up into the barrel. Catori grabbed the leather belt and wrapped it around her arm above the elbow. Kaedan took hold of her arm by wrapping his own over, around, then under it to hold it straight and still. She always flinched, and he always blew her vein; they didn't have enough dope to make mistakes.

He patted the inside crook of her elbow beneath yellowing, purplish bruises of previous needle punctures. She sunk her teeth into the belt to pull it tight, tighter, tugging it with her teeth, sweat beading on the grooves cut into her anxious forehead. The belt tasted burnt, acidic, bitter. She didn't care. She jerked it hard, harder, then harder still until, just as her frustration was about to spill over, the vein swelled.

He pierced the bulging vessel and pulled back the plunger, a gentle motion to keep from rupturing the fragile, pulsing rail. A swirl of blood. The barrel flooded. He pushed the plunger slow, steady, purposeful, running the amber colored liquid into her bloodstream with expert ease.

She let go the belt. A second passed. Then another. She lunged forward and vomited into the bucket by the couch. Her own, personal, puke pail. It was part of the ritual, unbearable if not competing against the savage pains of withdrawals. She wiped her lip with the back of her bare hand, slumped back and melted into the couch, eyes rolling upward.

"I think Death spoke to me tonight." Her words were tiny and sluggish. "He came in the winds of the storm."

Kaedan crumpled his eyebrows and pursed his thin, cracked lips, considered her words a minute, decided he didn't give a fuck, and turned his attention back to the spoon.

***

An eternal spirit, Amarinas came to be long before the creation of time, before the first birth crowned the horizon, created when the salty breath of the raging ocean coiled itself around the whisper of a silver-gray, storming sky. As the two parted with a lingering, silken sigh, Amarinas took the physical form of mist.

As ethereal as gossamer threads, the vapor of

beginnings edged across the drab and dreary globe, leaving smears of color in its wake and wrapped the all of nothing with its ghostly tendrils, converting abstract into actuality.

The quintessence of simplicity and profundity, neither male nor female, good nor evil, Amarinas was a being of all things, the core of which was to be the origin of all existence. She chose to appear as a young girl with hair to her ankles—youth is a thing unfeared, hair a symbol of femininity, a thing most trusted. The face, Amarinas kept hidden in darkness, for those who looked upon it gained immortality, a thing proven to be a curse.

For eons, Amarinas drifted along the lazy breeze between the oceans and the skies in a labyrinth of trails through nothingness. When eternity neared its end, nothingness became images, images transformed into thought patterns, thought patterns into abstract concepts, abstract concepts gave breath to self-awareness, and self-awareness led to the evolution of boredom.

Trapped within a perpetual state of boredom, Amarinas struggled to find meaning. A thousand years passed before the dawn of enlightenment; she realized life and death were the answer. Without death there could not be life, without life, no death, and without either, there could be no meaning, so she created both, brought them into existence as actual, tangible creatures.

Life and death were mere concepts, ideologies, philosophies varying in degrees of abstraction, and hers alone, as she alone existed. Both opposites and equals, she created one as light, the other darkness, one as female, the other male.

Life was a simple creation. Amarinas took the sterling sunlight of dawn and pressed it together as if silver clay, molded it into her idea of beauty, and life came into being. She named her Zahara.

Amarinas created death from shadows cast by fierce and raging storm clouds. The energy used for his creation was harsh and brutal, and through it death transformed into a physical being. She named him Draven.

Zahara appears as a blinding, white light, her features blurred by purity. The unborn are the only beings, which look upon her as she guides all into life.

Draven is a wraith, unseen in the realm of the living, showing himself only to those he is to usher into death.

Every life Zahara grants must succumb to death by the hand of Draven. This was Amarinas's condition upon creation. It defined meaning.

When Draven is to take a life, Zahara speaks the name.

Draped in darkness and shadow, he's often confused as both, but the dying first see Draven as a single droplet of blood.

Every life he snuffed, every death he dealt, once thought a gift, became savage, merciless punishments. His thirst for life turned insatiable, and Amarinas found it difficult to control his urges. He'd taken many lives without Zahara giving a name, and all he took without were stuck between the realm of life and that of death, lost, wandering. Amarinas threatened to destroy Draven if he took one more life without Zahara giving him a name. He gave his impulse over on condition he be allowed to keep the souls of the decrepit, the damaged and irreparable.

Amarinas agreed.

"Catori," Zahara whispered into the ear of Draven.

"Kaedan is for you," Amarinas whispered into the other.

Draven tilted his head, a simple nod, then turned to

mist. The winds of the storming night carried him away.

***

Catori blinked back into reality after an hour of heroin ecstasy, her high diluted down to short lived shivers slipping through her gut like sensual tingles. Then the itch came. The itch was enough for most addicts to become unhinged.

She scratched herself until she was bleeding in spots, unable to control it, and tried to wake the snoring filth on the couch beside her. She couldn't raise him. She relaxed and rethought her actions with the sudden realization leaving him in slumber meant she could sneak away without paying for her high. She detested his forced sexual favors more than she dreaded the pain of withdrawal. Following every fix, and used to determine if more would come, she paid with her body. It was difficult to choke back vomit when he crawled on top of her, but her need to feed her addiction reigned higher than her honor. Almost always.

Twenty-seven is too fucking old for this shit life. I'm so done—

The thought had not completed its formation; the same thought she thought upon every sobering moment, when she heard the low creak of the back porch door.

She sat ramrod straight and still, a dismal sense of foreboding looming over her. She sensed, as she had earlier, a presence, something as dark and threatening as the storm clouds.

Senses straining, she heard only a rattle, unaware it was the breath of the intruder, aware he was not far in the distance.

The porch door banged shut. Catori struggled to move, but her body turned to lead and sat frozen on the couch, rendered immovable by a force much stronger than fear.

At her feet, a single droplet of blood. Her brow raised into distressed, crinkled rifts and pulled her eyelids up with them.

The droplet grew into a thick pool of blackness at her feet. From it, a being rose upward like mist then solidified into a towering, monstrosity stripped of flesh with a skull that revolved as it searched all and everything for the owner of the name Zahara had given.

Unseeing, silver balls rolled around hollowed eye sockets until they landed on Catori. They fixated on the listless grays of her gaping stare. In the silver, she transfixed upon her reflection, fear as beaded sweat across her withering, pale face, tints of blue growing darker around the edge of her chapped mouth and sunken, black-stained eyes.

The silver balls began a slow rotation, each pass an image from her life. Catori was trapped in stillness, hypnotized by the reality of her bleak and meaningless years.

"Dear child, I gave meaning to your life. You didn't learn much on your journey, I'm afraid."

Her soul wept a deep sorrowful ache. He spoke truth.

His response was pushed into her mind with thought and reverberated through her skull: *You were given chance, and you destroyed it. You were given hope, and you abandoned it. You were given breath, and you choked it with poison. You were given life, and you mutilated it. I have come to release you but have been denied your soul. For that, I will make you suffer.*

Every word was a stabbing in her brain. The air of the room turned heavy and sticky with the putridness of rot, leaving a foul and sour taste on her tongue. She could smell her own death.

"Take me," she breathed and let go the struggle to move.

The last image shown through his reflective orbs was her lifeless, bloated body in the exact spot she now sat. Flies ate from the rotting sections on the side of her face and abdomen. Dead, blackened pieces of skin slipped off her frame, drooped from her jowls and neck.

She gave up in that moment and surrendered herself to Draven as a single tear squeezed itself from the edge of her unblinking eyes.

The heartbeat racing hard beneath her ribcage slowed to a stop as she quit her mental fight to hang onto a life long since dead. Draven reached through her chest and crushed it with a single squeeze of his skeletal hand. Her breath froze in her throat. Her eyes turned to milky spots.

Intense, searing pain pushed is way through every stitch of her physical being and, in her last flicker of brain activity, liquid darkness swallowed her silent screams.

Draven placed his mouth on hers and sucked her soul from her dead body.

Then he stood, turned his skull upward, and let go his breath in a steady, measured flow, and with it the soul of Catori. It was as fine and delicate as mist. He waved his hand toward the open back door, and the mist scattered into the howling winds of the storm.

Draven's craving then grew barbaric. Promised a soul for his own taking, a rare gift from Amarinas, he could taste its essence—numb, void of empathy, deprived of vitality. He ached for its depravity. He heard it snoring and whipped around to face the beast stretched outward from the corner of the couch.

His silvers came to rest on Kaedan, and Draven laughed a wild laugh. It had been more than a hundred years since he'd devoured and kept captive a soul inside the ghost of shadows that was his shell, one he could torment for eternity, and this one called for the harshest of punishments. Draven's eagerness grew into a violent lust for blood.

Draven now understood why his desire for Catori had been so vicious. Kaedan's energy had seeped into her like an infectious worm, decayed her from the inside out, bound her to him in servitude.

It was Kaedan who pulled at his hunger. Amarinas had known, had stopped him from taking the raped spirit of Catori, one that would only weaken his wrath, and offered him the thief instead. It was a fair and wise trade.

Draven would teach Kaedan how to destroy another the proper way, and he would be sure Kaedan felt every ounce of pain as he'd dealt unto others during his time in human life. Kaedan, like every other soul rewarded him, would suffer the same pain Draven inflicted upon each soul he severed from life from that moment forward.

Kaedan never opened his eyes, but his body convulsed from the silence of screams only Draven could hear, and each scream of terror and agony amped his energy until her contorted into a wild beast, tearing Kaedan apart in a feverish frenzy, shredding the writhing swine into bits and chunks of pulsating flesh, then consuming them all like a rabid, starving hound, contorting his sluggish essence into wild energy and merging it with his own.

When done, exhaustion took Draven, and he stumbled out into the night and dissolved back into mist. The storm carried him far into the blackness.

It would be many years before she'd award him another soul. Amarinas would be careful not to give so much power to Draven again. He needed kept bound by the laws of meaning as she set forth. He had severed many in the past months that did not belong to death, but Kaedan would keep him satisfied for some time.

Balance was one again restored.

***

Catori lay in wait, unaware of all and everything for a millennium until a blinding whiteness wrapped her, cleansed her soul with the purity of light, and twisted her into human form. Peace flowed across her consciousness like a river of blood and erased all memory.

"I am here to guide you into life. You will have many hardships, joys, adventures, and one love, your twin soul, should you find your way to him during your journey. Care for this gift of life dearly or you will be brought back to repeat it."

Zahara kissed Catori's soft, silk, newborn skin.

***

Catori strode down the vacant street in hurried, long, purposeful steps. She had one thing on her mind and hoped her fiancé had everything ready when she got home. They were due one good night. She picked up her pace...

THE END

Contributor's bio:

J Snow is a poet and author of psychological thrillers and tales of terror whose work has been described as disturbing, visceral, haunting, and powerfully evocative.

Snow pulls inspiration from personal experience to provide readers a peek inside the splintered psyche of an abuse and abduction survivor while utilizing her unique insight of the depravities hidden behind the smiling faces of sociopaths to breathe life into harrowing characters that have both horrified and fascinated those of conventional morality for generations. Snow has had six short stories and fourteen poems accepted for publication in various anthologies, is the founder of the *Scribblers Writing Organization*, editor of its newsletter, co-administrator of its online writing community, and private publisher of other's poetry and short fiction. Snow is also the co-founder of *Blood Puddles — Silent Screams in Liquid Darkness: A Literary Journal of Horror*, and still finds time to write daily. She is currently working on a debut novel and the first in a planned series of memoirs, a means to battle the stigma surrounding mental illness and give voice to abuse victims struggling to speak for themselves.

Follow J Snow on Facebook:
https://www.facebook.com/JSnowAuthorPoet/
Blood Puddles —Silent Screams in Liquid Darkness: A Literary Journal of Horror
Website: http://www.bloodpuddles.pub/
Facebook   page:
https://www.facebook.com/BloodPuddlesLitMag/
Scribblers Writing Organization
Website: https://jensnowauthor.blogspot.com/?m=1
Facebook   page:
https://www.facebook.com/SbribblersWritingOrg/
Facebook   group:
https://www.facebook.com/groups/1218065064964921/

THE STORM RIDER
By Gerri R. Gray

For three days and three nights, the rain fell with a vengeance. Riverside Parkway was closed due to flooding, and Reginald Madden was forced to follow a detour, which ultimately deposited his maroon Lincoln Continental sedan onto Twisted Oaks Road—a lonely and desolate stretch of unlit roadway that snaked around the outskirts of town.

He vehemently disliked traveling this particular thoroughfare; for the past twelve months he had avoided it at all costs. But, on this storm-filled night, he had no choice but to take it, even though it made him cringe. He continued down Twisted Oaks, driving in and out of ghostly patches of fog that swallowed him up and spit him out; and then, without warning, something darted in front of the vehicle. He swerved in an attempt to avoid hitting whatever it was.

Thump.

Thump.

He jammed his foot onto the brake pedal and his

body lurched forward. His chest made impact with the steering wheel as the tires screeched to a halt.

"Son of a bitch!" he yelled.

Wasting no time, he unbuckled his seatbelt. With his black umbrella in hand, he got out to inspect the front of the car for any damage. To his relief, there were no dents. He then took a quick look around, expecting to find a dead or dying animal—or something far worse. However, there was no sign of any road kill.

Madden started back to his car when a dazzling flash of lightning lit up the scenery around him. And it was then, when the fury of nature had transformed nighttime into daylight for one brief moment, he came to notice her at the side of the road, near a hedgerow rising up from a blanket of white mist. She stood there, poised like a statue, motionless, watching him.

He thought it odd that a woman should be standing alone in the proverbial middle-of-nowhere, and in the throes of a raging thunderstorm. Should he be daring and inquire if she was in need of help? Or should he play it safe and simply leave without getting involved? He studied her for a few moments, while weighing his options. Another flash of lightning illuminated her face enough for him to determine that she was young— probably in her early or middle twenties.

His mind suddenly reeled back to the mysterious thing that had run out in front of his car and the ensuing thumping sounds. Dread enshrouded him. Could he have accidentally run over a dog belonging to the woman at the side of the road? If he had, where did it go?

"Hey there!" he shouted to her. "Is everything all right? Do you need some help?"

A chilling wind whipped up as he waited for the woman to reply, but the constant swishing of the windshield wiper blades and the incessant pitter-patter of raindrops beating against the taut nylon of his umbrella were the only sounds that broke the silence.

Reginald Madden was not a man who advocated the practice of hitchhiking; he had never before picked up a hitchhiker, and was proud of the fact. He had always lectured people on the dangers of doing it. But for some queer reason that was unclear to him, he felt it was necessary to offer a ride to this particular stranger. Perhaps it was merely the unrelenting storm that compelled him. Or perhaps it was something far darker than the clouds looming above.

"Can I give you a lift into town?" He was astonished by the words spilling out of his mouth and could scarcely believe they were his, despite hearing them uttered in his own voice. "I'm heading in that direction, and I could sure use the company."

The woman still did not answer; Madden began to ponder her strange silence. Could she be deaf? Did she not speak English? Was she mad, perhaps? Strung out on drugs? Whatever the reason was, he no longer cared. He was tired of standing in the cold rain and growing anxious to return to his car and be on his way.

"Suit yourself," he sighed, feeling annoyed and relieved at the same time as he proceeded to get back into his waiting vehicle. However, no sooner had he gotten in and shut the door, the woman made her way over to his car, opened the passenger door, and climbed inside without so much as a single word.

"I'm glad you decided to take me up on my offer," Madden stated, dishonestly, as he put the car into drive, an artificial smile stretching his mustached-draped lips. "This is certainly no night for a lovely young woman to be roaming around, with the storm and all."

There was nothing 'lovely' about the woman to speak of. Her beady eyes of black possessed an almost rodent-like quality about them. Her hair, black and stringy and oozing with rainwater, dangled in front of her lumpy, colorless face like a wet, dirty string-mop veiling a blob of dough. She stared straight ahead at the dashboard, her face void of expression.

"So," Madden began, "if you don't mind me asking, what *were* you doing out in the storm? Did your car break down? Are you in some kind of trouble?"

The passenger maintained her stony silence.

Fed up with being ignored, Madden snarked. "You're not a very talkative person, are you? Cat got your tongue?"

At that moment, a trickle of blood issued from the woman nose, and then blood began to ooze from the inner corners of her vacant eyes. Within seconds, her eyes rolled up into her head; her body went limp as a rag doll, and her head slumped back. She began breathing rapidly, gasping for air.

"Oh my God!" Madden was seized with alarm. He could feel the hairs on his arms standing on end as his eyes frantically shifted from his passenger, to the road, and back again. "What the hell is going on? Are you freaking out on drugs or something?"

The woman let out an agonized groan, which rapidly developed into a loud and frightful growl, and her body launched into a cluster of violent spasms. A red wave of frothy blood washed over her lips and ran down her chin, contrasting the stark pallor of her skin in an appalling way.

"Jesus Christ almighty!" Madden bellowed, horrified. "You're bleeding all over the place! This is great. Just *fucking* great!"

His stomach quivered with nausea, and he turned his attention back to his driving. He was now regretting his decision to break his longstanding personal rule against picking up hitchhikers. He had always told himself that they were more trouble than they were worth, and tonight's events were proving him right. The urge then came upon him to stop the car and let the woman out. After all, she wasn't his responsibility, he told himself. She was little more than a stray animal, and probably a junkie, or perhaps even a carrier of some horrible disease. He felt if she were going to die, it was better that she does it on the side of the road in the storm instead of inside his precious Lincoln Continental and ruin the full leather interior.

A dense mass of fog appeared and then something again darted in front of Reginald Madden's vehicle; he swerved to the right to keep from hitting whatever it was. The rear of the car hydroplaned across the slick pavement for a second, and then there came an all-too-familiar sound...

Thump.

Thump.

This time, he did not stop to take a look; he continued down the road, increasing his speed at the very instant the fog dissipated. He again glanced over at his passenger. She was no longer growling or convulsing. To his surprise, she was sitting quietly and staring out at the road ahead with an eerie calmness, as if nothing had happened. He studied her face, startled to find that all traces of the blood had mysteriously vanished. Confusion ripped into his mind like the sharp claws of a cat upon a scratching post. *What the hell just happened? Did I simply imagine her bleeding? Perhaps,* he reasoned with himself, *I was far more tired than I realized.*

He took a deep breath in an effort to reinstate his composure. He cleared his throat. "Are you," he began, cautiously, "all right?"

The woman slowly turned her head and stared at him. Within the abyss of her eyes, a glaring hatred, like a seed, sprouted. She remained steadfast in her silence; her muteness was beginning to unnerve the man behind the steering wheel. He cleared his throat once again, feigned a meager smile, and attempted to carry on in a normal fashion in spite of the uncomfortable silent treatment he was receiving.

"Believe it or not, you're the first hitchhiker I've ever picked up. I normally don't give rides to strangers, you know. It's too risky—especially nowadays with nuts running around loose everywhere. If that dog, or whatever it was, hadn't run in front of my car, I would have never stopped. I wouldn't have even seen you standing there in the dark, in the storm. You're lucky that I did. Who knows what sort of creep might have picked you up if I hadn't come along? You know, a young woman like you really shouldn't be out at night, all by herself, thumbing rides from strangers. Don't you know it's dangerous? You could get hurt—or worse."

"You mean like that woman you killed in that hit-and-run accident last year?" the woman asked, while staring out the rain-blurred window at the passing scenery. Her voice was marred by hoarseness, and possessed an acrid quality.

Madden was somewhat startled to hear the woman finally speak, and stunned by her unexpected question. It rendered him momentarily speechless. His fingers tightened their grip on the steering wheel and his knuckles began to turn white. Once the initial shock passed, he regained his voice.

"What? Is this some kind of joke? I've never been involved in any hit-and-run accident! What the hell would make you accuse me of something like that?" he demanded; his tone was defensive and coupled with indignation. "Well? You'd better start explaining because I don't have any idea what you're talking about!"

"Don't you?"

Madden huffed. "Like I already told you: No! I don't!" He hurled a look of anger in his passenger's direction, and then added, "And I don't appreciate being accused of a crime. You've got some gall, lady. You don't even know me!"

"Oh, but I *do* know you. I know you all too well, Mister Reginald Madden. I've waited so long for this night... for this storm."

A crooked bolt of lightning split open the sky, followed by a booming crash of thunder. The rain now seemed to be falling with greater intensity—ferocity, if you will. The windshield wipers, even set to their quickest speed, could scarcely keep up with the barrage of pummeling water droplets.

"How do you know my name?" Madden inquired, coolly: his tone of anger overridden by curiosity and suspicion. "We've never met before. Just who the hell are you? What kind of twisted game are you playing?"

"A game with *my* rules."

"Don't talk to me in goddamn riddles," Madden snapped, an angry tone once again in his voice. "What, exactly, do you want from me?"

The woman threw her head back, gently, and replied with amused laughter. "What I want is for you to play this little game that I devised especially for you. I want to watch you squirm. I want to watch you suffer. I want to revel in the anguish that darkens your soulless eyes when this game concludes and the long-awaited moment arrives for you to pay in full."

"I see. So it's money you're after, is it?" Anger bubbled and coursed through his veins like a lava flow.

"Very well. You have me at a disadvantage, so I'll indulge you in your little game of blackmail. Let's cut to the chase. How much do you want?"

The woman did not offer a reply. She stared out the window, which only served to enrage Madden further.

"Well, come on then! I haven't got all night to play this goddamn game of yours! I'm keen to get this whole matter settled. Now, tell me. What's your price for silence?"

"You'll find out."

"What the hell is that supposed to mean? I've already told you I'm willing to meet your price, whatever it is. But don't take me for a fool. I'm warning you."

Several silent minutes, which felt more like hours to him, passed by. He slowed the car and then turned off onto a bumpy gravel road leading to a derelict textile mill that looked to be abandoned for decades. A flash of lightning transformed the ruins into an imposing and ominous silhouette. He proceeded to the rear of the mill, which overlooked a dark and turbulent river reaching flood stage, and stopped the car. It seemed the perfect place to dispose of a body.

"End of the line," he announced.

He flipped down his sun visor, revealing a pistol tucked into an elastic holster. Without hesitation, he took hold of the loaded firearm, cocked it, and pointed it at the woman in the seat next to him; she exhibited a blank expression. Madden's lips curled into a grin. He was back in control.

"Your little game has grown boring, so I'm changing the rules. We're going to play the rest of it by *my* rules now. *Capisce?* Now, be a good girl and get out of the car."

The woman obediently did as she was instructed without protest. Madden then exited the vehicle and approached her, clutching his umbrella in his left hand and the gun in his other. He aimed it at her chest. Another flash of lightning illuminated the night sky, and was followed by a long rumble of thunder. The rain was stinging Madden's hand; but, the feeling of having power over life and death was exhilarating to him, almost intoxicating.

"This is where we say goodbye. But, before we part company, I want you to explain to me how you know so much about that… incident."

"Because," the woman began in her hoarse voice, "that hitchhiker you killed in cold blood during that hit-and-run… was me."

Madden snorted. "You're as crazy as you are stupid. I don't know how you really obtained your dirt about me, but you know far too much for your own good, and for mine. You could easily destroy me, along with my business and my family. And I can't let that happen, now can I?"

He took a quick look around to ensure they were alone, and then squeezed the trigger of the pistol. The bullet exited the barrel and passed through the woman's body, leaving no wound. He fired a second shot, which yielded the same result. Madden's jaw dropped in disbelief.

"You can't kill me twice," she gloated with a grin before bursting into a fit of maniacal laughter. She tossed her head back and wailed and howled, her laughter growing so raucous that tears were streaming from her eyes. "You can't kill me twice!"

Her words were like swords that impaled the very fibers of Reginald Madden's being.

Horror-stricken and confused, he watched as the woman, like a mirage, gradually faded away into nothingness; only the sound of her laughter remained.

The loud revving of an eight-cylinder engine vibrated his eardrums, and he spun around to behold the sight of his Lincoln Continental barreling towards him at a lightning fast speed. It would be the last thing his eyes would ever see.

Thump.

Thump.

THE END

Contributor's bio:

Gerri R. Gray is a poet with a dark soul, and the author of the bizarre adventure novel, *The Amnesia Girl* (HellBound Books, 2017) and *Gray Skies of Dismal Dreams* (HellBound Books, 2018). Her writing has appeared in numerous literary journals and anthologies, including *Beautiful Tragedies; Demons, Devils & Denizens of Hell 2;* and *Deadman's Tome Cthulhu Christmas Special.* She has also contributed to the book, *Ghost Hunting the Mohawk Valley* by Lynda Lee Macken (Black Cat Press, 2012). She is currently working on a second bizarro novel. Among her passions are cemetery photography, paranormal investigating, and watching reruns of *Dark Shadows.* She is originally from the Chicago area, and currently lives in a haunted mansion in Upstate New York.

Links:
For more information, please visit Gerri's website at: http://gerrigray.webs.com.
Follow her on Facebook at:
https://www.facebook.com/AuthorGerriGray.
Goodreads:
https://www.goodreads.com/author/show/17311761.Gerri_R_Gray

VITA
Written by Evelyn Eve

My head hurt. God, it really, really hurt. Each beat of my heart sent a legion of metaphorical sledgehammers into my skull. Damn. It felt like someone smashed the back of my head in with a brick. Reaching back and touching the back of my head just at the base of my neck, I could feel my head was damp and wet. My hair was soaked. Bringing my hand forward again, I could see my fingers were stained with fresh blood. So my brick-to-the-skull theory may not have been too far off.

I tried to stand, but no such luck. I was strapped down into a chair at the waist, and before me was a large table. I was immediately taken back by how pristine and clean it was—like something you'd see at a dinner meant for nobility. The same could be said about the whole place, actually. In between my ever-fluctuating vision, it seemed I was being held captive in a palace or mansion of some kind.

I started to open my mouth to say "hello," but I couldn't speak. I touched my lips, and could feel thick metal wire laced tightly over them. It didn't take long for me to realize that my lips had been…had been…

Sewn shut?

I looked into a conveniently placed mirror on the wall across from me, and sure enough, there were numerous metal threads laced in a very clean pattern weaving in and out of my lips. I was taken back by not only the fact that my mouth was sealed by wire, but by how clean the job was done.

I wanted to panic, but couldn't find my fear. The metal running through my flesh should have hurt, but it did not. It was strange. Even if I wanted to hurt, I couldn't.

"I've given you a powerful sedative," a voice said, almost seemingly reading my mind. "It'll keep your mind clear, so I can chat with you peacefully. You see, I'm very rich… and bored. Very, very bored. My days of being a surgeon, tailor, sculptor, painter, and entertainer have brought great wealth for me. But after years of serving and pandering to everyone else who gave nothing in return, I've decided to make the most of my fellow man. I've decided to let him entertain and serve me. Now if you could kindly give me a moment, I'll be right down to remove your stitches…"

An awkward silence filled the room. Perhaps it was already there, but my awareness of it had increased due to the knowledge there was someone else nearby. I didn't know, to be honest. None of this made sense.

And even though I knew I should be a little distraught over this, I was not.

It felt like hours before the strange Other made his way into the room. I could hear a gentle tapping of his boots rapping against stone, slowly descending down what sounded like a flight of stairs. There, standing in the archway across the room, was a figure in a cloak and hood with a onyx mask with what appeared to be a single eye made from some form of precious stone, a cyclopean sphere slightly off-left. The flickering candles in the room somehow danced in a way that made the eye pulse with light, not unlike a heartbeat. After a closer evaluation, I noticed the eye would disappear for a moment, and suddenly reveal itself to have returned on another part of the onyx mask. It meant I could not keep eye contact with him for very long. If I wanted that, I'd have to follow the sphere. It was hypnotizing. And, had it not been under such strange and terrifying circumstances, I may have found it to be beautiful.

The figure slowly walked his way over to me, his blood-red cloak casually dancing side to side in an ethereal waltz. *Tap. Tap. Tap.* Between the moving eye, swaying of the robes, slow tapping and sedative, I began to nod off. Things went blurry for a moment, and before long, black.

When I came to, I smacked my lips, which meant my mouth was reopened. I looked about the room, but the figure was nowhere to be seen.

But soon, he spoke again.

"You're awake, I see. Good. Shall we talk a bit?"

I nodded without hesitation. My own compliance astonished me. Was it the drugs?

"Good, good. Excellent! If I may introduce myself, I am Vita. I am a cruel, cruel being…but not without class. My intention is to kill you, make no mistake. I have been watching you for some time, Mr. Jones. You have a very special family, do you not?"

At that moment, the mirror across from me quickly became a screen bearing an image—an image of my divorced wife, adult children, and dog. I couldn't help but feel anger well up in my stomach. Not towards the one who captured me, oh no, but at the sight of the whole ungrateful lot. I hated the whole of them, save for my girl, Mercy.

Mercy, of course, was my dog. Of all the things I lost in the divorce, the loss of Mercy hurt me the most. A man shouldn't be separated from his dog. It goes against all that is natural in the universe.

Vita chuckled, possibly from seeing the expression on my face. A quick flip of the screen back to the mirror revealed my own gaze, filled with anger and spite. I couldn't stand the sight of my contorted visage either, so I relaxed and went cold. I turned my head to the side, and stared off into some peripheral abyss.

"I know your story, Mr. Jones. A successful businessman that wanted nothing more than a good life for yourself, and your family. But your wife wasn't content, was she?"

I scoffed. "Nothing made her happy. When I was working, she hated that I was never home. When I quit work to be home, she left because I wasn't making money anymore. She turned everyone against me."

There was a moment of silence. Vita sighed, as if his pain was genuine. "I understand, Mr. Jones. I really do. What if I told you, you had the chance to kill her without ever getting caught by the police? Would you do it?"

I could feel the anger welling up in me, and then the thought of that stupid bitch choking on her own blood brought a smile to my face.

Karen…

"Absolutely!" I snarled, blind rage filling my vision with unspeakable things of what I would love to do to the woman. So much for inhibiting drugs!

Vita chuckled smugly. "Is that so? Truthfully? You would do…anything?"

"Yes, anything!" Shouting, I lunged forward and shook my shackles. Perhaps the sedative was wearing off? That, or my hatred for that stupid bitch was more powerful than I ever imagined.

There was another pause. "Very well." Vita's voice was calm and soothing. "Here you are."

Before me, the table began to swing slowly open like a casket. A long platform began to rise up from underneath, and on top of it, a white sheet was draped across. A quick glace revealed to me that there was a feminine form under it, faintly wiggling. A muffled cry came from underneath, before suddenly and without explanation, the sheet was snatched off by an unseen force. This revealed…

Karen. Karen, my ungrateful bitch of a wife! Laid out before me, nude, her pale skin faintly glowing in the light as her chest heaved up and down, frantically. Once upon a time, I might have desired to make love to her. But now, I couldn't even think about that. I wanted to do far worse.

It was almost too good to be true, like my wish was granted. Next to her, conveniently placed, was a tray full of a wide range of tools and weapons. This included a gun, axe, ice pick, knife, needle filled with a strange liquid, as well as a spade.

"Pick one," Vita said. "But only one. Then do what you know you've always wanted to do."

It didn't take me long to grab the sharpened spade. I already knew I was going to rip her heart out, just like she did mine.

Vita breathed in excitement. "A most excellent choice if I do so say so myself, Mr. Jones! Now, do it."

I didn't need much encouragement. I drove the spade straight into her chest. Her eyes went wide, and she screamed from under her gag. Blood shot from her chest as her flesh ripped, bones cracked, and fluids sloshed. I drove deeper and deeper as she tried to flail under her restraints, her screams quickly becoming gargled cries. I don't know if I found the heart or not, if she even had one, but I didn't care. I twisted and I thrust from my seat, well after she stopped moving. The gurgles stopped, and her head fell to the side. Again, that didn't stop me.

"Stop," Vita spoke softly. I complied. "Well done, Mr. Jones. I find your barbaric display to be most satisfying. Ahh, yes. The good husband finally gets his revenge. I always enjoy when a love story ends in bloodshed. But we don't want to ruin the meat, not yet. Say goodbye to Karen, Mr. Jones."

The slab began to lower back into the table. Before the lid could close, I spit on Karen's body and growled bitterly. I had a hunch I wasn't getting out of here alive, so I figured I might as well indulge in a little senseless vengeance.

Franklin…

Sometime after Karen's body was sealed away, sinking into the table in which she rose from, I must have nodded off. Soon, however, I was awakened by a sobbing sound. Across from me in a chair similar to mine was none other than my son, Franklin… and behind him stood Vita, his hands resting gently upon Franklin's shoulders. I wanted to say something, curse the little son of a bitch for being a traitorous ass, but found that yet again my lips were sewn shut.

"Ahhh...you're awake Mr. Jones," Vita sighed

lovingly. "Franklin here is a good boy. Really, he is. He wanted to tell you something. But he knows you have quite the temper, and he has quite the temper. He knew you wouldn't listen; he thought you would just get angry with him and then in turn he would get angry with you. So I made a deal with him. I told him I'd sew your mouth shut again so he could tell you something before he dies. What is it, Franklin? What is it you wanted to tell your father?"

Franklin sobbed, his eyes becoming more and more wet until steams of tears were streaming down his face and onto his chin. Franklin was a man, but at that point, for the first time in a long time, I saw my little boy. I wanted to hate him. Hell, after siding with that (now dead) bitch Karen and taking his share of bribe money from the divorce money, I should have just killed the lot of them.

I never once cheated on Karen. I never slept with that girl. And for him to lay claim that he witnessed me sleeping with my underage stepdaughter Jona, taking a picture (*that* picture... *the* picture) and posting it online and all – it ruined my life...cost me my job. It was a hell.

Sure, being a raving alcoholic, I made it easy. I was always snockered. But still, what the actual hell? I know I was never there for him before his biological mom died. And, sure, I was never there for him after she died either, but really? I didn't deserve that time in jail. I didn't deserve to lose my house and life's savings, or to have to put my name on that damn registry for the rest of my life, looking over my shoulder every time I went to the store for some damn milk in fear of some self-proclaimed vigilante deciding he's going to kick the holy hell out of me. And getting a job? Forget about it! Over!

Yet, there he was. Crying. My little boy was truly sad, remorseful. I could see it. Had it been anyone else but my son, I wouldn't have felt the twinge of guilt over carrying all that anger towards him. God or Nature or the Universe or whatever the piss sets the natural order of things didn't intend it to be this way. A father was supposed to give his life for his son if need be, not want to take it.

Vita made a soft moan. "Go ahead, Franklin. Tell him. It's okay. He'll listen. I've made sure of that."

Franklin's lips quivered and his bloodshot eyes grew large as grapefruits it seemed. "I'm…sorry…dad. Karen told me if I didn't do it, she'd have Jona say it was me that had sex with her. I was nineteen at the time, dad. And she was nine. Nine! You know as much as I do how crazy Karen was. I didn't know it would get that bad. I…"

Swiftly and without warning, Vita ran the knife across Franklin's throat. His blood shot out and splattered across the table and upon my face, into my eyes. My vision blurred, but I could hear Franklin's head smack dully into the table as he forcibly began gargling "grry" over and over.

I swear I could hear Vita smile from behind his mask. "He said he'd do anything to tell you the truth, Mr. Jones. Anything. So he died for that one. I offered to let him go, but alas. He loved you that much. And soon, very soon, you'll have to choose as well Mr. Jones. Very soon. But before that, you'll have another visitor. Just one more."

I started to cry. My emotions were swelling up, churning and burning in my whole body. I threw up in my mouth, but because my lips were sewn shut I had to swallow my own vomit. My body started to go into convulsions just moments before Vita slipped a needle

223

into my arm, and again, the world went away.

Jona...

She was the worst. She could have said something. She could have denied it. But no, she played along with it. Laid down next to me naked while I was passed out drunk in bed to frame me, she did. A minor, at that! I didn't think anyone could go so low.

I get it. She was young at the time, didn't know what to think. But now that she's a full-grown woman, she could have come forward. Cleared my name. Saved Franklin, perhaps.

God, I hated her more than Karen at times. Or maybe that's just easier to say now that Karen is dead?

When I came to, the slab that served as an impromptu sacrificial altar for Karen was now an extravagant banquet table. There was a fine red cloth laid out, and on it, a feast fit for a king. Fruits, breads, vegetables, and pastries of all kinds formed a culinary swarm around what appeared to be a large, succulent ham on a silver platter. I couldn't believe my eyes.

My stomach growled. Come to think of it, I hadn't eaten in what felt like days, so I couldn't help myself. Even in this place, I couldn't deny that my needs still were part of me. And even though I was facing imminent death, I still hungered. If I'm to die, let it not be due to starvation. I hear it's a long, unpleasant ordeal.

Again, Vita spoke to me over what, at this point, I still assumed was the intercom. "It's all for you, Mr. Jones. Eat up!"

I looked around for some silverware, but there was none. I could hear Vita chuckling again, much like he often did. It's like he could read my mind. That or he knew humans enough to know we've been conditioned to use tools for every little thing, even eating.

"Don't worry about such formalities here, Mr. Jones. While the food may be of the highest quality, prepared by gourmet chefs, I highly encourage all my guests to leave all the pretentious, so-called civilized pish posh behind. Use your hands, like Nature intended!"

I hesitated for a moment, but the lure of the meat ensured that my resistance didn't last long. Bypassing all the fruits and veggies, I grabbed the large ham with both hands and brought it up, while at the same time thrusting my face into it. I opened wide and then bit down; the flesh was soft and tender, with a slight sponginess to it. Juices exploded into my mouth as the meat fell apart easily with minimal effort from my teeth. It was absolutely delicious. Shame the best food I had ever tasted was under these circumstances.

I ate and I ate, for God knows how long. At some point, my stomach felt like it was going to burst and I knew if I took another bite I'd no doubt throw up. At least this time my mouth wouldn't be sewn shut.

Dropping the ham down back onto the silver platter, I leaned back onto the seat and let the food settle. I could feel another nap coming on. And, sure enough, sleep came.

And, again, I was brought to once more by the sound of Vita's voice.

"She told me she was hot for you, Mr. Jones. Said she wished you could eat her up. But she knew you never would, even when she was an adult woman. So I granted her wish. And granted yours. You wanted her dead, Mr. Jones. She is. And you ate her, just like she had long wanted you to do. Who am I to stop two consenting adults from engaging in some reciprocal indulgences?" He laughed. "Forgive me, Mr. Jones. I do tend to take things a little too literally sometimes."

There was a long silence. I stared at the Jona-ham with a slight unease at my stomach. I didn't know which was worse: the fact that I ate another human being, or the fact that I actually enjoyed doing so.

In my defense, I didn't know. But...

As much as I hated her, and wished she were dead, I wish I didn't have to go through that. It's not right. None of this is right. My whole life has been wrong. All wrong. I didn't ask for this. Why couldn't I have just been a regular guy, with regular problems?

Maybe it was the fact that it was my hatred that kept me alive all these years and was no good now that everyone I really wanted dead, was. Maybe it was all this torture. Perhaps it was just the fatigue. I don't know. I don't care. It was at this point I didn't want to live anymore.

If Vita didn't kill me, I was going to do it myself.

I started to cry. Dammit! Where are the drugs when you really need them?

Mercy...

Vita came in with two other hooded figures. As they began to clean the table, Vita once more spoke to me.

"You have no more guests, Mr. Jones. But there is someone else who would undoubtedly be happy to see you."

I looked up from my chair. "Who?"

"Why, your best friend, of course."

My eyes lit up. I wanted to smile. But this is Vita we are talking about here. There was a catch. Always, a catch!

"Mercy?"

Vita nodded. "Yes."

I felt anger welling up in my stomach. Mixed with

the Jona-ham, it didn't settle well with my nerves. "I swear if you've killed her, I'll…"

"You'll what, Mr. Jones?"

I went silent. I couldn't lie to myself. I was completely at this madman's mercy.

"It is as I thought. No hard feelings, Mr. Jones. I understand. You've been through a lot and perhaps I do deserve to be the recipient of your aggression. But I'm afraid your visit is nearing its end."

Vita held up a small stone-like object. On it was a button. After he clicked it, I felt my seat rattle a bit and detach from the floor beneath me. It started to rise up, slowly. The sounds of motors humming and gears turning rumbled and clattered as I was lifted up, seat and all, into the air. I looked up. The ceiling was drawing closer and closer; but it was soon apparent I was not going to be crushed. One of the stone tiles slid open. I passed through the portal, and as the motors stopped, the seat locked into place. Before me was a small pulpit, with an unsecured handgun resting on it. My shackles suddenly snapped loose and I instinctively shot up from the seat and secured the gun. I opened the chamber and realized there was only one bullet.

My stomach sank. I already didn't like the looks of this.

I was now in a room, not unlike the one I was in before, in design. But it lacked all the other accommodations of my previous place of occupation. It was empty, but a quick glance revealed a small gate built into the wall across the room as well as misters on the ceiling. From the darkness behind the bars, I could hear a faint set of whimpers and growls.

"Mercy?" I called out softly.

My greeting was met with a deep, rumbling snarl.

Vita spoke yet again. "Yes, it is Mercy. But I must

sincerely apologize, Mr. Jones. I wasn't prepared for a dog. How irresponsible of me. I fear I lacked proper accommodations for sweet little Mercy."

I chuckled over the choice of words. "Little" definitely was not Mercy. She came from Mastiff stock and at this point must have been tipping the 200 plus pounds mark. Last I seen her she was a puppy, but I met her parents during the adoption and they weren't exactly teacup poodles.

I growled, "If you hurt her, I swear…"

Vita sighed. "Again, I do apologize sincerely, Mr. Jones. I'd like to make it up to you both. I'll give you the chance to put her out of her misery, one way or another. Do the humane thing, and you'll walk free. I'll leave you be."

I looked down at the gun. There was no way in all the metaphorical or literal places between heaven and hell I was going to shoot my dog. I think Vita knew this. And the fact there was only one bullet? I knew he was up to something.

Looking towards the cage that contained Mercy, I sighed, "I can't. I just can't."

Seconds later, from seemingly nowhere, I was sprayed by a warm liquid from misters on the ceiling. It didn't take long for me to realize it was blood. It was fairly fresh blood.

"That's what's left of Karen, Mr. Jones. Waste not, want not."

Again, my Jona-ham-filled stomach churned. As I wiped the blood from my face, I couldn't help but feel I knew what was coming next.

Mercy's cage slowly rumbled open. And for the first time in years, I set eyes on my little baby. Except this time, she wasn't so little anymore.

But God, she looked like she was starving. Her eyes

settled on me as her head went low and her lips curled back, exposing her fangs. She uttered a deep, feral growl I would have thought impossible for a domestic breed. But there it was, that inner wolf coming forth to save her from the miserable grinding of starvation.

One way or another, I was going to put her out of her misery.

She started forward in a sprint, barking madly. I chucked a bit. Had Vita offered me to leave after eating Karen, I would have walked. Sure, I would have been scarred for life, but I would have latched onto the idea that those bitches got what was coming to them. I would have found solace in that.

But there was no way I could live with myself if I killed my dog to save my own life. No way. I would rather die.

I lifted my head and placed the gun under my chin. That's the way to do it, I've been told. I paused for a moment to take in the sight of Mercy barreling in towards me, and thought of what could have been had I not married that psychotic bitch. Mercy and I could have been sitting on the porch, with her eating a turkey neck from the Thanksgiving feast.

The thought of her teeth tearing apart a turkey throat gave me cold shivers, given the circumstances.

She was but feet away from me now. As she lunged, I closed my eyes and began to squeeze the trigger.

THE END

Contributor's bio:

Evelyn Eve grew up in a little town in the middle of nowhere, with little to do except play in the dirt and try to make fire with sticks with the other rural suburban cave-children. At some point, however, she found she had the power to create people and worlds with pen and paper and thus hid away from her other pint-size Neanderthal tribesmen, favoring Creation over eating bugs and avoiding predators.

To this day, she doesn't think they notice she's gone. But she likes it that way.

Alas, writing was not something that she could raise a family with. So she had someone else shave her head, have her march around with several other baldies, and eventually be trained to be a rambunctious grease monkey in a 5-ring circus. It wasn't glorious or pretty, but it paid the bills.

Eventually, her oily chimp handlers told her she had to go and sent her off with the promise of mailing her bananas every month if she'd leave them alone. So now, between periodic feedings from her former taskmasters, she has reclaimed her throne as Creator of her own Netherworld...acting as a sort of slightly imbalanced, partially blind, shaky-handed, dyslexic sculptor of Mana, Ether, and other Intangible mediums.

When she's not creating nonsense, she prefers the company of her four-legged friends, gawking over her numerous plastic idols, trying to make sense of other Ether-bender's works, and playing with sharp sticks.

You know what they say: once a Neanderthal, always a Neanderthal.

THE NECRAMANCERS
Written by Serena Daniels

She was still in pain, emotional and physical—the cause was those horrible memories of when she had been violated. She still remembered clearly his intrusion into her body and her soul. It had been a while since it had happened, but she still had not been soothed.

Because, although she had gotten away from and killed her attacker as soon as she had gotten the chance and had been cleared of any wrongdoing by the police, she still felt restless. Everything was going haywire within her very cells and nothing was settling them down—not therapy, not counseling, nothing.

The one feeling of pleasure that she had managed to dredge up during this whole ordeal was the euphoria that came with taking the life of the man who had caused her so much pain. Sure, she had thought about it a lot since then, but simply reminiscing about it didn't give her the same satisfaction as the act itself had.

She told no one of this; however, the last thing she needed was more intense mental treatment. She wanted to forget the whole thing had ever happened; and yet everything that she continued to do in her own home—hell, just still living there—caused constant reminders, but she could not afford to move.

Sandy sighed as she plopped into bed for another night of restless sleep. If only there was a way for her to kill him again—over and over and over...

* * *

The figure that was cloaked in darkness was jolted from her meditation as soon as the vision ended. Her formerly slumped-over posture straightened; she lifted her head to reveal a ghostly pale face; her gray hair spilled over her shoulders. She opened her old and tired eyes; the deep blue irises were invigorated—a stark contrast to the rest of her body. Her cracked lips tilted up in a grim smile, which meant there was work to be done.

"Mother Necra?" a young female voice asked softly as the sound of footsteps echoed off of the floor of the chamber that was the elder's sanctuary.

"Yes, Daughter Mortema?" Mother Necra asked as she slowly turned toward the voice. The female that stood in front of her was dressed like herself and the other daughters in a silky black cloak that was fastened with a gold broach. Her eyes were the exact same shade of blue as all the other daughters. She also had the pale flesh.

The only difference was that this daughter's hair was a rich brown.

"I haven't disturbed you, have I?" Mortema asked as she kneeled down onto one knee in deference.

"No." Mother Necra waved a hand and Mortema rose. "As a matter a fact, I've just received a vision, another job."

"Who am I to retrieve?" Mortema asked without missing a beat.

"Daughter Rapia," Mother Necra said in what could have been described as a sad voice if it wasn't so monotonal. Mortema could only shake her head in pity.

"Poor Sister Rapia has been overworked for as long as I can remember. Some men are so abhorrent;" Mortema whispered.

"That is one of our purposes for existing—to help women in trouble," Mother Necra said, calmly.

"True," Mortema whispered before her voice grew stronger. "As you command, Mother, I will go retrieve her." She turned to leave.

"One moment, Daughter Mortema," Mother Necra said as she held up a finger and Mortema stopped and waited. "You came to me initially for a reason, I assume?"

"Oh, yes." Mortema blinked once in remembrance of her original reason for coming. "I came to inform you that Sister Futurae has procured what you requested. She and Sister Puella are ready to begin at your request."

"Excellent." Mother Necra smiled and Mortema took that as her cue to leave. The mother sighed in bliss. "Wonderful. Everything is as it should be. Everything is going according to plan, as always."

* * *

When Sister Mortema returned to what would constitute as the family room, she found the rest of her sisters waiting patiently for her. She almost smiled at this comfortable routine; while awaiting her return, they normally would have been either reading or reminiscing of their past exploits.

"She has been informed that Sisters Futurae and Puella are ready to begin the next phase," she began slowly and the rest of her sisters seemed to sense that she had more to say, so they didn't even titter with excitement as they normally did around this time. "However," she continued, "she had come out of a vision when I saw her." The others began to squirm a little knowing what this meant. "And she has requested Sister Rapia."

The silence continued, but it was less out of respect and more out of discomfort. No one moved, even as the sister herself rose from her position on the floor. Her hood was down and her pale face was fully revealed along with her long blonde hair and disarmingly delicate features that belied the stoniness that was a requirement for their very natures.

"As she commands," Rapia said, coldly, as she pulled her hood over her head and swept out of the room with the rest of the sisters watching after her. When the door shut behind her, everyone turned her head expectantly to Mortema.

"We move on schedule," she announced, looking at Futurae and Puella in particular. "We must have everything prepared. We continue the tradition that has been done for Mother for countless centuries. We cannot falter or fail in any manner." This speech was familiar to all of them. She gave them the same one each time before the ritual was prepared for Mother.

The strange thing was that only Mother required such a ritual; they did not. Mother had always told them that it was because they were conceived out of magic, but she only used magic and that was what made the difference between something that was absolutely critical for Mother's health and yet not for theirs.

It was difficult work that always fell on Futurae and Puella, but they never complained as they were only doing their duty to their mother. She gave them life, their duties, their very purposes—so why should they not do what she commanded? They were not like humanity; they did not do things whenever the urge struck them. They did their duties when they were required.

The females of humanity needed them; that was what they were created for. Age, flesh color, rich or poor— nothing like that mattered to these admittedly superior beings. If a female was in some kind of trouble, it was their obligation to intervene, whether the victim was among the living or among the dead.

And the dead were often more grateful than the living. However, the living could surprise them from time to time.

* * *

Sandy woke up because she felt a presence in her room... just like last time; however, her senses didn't pick up anything dangerous about this second intruder. No, she felt more at peace. An unearthly glow had penetrated her closed eyelids and she only opened her eyes when the light had retreated into the darkness and the sound of soft footfalls against her carpet was heard coming toward her bed.

A normal person would have been frightened and screamed bloody murder at seeing a cloaked intruder in their bedroom; however, the first thing that Sandy thought to focus on was the chest area and she felt a bit of relief at the fact that it was a woman who had visited her—albeit an uninvited one. She felt little to no fear.

Instead, she waited for the visitor to make the first move.

"You have had some trouble recently," the cloaked figure stated. "You are angry and numb because of your victimization. I am here to aid you in your healing."

"What can you do that others haven't been able to do for me?" Sandy asked softly, but she felt intrigued, nonetheless.

"To grant your deepest wish," the female continued. "You may address me as Rapia. I aid women just like you. You are not the first and, tragically, will not be the last woman to suffer at the hands of a man. But I know just the thing that will help you."

"What?" Sandy asked more strongly as she carefully sat up in bed.

"What would you say if I told you that you can release your feelings onto your attacker over and over again?" Rapia asked in a rhetorical manner, as if she knew the procedure that she always went through with her women (which she did as it was always the same thing every time).

"I would wonder just how that was possible," Sandy replied as she got out of bed slowly and Rapia backed away to make room for her.

"Take my hand and I'll show you," Rapia said as she held out her hand in a way that made Sandy comfortable enough to actually take it. Before she knew it, everything had rushed around her, and when it all stopped and she got her bearings, she realized that they were in a cemetery and nearly fainted when she read the inscription on the grave of her attacker.

"Why are we here?" She asked pitifully, almost brokenly as she faced her rapist's final resting place.

"Pay close attention, child," was all Rapia told her as she took something out from beneath her cloak, something that resembled a glass ball. Rapia tossed the object onto the dirt that covered the parasite's grave and it began to glow. Within a couple of seconds, the man himself materialized beside the grave, lying down, and was as stiff and dead as he had been since she had taken his life. Sandy was too shocked to say anything.

"Let us go back now, child," Rapia announced, and again they were back in Sandy's bedroom; however, not only had he made the journey with them, but he was now situated in some kind of glass coffin.

"Why have you brought him back here?" Sandy asked as she shook away her shock and approached the coffin and stared at him.

"For you to do what you wish with him," Rapia said mildly as she approached Sandy from behind, and the mortal woman in question turned to face her with a quizzical look. Rapia said nothing and took out the same glass ball and held it out to Sandy.

"Would you want to make him feel the same pain that you are feeling inside? Would you like to do it over and over again until you feel that you are healed?" Rapia asked, and Sandy could only nod to both questions. "Take this and your desires will be fulfilled with no one the wiser."

"H-how?" Sandy stuttered as she reached for the ball, but halted her fingers just inches away from it.

"I have magicked this entire room so that you may reap your vengeance with no one else the wiser," Rapia began. "This ball holds his very essence. When you wish to awaken him, simply wish for the holding coffin to vanish and for his essence to be returned to him, and he will be resurrected somewhat. He will be paralyzed so he cannot escape and he will be invisible to whoever enters your room, save for yourself."

"Amazing," Sandy breathed. "This seems almost too

good to be true."

"All the women that I have visited have said the same thing," Rapia replied, calmly, as she looked Sandy squarely in the eyes. "They are also reluctant to visit their vengeance on their victims... at least at first. But I promise you that it will heal you. You have the time. I guarantee it. Now will you take back your life?"

Without any more hesitation, Sandy snatched the ball from Rapia's hand and looked it over in her own hands. Her face showed her fascination.

"All you need are your thoughts, and your strong desire to bring him back will awaken him for your pleasure," Rapia said, and Sandy looked up at her again. "I will be watching over you and will return once I have sensed that your healing has been completed."

"Thank you," Sandy whispered and watched as Rapia simply faded away into thin air. She didn't move for a few seconds; she just stood there, still holding the glass ball that now meant everything to her. For the first time in months, she felt something that was akin to hope. She finally moved in order to stare at the man that had ruined her life in more ways than one.

All the negativity came flooding back into her, smashing and breaking open the gates that she had so carefully constructed around her heart. The attack, the questioning by the police and being cleared, the death threats by the man's family that only stopped when the people that rallied around her drove them off (which she was grateful for), and, of course, all of her therapy sessions that dredged up the memories while doing nothing—she felt all the emotions at once and yet she was beginning to feel at peace now that she had the knowledge that she could be a mirror and reflect all that pain back at him.

She shook herself from her thoughts when she felt the

glass ball begin to heat up slightly as it glowed from her intense emotions. She also began to hear the sound of groaning. She took her attention away from the ball and looked over to the demon that ruined her life; he was beginning to stir, and her excitement grew when his eyes opened.

She smiled wide when he began to look around his glass prison, and she felt sheer excitement when she saw just how panicked he was becoming—especially when his faced twisted into terror and he began to bang on the sides of his new coffin, trying desperately to get out. She had no doubt that he was scared, waking up from Hell and not knowing where he was. She loved this, but she was really looking forward to making him pay.

Because killing him only one time wasn't enough.

* * *

"Will we have time to see how our latest lady in distress begins to take her vengeance?" Rapia asked Mortema as they viewed through the scrying pool the first of what they hoped would be the man's many awakenings from death.

"I believe we just might," Mortema said after thinking it over for a moment. "The moon will not arise for a few hours yet. Certainly, Mother will not mind if we indulge ourselves until it is time."

"We have the time," Sister Futurae told them as she crept up to them. Her nodding caused her flame-red hair to bounce a bit. Her twin, Puella, nodded in agreement; she was the quieter of the two and typically allowed her closest sister to speak for the two of them. "Mother has just informed us that we may watch."

'Mother is so benevolent!' was the collective thought as the Order settled in to watch.

* * *

"Hello there, you remember me, don't you?" Sandy's voice was sickly sweet as she addressed her rapist. The demon in question turned his head in her direction and his face became filled with rage when recognition had entered his eyes and he banged his hands even harder, but he seemingly gave up after a few minutes. But she wasn't fooled; he was just waiting to see if she would take the bait and let him out. He was in for a big surprise, though, when manacles suddenly appeared and clamped down hard onto his limbs, rendering him completely immobile.

"It seems that someone has been looking out for me after all," she told him softly as she gathered up her courage and walked closer to his cage. "I've been given something amazing, which I'm sure you've noticed by now." Her voice was now filled with awe as the full impact of what she had been given hit her.

"I can do whatever I want with you," she realized aloud, "and no one in the outside world would be the wiser, just like you did with me. I can hurt you...like you hurt me!" An idea suddenly struck her and she turned away from him and his now loud cursing that struck her eardrums, and headed to the kitchen. She came back with her utensil tray, in which were lots of sharp knives.

"What to do? How to start?" she wondered out loud as she carefully placed the tray on her bed, making it within reach of the box. She vaguely noticed that a gag had appeared in his mouth and that was just fine with her; she was annoyed at hearing him make noises that had nothing to do with being in pain. "I suppose some experimenting is in order?"

She hummed as she looked over what was available

to her and eventually settled on a small paring knife and turned it over in her hands thoughtfully.

"I can't help but wonder," she began in wonderment; "if the saying about cutting off one sense to make the others stronger is true. How about we test that out?" Without hesitation, she suddenly rushed over (barely noticing that the coffin sprung open on its own accord) and shoved the paring knife into the inside corner of his eye.

Her blood began pumping as the gag absorbed his screams of pain, and her adrenaline started surging as she carefully carved around the eye until she popped it right out and it fell to the floor of the coffin. She proceeded to do the same with its twin. Bloody tears ran down his already dead cheeks and she smiled almost serenely.

"That's a good look for you!" she shouted cheerfully as another idea struck her, and she took the paring knife and carefully wedged the tip under one of his pinky nails, ignoring his hiss of pain from how deep she had placed it. She pried it up, ripping the nail from the flesh. It was just barely hanging on by the cuticle, but she decided to leave it like that for him to watch.

She took her sweet time in doing the same with his other nine fingers. With their disgusting flesh exposed, his dirty nails were flying high like small flags that were putting pressure on their cuticle supports and he continued to cry out in pain and fear. She was finding it quite delicious, but she quickly grew bored with seeing them only minimally attached. She didn't want to end the horrifying sight in an easy manner, so instead of cutting off the nails, she braced her fingers on the sides of each nail and ripped them off.

His screams became like music to her and she listened to them intently as she tried to think of what to do next. She directed her gaze back and forth between his withering, undead body and her bloody knife when she noticed something out of the corner of her eye—the time on her alarm clock indicated that it was almost eleven p.m., and that meant she had to hurry this up as she had to be at work in about six hours and she needed all the sleep that she could get.

And I was just starting to have fun. She frowned as his thrashing became more frantic and loud enough that she wondered if the glass would break. *I guess I'll just have to plan better for another time when I would be able to play longer.* She sighed as she took her now quite trusted paring knife and decided to just get it all over with so she could go to bed, feeling marginally better than she had in a long time.

She plunged the knife into one of his empty eye sockets and rummaged around inside as if performing primitive brain surgery, not caring about the kind of reactions that was occurring (but filing it away in the back of her mind to experiment with at a later time) and only stopping when she felt him go limp and observed him for an extra few minutes to make sure that he wasn't bluffing.

She cleaned her paring knife on his flesh and placed it on her nightstand and made a note to buy a new one since she sure as hell wasn't going to be using it ever again. Then she took her tray back downstairs and put it back in its drawer before returning to her room to climb into bed without so much as another glance at him. But she did have one final thought: *I wonder if it would be suspicious if I rented a blowtorch.*

* * *

"Not bad for a first time," Rapia mused as the scrying

pool went dark, "but I have seen more enthusiastic vengeance seekers."

"You forget, Sister," Mortema began pointing out, "that most women are reluctant to exercise their right to vengeance, especially if their pain was at the hands of a man. Have you forgotten how many lost souls have had to receive multiple visits from us before they accepted our gifts?"

"True enough," Rapia sighed as she accepted Mortema's point. "I do sometimes forget that the women I govern are the ones who accept my gift more easily than the rest of you... even if they are still reluctant to reap the pain of the deserving men."

"In any case," Futurae said as she stood and looked at the large decorative hourglass that served as their clock, "it is almost time to begin." Without any argument, all the other daughters rose up and began to file out of the room, with Mortema and Puella heading toward Mother's sanctuary to bring her out.

It was time for Mother to be reborn once again.

* * *

As tradition stated, it was a new moon in the sky as they all stood in a circle inside of their ritual room. A normal human would not have noticed the difference in the contrasting darkness between the moon and the sky, but the Necramancers easily could. It was in their nature to be above humans in this way.

Mother stood, or rather stooped, at the head of the circle that surround a stone altar. It was decorated with carvings of skulls and was long and wide enough to stretch out two bodies, side by side. She looked up at the heavens and, despite her frailness and earlier need for aid from two of her daughters, managed to walk over to one side and hoist herself up and lay still while she waited.

Futurae and Puella then picked up a small wrapped figure that they had gathered up earlier and set it beside Mother, but that wasn't the end of it. They carefully unwrapped the package; Puella held it up as Futurae removed the sheets. When they were finished, the carefully preserved remains of a young girl were revealed. She showed no signs of decay or distress, just a peaceful expression on her pretty face. Her features were quite remarkable in the fact that she strongly resembled a young Mother Necra—hair black as night and delicate features that were untouched by wrinkles and gray hair.

"You have done well, my daughters," Mother managed to croak out. "Now let us begin!" She closed her eyes and she slowed her breathing to where it was barely noticeable. Futurae took Mother's place at the head of the altar and recited a spell that was deeply ingrained into her memory:

"Girl child, girl child,
Who died so young,
With a future cut short
Come back to us for now
We ask for your aid
Come to us, come to us, come to us!"

As she chanted, the others swayed to her soothing tone, except for Puella, who had a special job of her own of running her hands over the child's body, magic flowing from them and enveloping both of them in a golden glow. When everything stopped, the girl opened her eyes to reveal them a dark brown color, and they quickly filled with fear when she realized that she couldn't move.

"Where am I?" she squeaked out. "Why am I not in the nice place anymore?"

"It's alright child," Puella spoke in her soothing tone, as children were her specialty. "We will let you go back, but we would like to talk to you first."

"See this lady beside you?" Puella asked the girl after the latter had nodded to indicate that she was listening. Puella pointed to Mother Necra and the girl nodded again. "She's our mom and she's sick and you're the only one who can make her better."

The girl turned her head toward Mother and looked at her carefully; her face became sad as she got a good look at her dying face.

"You love your mommy?" the little girl asked Puella when she turned to face her again.

"So much," Puella replied as she reached out and carefully petted the girl's hair in a soothing motion.

"What can I do?" the girl asked, pitifully and unsurely.

"Just one thing," Puella said. "You need to promise that you will go back to the nice place and stay there forever and ever."

"I promise," the girl said without hesitation. "I don't want to be here. My daddy's here, and my mommy's in the nice place. I want to be with my mommy!"

"And you will be from now on," Puella said as she took the girls' hand. "You just need to grab onto my mom's hand and close your eyes. You'll never see your daddy again, I promise."

"Okay," the girl spoke for the final time before she did as Puella instructed. Her body went limp as soon as she closed her eyes and, at the same time, Mother Necra became a flesh statue; she wasn't even breathing.

Now for the waiting game.

After a moment that seemed excruciatingly long to the Daughters, the girl's eyes opened again but they revealed deep blue eyes this time. She sat up again and stretched out her limbs and wiggled her fingers and toes experimentally.

"Daughters," the voice that came from the small body was not meek like a child, but one that was filled with eons of wisdom. The child smiled at all of them as she made her way off of the altar and turned around to witness the old woman's body crumble into dust, which the daughters carefully collected into an urn that was prepared for this very thing as they made happy mutterings.

In her new body, as she watched her daughters place the urn with all of the others, Mother Necra smiled. It was good to be back and with the promise that she would be around for a good, long time.

THE END

Contributor's bio:

Serena Daniels has lived in Winnipeg, Manitoba her entire life and was introduced to the world of horror at a young age. At five she began with the "Goosebumps" series of books, before moving on to the "Arachnophobia" and "Pumpkinhead" movies at age six; she was scared but never regretted her head first dive into the morbid. In the ensuing years she began obsessing over "Nightmare on Elm Street" and "Friday the 13th" series among other horror classics in any media that she could find. She uses writing horror stories and poetry as a way to deal with her personal inner demons. She finds the horrors of fiction to be quite soothing for her pain; that monsters could be dealt with and sometimes they can't, they are fictional life lessons that can be reflected in the real world and finds beauty in the darkest moments.

THE ABANDONED
Written by S.E. Davis

Chapter 1: Lonely Ghost Girl

I awoke to noises in my room. I wasn't sure what they were, but I knew enough to be frightened. The rain was coming down hard outside. The wind was howling, thunder rolling. Lightning lit my room. On the first flash, I saw nothing. The second flash, however, revealed a shape. Some nameless, faceless man—the epitome of fear—was in my room, gazing upon my tiny form. I closed my eyes tight, hoping he'd go away. I was not to be so lucky. I was never to be so lucky.

This was my recurring nightmare. It was always the same.

I always thought I knew what I wanted. I thought the best thing in life was just to be left alone. I had always been told to be careful what you wish for. I just never knew how true that statement could be. I do not remember much about my life in the land of the living. I only get flashes now and again—pictures that seem more like someone else than of me. On the night of my recurring dream, however, my wish to be left alone was granted. I never knew how lonely, lonely could be until I was no longer a member of the living. All was about to change, however. A new family was moving into my house. It had been so long since I had someone to talk to, someone to make me feel not alone. Thinking back on it, I really can't remember ever not being alone. My only memory was of my haunting dream and painful loneliness. Why can't I remember anything?

Chapter 2: Ambrose

It is difficult for me to remember my life. It comes to me in pieces sometimes. There are images that play in my mind like a dream, though I no longer have a need to sleep.

I won't bore you with the details of my so-called life after death or the years between my death and meeting her. That time was so painfully lonely and boring that I could sum it up in just that one sentence and you'd be more satisfied than if I told you that I knew the exact number of every tile in the kitchen, every vine that grew up the side of our old house. But that's not the story you're here to hear. I believe you're here to learn about Ambrose, who, unlike me, had a mommy that loved her. I don't know exactly when she moved in, but I remember how I felt the exact moment I knew she was here. I saw her getting out of the car and was so excited there was to be another child in this house. She made me feel alive again because, from the moment she got out of the car with her tiny backpack and pink ribbon in her hair, she saw me.

"Mommy! Who's that girl?"

"Ambrose, honey go play," her mother said to her.

So she did. She smiled and waved at me. In that moment, I felt more real and alive than I had in my entire existence.

Ambrose was the first living thing I ever remembered seeing me, and I couldn't have been happier. She made me forget all the lonely days before she came. Ambrose's mother couldn't see me but she accepted me as Ambrose's imaginary friend, which I was okay with. She set me a place at the dinner table almost every night.

I pretended her mom was my mom, and Ambrose was my sister. Everything was going great until Ambrose's daddy came home from his business trip. I rationalized to myself that the uneasiness I felt was just because it was raining. Perhaps it was the wind or a general distrust with men because… well, I couldn't quite remember why I didn't like men, but something about her daddy made me very uneasy.

When he was around, I could never be in the same room with him.

"What's wrong Ana? Don't you want to meet my daddy, too?" Ambrose would ask me.

I would simply shake my head and we would continue telling stories to each other. Lucky for me, her dad traveled a lot.

I know you're thinking: Too easy. Ambrose's dad is the killer. Right? You'd be wrong. I didn't know then what I know now. Being dead is a learning process too. I do wish I had known why I was so uncomfortable around him at the time, but it wouldn't have changed anything.

Chapter 3: The Turn

"Why can't my mommy see you?"

"Because I'm dead."

"You're not dead; dead people don't talk."

"How do you know? Talk to any other dead people lately?"

"No, that's how I know they don't talk!"

I started feeling electricity, like static all around me.

"Ambrose, honey, who are you talking to?"

"Mike, it's her imaginary friend I told you about, remember?" Ambrose's mom, Marie, said.

"Oh, right. What's your friends name again?"

"Ana."

"Where is Ana?"

Ambrose giggled. "She's right next to you, silly daddy."

"Oh, right here?" Mike asked. He turned to look where Ambrose had pointed, but his smile faded right away. His hair stood up on the back of his neck. His face paled. The door to Ambrose's room slammed shut. Ambrose screamed. Mike shook his head and cleared his throat.

"Mike, what just happened" Marie asked, alarmed.

"It's nothing, hon. Just a draft."

I was alarmed. I had no idea what had just happened or why.

"Ana, why did you slam my door like that? That wasn't very nice of you." Ambrose said, seemingly angry with me.

"It wasn't me, Ambrose."

I stared at the closed door. No windows were open. I saw no other ghosts. I was just as confused as Mike had been.

Sometimes people are put in your path for a reason. Dead or alive, if your essence remains behind, there is a cosmic plan for you. It may not be evident until it's done, but believe me; the fates always have a plan. I followed behind Mike as he went into his room with Marie.

"Mike, what the hell was that?"

"I... I don't think Ana is imaginary."

"What do you mean? Of course she is."

"I saw her, Marie." Mike's eyes had been looking down this whole time until that comment. When his eyes met Marie's, there was something dark in them. It obviously scared her.

"What do you mean, you 'saw' her, Mike? Like, she's a ghost or something?"

"Do you remember me telling you that I had an imaginary friend when I was little?"

"Yes, but 'imaginary' is the operative word. You're scaring me."

"Yeah, well it's about to get even scarier. I didn't see my friend after my dad died. My mom took me to therapists when I was little because my dad died in the room that is now Ambrose's. I saw it happen and I wouldn't speak for months."

"Jesus, Mike. Why haven't you ever told me this?"

"Because the therapists convinced me that it was all made up in my head, and I blocked it all out. Tonight in Ambrose's room, I saw Ana, and I started to remember. She was here when my father died."

"Mike, this is insane. Is she dangerous?"

"I don't know, but I don't want to take that chance. We have to get out of here."

I was shocked at what I heard. I couldn't listen anymore. I left and went to sit alone in the living room. I thought long and hard. I didn't remember Mike and I definitely didn't remember being here when his dad died. I would never hurt anyone that I did know.

I wanted to believe that he was lying, but the feeling I got when he was around left me questioning if his story could really be true. In my mind's eye, I saw my nightmare. I saw myself in bed and the man towering over me. The lightning flashed, but that is where the vision ended. I could never get beyond that point and see who the man was or what happened next.

I knew I was dead, but had I really been dead that long? Time definitely moved differently in the spirit realm, but why couldn't I remember? I knew what I had to do, but I didn't know how I was going to do it.

I watched Mike for a couple of days before making my move. He seemed to be on edge and jumpy. He canceled the business trip he was supposed to go on for the coming week. I tried to imagine what I would say to him and how I could approach him. I knew I wanted him to be alone, but he was always moving and always looking over his shoulder. I finally found my opportunity. He went to the attic of the small house. I followed him up. I tried my best not to startle him, so I stayed behind him and spoke softly.

"Mike?"

Nothing. I tried once more, with a little more volume, but it was enough. He jumped and spun around, eyes wide.

"Ana."

"I wanted to talk to you."

"I'm sure you did, but I want you to stay away from my daughter."

"I can't do that, Mike. She is my friend."

"I was your friend once and she doesn't need your type of friendship; believe me."

"I don't recall being your friend. I only remember loneliness mostly, but I do have a nightmare of sorts that comes to me in times of loneliness and boredom. I remember laying in bed."

"Stop, I don't want to hear this."

"Why not?"

"Because I just don't. I spent years convincing myself that you weren't real, and here you are. You can cut the lonely little girl act, Ana. We're leaving just as soon as we can."

I walked over to him and put my hand on him. The vibrations coming from him were extreme. I couldn't even remember what feelings felt like, but here they were. My image started to waiver; the vibrations were so strong.

"Mike, help me remember," I said to him, pointing to a family photo album sitting next to where he was sitting.

"Mike?" I heard Marie calling from downstairs.

"Yeah, hon. I'll be down in a minute," he said, his eyes not leaving mine, but he did pull his hand away.

"Ana, we will continue this discussion later. In the meantime, please stay away from Ambrose. I need to figure this stuff out."

He did not await my response before descending the staircase from the attic. I was glad. I wanted to find out what he knew, but at the same time, I did not want to stop playing with Ambrose. I decided that, until we spoke next, I would try to stay away from her, just to placate Mike a little. It didn't take long. I watched her playing in the back yard. She felt my presence and called to me.

"Ana, come play with me. I miss you."

I went to play with her, but my mind was elsewhere.

"Ana, what's wrong? Don't you want to play with me?"

"Of course I do. I'm sorry. Where were we?"

"You were about to offer me a cookie and ask if I'd like to go swimming in the pond."

"The pond? Can you swim?"

"No, silly but it's not deep."

I had no way to measure if the water was deep or not, but I felt uncomfortable with the idea. I had once been a child of her age myself. However, the idea of having a permanent friend to share my afterlife with was starting to sound appealing. Was it wrong for me to wish her to be with me forever?

"I would love for you to have a cookie, milady, and afterwards, I would be honored if you would go for a swim with me," I said to her. We headed to the water, hand in hand.

Chapter 4: Coming Together

"Mike, What is she doing?" Marie asked, alarmed as she watched Ambrose near the water. She was frozen, unable to move.

Mike ran to the window that Marie was looking out of and, without saying a word, dashed outside.

"Come on, Ana. We can be mermaids!" Ana's tiny voice said as we waded a few more feet out into the water. Something nagged at my conscience, but I ignored it. Suddenly, I heard Mike screaming. I turned to look at him as Ambrose hit a deep spot and disappeared under the water. Bubbles swirled around her as I did nothing but stare at Mike, who seemed to be running in slow motion to me, trying desperately to make it to his daughter before it was too late.

Time moves differently in the spirit world. As Mike scrambled to get his daughter, the world around me stopped. I saw the bubbles, unmoving above Ambrose. I turned and saw Mike in mid stride. There was a butterfly in mid-flap a few inches from his head. I saw a lone, wet tear that had formulated on his panic-stricken face. The image brought me back years prior to a memory that I had long forgotten.

I saw another panic-stricken face, running toward me. He looked like Mike, only different. He had the same blue eyes and dark complexion, but his hair was longer. He was in the exact same spot that Mike was currently in. As if someone hit the un-pause button on a remote, the scene played out. I looked at the bubbles in the water; only, instead of Ambrose, there was a little boy, flailing in the water for a moment and then the flailing stopped as the boy began to sink.

The man made it to the little boy and dove under the water to get him.

"Mike! Oh God, Mike!" he yelled as he pulled the little boy up. He was unresponsive. The man pulled the little boy to the shoreline and checked his pulse. His lips were blue. The man ripped open the little boy's button-up shirt and began compressions. Soon, water came out of the little boy's mouth as he coughed, desperately gasping for air, like a fish out of water. I giggled at the imagery as I saw the little fish finally grab his first good gulp of air. He pointed at me.

"Daddy, she made me do it."

"Shh. Enough about that for now, son. I thought I lost you."

The man cradled his son in his arms. He couldn't have been any more than six or seven years old. Tears ran down his face as the mother ran out with blankets. The man wrapped his son in them and picked him up and carried him into the house. I followed them in, curious about this emotion I was sensing, but knew nothing about.

Chapter 5: Nightmares

I watched them for the day. I watched as a storm rolled in. The boy was near death. I was excited. Soon, he would join me. Soon, I would have a friend in my world and I would be lonely no more. I crawled into bed with the little boy as his breathing became labored. The lightning flashed and thunder rumbled in the room, but the boy slept still.

I heard the door open and saw a man standing in the doorway. I felt an emotion I was unfamiliar with. Fear. As the man neared the bed, he turned on the bedside lamp. He touched his child's head, with a worried look on his face.

"Don't worry, son. The doctor is on his way. The storm may make it take some time, but you hang in there," he said.

Doctor? I thought to myself. There was no way I was allowing them to take him from me. I was finally going to have a friend. There was finally someone for me to play with forever.

I was suddenly back in the present. I remembered everything. How could I have forgotten? I watched as Mike ran to his daughter; her hand reached out of the water as if she knew he was coming. He grabbed her little hand and brought her out, falling to his knees once his feet were past the water.

"Ambrose!" Marie screamed as she came running with blankets to wrap her daughter in. Mike made it to his daughter faster than I had anticipated. She was breathing and fine, but a little shaken. Mike turned his head and looked directly at me with an angry look on his face, but he said nothing. He picked up his daughter and carried her into the house. I followed.

Marie grabbed her daughter as soon as they got into the house and rocked her until she fell asleep. Once she was sure she was asleep, she spoke in whispers to Mike.

"Mike, what is going on?"

Mike looked at his wife and paused for a moment,

not speaking.

"Mike!" She said more urgently.

"Marie, I am not really sure, but I am going to figure this out. Don't worry."

"Don't worry? Mike, she just about drowned out there! Do we need a fence around the pond? She's never done something like this before."

"A fence won't help, Marie. I am going to figure this out. I promise." He kissed his wife on the lips and then kissed Ambrose on the forehead.

"Where are you going?"

"To figure this out."

Mike headed to the attic, knowing I would follow. I was curious to see what he was thinking. "Ana!"

"No need to yell, I am right here," I said to him. He turned to face me.

"What in the hell do you think you were doing? I asked you to stay away from her."

"She wanted me to play with her."

"She is seven years old. She doesn't know what she wants. Did you talk her into going into the water?"

I could tell that he was getting angry.

"I'd be careful if I were you, Mike. You wouldn't want to wind up like your father, now would you?" I looked him in the eyes, cold. I saw fear flash in his eyes, and then I saw a different emotion.

"You *did* kill him, didn't you?"

"I can't answer that question, Mike. Look at the album. Maybe we can figure it out together."

"You were my friend once, weren't you? If you ever cared about me at all, you will leave her alone."

"Look at the album, Mike."

Mike did as I asked. He pulled the dusty album from the stack next to the old trunk. There were many pictures of Mike doing various things, normal pictures. Something was odd about the pictures, though. In each picture of him, from the time he moved to this house, there was a blur behind him. I felt a rush as I started to remember the times spent with Mike.

"We were friends, but then you abandoned me."

"I had no choice, Ana. I was a child and my father..." He trailed off. Something was off about his voice.

"Why are you doing this to us?"

"I have no reason to do anything to anyone. I am lonely and I want someone to play with that won't leave me."

"Take me. I will play with you forever."

"Mike, you're too old now, silly." I said to him while turning to leave.

"Ana! Please! Take me. Take me instead."

"It's too late for that, Mike. You had your chance. Oh, and don't even think of trying to take her from me. You remember what happened when your father tried to take you from me. I'll know," I said to him. I felt a rush of exhilaration. I still did not quite remember what happened that night, but I now remembered that I had more power than any normal little girl. I had lived in this form for many years. I had no idea how many, but it was obviously even longer than I thought.

Chapter 6: Truth

I willed myself to the garden behind the house, content in what I was planning. I would find a way to make Ambrose my friend forever. She trusted me and wanted to play with me. The air around me grew still and I was suddenly back in that night.

The pictures had stirred something in me. I watched as Mike's dad talked to him. He couldn't see me and didn't even know I was there. How I would have loved to know this sort of love from a parent. I didn't remember anything about my life, but I felt certain that I had not had parents as attentive or loving as this.

Mike's mom brought in some tea.

"How's his fever?"

"He feels pretty warm and there is a rattling in his chest when he breathes that I hadn't heard before. What did the doctor say?"

"He said he would be here as soon as he could."

She sat on the bed right where I was. I watched as goose flesh crawled across her arms.

"It's drafty in here, Jake. Is there a window open?"

"No. It's just an old house, babe." Jake said, not moving.

Mike's mom put her hand on his head, just as Jake had done moments before. Lightning struck again. I heard the rain start suddenly and the wind picked up. The sound of the rain on the roof calmed me. I pretended for a moment that these were my own parents watching over me. Mike's mom fell asleep fast on the bed beside me. Jake dozed off, but awoke with a start when the lightning struck close and lit up the room, accompanied not long after with a loud crack. He looked immediately over to Mike and, instead, saw me.

"I must be dreaming," he said to himself, watching me cautiously.

"Who are you?" Jake asked me. I smiled, but did not speak.

Mike woke up, but his mother continued sleeping.

"Daddy, what's wrong?"

"Nothing, baby. Go back to sleep."

Mike turned and saw me. He smiled widely through his sickness.

"Hey, Ana," he said.

"This is Ana?" Jake asked.

"You see her, daddy?" Mike asked.

Jake kept his eyes on me but eased over to the bed, reaching his hands out to Mike.

"Come on, Mike. We're going to take you to the doctor."

"Nonsense," I told Mike.

"I will care for you. We'll be friends forever," I told him.

"Oh, God. I should have listened to you." Jake reached across me to take Mike.

"You will not take him!" I said. I touched his hand and he began to convulse.

"Daddy!" Mike yelled as his father fell to the floor with foam coming out of his mouth. Mike's mom finally woke up.

"Jake?! Honey, what's happening?" she screamed. A banging at the door startled Mike and his mother.

"Doctor, Oh God! In here! We're in here. Please hurry!" she said. I began to fade, unwillingly. I had used too much energy in backing Mike away. I was able to watch, but unable to act as the doctor pronounced Jake dead.

While I was reliving the past, Mike was being very naughty. He remained behind in the attic, digging up the past that had been so long forgotten, and I had unknowingly given him the key. Underneath the stack of family photo albums that went back a couple of generations, was another photo album that pre-dated the arrival of Jake and his family so many years ago.

The writing on the album listed it as "Joe and Jane's House of Shame." Inside were pictures that looked very old. It was hard to tell how old they were, but they were pictures taken of children with names and dates. Most were babies. There were letters inside from unwed mothers. What Mike gathered from the letters was that this house had been used as a sort-of halfway point. Wealthy families paid to have children stored here that were born to unwed mothers.

Newspaper clippings showed that in the 1930's this house had been used for this purpose. The horrifying part was that children's bodies were discovered on the property. When the families couldn't pay the dues, "Joe and Jane" murdered the children and buried them. Mike felt sick at the revelation. He saw that the house would send letters with pictures of the children. The article showed that one mother came to claim her child, only to be told that the child had passed away. Fearing that something was not right, she called the police; and that's when they made the gruesome discovery.

The back of the album contained the infamous "death photos" for many of the children. Mike gasped when he saw the first photo in the album titled: *Ana, January 1922.*

"What are you doing?"

Mike jumped at the sound of my voice.

"Ana, is this you?"

I didn't want to look. Deep down, I always knew but I didn't want to accept it.

"So what if it is? We both knew I was dead."

"Ana, is this what happened to you?"

"What happened to me? Hmm. Let's see. I only remember cruel parents and lots of beatings. I remember being the oldest in the house and watching them murder the younger ones. Some of them were lucky, though. Some of them went home with families."

"Ana, that's horrible!"

"Horrible, yes. It doesn't change anything, though."

"What do you mean?"

"I mean, Ambrose will be my friend forever. We will

play together with dolls and have tea parties forever."

Mike thought hard.

"Ana, what happens if you take Ambrose and she doesn't stay?"

"What do you mean?"

"I mean, there have been many other children who died here and I don't see any of them. What happens if you take her and she doesn't stay?"

"She has to! I can't be alone anymore."

"Ana, you've never had a mother or father to love you. What if I stayed with you? I could play tea party with you and tuck you in at night."

I thought for a moment. His offer did seem very intriguing.

"How do I know that you won't pass over?"

"You know because I know if I pass over, Ambrose will not be safe. Please, Ana. Take me. I will go willingly. We were friends once. You wanted me to stay with you. I am still that same boy. Please don't take our little girl from us."

"I will consider your offer," I said to him.

I had a lot to consider. I always wanted a friend to play with, but a daddy to love me was something special. I went to Ambrose and watched her sleep with her mother lying on her bed, much like Mike's mother had, so many years prior.

Chapter 7: Decisions

I let the lonely years replay in my head. All I wanted was someone to love me and never leave me. If this were what Mike was offering, then I would have the best of both worlds. He had known me as a child and he was now a grown-up, capable of giving me what every child I had known when I was alive wanted. There was another choice, though.

I could have everything I wanted if I just killed them all. I would have a family that loved me. A mom, a dad and a sister! We could be together forever. I felt happy at this thought. I was suddenly taken back to the time when I was living. I watched as though I were a casual observer in my own life.

"Ana, a hand, please," Jane said to me, holding a screaming child in her hands. I walked over to her with a hammer, and the baby screamed no longer. My face was covered in blood.

"Very good, Ana. You're proving quite useful. The daughter we never had," Joe said to me. I smiled, as I was the only one to ever get this sort of treatment. The forgotten memory stung a little. Had I really been so heartless? I didn't even wash the blood off. I walked over to the small table they bought just for me and began drawing and humming. I got irritated when the blood stained my drawing.

I heard a pounding on the door.

"It's the cops!" Jane said.

"Well, we always knew it would happen. Get the girl. She belongs with us."

We all ignored the pounding on the door. Joe went to his room and got a shotgun. Joe aimed at me first and pulled the trigger. I never saw them again.

I felt a swell of emotion at the betrayal, long forgotten but now fresh in my mind. I sat in Ambrose's room and rocked myself and hummed.

"Ana, what's wrong?" Ambrose said. This woke her mother. I continued humming.

"Ambrose, honey, go to sleep. There is no one here."

"Ana is. She's humming."

"It'll be okay, sweetie," Mike said, turning to me.

"Have you decided?"

"I have."

Many years later, a family moved in. There was a mother, a father and two little girls – twins! I was so excited to see them arrive.

"You may not play with them," Mike said to me. He was no fun.

"But daddy, they look like so much fun!" I exclaimed to him.

"Ana, daddy said no. You have Ambrose to play with, remember?"

"But she doesn't want to play with me much. All she wants to do is play in the garden by herself," I said to Marie, pouting.

"Ana, remember. You are our daughter now. You must do as we say," Mike said.

"Okay, Mama and Papa. I'll be good." I said.

"Promise?" Marie asked.

"I promise," I answered and danced away.

"Do you think she remembers?" Marie asked Mike.

"I hope not. When she forgets, she is good."

"Where are the albums?" Marie asked

"In the attic, but don't worry. She is forbidden to go in there."

"She is stubborn. With the new family, she may follow one of them up there."

"We will have to watch her, and if any of them can see us, perhaps we can get them to burn them."

"They have twins. Twins are normally very perceptive," Marie added.

They didn't think I could hear them, but I did. I wondered what was in the attic that they didn't want me to see. I made a mental note to find out as soon as they weren't watching.

THE END

Contributor's bio:

I am a married mother of three who also happens to run an automotive repair center. Time is something that I am seriously lacking, but I love to write every chance I get. When I am not juggling three kids and a full time career as a woman in a man's world, or throwing wrenches at grumpy mechanics, I love reading and writing. I am particularly a fan of horror and mystery novels. I also run a page on Facebook called Paranormal Fiction, where I post scary short stories in daily episodes for free. Follow my current stories at: www.facebook.com/paranormalandabnormal

IN HER IMAGE
Written by Anya Lee

*M*y sister had branded our entire family with a curse when she killed herself—our friends, even people nearby. She had stained them—figuratively, as well as literally. Splattered to bits.

"In front of the train. Boarding the Yamanote line that circles Tokyo, and then jumped. I forgot to mention it to you earlier, Sanae," my mother explained to me, her face as hard as glass.

Our mother was always withdrawn. I wanted to say I saw the cracks form, that perhaps, my mother was saddened. I can't say with certainty that she loved my sister or me. It hurt that my mother's face was so smooth, when mine was shattered with complete disbelief. A woman had told her that she saw Saya's head twist off her body from the impact of the train— just ripped right off.

She had told me that when someone died violently, it was like a curse. It was a curse that you had to remember their death, the loss, and the torture they experienced, as they died—a vivid recollection of each passing moment of their agony. If they were stabbed, beaten, cut, burned, drowned, choked, or splattered to bits, you would think of it. The pressure from hands against their throat, crushing their vocal cords as the blood ran cold in their bodies and oxygen stopped flowing to their brain. This was a curse, because once someone died, you were stuck with it. The curse would weave itself through your flesh, their bones, and the very association of it was a curse. You'd be haunted by it. The fact that we were all close to death and it was just a matter of circumstance that got us closer to it, or further from it, cursed us with the reminder that our lives could end swiftly, faster than they even started.

We were twins, Saya and I. As the cliché goes, we couldn't have been any more different. I felt it was my responsibility to help her, though. She barely made it past the high school entrance exams of her choosing, a choice she made just to follow me into it. She didn't go to college, spending about two years in our parents' house as a *hikkomori* (one who avoids social contact.)

Saya liked to live her life without complication, without choice. She wouldn't even remember to wear makeup unless I did it for her. I helped her study at my own time expense, and introduced her to a nice man from my friend's office. Saya's life, essentially, was a product of my help.

And yet, she chose to curse us. When I think about it, I can see her face. Calm, yet dulled. Eyes closed, plunging in front of the train, and splattering against it, pelting everyone with her blood. She was so helpless; it was hard not to pity her, unlike my mother.

"You're both too selfish," my mother said as I cried that morning.

Saya was selfish; she was so concerned with burdening herself, she never took action. She coasted. I was the pride of my father, and mother to an extent, because I didn't have that mentality. I did what I could, and I also tried hard to be a good sister. I pulled strings to get my sister a job at the company I worked for, and now, here she was… on the news, in the papers. Thankfully, they hadn't disclosed the office we worked at. That kind of damage would be irreparable.

I decided to ride the Yamanote Line tonight from my parents' house to go to the office. It was my day off, but the new girl in our office needed help with her paperwork, so I was obligated to help. As I neared thirty, I started getting a real kick out of being the mentor to the younger girls at work. They didn't come near me in terms of beauty or refinement, so I didn't feel old or burdened by it. It was almost kind of exciting, actually. "Miss Sanae, how *are* you still single?" they would ask, half attempting to insult me sometimes. They could never match me, though. Not in their wildest dreams. Not Hitomi from HR and her short skirts, and not even that half-breed Anna, with her wide eyes. Not ever.

My responses to these girls would remain the same: "I just prioritize promotions over pregnancies," I would respond, nasally—half joking, half insulting.

It was a fickle world of work, but despite minor jealousies, these girls would rely on me, and I would rely on them. Separating one's personal face from professional was essential, and the closer I got to promotion, the closer I was to shutting them up once and for all and winning their utmost respect. The men in my company were hardly a threat, after all. If anyone was in favor with the company president, it was I. Not once had I been asked to pour tea during a meeting. I never pour the tea, but I will always drink it.

But there was something I lacked: I was entering mid-life, still a virgin. There was something about me that I guessed was off-putting. Maybe it was my lack of attention to men?

I found a seat on the train, which wasn't particularly crammed today. I had looked into the crowd of people. A few *gyaru* schoolgirls sat together near me in a cluster, skirts pulled up to their waistlines, hems fluttering against the exposed flesh of their thighs. It was almost nostalgic seeing the cotton fibers of the bulky cardigans, plaid ribbons and skirts; they bobbed their bleached and dyed heads together in unison, chatting.

"Does that lady have a Thavasa bag? I wonder where she works."

I heard their conversation, directed at my purse. I was their ideal because I was once one of them. I had certainly become the woman I wanted to be, in more than image: successful, plenty of friends. I turned to the girls, tucking a section of hair behind my ear and exposing a gaudy earring. It gleamed appropriately, so it was a tactic to magnetize people to my jawline. Noticing I had turned towards them, the cluster of girls noisily turned inward.

I didn't usually take this train since I lived near my company, so it was a sense of spectacle for me. Usually people minded their business, so I quickly fell back into doing just that. The girls chattered amongst themselves as passengers boarded and left at the stations, and I couldn't help but find myself in the place of my sister once again. I found myself lost in thoughts of her laugh, her face—like those schoolgirls and the women at work; there was such a sense of adoration that would no longer be present in my life. Was I selfish for wanting it from her for so long? She was like a child to me, more than my sister—a product I had placed time and effort into. I mulled this over, thinking of her head ripping from her frail body. Her eyes going cold, losing their expression of gratitude, short bobbed hair brushing about her pale, angular face as her neck disconnected from torso, ripping away.

I was going to make myself sick. It wasn't an imaginary stretch to place my head in place of hers, and the thought that it could've been me instead was making me sick.

Snapping myself back into reality for a moment, the train was quite different—the bustle before was gone, and I had my headphones in my ear, gaze affixed to my phone, which displayed its lock screen. I gazed up to peer around myself, and quickly glanced back down, heat rising to my cheeks. It wasn't uncommon for *chikan* (molesters) to be on trains; it was their territory after all, especially at night. I peered up at a man, who looked to be in his early thirties.

He was slightly attractive, with a full head of hair. At this stage, I had heard it was important that a man had a full head of hair. I couldn't help but be disinterested. My lips curled with disgust, and interest, as I studied his movements. He brushed into a young woman, early twenties at most. Her back was facing me. She had short brown hair, cut in a fluffy bob—the style reminded me of my sister's. I peered down at my phone while they rustled about amidst a waning crowd, thinking they were unseen. I looked up; he had slid his hand up her skirt, fingertips pressing against the exposed flesh of her rear. Her skin was pale and flushed. He pulled her underwear down, dropping his briefcase against the side of an open seat. Everyone had to have seen this, yet nobody said a thing...

Or so I hoped. I felt like the only person there with a laser focus on them, crossing my legs. I felt a slight tingling start at my toes and travel up, feeling rather flushed myself. Was I blushing? I pretended to stare at my phone harder. I could practically see everything from my position, my throat becoming tight. He slid his fingers between her thighs, rubbing her furiously. I couldn't see her face as she was turned around, hand secured around a handrail. The train continued to move towards its destination, as did his fingers, working underneath her, rather aggressively.

My own knees buckled. I parted my lips, finding my mouth to be very dry. It was so dark in this tunnel, and the lights began to flicker. I attempted to turn my phone back on to distract myself, only to find it had died…

I just charged it.

I was ready to die right then and there. It was so embarrassing. How could anyone conduct themselves like that in public? I wanted to throw something at them, but instead I just pressed my legs together closer. I stared at them again, unable to take my eyes off of their… act.

I would be lying if I didn't say I was envious, but there was a level of disgust I was experiencing. The thought of offering myself to a man made me sick. Yet, right now, I felt anything but that. Heat was rising through my body, and my tongue felt stuck to my mouth. I pressed the hand not holding my cell phone against my waist, crossing my legs tightly again as the train passed through another tunnel. The tightness in my throat and body continued, and it felt as if my entire stomach was going to come up. I couldn't tell if I wanted to hurl or rip my stomach out. The pressure that was building continued, and I uncrossed my legs, preparing to rise and leave the train car.

Immediately after, I felt so disgusted with myself; hurling definitely seemed like a viable option. I had experienced arousal before, and to say it was definitely unpleasant was no understatement. I could feel my face drop as the realization that I was more than a little... unhinged at the moment. I felt so unclean. I couldn't control myself in that instant, and shouted at the couple, "I can SEE you!"

I huffed in embarrassment, and the figures turned to face me, obscured by the dark of the train tunnel, lined with red light.

Good. Stupid whore.

Her hair shifted briefly, her face coming to light. I was able to make out details, the red lights completely making her face visible. The clay-like face before me left me in horror. The large, angled eyes and sharp defined nose... small, yet pouty lips, and long neck that paralleled my own...

"S-Saya?" I stammered confusedly, the shadowy figures revealing themselves to have faces. What was shown before me in red light was a face of my own, like looking into a disgusting, slut mirror. However, that wasn't possible. Saya had been splattered to bits. Splattered, splattered, splattered, head ripped from her stupid shoulders and body pulverized like raw meat. I found myself staring harder. This girl just looked like Saya at a young age; yet, it was a face embedded in my memory. There was a crucial difference here, and that was that Saya lacked something.

Saya doesn't have a...

The train screeching to a halt interrupted my clarity of thought. I slammed into the floor of the train; my cell phone shook from my hand and onto the floor with my face, and shattered into plastic and metal fragments. This woman... Saya? She cracked a wide smile that snaked across her face and revealed blackened, sharp teeth. Her eyes twisted delightfully as she stood above me, terror filling my body like electricity. She withdrew from me and tightly grabbed onto the male figure.

She opened her mouth widely; biting into his face, blood splattering as he stood, willingly consumed by her. I screamed immediately, crawled, and stumbled into a standing position, and quickly ran to the door of the next train car, sliding it open roughly and running through, and then slamming the sliding door shut, sweat pooling at my forehead as I contemplated what I had just saw.

My eyes widened as I turned around. My jaw trembled, and I immediately raised my hand to cover my face. My body tightened. The train car was bustling with women all staring at me, naked with bulging eyes, all with the same face: Our face—my face. I wanted out of the depths of the subway station.

"Big sis," they hummed lowly in a chorus.

"Big sis, I missed you," they moaned. *"Big sis, big sis."*

The train screeched loudly, a low buzz filling the air as the lights flickered from red to nothing, the darkness of the space pulsing and filling. They moved with each flicker, gyrating aimlessly and sluggish, exposing to me the filth of their thin bodies, and touching one another. Heads thrashing about with the rhythm of the light, plastering their sweaty palms and soles against the train windows, slamming, blissfully moaning, calling to me.

"Big sis, big sis, big sis, big sis..." The noise overpowered me as I stood in silence, my throat so tense I could hardly do anything but watch in disbelief. I couldn't conclude I was dreaming. I couldn't think. My mind went blank, buzzing with the noises filling the tunnel. I didn't notice the slide of the door behind me, but I registered it immediately when my neck felt moist. A slight tickle, a humid pulse trickling against the nape

of my exposed neck and chain jewelry. A tongue had glided across the base of my neck to earlobe, my entire body going cold, and goose bumps rising painfully along the lengths of my legs and up my spine.

"I only had you," a woman's voice slithered into my ear. She placed her hands around my body as she spoke, pressing her now naked body against me. It was the woman I had evaded, now disrobed. Her body felt wet and slick, staining my white blouse with a reddish brown substance as if she was made of shit, guts and blood. Her hands found their way to my chest, pressing tightly against me as I whimpered. I could only cry, tears and mascara stinging my eyes as they welled up, a droplet sliding down my face as my breath went erratic.

"Big sis, big sis, big sis," they hummed, thrashing still, eyes turned towards me without so much as a blink.

Her hands slid downward, curling around my pelvis tightly. I screamed violently, shoving my elbow into her with the weight of my body, only to slam down backwards into nothing, falling onto my side and out of the car filled with doppelgangers into the one I had just left.

I looked up sharply, seeing the car I had left filled with nothing. This vanishing act was opportune for me, as I scrambled to my feet, running across the aisle and to the exit. I banged on it helplessly.

"Let me out! Let me out! Open up!" I fruitlessly screamed, banging on a door that didn't even respond or shake. I felt defeated, and immediately ran to the next car, hoping my luck there would be better than in the last two, heading towards the back of the train. The security door hung open. I sobbed, tears filling up my vision as I descended the train car into the depths of the subway tunnel. The space around me was not the sprawling station I had seen before, as if I was walking through someone's dark dream.

Why won't this nightmare stop?

The depths of the tunnel were rustic and browned, covered in dried brown crusts and stains, and paired against black streaks and red pools of what I was going to say was blood. I had been plunged deeper into the subway, buried underground. Buried in hell. Numerous faceless corpses lined the ground, having the appearance of decayed, rotting carcasses left out in the summertime. Some were bloated, with slick, wet, brown flesh that had deteriorated into a chunky mold, singed and exposed insides visible through several large cuts in their torso, and others were thin, merely bruised skin clinging to bone. They lined the floor intermittently, haphazardly placed chains of bodies scattered on the dirt ground.

I heard raspy, haggard breathing, although these bodies had not mouths, noses, or eyes. Huffing and extremely labored inhalations could be heard, crackling present in the room. I felt I had to get to the other side of this cavern; to keep going was safety, and the only instinct I presently had. I stepped around the bodies, which began to growl lowly, shredding noises coming from the depths of their throats, but muffled, their mouthless faces buzzing with subdued noise. They didn't move. The smell was overwhelming. The space was humid and reeked, likely from the bodies, the smell resembling rotten fish or a fetid dumpster. Sweat drenched my body, but I couldn't stop going. The faceless bodies seemed to be staring at me, watching my movement, necks craned towards me.

"Do…" The air filled with light noises, like someone struggling to speak. There were whispers amidst the growls and low hum. *"Steal… om… ck…. DIE."* The voices crackled and broke.

A bout of sobbing escaped me, gasps slipping

through my lips. I was finally clearing the lot of faceless bodies; as the cavern stretched it became darker, and darker. There was a light in the distance, perhaps another subway station? I drew closer to the light, my heart skipping several beats as more tension built in my chest, exasperated to come to the light and make out not a crowded, safe station, but rather a child's bedroom. A bunk bed stood firm against a wall, clashing colors of blue and pink decorating everything in sight, plush lambs and ribbon lining the floor. I had spotted a familiarity.

A young girl, faceless, had pinned down a boy, with his pants around his ankles. She held a pair of scissors dangerously over his lower body, laughing in a shrill, distorted child voice, crackling with a low buzzing sound. The tears continued to flow from my face, guilt and shame being the only things I could feel, aside from fear, as my breathing became heavy, almost a pant. I remembered this scene as vividly as it was being portrayed to me.

"Hold still. You'll be like me, Sho. My real sister." The scissor-wielding girl stretched her fingers, the blades gleaming as she lowered them to his penis. She began to close down on them, grinding away at his flesh violently, attempting to apply enough pressure to completely remove it, blood spurting forth as screams filled the air

"It hurts! It hurts! Stop it!" the other howled, scrambling, throttling about, kicking and stomping. The girl didn't relent, her faceless expression emitting a determined seriousness.

I hated this scene. It had haunted me for a long time, repressing itself. I knew what I had done, and what it meant for my family. I shouldn't have felt shame, though. I had fixed Saya's life. She had wanted to be just like me, so I had to remove it… She had something there that wasn't like mine, and we had the same face. We had to be the same then—sisters.

The faceless girl continued to hack away at the other, the screams pounding away at my head. I collapsed to my knees, clutching my mess of brown curls and digging my nails into my scalp.

"Stop screaming," I whispered as the little girl, a parallel to me, shouted. "Dad will hear you," we said in unison. I hadn't recalled the words, yet they escaped my lips verbatim.

My mouth actively betrayed my thoughts. It didn't stop. I closed my eyes tightly, and she still cut away at the other despite his protest, screams, resistance, thrashing. I could hear the scissors open and close, hacking into the boy's flesh. I could hear the struggle, the ripping, the insanity, and numerous sounds of the metal closing and opening, each accompanied by a scream, a sob.

I felt so dizzy, like my body was going numb. Voices cluttered my head, as I recalled a conversation from my parents.

"They're not really twins, should we tell them?" My mother mused quietly in a hushed tone, unaware I had heard her.

We had the same eyes, nose, lips, hair texture, height… Every day was like looking in a mirror, especially after I mutilated her. She wasn't my twin, but the second I made her that, she had become constant in my life.

It was like looking into a mirror. I never considered her born male, or anything. She was my doppelganger in every sense of the word, which is why I had to care for her. I was certain she had split off from me at birth, a half of me that just didn't end up in the same place at first. But she was as drawn to me as I was to her—and I had always wanted a sister. I had wished every night for a sister, and finally, one had come to us. I granted my own wish.

The voices seemed to cease momentarily, along with my tears—all was quiet, except for the sounds of creaking and air filling the damp area. I dared to open my eyes, only to meet with a smooth parallel to myself, with bobbed hair. Her broad shoulders glistened nakedly, scars of mutilation adorning what was otherwise a slender and beautiful form. I admired it like handiwork, but the terror I felt was too much for me to handle, my eyes throbbing, mouth creeping into a smile as her hands touched my head very tenderly, sisterly love, I had felt.

But then her hands wrapped tightly around my throat, and reality hit me once again. I struggled to remove her hands from me, but they had gained a monstrous strength unlike the frail sister I knew. She violently throttled me, shaking my body as I felt my throat crush underneath her palms. My entire neck tightened, a faint crackling emitting from my mouth as I tried to scream. It throbbed, heating up, but a particular coldness began to start in my lips, trickling through the rest of my face as my eyes rolled. My face began to numb, stinging in several small sections, which seemed to pop and then migrate elsewhere, like fireworks. My entire face felt like it was enlarged, my lips feeling as if they would burst any second. I didn't stop staring at my sister's smooth face, unable to remove my eyes from the horror of seeing nothing back at me instead of my own reflection.

That smooth face soon ceased to be, skin ripping as it changed shape, bone melding and forming as its jaw stretched, the skin splitting and ripping, blood splattering against me as my vision faded. I only heard a white noise, a loud ringing filling my ears. A mouth formed on her face, straight white teeth ripping through bloody gums as her jaw widened, stretching like a canine's and preparing to consume my face. I couldn't scream or do much, the last thing filling my vision being the darkness of its mouth.

It was a long darkness. The white noise didn't cease, however, sounds filling my head as I drifted from unconsciousness. I could hear the clamor of people, a baby wailing, and the stirring of numerous conversations around me. I felt as if I could finally open my eyes, stirring awake amidst the bustling of the train platform, sitting on a bench with my purse by my side and phone tightly clutched in hand. I stared at a large clock, instinctively, and it was mid-afternoon. My heart trembled, a sigh of relief escaping my mouth, horror lifting itself from my body. I had dozed off at the train station! I clutched my chest, my breathing increasing in speed as I stood up, trying my hardest not to cry at my horribly disturbing nightmare. I tried to brush it off, but the feeling of melancholy hadn't left me just yet. It was terrifying, after all. I looked at the clock again. The train would arrive soon, and I definitely needed to go home and shower since I had slept at the station all night.

I glanced at my phone. There were no new text messages, nothing. I had certainly expected a few calls from the office or something since I hadn't shown up last night. I dismissed it quickly, figuring that she probably did the work herself. I brushed past a few people in the noisy crowd of the bustling train station, a smile finally returning to my face. I was so glad to be out of that dream, lost in the memories of helping my sister live a better life in my image.

The trademark screech of metal could be heard as the

subway train approached, loud roars echoing from the tunnels. I turned to face the source of the noise, speeding up my approach in the crowd to find a good spot so I could get a seat, but bumped into a dark coated figure. My face pressed against a black fur-lined hood, and I quickly withdrew myself.

"I'm very sorry!" I apologized hastily for bumping into this woman, who was about the same height as me. Our heads nearly clashed.

My throat went dry as she turned to face me, her skin as pale as mine. Lips shaped as mine, and her eyes, fierce and as angled as mine. My heart stopped immediately, chills running through my body as the woman took my hand, pulling me through the crowd.

I whimpered as I tried to resist, her strength monstrous. I struggled amongst the crowd, my hair tossing about, garnering looks of scorn from people as we cut through the line. My hand was obviously being pulled, yet everyone glared. I tried to call for help or hold onto someone, but my body wouldn't move, frozen by Saya's touch. Her hands were cold, as if she were already dead. We neared the front of the platform, and I stared into the darkness of the tracks embedded down below, trembling with fear. The broken voices from the hall of faceless corpses filled my head again, with clarity…

"Don't go. It stole your face. Come back. YOU'LL DIE WITH IT."

"N-No!" my voice shook, trying to respond to them, but Saya turned and the voices cleared. She offered me a smile, hand tightening around my wrist. Her eyes were happy, lighting up with a joy I had never seen on her face. She lunged backwards as the train approached, swiftly, pulling me in with her. Terror filled my body, shaking me to my core, the train speeding as my heels left my feet, my body propelled by Saya's pull. The force left as I blinked. The next thing I registered was spotting myself, faceless, standing where Saya had. My clothes had changed. My body had changed, replaced with Saya's. A searing sensation enveloped my face as I hit the ground, the subway crowd screaming in terror as the ground rumbled from the train speeding to dock. I couldn't move. There wasn't time. I'm sure that, as my head flung from my body upon impact, it looked like mine, not Saya's. I'm sure that our face was always mine, and never hers, as I had shaped her in my image.

I regret wishing for a sister.

THE END

Contributor's bio:

Anya Lee resides in Louisville, Kentucky, and in addition to consistently being frenzied at all times due to an existential complex, this is her first publication! Attempting to blend her anxious woes with extreme physical discontent, Anya utilizes
body horror and dysmorphic imagery to convey herself in her writing. When she isn't a walking advertisement for treating your children for ADHD, she can be found abusing her Amazon prime subscription or watching Japanese b-horror (and yes, these hobbies do overlap.)

THE FAT OF THE LAND
Written by Sam Hill

Annie pinched the extra inch of pale flesh on her stomach, so fiercely that she drew blood. She wished that she was strong willed enough to rip it off entirely, but concluded that she did not have the resolve.

I'm too weak, she thought. *I can't even say no to a biscuit at break time or a slice of cake brought in for someone's birthday at work.*

Frowning into the mirror, she took one last look at her pale, pudgy thighs and sinking breasts. *Adam's right,* she told herself. *I am disgusting. I am a fucking pig.*

Before Annie had met Adam, she'd thought she was all right looking. Not exactly pretty, maybe, but attractive. Her hair was long and dark, her eyes a chocolaty brown. She'd always been slim, but what she hadn't known before Adam was that there is such a thing as being skinny fat.

"Your tits are saggy," he'd say. "You're thin, but you're flabby."

Almost immediately after meeting him, Annie set to work on changing herself. She needed him to want her as much as she craved every part of him. She banished carbs from her diet and bought a pedometer, striving hungrily for those coveted ten thousand steps. She lost weight, of course, but was still flabby. Sighing, she pulled on her work clothes and headed downstairs to make breakfast.

Adam was already at the table, his herbal tea and muesli in front of him, reading the paper. Annie popped a slice of toast into the toaster and felt him eyeing her disapprovingly as she opened the fridge and took out the butter, while waiting for the toast to pop. Self-consciously, she pulled her T-shirt down further over the slight bulge of her stomach.

"I'm off," Adam said, kissing her forehead as he grabbed his coat. "Perhaps you should walk to the office today. Get some exercise." He looked down at her plate of toast and added, "Maybe lay off the butter too, eh? You can hardly afford the extra calories, love."

It's true that she'd been a little lighter when they'd first met, but she was hardly a heifer. Adam, on the other hand, never seemed to gain any weight. He hit the gym regularly and ate well most of the time, as did she, but their weekend pizzas and take away curries never seemed to cling to his waistline as they did to hers.

Adam was a popular sort of guy—a man's man, but also very popular with the ladies. Extremely handsome with short blond hair, blue eyes, a square jaw and a killer smile. He knew this, and liked to rub it her face. Just little digs here and there about girls who flirted with him, how pretty and slim they were, and how lucky she was that he stuck with her instead. Little digs became bigger ones; he was increasingly crueler every day. The more hideous he was to her, the tighter she clung to him. She was developing an insane jealous streak, which didn't suit her, and she didn't know how long she could live that way.

* * *

Later that day, Annie arrived home from work to get changed. She was meeting Adam's mother for the first time that night and was terrified. Adam was a real mummy's boy, on the phone to her at least twice a day, running every little thing by her. If Annie didn't make a good impression on Mrs. White, she was pretty sure she would be kicked to the curb, making space for one of Adam's slim and sexy sidekicks to move right in.

As she walked up the stairs, she could hear the shower going. Adam's clothes were folded neatly on the bed; his phone, which was on top of the clothes, was ringing. Annie couldn't remember the last time he had left his phone lying around. He always took it with him everywhere, even to the loo.

Curiosity got the better of her and she glanced toward the screen of the phone. The words, '*Camila calling*' were displayed across a picture of a scantily clad brunette. Annie's heart began to pound in her chest. She felt sick. Her hand moved to answer the call, but she couldn't quite bring herself to do it. Couldn't face the confrontation.

In a zombie-like fashion, she reached for the dress she'd picked out for the evening and laid it on the bed. She knew that Adam liked this particular dress; he always said that the bell sleeves hid her bingo wings.

The sound the running water stopped and the bathroom door opened; Adam appeared in the doorway with a towel around his waist, his taut muscles glistening with water. He flashed her the grin that God gave him so that he'd get away with anything, and, involuntarily she smiled back.

"Hello, love," he said. "Jump in, your turn. Don't want to keep Mumsy waiting, do we?"

Annie regained as much of her composure as she could and walked into the bathroom, pausing to kiss him on the cheek as she passed. As she let the warm, soapy water wash over her, she pondered what to do. She'd always known Adam was a flirt, but was he acting on it? Who was Camila? Strangely, she felt more hurt than angry. *Weak. No backbone.*

* * *

They arrived at Adam's mother's place promptly at seven o'clock as requested, and were greeted by the most enormous woman that Annie had ever seen. Mrs. Mallory White must have weighed at least thirty stone. Annie, quite in shock, reached clumsily to shake the ginormous woman's hand, but instead was pulled into a soft maternal hug and the smell of freshly laundered clothes. This, unbeknownst to Annie, was a ploy to put her falsely at ease, for Mrs. Mallory White was not a nice person.

Annie was led into a large living room and ushered into an armchair whilst Adam sat down next to his mother on the sofa, kissing her ample cheek.

"What a lovely room, Mrs. White."

"Call me Mallory, dear. It's lovely to meet you. Annie is it? Well, aren't you lovely? Not quite as beautiful as the others he's had, but sort of pretty, in an understated way."

Adam put a hand over his mouth to stifle an

imminent chuckle and Annie found herself red faced and wondering whether this was all a big joke. She attempted to change the subject.

"What is it that you do, Mrs. White? Mallory."

"Do? Well, I'm a mother aren't I? And that's quite enough I believe. I don't understand all these women who want everything at once: children, husband, career. If you want to be good at the first two, I suggest you don't embark on the third. That's I way I see it. Of course, you're a career woman aren't you? Shame."

Annie scanned the room trying to think of a way to change the subject when her gaze fell upon a framed picture on the mantelpiece; she got up for a closer look. It was Adam when he was about ten years old, and boy, if he wasn't the porkiest little thing Annie had ever seen. Huge cheeks with those beautiful blue eyes sunk so far into them, it was surprising he could see.

"Adam, is this you?" she asked, barely able to control her happiness at this new discovery.

"It is." he admitted. "I wasn't quite the stud I am today, was I?"

"Nonsense," Mallory insisted. "You were a bonnie boy then and you still are now. You could use a bit more meat on your bones, though. Talking of which, I think it's about time to eat."

* * *

Annie and Adam sat at the green Formica table in the kitchen, and the aroma in the room was wonderful. They were served crispy skinned roast chicken, creamy mashed potatoes, Yorkshire puddings, buttered vegetables, stuffing balls and cocktail sausages wrapped in bacon.

Whatever Annie thought of Adam's mother on a

personal level, she was undeniably a marvelous cook. *No wonder Adam had been such a pudgy child*, she thought. *Who could resist all this?*

She began digging into the huge plate of food in front of her, Adam's judging looks for once absent as he concentrated on his own meal, seemingly transported back to another time and place. Mrs. Mallory White gazed fondly at her son.

"Good boy," she said, soothingly. "Eat it all up. There's a lovely crumble for desert."

The crumble was just as good as the main course, sweet warm apples coated in a buttery, crispy crumble and topped with ice cold homemade ice cream. By the time they'd all finished, Annie could hardly move.

* * *

On the way out, Annie thanked Mallory for her hospitality, and pulled on her coat, when Adam announced that he needed the loo quickly before they left.

There was an awkward silence between the two women left standing in the hallway until Adam's mother turned to Annie and smirked, a menacing grin exposing rotting teeth.

"It won't last you know. You're not good enough for my boy. I'll tell him so, and I'll tell him over and over again until he listens. Mother knows best."

Annie held back tears and bit her tongue, knowing that it was best not to respond.

"Look at you. How would you ever think you were good enough?"

Mallory stared directly into Annie's eyes.

"You're trash, little girl. Dirty, stinking trash. He'll be done with you soon. I'll see to that."

Adam clambered back down the stairs and gave his mother a big bear hug.

"See you soon, Mumsy."

He grabbed Annie by the arm and practically pushed her through the door and into the passenger seat of the car.

"Well that didn't go very well, did it Annie? You were thoroughly rude and obnoxious when Mumsy was trying so hard to be nice."

"Are you kidding?"

"No. I should have known you'd let me down. You ate enough of her food though, didn't you, Fatso?"

"Excuse me? Your mother isn't exactly svelte, is she?'

"You leave her out of this; she has a slow metabolism; it's a medical thing. What's your excuse?"

Annie knew better than to try and argue with him, and the rest of the journey was spent in stony silence.

* * *

The next morning, as was his way, the Adam she'd fallen for was back. They'd made love before breakfast, eaten together—with Annie avoiding the butter—and kissed each other goodbye before heading out to their separate work places. Annie so loved feeling cherished by this stunning, funny man that she managed to keep all sinister matters out of her head, at least until after lunch.

Her colleague, Sarah, bought her a chicken baguette to eat at her desk, and as she pulled it apart, scraping off the greasy mayo, memories of the previous night's chicken dish came into her head, prompting thoughts of overbearing mothers and possible mistresses. Not just one woman to compete with—but two, if not more. She decided that after work she'd go shopping for the ingredients to cook her man a dinner, healthy though, not like last night, and she'd buy enough wine to ensure he'd pass out early, the lightweight that he was, and she could begin an investigation.

The afternoon passed slowly and at five p.m. she bought some salmon fillets, the ingredients for a Greek salad, and three bottles of crisp white wine from the local supermarket.

She returned home, showered, and got into denim cut-offs and a gypsy blouse, which Adam had always said he'd liked. By the time he got home, she was in the kitchen, putting together the salad.

"What's all this in aid of?" asked Adam, wrapping his arms around her from behind and kissing her neck.

"Well, my love. It occurred to me last night during the spectacular meal your mother served up that I really ought to cook for you more often."

"I like your style, baby."

"Go take your shower and by the time you come down it'll be ready. I'll pour you a glass of wine to take up with you."

She coated the salmon in lemon juice and pepper and lightly fried it, making sure that the skin was nice and crispy. It was dished up and on the plate by the time Adam returned to the kitchen.

"Smells good," he said.

"I hope you enjoy it. It's not exactly up to your mother's standards, but I tried."

He took a mouthful and smiled.

"Not bad."

"Thanks. You know, I don't know how you're so slim and fit, the way your mother cooks. I mean, it's delicious food for sure, but how did you lose all the weight you were carrying as a kid? No offence, but you were huge."

"It wasn't easy. I got into sports and discovered I was good at it, so I wanted to be fitter. I trained hard, which got rid of a lot of the blubber, and then, when I went away to Sports College, I weaned myself off of the rubbish and started eating better. It was really, really hard; I think I was a bit addicted to food in some ways. Eating round at Mumsy's is hard; it's almost like a trigger to get me eating anything I want again and not caring about the consequences. That's why I don't visit as much as I should, and when I do, I try to avoid meal times."

"It must be hard for you. More wine?"

Adam didn't take his alcohol very well and so it was not long before he looked tired and she suggested he go to bed. He didn't argue. It had been such a nice evening that Annie almost felt sorry about what she was about to do, but she needed to know the truth. She watched TV for a bit and then crept up the stairs, quietly grabbing the phone from Adam's bedside table and tiptoeing back downstairs. She knew the code to his phone because she'd once watched over his shoulder when he'd typed it in and had stored the information in her head in case of future need.

First, she checked the photos. The initial few were standard selfies, the likes of which he continuously posted on social networking sites. The following ones made her want to be sick. She recognized the woman as Camila. There were pictures of her in underwear, then naked, then some of her and Adam together. Annie's heart pounded as she flicked through the others, unable to bear looking at them for long.

She put the phone down and felt the room start spinning; she willed herself not to be sick. She really didn't want to lose him, but she wasn't going to share him. A plan began to take shape. He was her addiction; she knew that. But now she knew his addiction, and she would feed it, slowly adding ingredients to their dinners to make them richer and more fatty. So slowly that he wouldn't notice until he was once again hooked. He would be the fat one that nobody wanted and she would be the svelte goddess he clung to. He'd need her. And that was what she wanted. She walked upstairs to bed, making a mental shopping list as she went.

* * *

It was easier than she thought, and the plan went smoothly. She added cream to sauces and butter to vegetables, swapped his bottles of Pepsi Max to regular ones, and added sugar to anything she could. She stuck to small portions herself, after all he'd told her she needed to diet. As the weeks went on, there were sumptuous meals every night, and even pudding. Of course, Adam had noticed what was happening eventually, but he was firmly back in the throes of addiction by then and said nothing. Annie reveled in the ever-increasing fleshy folds on his body, the little white pimples appearing in the crevices of his sweaty face. She watched, delighted as he struggled to climb the stairs, enjoying the sounds of his labored breathing. She began to feel disgusted when he made love to her, his once-toned belly a jelly of white, flaccid flesh. Still, at least he was now all hers. Nobody else would want him now, would they? The notion that that may not be true niggled at her incessantly until one day, several months into the experiment, the curiosity got too much and once again she typed the security code into Adams' phone.

What she found was not at all what she'd expected.

There were still copious amounts of texts and photos

from Camila:

I love u Cam xxxx
Love u too babes. Can't wait 2 be with you xxxx
Won't be long. Just need to stick it out with the ugly dog a bit longer. Longer I stay here rent free longer I can over charge the tenants in my flat.
Make it soon Ads xxxxx
More dollar I save. Bigger better place for us xxxxxx

Annie stared at the phone screen for a long time, trying to let it sink in. She'd been wrong about everything. He'd been using her. She changed his appearance completely, turned him into a monster, and he could still hurt her. And Camila, unbelievably, *still* wanted him. Why? What could a stunning woman like that want with him? It made no sense. The jealous energy she'd been harboring turned almost instantly to anger. Annie realized now that she could never have Adam, but that didn't mean that Camila could either. She was going to confront her.

* * *

Before going to bed the previous night, Annie had scrolled through the myriad text messages on Adam's phone to find the information she needed, and now knew that Camila ran a plastic surgery clinic on the opposite side of town to her office. After a long day of filing and answering phones, she freshened up, brushed her hair, retouched her make-up and sprayed herself with perfume. If she was coming face to face with her rival, she wanted to look the part.

Heading across town, Annie felt her heart quicken and her palms become moist with sweat. She couldn't believe that she was actually going to do this. It wasn't like her at all to be confrontational, but the control she'd gained from her culinary torture of Adam these past weeks had given her the stirrings of a confidence she never felt possible. Fifteen minutes later, she was outside the entrance to the clinic, prepared as well as she could be for battle.

As luck would have it, Camila was at the reception desk when Annie walked in. She was even more beautiful in the flesh than in the pictures, and Annie felt a curious mixture of inadequacy and desire upon seeing her. Despite herself, she could see why Adam was drawn to her. She seemed almost otherworldly.

"Camila?"

"Yes. May I help you?"

"I think you can. My name is Annie and my boyfriend's name is Adam White. I believe the two of you are acquainted?"

Camila showed no signs of being ruffled by any of these details. She smiled.

"I believe we are. I suppose we should talk. Give me half an hour to sign out the last patient and I'll meet you in the pub over the road. Mine's a Chianti. Large."

Annie didn't really know how to react. She was shocked by the brazenness of the other woman, but also intrigued. She did as she was told and headed to the pub, ordered herself a large gin and tonic and hesitated a moment before ordering Camila what she'd asked for and taking the drinks over to a quiet table in the corner. She was already on her second drink by the time Camila swanned into the room, turning every head on her way over to their table. She took the seat opposite Annie and stared alluringly at her for a moment before speaking.

"So, you know that I'm fucking your boyfriend?"

"I do. And I'm here to ask you woman-to-woman to

leave him alone. I'm not even sure why you want him. I mean, I get why you did at first, but now… Well, he's so fat. I've made him… I mean, he's eaten so much, put on so much weight. Why are you even interested?"

Camila looked Annie in the eye as if weighing up what to tell her. She sighed.

"I wasn't interested in him to begin with. I'm not really interested in him now as much more than a resource, but I'm growing more interested as he grows larger."

"I don't understand. If you weren't into him, why sleep with him? Why all these texts about him leaving me for you?"

"I was using him to get to someone else."

"Who?"

"Mallory White."

Annie was incredulous.

"What? Why? She's so awful. So *disgusting*. So fat."

"She's not disgusting, Annie. To me, she is beautiful. She is bountiful. She is life."

"I don't get it. You're *attracted* to her?"

"Yes. But not in the way you think. Annie, for you to truly understand the situation, I'm going to have to tell you some things that you'll find nigh on impossible to believe. Are you ready to listen, keeping your mind wide open?"

Annie thought about it. She was already intrigued, and part of her already believed whatever it was she was about to hear. She felt slightly hypnotized.

"Yes," she said, "I am."

"Okay. Here goes. Many, many years ago, I was a young girl living in a tiny village in Peru with my mother, who, just like Mallory White, was grossly obese. There were rumors when I was growing up about demons called *Pishtaco*, who appeared in the form of white, bearded strangers. These demons would suck the fat out of their victims, sometimes just a little to sustain their appetite, and sometimes, especially the most fleshy victims, they would suck out the entirety of the body's fat, leaving nothing but a pile of soggy flesh covering the skeleton. In Peruvian culture, body fat is thought of as a symbol of health and longevity. Being fat is being strong and beautiful. Being thin, a sign of weakness. And so by consuming all of the fat from a person who had an abundance of it, the *Pishtaco* was stealing the victim's life force, making them themselves stronger. Some say immortal."

Annie felt impatient.

"This is all very interesting, Camila, but what does it have to do with Adam and Mallory?"

"Be patient, Annie, I'm getting there. One day when I was hanging out washing for my mother, who, by that point, could barely move, I saw him. A tall, bearded, pale-faced stranger. A *Pishtaco*. I knew straight away that he was there for my mother. I was just a child and I was terrified for her, so I ran into the little house and flung myself onto her, screaming between sobs that the *Pishtaco* was there to get her. She held me to her, soothing me. And that's when she told me."

"Told you what?"

"That I was the demon's daughter—half human, half *Pishtaco*. Apparently, twelve years before, the demon had come for her but had inexplicably changed his mind. Perhaps he fell in love with her. Who knows? But instead of taking all of her, he fed from her just a little and told her he'd keep coming back, bringing food to keep her mighty girth intact, and feeding from her a little more. For some reason she agreed. Perhaps she was frightened. Perhaps she loved him too. They consummated their deal with a sexual union which resulted in me."

"This is ridiculous..."

"Annie, shut up. I'm nearly done. I asked her that if this was true, why was I not out all the time, sucking folk dry. She said it was because I was only half *Pishtaco*. That my 'father' had been bringing back supplies of human fat to be added to my meals, keeping me going, and that there was a part of me, a kind of feeding tube with a sucker on the end that would be released from my throat if I were to ever feed on a live person. I was so angry with her. All this time I'd been not a child, but a monster—a monster that had been trapped and fed on scraps, instead of being let out into the wild to hunt.

"My mother was my first meal. So ginormous was she, so full of lifeblood, that my little body became almost super human. The power inside me was immense. I've been chasing that feeling ever since, and here I am."

Annie felt the urge to laugh. This was all so ridiculous. Was she really expected to buy it?

"So, okay. Why did you need Adam to get to his mum?"

"I wanted him to introduce us, but he wouldn't until he'd got rid of you. I couldn't just knock on her door and say, 'Hello, here to suck the fat from your body!' I also had to know that she was the right one, so I needed to get close to her."

"So let me get this straight: I'm to believe that you are a demon, who wants an introduction to Mallory White, so that you can suck out all of her fat and get high. Thereby causing her to suffer a horrific and painful death. You didn't really want Adam, but now that I've fattened him up—I presume you know I've been doing this—you're quite interested after all."

"That's about the size of it, yes."

Annie laughed loudly from her very core, for the first time in a while. It was all so deliciously curious.

"Camila," I don't know if I believe what you're saying is true, or if I just want it be. But grab your coat; we've got a blubbery old harridan to visit."

* * *

Annie rang the doorbell of Adam's childhood home and waited patiently for Mrs. Mallory White to heave herself out of her armchair and answer the door. Eventually, the door opened and her porcine face peered suspiciously at them through a small gap.

"Yes? What do *you* want?"

"Mallory," said Annie, sweetly, "I was in the neighborhood and realized I haven't seen you for a while. I bought my friend, Camila, with me. Could we come in?"

Mallory turned towards Camila and looked her up and down. She seemed impressed enough with what she saw, and so she ushered them through to the living room.

"What a lovely home you have, Mrs. White."

"Thank you, dear. Would you like some tea? Coffee?"

"Why yes, I'd love a nice cup of tea."

As their hostess waddled off to the kitchen, Camila whispered, "When she comes back with the tea, excuse yourself and go to the bathroom. I have a plan."

Annie nodded her compliance and did just that when the tea and biscuits arrived. She took her time, using the toilet, washing her hands, reapplying make-up, and when she got back downstairs, she had barely time for one sip of tea and a bite of a biscuit before Camila was pulling her through the front door.

Apparently, Camila had told Mallory White that she'd only been pretending to befriend Annie to get to Adam. She'd told her that she was cooking dinner for Annie and Adam the next evening at Annie's house, and that she'd love for Mallory to come. Mallory had agreed to arrive at six o'clock; Adam would not be home until eight.

* * *

Annie was too excited to go to work the next day. When Adam had gone to bed, she'd spent hours on the phone with Camila, finalizing their plan. She'd hardly been able to sleep, still unsure of what she really believed, but excited to be part of something so thrilling nonetheless.

Camila arrived at four in the afternoon, flawlessly made up and meaning business, and they got to work getting things ready. They cleared up the cellar of Annie's house; there was an old armchair down there already, and they set up an old TV set in front of it on a cardboard box. Next, Camila brought down the sets of strong rope she'd bought, cut a hole in the seat of the armchair and placed a large potty underneath it. Just before six, they emptied some cans of soup into a saucepan and let the aroma of vegetables, herbs, and spices get ready to fool Mallory that dinner was bubbling away on the stove.

Mallory arrived on time, dressed for the occasion in a flowery tent of a dress and was heralded in like the guest of honor that she was.

"Oh, well, this all looks lovely," she said, smiling at Camila, as she was handed a glass of wine.

"I'm delighted to have you here for dinner," said

Camila.

Camila chatted with the older woman, who seemed quite delighted with her charming host, as Annie pottered around, setting up plates and cutlery that would not be used at all that evening.

"Mrs. White, Mallory, Adam will be here soon and we will all sit down to eat, but first of all, I'd like to show you something. It's in the cellar," said Camila.

Annie felt excitement flutter in her belly.

"The cellar? I'm too old to go looking around in cellars. Can't you show it to me up here?"

"I'm afraid not, it's too big to bring up. Please, Mrs. White, I *really* want you to see it."

Mallory looked flattered; it wasn't often a woman like Camila paid attention to her, and after all, once they were rid of the awful Annie, Camila could be part of her family. Finally, the perfect match her precious Adam deserved.

"Okay then," she agreed.

Camila took her by the arm and led her down the dark narrow staircase to the cellar. Annie followed, heart pounding.

Mallory looked around, confused. "Well, where is it then?"

Camila grinned. "Here it is."

Annie could not believe what she was seeing, as a proboscis appendage lurched out of Camila's throat and attached itself to Mallory's ample stomach. Mallory screamed, an agonizing, guttural noise, as she deflated before Annie's eyes, until she was nothing but a pool of blood and a sack of droopy flesh covering bones.

Annie struggled to hold in vomit, breathing deeply, unable even still to look away from what had once been Adam's mother. Camila stood with her arms stretched out at her side, her head leaning backwards, looking euphoric. She looked younger, vibrant, satiated. Annie had never seen anything more captivating. She suddenly felt scared for her life.

"Camila?"

"Annie. Thank you. There is no need to be afraid; I won't hurt you. Now it's time for you to get what you want at last."

* * *

When Adam arrived home, the two women were sitting amiably at the dining table, waiting for him. He looked momentarily confused. And then cocky.

"What's all this then, ladies? Judgment Day?" he laughed.

"Something like that," replied Camila.

"I know about you two, Adam. I've seen the text messages, and Camila has confessed."

"Has she now? Well, you can hardly blame me. Look at her and look at you. It's a no-brainer."

"Adam," said Camila, "I've decided that, just like Annie, I'm not a fan of how you treat women. I've come here to join her in confronting you about it. And so has your mother."

Adam's face lost its smugness and he started to look worried.

"Where is she?"

"She's in the basement."

"The basement? Why on earth is she down there?"

"Follow us; we'll show you."

Camila led the way, followed by Adam and then Annie. They stepped together into the dank cellar.

"What's that smell? Where is she?"

Annie nodded toward the stinking puddle on the floor. Adam looked confused for a moment, then vomited, falling to his knees, sobbing.

"Mumsy, oh Mumsy, what have they done?"

"Mumsy finally did something good in her life, and one day you will too, but you're not quite ready."

With that, Camila picked him up as if he were as light as a baby and forced him into the armchair, using the rope to tie him up with ease. He stopped fighting back. There was no point.

* * *

After leaving Adam to get hungry for a day or two, Annie and Camila went down to the cellar to see him. He hadn't the strength to fight them when they loosened the ties to his hands so he'd be able to eat, and when they removed his gag, he didn't cry out.

Every day, Annie would bring him heartening meals, spaghetti Bolognese, macaroni cheese, pasta carbonara, ice cream, trifles, and doughnuts, and he'd eat it hungrily. Annie and Camila took turns to empty the potty, which was a particularly vile job.

Adam didn't really talk anymore; most of the time he sat transfixed in front of the telly, no matter what was on. So Annie chatted to him instead about how well she was doing at work, the dates she was being asked on, about how the resignation letter she'd sent to his work on his behalf had been accepted eagerly—after all, he was to fat to work really—and about how the tenants he'd overcharged so maliciously had been made up about his generous reduction in rent. She told him that, as far as she knew, no one had even noticed his mother was missing. Poor, unpopular Mumsy.

It got so that Adam was too big for the chair, and now lay languishing on a mattress on the floor, no need for restraints, as he couldn't move. Camila had begun to salivate around him. It was nearly time.

Annie had no desire to stay around for the final act. She'd thoroughly enjoyed the control she'd gained over Adam, but she'd grown tired of him. There was a profound satisfaction in the knowledge than she'd overcome her addiction when he hadn't been able to kick his.

She told Camila that she was planning on selling the house and leaving town, but that it would be hard to do so with a corpse and a tortured fat man in the basement. Camila paid the asking price without batting an eyelid.

The small amounts of fat that Camila sucked out of her, weekly, whilst waiting for the main course to be ready, had finally given Annie the figure that she'd always wanted; and, full of newly found confidence, she went out into the world feeling anything was possible.

* * *

A few months later, Annie was enjoying a Sunday lay-in with Tom, an attractive man she'd met at her new office job, which she loved. Her newfound assertiveness had given her the courage to apply for a managerial role, which she had got, and was good at.

Tom had seemed sweet at first, pulling out all the stops to woo her, but his enthusiasm was waning and alarm bells were distantly ringing in her head.

She rolled over and kissed him, before getting out of bed to put on her robe.

"Cor! That arse is on the grow, love. Maybe you ought to come to the gym with me today. Get some inspiration from the major hotties there. Get us a coffee will ya?"

Annie took a deep breath and tied up her robe.

"Of course, darling. Would you like a slice of cake

with it? A large one."

THE END

Contributor's bio:

Sam Hill lives in Windsor in the United Kingdom. She has had several short stories published, the latest of which can be found in the Burdizzo Books anthology, Sparks. *Sam is currently writing a novel, and working on a project with the horror novelist, Jasper Bark.*

CRÈME BRULEE
Written by J. C. Raye

Make them see what cannot be
Flames to leap and make them flee

Hayton Beecher grabbed up the dainty teaspoon. Certainly an instrument never meant for his bulky, calloused, toolmaker hands. He cracked the sugar-crusted crown of the crème brulee, plunging deeply into the heart of the white ramekin. Actually, it was more of a violent stab than any serious attempt to scoop up a first bite. Hayton was seething. Much like the viscera of his $12 dessert. What was the big damn deal anyway? All he had wanted was to order the chocolate brownie. Because he *liked* chocolate brownies. Because brownies in restaurants never disappointed. He figured his wife would toss him this infinitesimal bone. Because Kyra had already made him suffer through the stupid rubbed quail with Israeli couscous thing, which successfully emulated a dead pigeon lying in a bed of its own poop, served atop some ridiculous slate-colored roof shingle. Because Kyra had mandated they'd vacation in New England rather than on some nice Carribbean island. And because she made them stay *here*, in *this* place, The Hawthorne Hotel, rather than the no-frills jobber a few blocks away at half the price, and right on the dock.

The dock would have been nice for Hayton. It would have made the vacation bearable. A harbor view... the occasional *huoh-huoh* of the gulls... a breeze, for God's sake. But, *no*, his wife had insisted on the century old brick monstrosity smack in the middle of town, oozing overpriced charm, claustrophobic bathrooms and narrow glass windows which rattled explosively should a ladybug beat its wings over in China. The mere thought of another three nights, victimized by nippy, nomadic drafts and the maddening sight of blue and gold wallpaper vines in every direction of his resting head made Hayton's jaw ache.

He chipped away at the remaining shelves of sugar grit clinging to the sides of the ramekin. He muddled over his familiar circumstance. Even with something as small as dessert, he had again allowed Ky to talk him out of a firm decision. *We're on vacation, hon. It's the Hawthorne. A little elegance, you know? You can have some old chocolate brownie any time.* But before Hayton was able to swallow his dander and gently explain to his younger, gorgeous, control-freak of a wife that perhaps vacation *was* indeed the time to have what one wanted (especially when that *one* was doing all the paying), or that if the fanciest restaurant in Salem, Massachusetts, had listed a brownie a' la mode on their little parchment paper menu, it was not such an uncouth choice to make, Kyra swiftly ordered them both the Crème Brulee and some sort of fancy pants latte.

He looked down at his spoon, submerged yellow goo, and then at the back of Kyra's head. She had already wheedled herself into a conversation with a good looking white couple at the next table. Poor things. Just innocently trying to enjoy their dessert (they had the brownie), and now having to endure his wife's New England bucket list manifesto. His right nostril itched. He caught the faint unpleasant odor of the honey-hemp spritz dousing her corkscrew curls. It was a scent he would have welcomed enveloping his face, were she to get bored enough to condone sex with him two evenings in a row. But that was doubtful. More likely it would be another night of listening to her excitedly plan day four's big adventures: Boutiques on the wharf, and mansion tours. Witch shops and art museums. Reading to him aloud, directly from the hotel travel guide, while noisily munching on almond bark she'd picked up from one of the countless sweet shops besieging the cobblestone streets around the hotel. Hayton would spend most of the night lying against a quilted headboard, uncomfortably undersized for his 6'2" wide shouldered frame, pretending to listen to her and desperately searching for any TV show that was not an 80's sitcom, or God help him, *The Jeffersons.*

Hayton finally brought a taste of the goop to his mouth, never imagining for a moment that his previous few minutes of crem-autopsy would not have been enough activity to bring the concoction to a satisfactory temperature. The fiery paste instantly scorched him. A squeak escaped him and he bumped one of his bony knees to the underside of the table. His tongue shot out automatically to soothe his lower lip. Quickly lifting his water glass, he tipped it so the remaining ice crescents floated towards the burn. In his haste, a few dribbles of water dropped onto his dark wash jeans. Unluckily, his yelp had not gone unnoticed by his wife, still yapping away at her captive audience. Kyra shot him a quick, *you're embarrassing me,* dagger of a look. And in that moment, oh how he secretly prayed to the restaurant gods in the sky she'd go for her dessert in the next minute, and burn her whole frigging tongue. *No travel guide readings tonight, baby? Brulee got your tongue? Damn, now that's disappointment! I sure love to hear you read'em to me. I mean, who needs sex when I've got Fodors.*

Hayton dug in for another spoonful. The metal spasmed in his hand. Then, it *tugged.* And Jesus, if it didn't feel like a grown man was on its other end. But, no. *No.* It wasn't the spoon at all. It was the brulee. The crème brulee was *pulling* on the spoon. Instead of letting go, as any rational person might when food decides to move of its own volition, Hayton made a mistake. He instinctively brought his other hand around the ramekin to get a better grip on the utensil, attempting to wrest it back from his gloppy adversary. But the double grasp fared him no better, and only seemed to result in even more of a yank from the brulee.

Hayton looked up instinctively, quickly scanning the oak-paneled room awash in candlelight and capital to see if anyone was watching him, sure that by now as least one dining patron had eyeballed his two-handed tug-o-war with a dessert. Perhaps even Kyra had taken a breath from her intense conversation to notice her husband's custardly plight. But, for just that moment, it seemed that Hayton Beecher was still having an intensely private moment, battling with his crème brulee. Well...until it exploded, that is.

A spray of golden, gelatinous appendages, at least a foot long, *shot* out from the center of the ramekin and latched onto both of Hayton's muscular forearms, searing deep impressions into his cocoa skin. Before Hayton could react, more syrupy tentacles appeared, erupting from the backs of the first ones. These were darker, veiny, purplish. They encircled his wrists with the speed and precision of a bullwhip. He yowled in agony, and then bit down on his tongue, involuntarily, violently, severing it at the tip. Warm blood squirted into his cheeks, and advanced downwards clogging up his throat. Hayton was choking. Burning and choking.

Kyra was facing him now. In her eyes, he saw the terror and revulsion, which confirmed he was truly in trouble. Bad trouble. The fiery strands gripping his arms had burned through both of them and reached bone. Bone he could see through the slashes of shirtsleeve. The veiny brulee handcuffs began to pulse. Then, unbelievably, and what could only be described as tiny rows of oscillating teeth emerged, and began to saw off his hands. But of course, any verbal description, or utterance of comprehensible communication, was now far beyond Hayton's abilities, as was any doubt that other diners were noticing him. His mind was racing. The thoughts were senseless, disconnected, crazy: *How to hide his wrist stumps from the foreman at work...Selling all his roof shingles to 4-star restaurants... Kyra scolding him for acting undignified in front of all these white people.*

Hayton was desperately trying to rise, to run, to just pull away, but one of his long legs caught the ornate metal scroll under his wife's chair, sending both him and her crashing to the hard wood floor. The crème brulee came with them, of course. The gooey tentacles audibly snapped off the brulee cup, their other ends now squiggling to gain hold of his thighs, while the white pottery itself spiraled into the air and landed not a foot from his face.

Kyra jumped away from him. Her hands flew to her ears. Her mouth, frozen in a silent scream, reminded him of a hear-no-evil monkey figurine he saw once saw in a Voodoo shop when she had dragged him to New Orleans. Hayton heard shouts from other parts of the restaurant now, though he couldn't get a fix on what was being said. A child was crying. Someone dropped a tray. Insane as it was, he could also hear his own arms sizzling.

There was no temptation to look down at his hands any longer. He knew they were gone. Even through the mind-numbing pain, he felt the sensation of tears flowing generously over his nose and cheeks, etching small rivulets into the bloodstains around his lips. He jerked his body in every direction. Slowly losing consciousness from the agony, gasping and glucking for air, Hayton Beecher watched in absolute horror, as little crackles materialized on the outside of the overturned ramekin quite near his face. The remaining custard inside it began to squeeze outward, like a newborn chick shedding an eggshell. As it came forth, the blob of crème brulee increased in size, blackened, and slowly advanced towards Hayton's head, leaving behind a trail of unctuous, glistening gunge. Little white fizzy bubbles were budding from every inch of its blobby essence. The fizzles bulged, and then opened. They were eyes. All eyes.

The last thing Hayton Beecher saw before the creature attacked, encasing his face in a blanket of burning slime and punching its way down his gullet, was not what one would expect in the dramatic final moments of life. For it was not his wife's grief-stricken, beautiful face as she tenderly held his head in her lap, weeping with anguish. It was also not a heroic Hawthorne wait-staff rescue party armed with kitchen cutlery. It wasn't even the visage of an angel, come to take his chocolate brownie a la mode ass home to his maker. It was a woman. A woman casually leaning on the gleaming bronze bar at the far corner of the historic restaurant. She had short white hair. She was familiar. And, she was smiling at him.

* * *

Burt Toleran was leaning on the register counter in Crista's shop. Leaning in fact, on her most prized possession, The F.C Jorgeson, slant oak and glass number, circa 1920, she'd paid hell to ship from the bowels of Pennsylvania Dutch Country just last year. One of Burt's smelly, ancient, annoying elbows was practically stroking the wooden tabletop sign that read, *Do NOT Lean on Glass. Trespassers will be Melted!* But Burt *was* leaning—with both arms. Probably half his damn weight, dead center on the glass. He was rifling through a fishbowl of rubbery, wart-garnished noses with elastic ear strapping. Set behind the bowl, a female mannequin head with blue glitter eye shadow displayed one of noses, along with a vinyl-sheer pointy black hat, and a pair of mini-rhinestone skull earrings (on sale in the display case for $11.99). Burt was leaning there on purpose, of course. Not because he was nearing eighty-three and needed the rest, and certainly not because he felt the sudden desire to add a rubber witch nose to his fine 80's windbreaker, elastic-waist, cargo short ensemble on this sunshiny Halloween morning by the sea. He was also not there to flirt. Burt was leaning on the counter because he wanted Crista to stop what *she* was currently doing (taking down the large resin sand timer from a high wall shelf for a customer) and come over to *him*, for what she could only presume would be a lecture of some sort. Or, what a few of the spirit shop owners in town referred to, as a Burt *Tolerrational.*

Crista climbed down from the stepstool and placed the heavy sand timer in the customer's arms with the delicacy of a young mother entrusting someone with her newborn. The piece was decorated on all sides with rose accents and runic symbols. She smiled as the heavy-set woman, dressed in a lime green pantsuit, carefully held the item, and read the *Symbol Explanation* card.

"I've only ever had two in the shop…they're pretty unique," Crista said, pushing her pink tortoise frames further up on the bridge of her skinny nose, and pressing a rogue strand of her white pixie cut hair behind one ear. "Probably the largest sand timer you'll find, even if you check out the rest of the shops in town," she added, after a short pause. Crista, a seasoned salesperson, was now executing her almost no-fail strategy for selling expensive items. Get it in their hands. Convince them it was the only one left on the planet. And then, give them space. Lots of space.

"I didn't really see all the detail when it was up on the shelf," the woman gushed. "It's magnificent."

Magnificent was overdoing it a bit, but Crista smiled, nodded in agreement, and remained silent. Judging by the thickness of both the dialect and the polyester, she figured the woman was most likely from North Jersey. They didn't sell pieces like this at the mall, that's for sure. She watched the customer's eyes, confident the sale was in the bag, but shifted her stance so she could also observe Burt. He was still bent over, back to her, subjecting her to the sight of his greasy, gray ponytail and delightful black dress socks stuffed into white running shoes. She knew he felt her gaze upon him. Reaching into his pocket, he plucked out a crusty blue handkerchief, and blew his nose quite loudly, quite wetly, thus christening his immediate surroundings with who knew what bacilli and momentarily turning every head in the store. He then snuffled for what seemed like half an eternity as he wiped his upper lip with the cloth.

Crista had no intention of losing this $120 sale. *Burt could blow brain tissue out his butt for all I care.* He'd have to wait until she made the sale. She made a mental note to give the fishbowl and rubber noses a soak later, after having being violated by his pickled fingers and flying microorganisms.

* * *

Ten minutes later, the pantsuit lady was leaving. Her sand timer was thickly entombed in bubble wrap, black tissue and a recycled brown shopping bag touting the shop's imprint: *Witch-Pop...For the Magically Inclined.* Crista lifted the velvet brocade record book from under the register counter and noted the purchase inside it with a crow-feathered pen. She pushed the book to the center of the counter to do so, consequently forcing Burt to finally stop leaning on it. She enjoyed that particular moment immensely. Crista had not yet made eye contact with him at all. She feigned some calculations in the book, simply waiting for him to impart whatever had his goat this morning. But no matter what the topic, she'd need to tread carefully.

Toleran was an Elder. Not the most powerful, or one with any wisdom or advice worth a damn. Just the oldest, the most connected, and by far, the most aggravating witch in Essex County, Massachusetts. And, he was a dying breed. Not only because most of the Wiccans and pagans streaming in to take up residence or start businesses in Salem these days were a younger, more Neo, eclectic crowd, and not a Trad like himself, but also because Burt was *literally* dying. Some sort of low-grade, non-Hodgkins lymphoma, usually taking its host within six or seven years. Word had it, though, that dear old Burt was now pulling his ninth, on a regimen of spiritual bathing and a mojo sleeping quilt laced with sweet woodruff and goldenseal.

Crista knew Burt did not like her. Certainly Burt never accused her of anything directly. His conversations with her always took more of a "read between the shadows" rant about "do-it-yourself witch-crafters" or "watered down practicing."

The only remaining customers in her store now were two teens lingering in the *"Inquisition Corner"* library cubby. The girls seemed to be devouring dream interpretation handbooks, and cracking themselves up by taking turns reading each other the bad news. If there was going to be a good time to talk to Burt without driving away business, it was now.

"Oughta get that front porch fixed," he started. "Planks seem a little wobbly."

Crista softly bit the bottom of her lip. Burt had voiced the comment as if he was actually concerned about the safety of her customers. *Yeah. Okay.* Like he wasn't secretly wishing she'd give up this prime piece of commercial real estate on Essex Street and sell out to another ice cream parlor.

Crista sighed. *Here we go*, she thought. *Here. We. Go.* She closed the sales book, folded her arms and finally met his waiting gaze. Except for eyes that were piercingly black, it occurred to her now that Burt Toleran actually looked a lot like Karl Malden, the actor. Well, Karl Malden in his has-been American Express Card commercial years, not his virulent *Streetcar Named Desire* years. Bulbous nose. Sagging skin obeying years of gravitational motivation. The pallor of pre-cooked Thanksgiving turkey. Burt was the spitting image of Karl. Including the spit.

"Did speak with the town," Crista said, smiling thinly, "You know, right after you mentioned it to me last month, K- Burt." (*Hells bells I almost called him Karl…*) "Noel said the steps to the shop are fine and up to code."

"Whose that? That fluffy bunny, Hargis? Burt blew some air and spittle from his lips as he made the creature reference. "That kid couldn't find a dagger in an army-navy store." Burt then guffawed at his own joke, sending even more spit over her counter.

Crista's mouth was hanging open a bit. She knew the expression was a reference to "fake Wiccans" of a sort, or those that were given to believe in fairies and unicorns and the like. She just never heard anyone use the deeply derogatory term in public before. She curbed her surprise, and nodded thoughtfully before speaking.

"Well, Burt… to me," Crista said, "Noel Hargis is the grown man who happens to run Planning and Zoning. So I am fairly comfortable going with his call on these types of issues."

Toleran grunted and snuffled. Crista thought perhaps she had misread him. Maybe he *was* just grumping around town today, complaining about the sun, moon and stars to anyone who'd listen. Maybe today, he was just what he was—an old man in pain, who needed to talk.

Crista wanted out from behind the counter now. She needed to get more merchandise up on that wall shelf, and maybe talk the teens into a few of the bargain spell kits at least. Before walking away, she asked Burt, "So was there something you wanted, because I've got some inventory to…"

"You are the only one in town still doing it," he said.

Crista froze.

"I-" she started, "I'm not sure what you…"

"You are being *disrespectful*," Burt cut her off, louder than he really needed to.

He was talking about the illusions. Burt knew about her illusions.

He knew, meaning *others* knew. *Others* were talking about her. And whether those others were from the Wrens, the Death Metals, the more tolerant Witches Education Leaguers, or some frightening activist Trad group Toleran might be leading, Crista could barely speculate. But, she could end up in a lot of real trouble should it turn out to be the latter.

Crista glanced around the shop. The two girls had moved on from the bookshelf to the human figure candles section. The exchange between Burt and herself still not a blip on their radar. Crista's eyes returned to Burt's face and folded arms. He was expecting a response. A twinkling of bells and the shop door opened. A few soccer mom types strolled in, laden with shopping bags and carrying on breathlessly about some blood-red Timberlands they saw in a store window.

"Welcome to Witch-Pop!" Crista heralded, smiling broadly at the women, hoping it was enough to send Burt packing. "Almost everything is on sale this week, ladies, so please grab a cup of our complimentary witch brew in the back and enjoy!" Some of them made an immediate bee-line for the crock-pot; its intoxicating aroma of apple and cinnamon permeated the shop was hard to pass up.

But Burt Toleran remained. "An it harm none, do what ye will," he declared, raising his hand dramatically as he did so. There was something about his face now that was different. More grave. Something in his voice. This was not the usual Burt Tolerrational shop owners chuckled over. Burt was not blowing off steam about *Neos* and their *limited understanding of occult principles.* He was *telling* her something.

More bells, and over his shoulder, Crista saw her friend, Aggey, come in. Aggey owned Potions & Pamperings, an elegant Wiccan boutique half the size of Crista's shop, on the other side of the wall. The ladies made eye contact, and in one second, Aggey knew to hang back, that (as the kids all say) something was going down. Aggey smiled sardonically, rolled her eyes and started straightening a display of Voodoo dolls and poppets on a small circular table near the register, and directly behind Burt.

"Burt, I know the Law of Threefold, okay? I am not a child." Crista was feeling anger rising up, or perhaps, it was fear. Her voice was taking on a shaky tone that she did not like at all. She was sounding bitchy, pissed, rattled. "And I am not sure why you're hassling *me*. You know there are folks up and down this street who conjure all day long, and for cash. They've got signs in their damn windows advertising it."

"Readings," Toleran said, "Circles of Healing. Not vendettas. Not dispensing punishments." Crista and Burt then spent a few very uncomfortable minutes going back and forth. She, emphatically denying using illusions for personal gain. He, sounding more and more like some imprudent AA sponsor helping her to see the light (or the dark of it), and not taking refutation for an answer. Probably, because he knew he *was*, in fact, correct about the whole thing.

And, it was while Burt was droning, on and on, about the "old time" and socio-pop culture bull, that Aggey caught her eye. Her friend had taken about a dozen Dove Blood quills and poked them all into her frizzy red hair and, just staring at Burt from behind with a deadpan expression. Aggey then removed one quill and was pretending to fan it behind him, while holding her nose, as if driving away some obnoxious odor. Crista could barely keep a straight face. She briefly wrinkled her eyebrows at Aggey. *Cut the crap Ag, he's gonna see you.* But her friend would not be impeded. Aggey grabbed one of the novelty Instamatics housed in a black and white spider-webbed cardboard and began snapping pics of Crista and Burt.

"Hey you two! Say stinky cheese!" Aggey shouted. Snap! Flash. Wind. Snap! Flash. Wind. "Crista!" she said, "Let's get an action shot! Why don't you climb up onto the counter?" *Dear Aggey, to the rescue again.*

"What in the name of…!" Burt hollered, blocking his face with arms and hands. "What are you doing that for?"

"Oh come on Burt-" Snap! Flash. Wind "You can see the lady has a full house here," Aggey teased. "She's got work to do. Now how about you come next door and I will make you one of my especially spicy hot cocoas and give you an erotic reading."

This time, Crista did laugh out loud. Burt glowered at her.

"Oh dear, I think this one's cooked Crista," Aggey said, projecting some over-the-top vocal distress about running short of film. She violently shook the camera as if to revive it from being used up. "Awww! No more shots. No worries Burt, I'll just grab another…"

Burt, deeply embarrassed by the whole spectacle and genuinely pouting over the interruption, made his exit; but not before swearing and muttering, "New Agers," under his breath.

Crista looked at her friend, who was absolutely beaming. "Thanks, Aggey," she said, smiling. "*You* are the best."

"Anytime Cupcake," Aggey said, "Now, why don't you offer all these nice folks in here a 5% discount for the disruption? You know we all gouge our prices anyway, right kiddo?" Aggey bumped Crista's elbow with her own. "I'm just gonna go and soften the guy before he gets away or complains to some of his troll friends and we have to make it up to them by buying some crappy t-shirts in *their* stores."

* * *

It's not like Crista knew this wasn't eventually coming. Some high up, self-appointed, Wiccan community rep giving her flack. She wasn't exactly cloak and dagger about her little *problem*. Burt wasn't the first witch to mention it to her either, just the oldest and most vexing. Most of the spiritual folks in town probably had identified some of her handiwork since she'd moved in and opened the shop. If one wanted to keep track, Crista's batting average was at least two "scenes" a week. Maybe, even more. Aggey had told her straight out over lunch once that she might even be *addicted*. But sometimes, she just couldn't help herself. And, it didn't make matters any easier that Crista was quite a connoisseur in casting incredibly realistic deceptions. That she had the kind of concentration and creativity in her craft, which made others eat their heart out with jealousy. Crista did not deny that witches could become addicted to performing certain kinds of spells. Aggey had pulled up a few recent articles on spell dependence off the net, many, written by credible researchers with strings of letters after their names. Not that reading about it was doing Crista any good, or easing the compulsion in any way. If anything, her desires to cast these chimeras on others were *growing.*

Crista's illusions, or befuddlements (as they were sometimes called), were temporary, of course. And she didn't feel they did any *real* harm to anyone. In fact, she viewed herself as more of a half-baked superhero type. Just doling out a little justice to persons that needed *perspective*. Little figment-ations that set the confused on a much better path: A young mother too busy yapping on her cell to take her youngster's hand while crossing the street, offered a fleeting mirage of her child flattened by a Hummer; a teenage boy attempting a four-finger discount on a trinket from her shop, seeing and feeling the chomp of a cobra's fangs on his offending digits; tourists, discourteously picnicking at Burying Point, and having the underground residents take a small nibble out of their ankles—just a little quid-pro-quo, Salem style. *And don't tell me it doesn't help our visitor count either. Mysterious happenings, right?*

Crista couldn't help it if that guy at the Hawthorne yesterday had a bad heart. It wasn't her fault he was dead. Probably would have had the MI anyway. Coronary artery disease built up from years of being a complete jackass to his wife. Crista certainly had a front row seat to a tasty share of that when he knocked over the crystal ball in Aggey's shop the other day. *He* bumped into it and broke it. The wife immediately apologized and offered to pay for it. But he's whining to Aggey about how cramped the store was, and how she probably set "this garbage" on the edges of table "intentionally"—"the only way to get someone to buy it." Crista could plainly see what that poor woman's marriage must have been like with him in tow. That's why she followed him to the restaurant. Anyone would have agreed that the guy needed a bit of comeuppance. Aggey didn't even try to stop her that time.

At least Crista knew *what* she was. At least she

wasn't a pretender. She was a witch, who was a businesswoman at heart, and not the reverse. She didn't have a great deal of respect for the ones always touting how their main priorities were "educating the public" rather than raking in a comfortable living selling spells, potions and magical charms. Witchcraft was a craft, an art, and though one might be very skilled at it, everyone knew there was no living to be made by simply doings readings and running Wicca 101 classes for newbies and bored housewives. To make any real money, you had to sell physical product.

She had arrived in Salem a little over a year ago, like the many who had come before, to glam off the thriving tourist trade. Crista never pretended it was a search for sisterly solidarity or to run from mainstream persecution. She was always honest with others about why she had come. After owning a successful candle shop in Marblehead for many years, she had done her homework and saw real potential in the shift to Salem and expanding into the spirit store arena. When the Essex Street property came up for sale, the stars lined up perfectly for her. Crista had the cash, the experience, and the mobility to open Witch Pop!—a store that blended real Wiccan and pagan merchandise with the typical Hollywood gobbledygook that vacationers in Witch City were on the prowl for.

And Crista learned quickly what moved and what didn't. Strategic marketing was in her blood. Cheap stuff, such as sage bundles, only a couple dollars each, literally flew out of the store when she added tea-stained labels listing potential uses in a pretty Burch font. *Thank you community college graphic design class.* Crystals and gemstones were big sellers too, and sometimes hard to keep in stock. Altar cloths seemed to be having a heyday as well. Customers confessing their bizarre plans to use the sacred fabric for clothing, gift wrap, potholders and dog beds. *Whatever makes your monkeys fly, dear.* Crista had every intention of continuing to peddle whatever sold and beam her practiced smile when the customer explained she was using four tarot reading cloths for picnic placemats. Purification, Cleansing, Balance and Blessing spell kits were hot with moms, especially when she displayed personal thank you letters addressed to the shop next to them. One, from a Bostonian who used the spells to bring peace to her home of four teenage boys, a meddling mother-in-law and two German Shepherds (completely made up by Crista, of course. The wasted stamp on the fake envelope was well worth it.)

She also sold mid-range products. The leather-bound blank journals, pyro-graphed with intertwining dragons or Celtic knots, intended for practitioner's private notes, seemed more destined to the category of unique birthday gifts for teen boys. In the early days, it was all Crista could do to hold her nose from angrily twitching as some grandparent inquired if she also sold colored pencils to go with the "sketchbook," and if she could gift-wrap it. But Crista, an avid reader of business blogs, found a Josh Billings quote about how a little taste of adversity brings prosperity, and was soon ordering artist packs of pencils and pastels, and a particle board, full-function gift wrap station, equipping it with Witch Pop! tissue.

Yep. There was no doubt Crista was thriving as a successful businessperson in Salem, Massachusetts. So what if she didn't exactly subscribe to the Gerald Gardner *Rede* for ethical conduct. She was taught, long ago, that the Craft was about following your own heart more than anything else. *Sorry Burt, maybe you lost that organ to the bad old Hodge?*

* * *

Crista was in her Mazda, racing up Derby Avenue. Well, it was more her *mind* doing the racing. Her car was barely hitting 15 mph before she would pump the brakes to avoid mowing down small swarms of costumed out-of-towners, those who shook off obedience to traffic signals and crosswalk paint long ago. Vampire wedding parties, Ninja Turtles, dead Girl Scouts selling maggot cookies, Chewbacca. Twerking Grinches. Skateboarding Reapers. *Was that a bloodied Derek Jeter outside the Pirate Museum?* All were out in force tonight, joyously injecting greenbacks into the Salem economy. All lit by glow bling, or the blue beam of a cell screen greedily sucking away melatonin, as they interacted with the town's new travel guide app. Attempting to navigate the streets of Salem proper on Halloween night in a vehicle of any kind was something Crista knew better than to do. Witnessing the throngs of tourists milling about, shouting, screaming, singing, falling over, oblivious to anything but their own merrymaking, many of whom would sleep well past hotel check-out tomorrow, might be the closest anyone could ever come to envisioning the pandemonium of what a zombie apocalypse might be like. Traffic was bumper-to-bumper from as far back as Engine House Pub all the way up to Ye Olde Pepper Candy across from Seven Gables. As Crista inched her way north, a particularly sozzled group of adults in their 50's, all dressed as Dalmatians, were pouring out of the Pig's Eye Tavern as she passed it on the left. One of them ran alongside the Mazda for a moment, pretending to chase it, while barking. *Arguably, not one of his more attractive moments*, Crista thought. He was bouncing up and down on (his version) of all fours about two feet from her driver side window. She could now see the detail of the dog costume. It had looked more realistic from afar. A cheap, white, zip-up HAZMAT suit covered with stick-on foam spots. Then the man abruptly vanished from sight. Crista was unlucky enough to catch his next canine caper in her rearview; bending over to hurl onto the asphalt. *Dalmatians just can't handle their pilsner, I guess.*

Past India and English streets and the Salem power plant, the road opened up. She had expected her hands to stop shaking by now, as she got further and further away from her own apartment. They didn't. Very few bodies on the street up this way, though she spotted some trick-or-treaters pulling a red wagon almost overflowing with the night's bounty. Crista tagged them as locals. Dressed for warmth rather than scare, fortified with pillow cases rather than plastic shopping bags, and of course, their wheels. Those little Salem crumb-gobblers knew how to do it right, even though these were doing it right more than an hour past town curfew.

A few fat droplets of rain thumped the windshield at the Forte Avenue merge, knocking hard at Crista's heart and almost causing her to run over the small flowerbed island facing Salem Fire Company. *Oh yeah, now that would have been perfect.* She could already see the headline and photo in tomorrow's *WickedLocal*: *"Why Didn't She Take the Broom?"* Crista had to get to Aggey's place. But she also needed to get there in one piece. She took a breath, and dropped her speed a bit. She so badly needed her friend to shove a drink in her hands and help her sort out what just happened. Or more so, what *didn't* just happen. She kept turning it all over in her head.

* * *

Crista had shooed the last of the customers from Witch-Pop! around 9:30 p.m. Just two college-aged men, dressed as full-on Oktoberfest characters, complete with lederhosen and Bavarian felt hats. They had been sniffing incense sticks for 15 minutes and ended up buying two boxes of novelty chewing gum: *Hormonal and Loving it!* and *Cute but Psycho.* Crista wondered what lucky ladies would be the recipients of all that admiration. She flipped the *"We're Closed: But Still Open-Minded"* sign hanging from a thick braid of orange and black organza. A dozen mini cowbells, hand-stitched into the ribbon, jingled sweetly. She yanked the heavy door shut and locked up for the night.

Few of the curiosity shops lining the historic cobblestone and brick walk of Essex Street stayed open much past ten, even during these magical thirty-one days, which pulled in more than half the year's profit. Anyone in your shop that late was either buzzed, cold, or didn't have spending money to hit a ghost tour or late night masquerade parties. No big-ticket sales. Just the aimless, not yet ready to call it a night and head home, or to whatever overbooked hotel or B&B was lodging them.

Crista's apartment on Norman was a six-minute walk from the shop. With no errands to run on Washington Street, she planned to cut down Derby Square, around town hall, and maybe pick up a Margherita pizza if the Adriatic wasn't insane tonight. *Of course it probably was insane.* She might even be liable for herding some of the drunk, cold, and broke to the pizzeria, by locking them out of her own store. *Did she have any microwave ravioli still left in the pantry?* She listened to the echo of her footfalls descending the burnt orange stones steps in the square. The lonely sound was temporarily trounced by a 60's jukebox blaring *Wild Thing*, and some chaotic flavor-ordering in Sweet Something's Ice Cream as she walked by. *Now that has got to be a hellish business to run this week.*

Crista began to take stock in just how much her shoulders and feet were aching and how nice it would be to sleep. *My own damn fault for wearing platform wedges on the biggest sale day of the year. Idiot.* The night air was warm, but damp and close. She felt a bead of sweat forming on her forehead and at the base of her spine. The thought of warm red sauce and gooey cheese was still pulling at her. *Screw it.* She'd stand in line at the Adriatic.

* * *

Crista turned the bolt on the door to her loft condo. It was an intimate one bedroom with hardwood floors and exposed beams. Two walls white stucco and two walls brick. Three tall windows were dressed in espresso cellular shades and black interior shutters. The "loft" part of her condo was not a full bedroom, but a platform over the entranceway, accessible by a wrought iron spiral stair. While the Witch Pop! was tchotchke out of necessity, Crista preferred her home to be barren. Aggey lovingly referred to it as "The Spa." Some people need refrigerator magnets, stacks of magazines and a windowsill chock-full of green glass bottles to make their habitat homey. Crista just needed a white leather sectional and a flat-screen TV to find serenity.

Hurrying to get the pizza over the sink (the box had been leaking olive oil for a city block), she had not realized that the light was already on over the tiny galley space. She shoved a dishtowel under her dinner. But now, something smelled...well...*off.* She lifted the carton lid, hoping the odor was a weird new topping and not a spoiled dinner. But the odor wasn't coming from there at all. The pizza looked a little oily, but...

Crista lifted her head and took another whiff. The smell was *familiar:* a mix of newly mown grass or vanilla or...sweet woodruff! A creak, above and behind her—the unmistakable sound of shifting weight. Crista slowly turned and looked up. Burt Toleran was perched on the wooden rail of her bed platform at an unnatural angle. Perched like a gargoyle. Perched like a predator. Crista screamed. His jaws opened wide and discharged an ungodly substance. Gelatinous. Loaded with crusty brown bits. The amorphous jelly smacked the floor around her feet. A fiery spray of airborne smidgeons scorched her slacks and seared pencil point sized holes into her exposed ankles. *Is that the smell of my own skin burning?*

Crista made a dive under the platform towards the front door. It was still open and her keys were still in the lock. She grabbed them. Tearing down the back stairwell of the apartment building, Crista felt a terror she had never known. And, she could hear the Burt-thing yowling for her.

* * *

As Crista took the right down Lowell, she momentarily forgot her panic and her plight. An unconscious, wry smile was forming on her lips. She snorted. It felt good. Even in the gloom, the sight of her friend's abode could make a terrorist chuckle. Aggey's two level, cedar shake saltbox, coated in bright cranberry apple paint, seemed nervily pressed between half a dozen unexceptional, white colonial revivals. It was quite the neighborhood eyesore, but to Crista, tonight, it was an oasis of sanity.

The front and sides of the house were a comical overgrown nightmare. Clumps of rugosa and glossy green buckthorn flanked the property on all sides, rising to almost three feet in some places and clearly threatening potential invasion to the meticulously manicured neighboring yards. Both species of the tangled dense undergrowth, more meant for strategically keeping tourists off sand dunes rather than spotlighting in a *Home & Garden* photo shoot, were remarkably tolerant of sea spray, sun and shade, and had no natural predators. Their import, distribution or sale had been banned in Massachusetts since about 2009. Well, unless you were Aggey.

There were only three two lampposts on Lowell. The one closest to Aggey's, two homes down and across, was enveloped in a maddening crisscross of tree branches. Rather than cast any useable light on the road surface or sidewalk, the beam appeared to be constantly winking off tree branches at the mercy of seaside October gusts. Crista carefully negotiated the Mazda into the skinny and disintegrating stone driveway to the right of her friend's house.

Just two weeks ago, Crista had helped Aggey wrap four sets of blinking skeleton lights around the tapered posts of the Georgian style porch. It was mostly Crista doing the work, teetering on a wobbly four-foot painter's ladder, pushing red thumbtacks into splintery wood, while her friend pumped her full of hot cocoa and pistachio sea salt cookies. While handing Crista a third string of skellies, Aggey made a comment about receiving notice from Public Works requiring the removal, or at least a sober pruning of her insidious shrubbery. Aggey said she'd make a note in her journal to sleep with some Chamber of Commerce Admin to avoid the impending bush crisis. It caught Crista so off guard, she almost fell off the ladder laughing.

Aggey had been born in Salem, and looked the part: Long, red, wild hair. Green eyes. Killer boots. Delicate moon midi rings on every finger. A silver Ouija planchette pendant on a black velvet choker against milk-white skin. Crista, even in the short time of knowing her, really grew to admire Aggey. As a young child she could never remember having such a good friend—one that made her feel more brave and more confident in herself, one that cracked her up on a daily basis. Since setting up shop in Salem, Crista seemed to hit it off with her right away. Aggey didn't seem to feel threatened by Crista's competing shop over the wall. In fact, whenever Aggey wasn't in her own shop (she did have two young novices working there part time) she was in Crista's shop, helping hang décor and even assisting customers with questions about the more legit merchandise.

Directly centered in the front of Aggey's house and pitching streetward, was a single, overly mature Norway maple jutting up from the front walk. To Crista, its root system was seemingly embroiled in the most sluggish prison break of all time, transforming the sidewalk into an obstacle course of hazardously bumpy, concrete crumbles. The snakelike interior branches were devoid of growth; precious sunlight having been hijacked long ago by the impenetrable wide-loaded leaf tufts at the outer ends and top of the tree.

Crista reached the top step of Aggey's porch, and the strong grip she already had on the railing was perhaps the only reason she did not Jack-and-Jill right back down again when she saw it. A life-sized, stuffed scarecrow figure was seated on the white wicker rocker near the front door. Aggey, maniac that she was, had put the scarecrow in a midnight blue, three piece suit and top hat. It had a cane in one hand and large, foam, feathered crow on the opposite shoulder. *Nice Aggey. Hysterical. Thanks a lot.* The conflicting breezes off Juniper Cove and Ram's Horn Channel often turned Lowell Street into a wind tunnel, and tonight was no different. Twisting and turning breezes were animating the rocker in just about the creepiest way possible. Arranged around the figure's dress shoes were several mid-size gourds, carved with the names of Aggey's favorite 80's hair bands: Quiet Riot. Aerosmith. Def Leppard. Their votives glowed in the deep shadows on the porch.

Crista approached the front door. She turned the antique Victorian doorbell, and angled her body so as not to have her back to the scarecrow. She started to feel a little childish in doing this. It's not like Mr. Brooks Brothers here was going to *get* her. In fact, waiting for a light to come on in Aggey's front room, Crista started to giggle at the thought of her friend opening the door only to witness Crista in full-on mixed martial arts with a sock-stuffed Halloween decoration. She turned the bell again. She was feeling a little more calm and comfortable here at Aggey's. She was realizing now that what happened in the apartment was more than likely a dream. She *was* dead tired when she got home from the Adriatic. And, the convo with Burt in her store today had troubled her—that was a definite.

Crista was imagining Aggey filling her mouth with orange juice and attempting to reenact the crime, *Law & Order* style, by spitting it into the sink. *So tell me ma'am, did it come out of his mouth like a fountain, like this? Or was it more of a geyser spray, like Old Faithful?* Crista laughed aloud, and heard it echo down the street.

The lights inside the house were still off. *Aggey, where the hell...?* Crista could clearly make out two green eyes peering up at her through the glass panel aside the door. The bell had driven Lavender, Aggey's cat, from his quilted basket in the parlor. It's tail began to twitch: cat-talk for *I'm excited to see you Crista,* or, *Finally! Something to break up the boredom around here.*

"Sorry Lavendar," Crista started, apologizing to a cat that could neither understand English nor hear through 19th century glass panes. "Doesn't look like your mommy is-"

Something was wrong with the cat. Lavender's head looked a little strange. Bigger. Flatter and kind of *gooey.* Like he had dipped his face in paste. She hadn't noticed that about him a few seconds ago. Crista squatted down to get a closer look, because she really didn't understand what she was seeing, or what the tabby had gotten itself into. "Lav-?"

And then, the goo on its face, *moved.* The cat started mewling, first softly and then quickly rising to an unmistakable screel of agony, as its goo face suctioned onto the windowpane. Though futile, Crista hopped up and started pulled on the doorknob; desperate to get inside and help him, though she had no idea how she would do that exactly. More and more of the face and neck were becoming goo and sticking to the glass, while the cat's paws and back legs were pulling like mad in the opposite direction, backwards. But the worst of it was when she finally comprehended that the cat was no longer sticking *to* the inside glass, but in fact, was *penetrating* it. Moving through it. The cat was extruding through the glass towards Crista.

Crista knew she should get away now, bang on a

neighbor's door, or shove Mr. Brook's Brother into the hole to stop the creature from reaching its intended destination. But she couldn't do any of those things. Not one of them. She could only keep looking. Of course, she did think about her feet, and about moving them. She also contemplated her car keys, dropped somewhere behind her in the darkness of the porch. And now the gooey cat's head, pushed fully through the pane, much enlarged and slushily translucent, sagged under its own weight. The face fell forward, hidden from view. It was no longer crying out in pain, but emitting a strange new gurgling noise, the sound of goo-ified lungs or slushified cheeks and tongue. And what was left of its furry little hind legs, still more cat than goo, quivered, mimicking some dark horizontal ballet allegro.

Lavender the cat was gone, and the thing, which remained, heaved the rest of its torso through the glass pane and dropped to the wooden porch with a sickening thud. As it struggled to raise its oily head and look at her, to her horror, Crista began to make out Karl Malden's bulbous nose. She had no trouble moving her legs after that.

* * *

She was running. Running towards Juniper Cove. Towards the water. Running from Burt Toleran. Or maybe from his whole coven. She couldn't remember exactly how she got out of Aggey's front yard, though her thorn-torn slacks and savagely grated knee caps offered some clue that it hadn't been via the walkway. Even now, tears streaming down her face, chest heaving, damp air invading the wide open cuts on her arms and hands, she seemed to be driven by a force other than herself. Running away from, and not toward, the places that promised more activity, and more people who could help, like Willows or Restaurant Row. An unseen, sinister, and relentless autopilot, steering her to the cove.

In the distance, far out on the rocky beach, Crista spotted a small light—*a lantern?*—and a few figures around it, just beyond the fringing salt marsh. She thought she heard country music. Relief washed over her wholesale and she darted towards it. Maybe even Aggey was there. Raising both hands high, as if under arrest, she called out, "Please! Please. I'm…" And, in that one precious moment, she grasped two equally dreadful realizations: First, that the light was not emanating from a lantern at all, but from a white plastic shopping bag, snagged on a rock, reflecting the moon glow. Second, that she had completely forgotten the low, pointed stone wall that lined the beach and marsh of Juniper. She was running right at it.

The unforgiving barrier of stone fangs collided with both of her shins simultaneously, and sent her flying. Crista came down hard on the other side of the wall. Her face hit first, violently driving a fist of gravel into her mouth and dislodging one of her front teeth. Crista lay there for a moment, shaking. She tasted a salty warmness creeping over her bottom lip. Stretching her arms out to either side, she pressed her hands into the sand and grit to gain some traction. She had to try and pull herself up. But the wet silt swallowed her arms and she screamed. Her mouth took in even more sand and she struggled, rolling her body back and forth to break free. It was no use. Even in her terror, she could sense vibrations around her legs, and could feel the lower part of her body too, being drawn down into the sand. For all her twitching and wrenching, she was only getting deeper, only making it so much worse, reminding her of the runic sand timer she had just sold. There was no reversing what was happening to her now. She wasn't expecting a rescue any longer, and knew she'd never see Aggey's face again. With every effort of her being, she moved the only part of her body still under her control—her head. She pushed out her chin, leaving shavings of jaw flesh on the sand, and slowly raised her head. There, advancing in the damp glimmer was an army of small rocks, about the size of a rubber nose. They were directly ahead and rolling towards her face.

For just one moment, all the little Karl Maldens halted. They were looking at her hungrily through black piercing eyes. Crista saw all their bulbous noses. All their drooping fleshy faces. Some were smiling. Some had teeth. Then, one by one, they hit her. Over and over.

* * *

Witch Pop! did not open the day after Halloween. It was the only store on Essex that didn't, despite the fact that many leftover tourists preferred to do their "store research" and partying on the 31st, while saving their hardcore shopping for the next day. But Crista did not open the shop because she could afford to miss the sales. Crista did not open the shop simply because she was no longer in Salem. She was somewhere in Boston already making arrangements to get her merchandise shipped and put both the shop and her loft on the market, stat.

Over the next few weeks, Aggey was a true friend to Crista. She helped her coordinate it all – closing the shop, oversee the packing of her apartment furniture and whatever else was needed – so the poor girl, clearly experiencing some sort of trauma she would not share, could do everything remotely. When it was all said and done, Aggey knew she would most likely never hear from Crista again. She also began to see Burt Toleran less and less. Some of the sisters in Aggey's crowd said the mojo sleeping bag was no longer enough to keep the cancer from ravaging the old man's organs.

But that was okay with Aggey. She didn't need to see Burt again. She could conjure up ol' Burt's face anytime she wanted to. Just like she did that night.

* * *

Aggey's much larger shop opened December 1st. Turned out there were no bearing walls between Crista's and her own, so the renovations joining the two spaces were a snap. Lavender was the guest of honor at the opening party. Everyone got a free rubber nose and a cup of cider.

THE END

Contributor's bio:

J.C. Raye is a Professor of Communication at a small New Jersey college. She teaches the most feared course on the planet: Public Speaking. Witnessing grown people cry, beg, freak out and pass out is just another delightful day on the job for her, so she does know a little something about real terror. She has won numerous artistic and academic awards for her projects in the field of Communication and Media, and seats in her classes sell quicker than tickets to a Rolling Stones concert. Her short fiction can be found in anthologies with Scary Dairy Press, Books & Boos Press, HellBound Books, and Franklin/Kerr. When not teaching or writing horror, Ms. Raye creates disturbing short films for her friends using found family footage. She also loves goats of any kind, even the ones that faint.

HELL IS OTHER PEOPLE
Written by Donna J. W. Munro

Paulette pulled the door shut on her cinder block house. The handle didn't work right anymore. No one would break in. The smell kept them away. She smoothed her thin brown hair down; though she'd not brushed it for... she couldn't remember how long. No need. Her hair clung to her round head in a greasy hug, slung back in a hasty knot at the nape of her neck.

"God, watch over me through this day," she said, clutching her mother's black bag close into her soft, round middle. Then she set off down the snow-crusted shoulder of the two-lane road she lived on, next to the lake her dad had fished, and down the road from the shrine her mother had spent hours every day at until her heart gave out.

Her mother and father had been the only people she'd believed in. The only ones she'd ever understood. Then they died.

A bright silver car with crunching tires sped past,

plowing through a pile of gray slush, splashing it up on her boots and her brown winter habit. Not that it had been clean before, but it had at least been warm. The car slowed for a moment, as if the driver had realized what he'd done; but after a moment of eyes reflected from the rearview mirror catching and holding Paulette's muddy gaze, marble-hard and set back in the sagging hard wrinkles creasing the corners of her eyes, they sped off, their wheels spinning in the soup of slush and grit. God's armor, her mother had told her time and again, was age and fading beauty.

Paulette had never been beautiful.

As she walked in the sloppy melt of a Wisconsin spring toward town and the courthouse, she remembered the pictures she often took out to look at: Pictures of she and her traitor brother when they were kids. Mother, back when her hair flowed down her slim back—before she found forgiveness at the shrine for those early indiscretions with Uncle Lee, her dad's brother. Dad, before he'd become Mother's keeper. And the bright picture that always swam up was the picture of herself in a lovely pink dress, modest but sweet with curled hair and a bangle bracelet, clutching the Confirmation Bible she'd just gotten. Her cheeks had been rosy and her smile so proud. Mother had beaten that out of her that night, dragged her back to the whittling stone and made her listen to rants from random spots in the Bible. But in that picture, that moment was the moment she'd been the closest to pretty she'd ever be.

After that, she learned to fear everyone.

Mother had chosen to send her to the convent, to be the only child that would live up to her holy aspirations. Clothing with color had been taken away, replaced with a Carmelite brown, thick habit, cinched with wool and a scapular covering to hide her figure. A wimple and veil covered her head, and soon, she stopped bathing because who would see anyway?

Those last few months of school had been hell. Students hurling insults was bad enough, but in a moderate Catholic school, where her brother had been such a suave tough, such a dreamy boy, she'd shown up in full habit, and her friends, few that there were, scattered. Like what she had was catching. She'd felt like a dull tugboat parting the colorful waves of teens flowing through the halls of her high school. Even the nuns treated her like an oddity. Sister Elizabeth Martha set her in the back of the class with a circling row of desks around her separating her from the others. She'd refer to Paulette's chastity and her sacrifices as an example, but then wouldn't want to discuss Paulette's interpretations of the Gospels.

But soon it was over. Graduation.

Walking along the cold Wisconsin county highway, Paulette let her teeth grind and her ragged nail tips bite into her fleshy palms. Eddie, her oversexed brother, had brought home his pick for a wife and Mother lost her mind.

Another car, driving more slowly, deliberately swerving to miss puddles, slowed. The driver rolled down the window and said, without seeing Paulette's face, "Headed to Necedah? Hop in.... Oh."

Paulette glanced at the driver and watched the pantomime of kindness stretched across the rigid bones, sharp as knives, collapse on itself. The woman's head jerked back, placing her gaze on the road, and without another word, she rolled up her window and slammed on the gas, spraying sludge and fishtailing. Kindness was a false idol worshiped by small minded, faithless people.

She bit her tongue until she bled; the taste of bitter metal trickled down her throat. Her feet were lead and her legs felt like cement pillars sinking into the ground. Her body didn't want to go to town and fought against every foot-dragging step. People. The thought of them made her skin bubble up and her eyes water. She bit her tongue again to drive out the weakness. Mother taught her that. Pain made the fear creep back from her skin and hide in the dark places. Anger helped too.

Around the curve and across the bridge that split the lake in two, and then into the cesspit of a town. Past dirty gas stations filled with liquor and porn. Past restaurants with food she couldn't afford and people who didn't care. Into the converted ranch house that served as the county seat for the bi-weekly traffic court where the orange plastic seats hooked together and made bodies press close. Paulette chose the very back and spread her bulk across two chairs and put her bag on the one next to that.

As always, Mother's voice in her head reminded her, "touching anyone without pure thoughts or having them touch you, even an accidental brush in chairs set so close, was a sin."

Not that she had to worry. They always took one look at her and moved away, choosing to stand rather than test her over the seats she took up. That was fine with her. She did her best to avoid everything Mother told her would send her to hell. People would send her to hell faster than anything else.

"All rise," said the short, skinny bottle-blonde at the front of the makeshift court, her nasal upper Midwest cutting the air rudely. She'd stuffed her body into the court deputy uniform until the buttons strained and the skin climbed out of the top and over itself to be visible. On display.

From one of the converted bedrooms, an old man in a threadbare robe shuffled to the rickety wooden desk that served as a judge's bench, worn out from his years of service. Paulette bit her lips, pulling bits of skin from them. Judge Gorgen. He hated her. He never tried to understand. He always told her things that didn't make any sense.

"Paulette," he said, pulling his thick-lensed glasses down his swollen, porous nose. Paulette pulled herself up and made her way to the back row. He shook his head as she approached, though what hurt just as much as his open sneer were the reactions of the others waiting to plead their case.

"Oh my God, it's her."

"What is that smell?"

"Why does she dress like that, Mama?"

There were mutters and laughs and even gags. Paulette reached up and adjusted her wimple, then sniffed through her slightly upturned nose, just as Mother had described Saint Christina when she rose out of her coffin into the church rafters to escape the stench of sin. She stared at each of them, as they pulled back from her, eyes round and rolling in their sinning heads. Mouths covered with their inconstant, clawed hands. Paulette shuffled past them and stood at the podium near the front. The deputy woman leaned in to give her a paper outlining the fines and possible punishments for her offenses.

Paulette found that mumbling often helped drive them back when they got too close. "Let he among you cast the stone at the innocent. I turned the cheek. I gave the loaves."

The deputy's stretched arm trembled, holding the paper out at Paulette like some shield. But her face, usually set in the stern, polite grumpiness of court officials, wavered and collapsed around her crinkling nose. Paulette pushed back her urge to giggle. Her armor was working.

"Get back, Barbara. No need. She knows what's on the paper," Judge Gorgen said. Then he turned back to her and frowned, eyes lingering so long on her that she fought the urge to scream. The gaze had weight—the sinful weight of hands on her, touching what God didn't mean to be touched.

Mother's voice in her head said, *If only you'd taken orders in Spain, there wouldn't be any need for this.*

Spain. Her greatest failure.

"I'm sorry, Mother," Paulette said under her breath, though the judge's gaze caught the movement of her mumbling lips.

"Look here, Miss Paulette, you've been in here at least ten times in the last two years."

She nodded one sharp jerk and then she tilted her head and found the cross hanging behind the judge's shoulder to stare at. Our Lord and Savior perched there in the perfect agony of his death—a good, old crucifix. Of course, it would be. Necedah was a good Catholic town. That's why her mother and dad brought her here after her failure at the convent in Spain. The nuns had talked and invaded her space until she screamed and rocked and ran to a cave to hide. Her mother had to fly out and remove her, drugged her to get her on the plane and back home. If she couldn't make it in a convent, maybe a shrine town would be better with its old fashion priests; none of that Vatican II nonsense, and away from Eddie and his whore wife. None of that.

"Let's see, we took your license for driving without insurance in October last," he said, scanning the file in front of him. He pulled a cotton hankie out of his sleeve and held it up to his nose.

"I can't afford insurance, Judge. My brother won't pay and I can't work."

"Can't or won't?"

"I took care of my parents. I paint sometimes and sell at the church bazaar, but it's only enough to get some gas or repairs on my house."

His face softened for a minute, then he turned back to reading the chart.

"This time, you insulted the officer."

Paulette felt her hand shaking as she gripped the podium. They all were against her. Like the saints, she was pursued by these demons every day.

"He had no right to pull me over."

"You had no tags on your plates."

"I can't afford them and I needed to get to church." She wanted to add, "for the food pantry," but knew it would make no never mind to his hard heart.

"Miss Paulette, you have no license and therefore you cannot drive. He was right to pull you over and you called him..." Papers rustled as he looked for the words. "A sinning sack of pig guts and a Joseph Stalin?"

She gripped the podium so hard, hating the feel of the eyes on her back, hating the words she had to hear and the fact that there was no way to avoid these terrible scenes.

"He touched me." It was her only defense, but she knew they wouldn't accept it. They never accepted it.

The judge stared at her for a moment and sighed. "He didn't touch you inappropriately, right?"

"Every touch is inappropriate," Paulette thundered. The words felt like medicine soothing the burning hurt that was other people. If she could just scream until they walked away, she'd feel better. But that was not possible. They'd lock her up if she did that; Mother warned her. "I can't be touched. I'm a wife of Jesus."

The judge stared at her, nodding but not in agreement. He'd been told this before and Paulette was sure she'd have to tell him again. If they'd just leave her alone, she'd never bother them. She'd pray in her house, feed her cats, and wait for God. But there were taxes and building codes and policemen ticketing her for not having the right stickers or blinkers or whatever expensive blame thing they'd saddle her with. Back when Dad and Mother had been alive, she'd been able to just sit in her little room, pray on her cot, and go to the shrine without ever having to deal with the others. Like Saint Katherine, she'd rise above and float away on her prayers. But then Dad put his hand on her. Mother had flown into a jealous rage, screaming, scratching her eyes and cheeks, ranting about Paulette's virtue.

Dad started sleeping in the car then, even on freezing Wisconsin nights, but Mother believed the worst.

Paulette wished she hadn't stumbled into him in the first place. Just an accident, but Mother would not be persuaded.

When Eddie called, Dad and Mother had acted like all was well, even if he sat bleeding from the beatings that she and Mother gave him. When Mother told her to send him to God, she'd done it—shoving him down on the icy steps so his neck broke. Paulette sat next to him as the breath left him, glad that there was one less person in the world—one less person that made her stomach crawl. But she found, without him, Mother's rages had no other place to go but toward her. The days filled with touches and words from Mother—beatings and punishments that lasted days.

When Dad's money came, Mother would make Paulette walk into town to buy supplies. It was torture, and she knew it—torture with every word and every interaction. And the people knew how Paulette felt about them. She made them uncomfortable as they pretended to be polite. Jerking back from their hands. Ignoring their comments about how she smelled, even smiling. She and Mother built their hoard of things so they had walls inside their walls. People stayed away. Neighbors could smell their house from a mile away. The roof had blown off and the church sent out men to fix it for the poor widow and her crazy, failed nun of a daughter. Mother ranted the entire time they worked, and Paulette hid in her closet.

The ranting and accusations went on for days, punctuated my Mother's fists and tears. When she could take no more, Paulette shoved a knitting needle in the space next to her mother's eye until she stopped her screaming.

No one questioned her death. Paulette thought they were likely relieved.

She was.

So it went for a while. Dad's checks came but she didn't want to go to town. The people from the church brought her food sometimes. She took Dad's car out to the shrine at night when no other people were there. She made her own sacraments—anything to stay away from them and their careful questions about her life. Except on days like this one, where the world reached out and grabbed her, pulling her into its madness, demanding taxes, payment for water, or sending police to harass her as she drove or sat in her house contemplating God.

And here they were again, pulling her into their insignificant rules, infractions and punishments. Didn't this judge recognize a live saint? Saints don't pay bills or taxes or tickets. Saints float above the distractions of human frailty.

"He touched my hand. I will not be touched." Each word spilled out of Paulette's mouth, edged with all the fire of her fear.

Judge Gorgen audibly sucked at his teeth as he

thought.

The things he did, the proximity of these people, ached like bruises.

"Look here, Miss Paulette..."

"Sister Paulette, if you must," she said with a sniff, brushing her hands across the wide sleeve of her brown habit. Then she reached down and grabbed the beads of her rosary, counting each, saying a prayer, trying to distract herself with how much this talking, standing and muttering hurt.

"Fine, Sister Paulette. You have been before me for everything from tax bills to speeding tickets. You're in here every few weeks. I don't put you in jail because, honestly... Who wants to put an ex-nun in jail?"

Paulette's stomach flipped as he talked. God wouldn't allow him to do that, would He? Being forced to live inside a cell with people watching her, forcing her to interact and talk. She flattened out the tension on her face and formed her gaze into something piteous. She had to convince him, quick.

"Just... let me go," she started to ask, her false gravitas shrinking under the weight of this reality. She couldn't get away fast enough. His mouth assaulted her with words she didn't want to know or hear. His eyes were on her, like fingers touching her skin. And suddenly it was all sinning, all against God's plan. "Let me go home, please."

The judge's gaze softened as he watched her shift on her feet. Paulette knew how to get rid of people, but the judge had power over her. He'd sent her away before. Three years with Eddie back in the city. She'd had to fight her way home. Eddie and his loose daughter had made her dress like everyone else and tried to sign her up for school. Eddie sent her back before she used the rat poison in the dinners she made them. He told her that she wasn't welcome and gave her a bus ticket, probably because she'd burned her niece's soccer shorts, whore-red and silky as they were. He sent her money sometimes, never enough. Dad would be ashamed.

On a bus, all those people, trapped for eight hours of driving. She'd nearly died, but she floated above it all, praying so hard that she disconnected. It wasn't until they were twenty minutes from Necedah that she realized a man had reached his hand up her robes and onto her leg, running his filthy hand on her calf. They were the only ones on the bus besides the driver at that point. Paulette pulled a knife she'd taken from her brother's house and plunged it into his neck. He bled out quietly, gurgling as the blood flowed down his tan coat, but his hand left her, clutching at his wound. The bus rumbled on for the last few miles and when the driver pulled up at the lonely depot, Paulette stood, clutching her hard-sided suitcase in front of her, blocking the view of the knife. The driver never saw it coming.

"Sister Paulette, I'm afraid if I let you go home, you'll just be in here another time next week. What if we, got you a job? Maybe caring for the elderly?"

Paulette shook her head, knowing that the result would be a bad one. Having to touch some elderly person so... intimately. Wiping them, listening to them, smelling them. Tears floated behind her eyes, so she turned to her anger to cover her fears.

"I will not do any such thing. I have a job. I worship God."

The judge leaned forward, eyes magnified in his thick glasses like some fantastic beast. "You can't continue to keep living off the dole, Paulette. There's no money left for your taxes and your tickets and all of the other things you need."

"Would you ask St. Sebastian to worry about your

laws as the arrows rained down on him? Or St. Cecilia to pay taxes as the sword fell on her neck?"

The others in the room, mostly good Catholics, muttered as she spoke. Paulette knew they couldn't understand her. God had made her different than them. Made her so that she stood apart. Made her hate their lives lived in the ways of Satan. Laws outside of the Book. Traditions forgotten. If only she'd lived back in the days of the Saints, when she could live in a cave and the penitent would come to leave her food. If only they understood what she was... and left her alone.

"I will not answer to your sickness, nor will my pure hands touch another sinning creature." At that moment, Paulette's trembling and suppressed fear came out in a babbling rage and she kicked the nearest chair as hard as she could. They'd let her alone. They'd get away from her if it were the last thing she did. She swept her hands across the paper-littered table beside the podium she stood at, scattering every paper piled there. "I am not of this place. I am not of Caesar. You shall not have me."

Her rage was alive in her belly, eating the pain that swirled in all the skin that was exposed to their judgment, to their creeping eyes. Her face, her hands, her neck, all burned with shame. She had to get away from them. Without another word, she turned out of the courtroom and trotted back to her home as fast as her bulk and her habit would allow, passing the casual fishermen cussing and drinking beer, the jogging teen girls with legs exposed in tight running pants, and the cars, and the wires, and the words and all of the humming, jittery loudness of them doing the things they did on phones and computers and televisions. They built their Sodom all around her. Every step took her through hell.

On the stoop of her house, silence and prayer within

reach and the buffer of the stink and the walls she'd built to keep them out, just past the threshold, there he stood, Judge Gorgen. He must've jumped in his car and sped past her as she wove through the people littering the main streets of Necedah on the unseasonably warm midwinter afternoon. He stood there inside her house, past the front door she never bothered to lock, looking at her personal life. Touching the collection she'd made of the old and rejected things from before. He pressed a white hankie to his mouth, but she knew that the smell of her waste buckets, scattered like bombs among the debris of her years, got through that thin, white cloth. His hands were there, touching. His breath through that hankie. This was Paulette's shrine to her mother and dad and all those she'd sent to God. Her church to what should be. To what only God sent her for.

But here he was... in her home. Paulette's rage came back like a black god, riding her into the house. She smiled, a mask to hide the loathing she felt for every whorl on his fingers, for every hair on his head. He represented everything sick, everything forbidden. God turned Lot's wife into a pillar of salt for looking back into the sin of the world, for longing for society and its sins.

"Sister," the judge said as he turned toward her, the picture of her whore niece clutched in his crepe, thin-skinned fingers. Touching her things. Claiming them for this world. Why didn't they understand that she wasn't of this world?

"Judge Gorgen, I need you to leave. This is my house, my place, and no one comes in here but me and God. Just me and God!"

The judge's face stretched into the mockery of regret, eyebrows close and lips tight. Judging. It was his job.

"Listen, Paulette..."

"Sister Paulette."

"Sister, you are living in filth. This place must violate every safety standard, every township law..."

"Your laws don't mean anything to God, Judge. You people are..." Paulette tried to move around him, keeping a wide orbit as she moved into the safety of her nest. Her shrine to all that wasn't what Gorgen wanted her to have. She'd learned to hate and to fear everything he stood for. Just watching his eyes sliding across the surface of each ledge, each pile, noting the saint statues, the icons, and medals.

"It's like you're living in the Middle Ages or something, Sister." Judge Gorgen's voice was muffled by his handkerchief.

"Judge Gorgen, I try not to cause problems. Jesus said not to cause problems with the government. God knows I try to stay away from you people. Your hobby lives. Your marriages that are only for now. Your pastimes and jobs. How little it all matters. How little it adds to God's calculations. I am a creature of eternity. My mother and my dad and my brother and my niece all knew I was different by degrees. I can't be what you want as much as I couldn't be what they wanted. What they tried to make me. God make me quiet and inward facing, and you... you want me to be some kind of shade of you, but just knowing you, knowing you and the others makes my skin burn."

Paulette paced back and forth in front of the little room with the cot, between the kitchen with the collapsed table and the blackened, sprung living room Lazyboy, flipping its seat forward in a collapse. The stink mattered not to her, but Gorgen's eye wept and he coughed as she paced. The smell was ancient. Deep as hell and real—years of collecting, dead cats buried beneath collapsed bundles, plastic buckets filled with her body's foul makings. The smell kept most of them away.

"How can I allow you to stay here? In this? This is hell on earth, Paulette. You need help." He reached out a kind hand, withered by his age with standing blue veins and brown spots.

The rage and fear whipped together into a tower, lifting her above his judgments. Above the offensive sound of his breath and the beat of his heart. He'd take her and force her to live among them. Among them with their sins and their touches and their bathing and their laws. In the same space. Assaulting her with words and questions when she should be alone with her thoughts and prayers. She'd worked so hard to be left alone to do the work of God.

"No," she said, though inside she screamed and ranted, blood boiling against the walls of vessels and battering her heart. Her bellowing lungs fought against the calm she projected. She had to keep him from running for the others. She had to. "Judge Gorgen, you all frighten me. Since I was young, since my mother taught me that touches would lead me to hell. Since the nuns wouldn't leave me in my cell with God. Since my dad used to tell me to go hide from Mother. Every moment I'm alone, I pray for the souls that are trapped in your false world. I save you in my loneliness. But you... you and your kind—the social workers, the police, the teachers—you are sent as special demons to torment me. To test me. You and your 'help.'"

Paulette's voice began to escalate, but she'd put herself between him and the door. Of course, it would have been so much easier to let him go. For a moment of quiet, she'd give almost anything. But if he went, he'd bring back so much more. They'd invade like rats. They'd swarm on her, touching and talking and demanding.

In that moment, everything slowed. Dust motes floating on the banded ray of sunlight stopped their dance and the judge's eyes froze mid-blink. God would speak.

There is no choice, my child. He would close you off from me. You can't allow them to take you. To make you one of them. Send him to me.

God always told her when it was time to take a life.

Paulette picked up her father's knotty wood cane, a remembrance of him she kept by the door.

"Judge Gorgen, make your peace with God," she said. Before he could do any reacting, before he was even back to his normal speed, Paulette swung the cane, cracking the judge's temple with the handle. The blow knocked him sideways, against the wall, and he slid to the floor, a trickle of blood dribbling down his cheek.

"Wha..."

"No more of your words. They make me sick," she said, as she arched back and brought the cane down again on his head. The second time, his skull crunched and his words became the groans and natters of someone dying. A third and fourth blow ended his breath.

She panted, catching her breath as she watched the blood pooling in the broken cavern Dad's cane had made. The hard part was next. Touching him. She grabbed his ankles and pulled, fighting the urge to vomit as his skin brushed her chaste fingertips. She knew God would forgive her this touch, but it still made her fear well up like a wave.

"Just a few minutes," she told herself, "then you will be safe and alone again."

She pulled him out the side door and wrapped his body in an old sheet. She lived far enough out that no neighbors could see. And as she dragged him around to the front of the house where his car waited, she checked the road for cars. Nothing. She loaded the judge's body into his car in the front passenger seat, and then drove him deep into the Wisconsin woods. She found the spot her dad had shown her, so many years before. It was behind the shrine, about three miles up into the woods. A little access road, overgrown with bush honeysuckle and sprouting pines, led to the deep-channeled creek that her dad used to fish. Cold, spring-fed water kept swimmers away in the summer and the remote road camouflaged the spot for all else. Perfect. A miracle from God.

Paulette pulled up to the high lip of the creek and dragged the judge over into the driver seat. She didn't bother to take off the sheet because, by the time they found him, it would be gone to river rot. Besides, it wasn't fitting to have even his dead eyes watch her as she toiled and sweated so. Once he was wedged into the seat, she put the car into neutral, slammed the door and gave it a hard push from behind until it tipped over the lip, sliding down the muddy bank into the channel. It bobbed there for a second, a little tugboat in a tiny sea, and then it sank, stirred water sealing over him and drawing him down where he should be.

Paulette smiled. Around her, the trees waved and the bird tittered in the gentle winter wind. A note of frost. A breath of spring. No people to jumble up her thoughts or violate her peace. She kneeled there in the mud and clutched her folded hands to her nose and lips. She whispered the prayers and all the words given to her for the poor judge's soul. He'd go to hell, sure enough. That didn't mean she shouldn't do what she was sent to do.

"Forgive them, Heavenly Father. Forgive their rules and their talking and all their touches. Give me silence and peace." She crossed herself and stood, staring into the deep water. Sometimes she thought death would be better than the continual war she fought against them and their laws, their misguided demands on her life. She thought about throwing her body into the water and sucking it into her lungs to end the fear. But, God spoke to her then. Stopped her from committing that ultimate sin. God showed her what hell would look like for her. Bodies pressed together like cattle in slaughter shoots, naked and touching and talking all the time.

God said to her, *Hell is other people.*

Paulette nodded and headed back home to pray. Alone.

THE END

Contributor's bio:

Donna J. W. Munro has spent the last seventeen years teaching high school social studies. Her students inspire her every day. An alumni of the Seton Hill Writing Popular Fiction program, she published pieces in *Every Day Fiction*, *Syntax and Salt*, *Dark Matter Journal*, the Seton Hill Kindle anthology, *Hazard Yet Forward* (2012), *Enter the Apocalypse* (2017), *Killing It Softly 2* (2017), *Beautiful Lies, Painful Truths II* (2018), and several upcoming 13 Press anthologies. Contact her at https://www.donnajwmunro.com

THE HAUS OF DOLLS
Written by R. J. Murray

Gertrud Von Mueller was a peculiar woman of a somewhat mature age, who had never married. She resided on the small island of Wikonsia, which lay on the most southerly stretch of the Red Sea, one hundred miles from any mainland. Within the centre of the Island, Gertrud owned a small doll shop in a quaint old building of three stories, which was situated to the east of Main Street. The Haus of Dolls sat between two fine establishments: namely Bryers Bakery and The Hat Emporium.

Since 1704, the island had inhabited a small interwoven population, which included four generations of Von Muellers. After a mysterious tragedy had taken the lives of both her mother and father, Gertrud had grown up with her aunt in a rickety old house by the sea. When she grew older and her aunt passed away, Gertrud used her inheritance to purchase the Haus of Dolls, wherein she spent her proceeding days and nights.

On a wintry Saturday, if you looked along these

winding cobbled streets, you would see the hustle and bustle of bodies as the islanders went about their day, running errands and collecting groceries. The ladies would be socializing inside Glynda's Tea Room, enjoying a hot drink and strawberry tart, whilst the men could be seen lurking inside Foyle's Public House with an eye on a sporting event, ale in hand.

As day slipped into night, the streets would turn dark and grey, rain lashing down on the narrow roads as the crooked trees swayed to the rhythm of the blustery winds. Windows and doors would slam shut as thirsty bats took flight from the tall trees hidden in the valley below.

To the annoyance of one Gertrud Von Mueller, the clatter of metal bin lids was a regular occurrence as sneering alley cats foraged for leftovers outside the bakery. You see, Gertrud had more than a strong dislike for felines, due to a most unforgettable and bitter memory: On her fifth birthday, her aunt had given her a most treasured doll, which she lovingly named Patty. Patty possessed golden ringlets and lace pantaloons and the most delicately fair complexion. Immediately, she had shown a peculiar attachment to the doll and would cling to it with fierce possessiveness, as if sensing some impending peril. And indeed, this foresight was confirmed a week later when a cat prowled into the garden and attacked Patty, tearing her piece by piece until she was tattered and unrecognisable. Gertrud screamed and wailed and stomped her feet as her parents attempted to salvage her, but nothing could be done. Of course, the following day she was given another doll; but, to Gertrud, it did not possess any of Patty's charm or grace, and she was left with a feeling of loss, a desperate void she had to somehow fill.

As the years went by, Gertrud collected more dolls.

Every birthday and Christmas, when asked which gift she would like, the answer was another doll. She was constantly searching for one just like Patty: perfect and untainted—destined only for her. She began to grow a disdain for her mother and father, who prevented this growing collection, insisting instead on books and educational games. She rarely had friends and preferred it so. The other children would whisper and laugh and call her a baby, but this only made Gertrud more introverted and attached to the dolls.

After the fatal accident, Gertrud showed little emotion or grief about the loss of her parents and seemed perfectly happy to live with her aunt and the dolls. When she came of age and her aunt passed away, she continued happily in her solitary existence, her passion for dolls as strong and unwavering as the resentment she had for the world around her.

Day to day in the shop, she would arrange the window display meticulously, continually attracting admiration from passersby. She stocked a manner of antique dolls, many of which were so rare that collectors and enthusiasts would flock from far and wide to obtain them.

By evening, Gertrud would retire to bed and stay awake into the night, reading supernatural, strange tales. From a young age, these had been her escape, her salvation from the cruel reality she had come to despise. She had stacks of fantasy books and comics, all of which explored the unimaginable: outer realms, monsters and unknown entities. Curled up in her old wooden bed, her bedside lamp crackled and flickered as she scoffed venomously at the sound of cats outside, willing for some powerful entity to eradicate them all.

Since her teenage years, there had been one particular story that had captivated Gertrud's imagination and ignited a deep yearning: *Living Doll* was a comic she had treasured for many years and although each edition was now well faded and dog-eared, she re-read it over and over again, finding comfort and hope in the pages.

To breathe life into an inanimate object through science and formula. Through focused will.

For months she researched the idea, wishing for it to be possible that science had really come this far. She frowned at the memory of her parents, trying to dispose of these comics, complete disappointment on their faces when realizing she had no interest in academia.

But that was then. They can't stop me now.

Over time, Gertrud had concocted a vague plan, a theory born out of her own fragmented imaginings and beliefs. Yet, she still had not found the subject. The one she would breathe life into. Yet, she had to somehow act, create a prototype. She knew she must strengthen her ability in order to succeed.

As she read the opening pages from her favourite volume, the cats outside squealed and scratched in cahoots with the rain, which lashed aggressively on the window. Gertrud felt her anger begin to surface and in frustration she picked up a heavy book and tossed it at the window.

"Shut up!" she screamed.

The glass shattered loudly, multiple shards falling like glistening snowflakes into the street below. She leapt out of bed and dashed down the winding stairs, each one squealing with mercy as she stomped in manic haste. As she pushed open the heavy door, a gust of wind blew forwards, forcing her to cower to the side. A scruffy tabby loitered on the step below, a half dead mouse between its jaws. Alongside it, on the cold stone, laid a gleaming shard of glass. A black mist descended on Gertrud, and as the wind howled, she grabbed the weapon in one hand and the squirming animal in the other. With savage ease she pierced through the matted flesh, her eyes glowing like sniper targets. She repeated the motion like a machine, spurts of liquid seeping into her nightdress, her face, and the crooked step.

Turning back into the house, she slammed the door, scurrying through the shop and into the utility room to the rear. Inside were a refrigerator, a work surface and several oak dressers.

With the light of moon shining through the narrow curtain-less windows, she dropped the dripping carcass on the wooden slats and picked up the scissors, tearing away flesh and fur to extract the heart. *Snip. Snip.* Pink and fresh, it bounced slightly on the surface, a putrid odour whisking the air. With a scalpel, she carefully removed the eyeballs and placed them with the heart into the top compartment of the freezer. The drawer below contained further specimens, pieces of apparatus she had been saving. She hesitated as she traced her forefinger under the plastic arch.

Not now. Not Yet.

At the rear were stairs to the basement, which housed the furnace. She gathered the unruly remains, cradled them in her arms and carefully descended down the narrow steps. With one hand, she pulled down the metal grate and revved the lever before delicately peeling the bloodied nightdress from her damp skin. She wrapped it over the dripping flesh and bone, her stocky form naked and pulsating as she placed the heap onto the coals and tugged the rusty crank.

Out in the dark street, The Haus of Dolls glowed luminous as the wind whimpered its woes to the shrinking shadows. A gang of petrified moggies could be seen running down the valley, taunted by the murderous smoke which chased them down the dark cobbles and into the trees.

After the flames were extinguished and Gertrud returned to the ground floor, she suddenly felt an urge to begin something. Now with numerous supplies, she knew she should make a start, a trial run. She opened the airing cupboard and slipped into a black nightshirt, then proceeded to pull out a drawer from the dresser. Inside were accessories she had acquired over the years: buttons, hair, and odd pieces of clothing. In another were mechanical parts and tools, battery packs, tiny power circuits, and voice boxes.

She began picking out items in a frantic manner and placed them onto the worktop. She grabbed a gas lamp from the shelf above, ignited it and scurried through to the shop. There were shutters on the windows rendering the room pitch black. She scanned the stock with the lamp as multiple eyes gazed from the shelves above. *Pick me, pick me*, she imagined them pleading. She grabbed a rather unremarkable doll, a baby Tiffany from the modern collection. She had been thinking of replacing the modern ones to make way for more valuable antique models anyway. *Yes, she will do nicely.*

She placed the doll on the worktop and gathering the items together she cut, weaved, stuffed and sewed. *All done.*

Of course, it was not until all parts were thawed that she could measure its success. She would decide in the morning when to carry out the birthing, so to speak. She knew she should sleep now, that she got complacent when she was tired. But she felt so energized and eager to carry on. She crept back into the dark shop. Above the general displays sat mounted glass cases containing older dolls, many of which Gertrud had personally preserved and modified. These dolls had been difficult to acquire and she took great pride in restoring each one to its previous glory.

There was one in particular whose complexion reminded her of Patty, and although not identical, it provided an air of comfort and familiarity, and as she gazed at it, she knew what she had to do.

Just a start. To satisfy my hunger.

Her eyes were luminous, her mouth frothing with excitement.

* * *

One hour later, an exhausted Gertrud trod back upstairs to a blustery, cold bedroom. She had forgotten about the broken window and so hastily cut some cardboard from an old box and taped it over the frame. As she got into bed, she noticed the book still open on the pillow. She gazed at the illustration that had been planted in her for so long – her one true vision. With a satisfied breath, she held it close to her chest and fell asleep.

The next day, Gertrud opened The Haus of Dolls as usual at precisely nine o'clock. A customer was arriving from the mainland to collect a fifteenth-century Russian model, so she set about preparing the shop.

She had risen early to wash away the remnants of her temper from the night before and vigorously scrubbed the outside step, the stairs, the inside surfaces. She knew she must be thorough. Just like before. Working into the night had brought darkness to her mood, but she knew not to be complacent, nor show any sign of her activities.

The customer arrived promptly and the doorbell tinkled as she let herself into the shop. Gertrud welcomed her as she entered, inviting her to take a seat whilst she fetched the reserved doll from the back.

When Gertrud returned, the woman was peering into the glass displays with fascination. Expressing a mild aggravation, Gertrud summoned her to the counter.

"Here is your order. Please check before I wrap," she ordered in a stern tone.

The woman took a moment to approve the doll, and then turned back to the display cabinet she had been viewing.

"That is a remarkable doll – the eyes look almost lifelike," she said, pointing to the mounted display case. "I would've guessed German eighteenth century; am I correct?"

"That's correct. Those are the models which have been... restored," said Gertrud, with a nervous hesitation.

"How much for that one?" she asked, still transfixed.

"Unfortunately that one isn't for sale," answered Gertrud, speeding up the wrapping as if to hurry her departure.

"Oh, that's a pity," she said, looking back at the case. She seemed dazed as she handed Gertrud a cheque and left the shop.

* * *

In the city of Senago, Eleanor Wagstaff was in her office. A props manager for the Majestic Theatre Company, they were currently in pre-production of the show, *Island of Dolls*.

"I'm telling you, this was supernatural, like nothing I've seen before," she gushed, twirling the telephone cord around her slender fingers. On her desk sat a collection of odd-looking dolls, recently acquired from a range of specialist suppliers. "Don't get me wrong, this one is perfect, but that other one with the realistic eyes would really push the limits of creativity, you know?"

She paused before continuing.

"Well that's just it," she said, "they weren't for sale - which I thought odd for a shop to display something that isn't."

Another pause.

"Yes, Von Mueller, apparently.   A very strange woman indeed." She laughed before continuing. "Okay, but you'll believe me when you see it. Yes, sure, I'll do the research. Right, see you then."

* * *

That night, Getrud knew what she had to do. She craved violently for results, the one thing which would satisfy her ambition, her only purpose.

After retrieving the doll from the display cabinet, she set to work again to finish the modifications. She looked at her on the worktop, motionless yet her eyes twinkled with secrets, with affection.

As she worked on the doll, snipping, sewing, threading, pumping into her from the now thawed vial, she scolded herself for being so complacent, allowing her excitement and pride in the doll to cause her to place her within sight of a customer. She didn't want to consider what *could* have occurred.

How careless of me to jeopardise our life together. I will now focus entirely on your birth. On protecting you.

With methodical concentration, she cut the last pieces of thread and positioned the clothing—Patty's original outfit, which had now thawed perfectly—into place. She could instantly tell the operation had been a success.

The doll blinked its eyes and Gertrud watched as the air began to filter through the installed mechanism and she took her very first breath.

"Patty!" she announced in glee, like a proud mother.

But as she admired her perfect work, the Tiffany doll began to twitch on the surface alongside Patty. It let out a vengeful *miaow* as it jerked up on its feet and swung violently towards Gertrud's face.

Gertrud grabbed the squirming doll and bashed it down onto the cold floor. In a protective stupor, she cradled Patty in her arms and rushed through to the shop. Still overcome with accomplishment and joy, she sat on a chair and placed Patty on her knee to gush and admire her work. The doll slowly opened its perfectly formed mouth.

"Gertie," it said, in a voice that Gertrud instantly recognized.

Gertrud froze, her smile shattering into a frown of disbelief. A flash of pain shot up her arm to her chest. *Gertie. The only person to ever call her that.* She instantly placed the doll down on the cold floor and backed away as it slowly brought itself to its feet.

"Gertie," it repeated, "how could you, Gertie?" Its eyes were like sirens, blinking rhythmically. Unsteady limbs plodded forwards, arms twitching, plastic feet dragging against the frayed rug.

She had tried to stop the memories of those eyes revealing themselves, showing their truth to her. Every ounce of her fought to keep out that knowing. Yet, with that voice, she was thrown back to those feelings, to that existence.

"Impossible!" she spat, her flushed cheeks swelling with anger.

In Gertrud's eyes, her beloved Patty had now transformed from the perfect creation into something that she had instant hatred for.

"It wasn't meant to be this way," she spat.

"Don't be like that, Gertie," the doll spoke slowly, edging closer.

"You've ruined it all!" she howled, hurling the doll against the far wall. Its face took the impact and cracked, one eyeball bouncing to the floor.

Meanwhile, the Tiffany doll had been quietly creeping into the shop, grasping the kitchen knife, still bloody from slaughter. As Gertrud knelt down, exasperated, the doll quickly leapt onto her from behind, piercing the blade into her back. She fell forward, struggling for breath as the doll clambered upon her wide torso, stabbing again and again until a pool of red covered the shop floor.

Outside, the streets were dark and the wind foreboding as the two dolls made their escape, hand in hand, down the cobbled lane and into the hidden place where the lost and undead dwelt.

That night, as the hours passed in dark stillness, the islanders remained unaware of the terrifying occurrences on Main Street. But the next day a truth would be discovered from within The Haus of Dolls—a truth that would forever taint Wikonsia, bringing endless nightmares to all who heard.

And in the research library of Senago, Eleanor Wagstaff gasped in disbelief as she read an old Wikonsia newspaper article describing the unsolved death of a Mr. and Mrs. Von Mueller, whose mutilated bodies were found forty years prior, their eyes and hearts never to be found.

THE END

Contributor's bio:

R. J. Murray is a Scottish writer of mostly speculative fiction with stories published in Hello Horror, Penny Zine, Horror Addicts and Ink Stains Anthology, amongst others. She lives in Glasgow and when not writing is usually playing in her rock n roll band or hanging around cemeteries. News, poetry and art can be found on her blog:

https://rebeccajmurray.wordpress.com/

THE BLISTER
Written by C. Bailey-Bacchus

The blister appeared from nowhere in the perfectly hung wallpaper. It was only a thumb's width but formed a glaring pustule just above the skirting of the living room wall.

Once Kate had seen it, it refused to be unseen.

Kate pointed to the wall. "John, what is that?"

He frowned and followed her finger. "What? I don't see anything."

Kate raised her eyebrows, concerned that only she could see it. "It's a blister in the wallpaper, just above the skirting board."

"Like a bubble?" John battled to draw his attention away from the television. His eyes flicked between the two, as though they were rallying a tennis ball. "They happen sometimes. It's usually moisture. Maybe I didn't paste that part... it's probably always been there."

Unconvinced, Kate walked to the wall and crouched to get a better look. Maybe John was right. There could be something trapped beneath it. Somewhere inside, a spasm of dread began as she pressed a shaky finger to the blister. It broke as easily as an eggshell. As she went to move her finger, the blister clamped it and began to suckle like a nursing child. She screamed and recoiled from the wall.

"What happened?" John asked.

Kate looked at the oozing pinprick on her finger and turned to John. "It bit me!"

Red blotches erupted over his cheeks as he burst into laughter. "It… bit… you," he scoffed.

Kate turned to show him the growing bead of blood on her finger. "Look!"

"Babe, there's probably a splinter of wood underneath." He drew breath to calm himself. "Just leave it. It will probably go down on its own. You're such a drama queen."

Kate felt her cheeks warm in the glow of John's ridicule. His indifference caused frustration to bloom as she instinctively sucked her finger. He never missed an opportunity to mock what he considered to be her tendency to overreact. Whatever had happened, she was hurt, and he showed no concern. Instead, he laughed.

Kate saw it.

The crack in the blister healed. Its dome stretched and pulsated, as though beneath it, a rumbling stomach was filling. The skin was stretched close to its tolerance. She winced in anticipation of what would burst through. Instead of rupturing—with a sound not unlike a kiss—it grew.

* * *

John was wrong about the blister. Two days had passed, and it still blighted the wall.

Kate had spent those days rationalizing what she had seen. She felt silly after thinking about Occam's razor: *All things being equal, the simplest explanation is usually the correct one.* There must have been a splinter beneath the blister. The wallpaper did not crack; it creased. And she had mistaken the air rushing back in as growth.

Yet, as she rolled her thumb over the little scab on her finger, the blister's continued presence unsettled her. No matter what she did, even when she wasn't in the room, it lingered in the periphery of her conscious thought.

She denied the instinct to make a fuss. If she received a pound every time John berated her for being too melodramatic, or for thinking illogically, her shoe addiction would be fully funded. Despite his assertions to the contrary, Kate did consider herself capable of rational thought. If life had taught her one thing, it was that misery came from following her heart and not her head.

As her eyes circled the blister, Kate wanted her head to guide her, but it was intuition that sensed an inexplicable hateful promise seeping from the blister. The foreboding conjured a sick feeling in the pit of her stomach.

After another glance at the blister, she switched on the television to distract herself. Filling the screen was a sickly man, with a map of broken capillaries on his sallow skin. He was nervously recounting his descent into alcoholism, starting with how he had reached rock bottom after the death of his wife and son in a car accident.

His heartsickness, it seemed, grew from regret. Had he not decided to work late that evening, he would have been the one to drive his son to Scouts. In his mind, this was tantamount to killing them himself.

The alcohol had quickly moved from a crutch to get through the day, to the sole reason to get out of bed. With every day that passed, his dependency grew, and after six months, his guilt began to haunt him.

"I started to see things," he said.

"What sort of things?" the faceless interviewer asked.

The man frowned. He clearly regretted mentioning this part of the story. "The things I couldn't forgive myself for... the horrible thoughts within me... all the guilt I was carrying... fed something... made it real."

"Made what real?" the interviewer asked nervously. Seemingly concerned that the answer would not be suitable for pre-watershed viewing.

"A demon."

Kate didn't hear the rest of the interview. The man's tale hooked a thought buried deep within her mind and was reeling it in. The years subjugating the guilt within her had, in some ways, made it a living thing. Its heartbeat sounded between hers as it went about its daily grind—gnawing away at her conscience—never letting her forget.

If an innocent man can make his demons real, what punishment could guilty people unleash on themselves?

Her eyes drifted to the blister. Staring at it was like staring into an abyss, and sure enough, she soon felt the abyss staring back at her. It evoked a memory she had long forgotten...

Her mother was kneeling on the floor as she dressed Lucy, Kate's younger sister, for bed. Her mother took Lucy's hands into her own. "When the sun has said goodnight, and the moon has said hello," she gently kissed Lucy's forehead, "it's time to get into bed, little one, and it's time—"

"No Mummy! That's my story," Kate whined, no

longer able to stem the flow of jealousy.

Kate's mother sighed. "When I was a little girl, your Nanna told me and Auntie Celeste this story. I want to share it with both of you."

Kate's jealousy became frustration. "But it's *my* story!"

Her mother started to brush Lucy's hair. "That's enough Kate. Go to your room and put your pajamas on. I'll be there in a minute to tell you the story."

"No. I want you to put them on me."

"You're nearly five. You know how to dress yourself. Go on Kate, go."

The frustration became anger. As Kate stomped out of the room, she saw Bunny, Lucy's stuffed rabbit, on the cabinet beside the door. He was Lucy's favorite and went everywhere with her. She looked back. Her mother was plaiting Lucy's hair. Kate pulled the rabbit down and took it to her room.

She stared at Bunny through her welling tears and could not help but imagine he was Lucy. "Stop taking my mummy away," she hissed. She threw Bunny to the floor with all her might. "I hate you," she sobbed.

Kate stood on Bunny's neck and pulled his ear. Even in hindsight, she could not say why she did it. But she knew why she did not stop, for as she tugged, she felt the frustration drain away.

Then he came unsewn. Kate forced Bunny's ear, and then his body beneath her bed.

Kate's heart pounded as her mind meandered from the memory.

That was just childish sibling rivalry. She couldn't fathom why she had thought of that moment with such startling clarity.

The things I couldn't forgive myself for… the horrible thoughts within me… all the guilt I was carrying… fed something... made it real. The man's words echoed in Kate's head.

Though she denied the thought time to fully form, she sensed the blister had shown her the start of it all. What if it was her demon conveying its disdain for her actions?

The living room door opened.

"Okay, that's it. I'm going to fix it," John said.

"Fix it?"

"Yes, you're obsessed with that bubble. I was calling you for ages," he said flatly. "Didn't you hear me?"

"No... sorry."

"I'll get my toolbox." John shook his head as he left the room.

Kate's stomach churned. The blister summoned her wordlessly. Kate's need to obey was innate, like a mother bird bringing food in answer to the hungry squawks of her hatchling.

Everywhere, a thundering heartbeat—coursing through her chest, throbbing in her head and beating in her ears. Not hers, but the blister's. Kate crawled toward the blister. It was pulsating, and intuitively she knew it was baying for her blood. Against her will, her hand was moving towards it. As she came within a hair's breadth of touching it, she heard John come back into the room.

"Okay," John said, kneeling beside her.

Kate sat back on her haunches and watched him work.

He opened the toolbox and pulled out his utility knife. He moved meticulously to pierce the blister. Air huffed from the hole. John dripped glue into the gaping cavity and pressed a damp cloth against the wall. Their eyes met briefly, and he smiled. He turned back to lift the cloth.

"What the hell?" John said.

Kate was riddled with panic as they wordlessly watched the blister twitch and rise.

* * *

John insisted that there was a rational explanation for the blister. He had decided that the glue had sealed the cut and allowed the paper to swell again. But after he fervently stripped the blister away, Kate knew, for a moment at least, he had shared the fear lingering in her chest.

Smudge, her Kitten, was doing his best to distract her. She knelt and tugged the string attached to his toy mouse. He stalked behind and then pounced. The tinkling bell inside the mouse signaled its capture. She smiled at his joyful mews as he reveled in the spoils of his hunt.

As the mouse's bell chimed out, Kate's eyes drifted beyond Smudge to the scar left after John eviscerated the blister. It was gone, but not forgotten. The memory it had brought forth had been playing over in her mind. *Lucy.* Kate couldn't even think her name without feeling deep regret. It was better to swallow the guilt. Keep it distant from her thoughts.

Then, just to the right of the exposed plaster, there was movement. An area of untouched paper was rippling. As though a finger was pushing from the other side, a blister jutted out from the wall. It moved in a sweeping motion. First upwards, then back down. Stopping when it found its new position.

Kate stared out from her frozen body, unable to blink or breathe.

A pang of panic started in her stomach. The blister rose and fell like it was calling to her in Morse code. The message forced its way into her mind and sent it delving into the past again…

The toilets at school were supposedly cleaned daily, but they always smelled foul, even first thing in the morning. It seemed there were still some teenage girls not yet potty-trained. It was only absolute desperation that compelled Kate to go. She held her breath, ran into a cubicle, and relieved her aching bladder. As she finished buttoning up her trousers, familiar giggles reverberated through the room. After a moment, she realized they were Lucy's best friends, Jodi and Mia.

"Seriously?" Jodi asked.

"That's what Lucy told me," Mia said.

Her curiosity piqued, Kate leaned forward, hoping for a juicy tidbit of gossip about her sister.

"I feel sorry for her," Jodi said, making spluttering attempts to stifle her laughter. "I mean, there's nothing wrong with never having had a boyfriend. But when your younger sister gets one before you do, well, that's got to be embarrassing."

"I know," Mia's voice was throaty, after being harried by laughter. "When the boys in her class hear about it, they'll torture her!"

Kate would soon be the school's new punching bag. She would be harassed daily for the rest of the year. The realization struck her like a blow to the stomach. She wanted to run but could not face them. Kate pressed her hands to her mouth to suppress her mounting sobs.

"It won't be that bad," Jodi said.

"Oh really? You try telling that to Ten-Ton-Tessa, Fugly Fiona and what was the name of that girl that changed schools?" Mia asked.

"Donna the Dyke?"

"Exactly! The whole school will know about Frigid Kate by lunchtime."

"It doesn't fit the pattern. It has to have a Kah

sound." Jodi said.

Mia paused. "Fine then—Cunt-less Kate."

They erupted into bawling laughter.

When Kate heard the door close as they exited, so saturated with betrayal and terror, she could not control her colliding thoughts.

The girls they spoke of were hounded daily. Their friends had slowly left them for fear of association. They haunted the corridors, alone and distraught, like tearful ghosts. Kate knew that she wasn't strong enough to stand up to the bullies.

Her stomach churned furiously. There was no fighting the urge. She fell to her knees and expelled the contents of her stomach.

There was no one she could turn to. Even her own friends would mock her. She was alone in the nightmare. *Why didn't Lucy just lie for me?*

Wiping the vomit from her mouth and the tears from her eyes, she staggered to her feet. A streak of daylight beamed from overhead and lit the faded graffiti on the cubicle wall. Kate reached into her bag and retrieved her pencil case. Her fingers found a pen first, but she kept looking until she found her compass. Kate couldn't risk it being faded by scrubbing. No, this required permanence.

Kate took the compass and pressed it into the wood. Slowly, she made short sharp cuts to etch the words: *Lucy Owen is a slut.*

It was Smudge tugging against the string that sent the memories scattering back to the deepest recesses of Kate's mind.

She ran into the kitchen and splashed her face with cold water, hoping to shock her senses and wash away the sorrow. The dousing did not have the desired effect. Without bothering to dry off, the only thing left to do with the sorrow was to drown it. With a shaking hand, she poured a large brandy.

Carving the words was a thoughtless act, born out of anger rather than hatred. As a teenager, perhaps typically, she reacted without the ability to even imagine the consequences of her actions. Had she taken a moment, just one breath, Kate was sure she would not have done it. The anger was transient, the regret long-lasting. Whatever lurked within the blister didn't want her to forget that.

* * *

"I quite like this one, the classic gold pattern. What do you think?" Kate asked, pointing to the wallpaper in the hardware store's catalogue.

John blinked, at a loss. "A new pattern? I'm just replacing the paper on that one wall, aren't I?"

"Yes, I thought we could make that a feature wall. This pattern will go nicely with the plain magnolia paper."

John didn't seem to hear anything beyond yes. "Whatever you think is best." His mind turned to the practical. "If it's in stock, we'll get it. Hopefully I'll be able to hang it today."

"What do you mean? I want the thing gone."

John sighed. "Me too, but another bubble could mean something's wrong, like damp. I won't know until I strip the wall. Come on, let's go. If I can, I want to finish hanging the wallpaper by lunchtime. Kickoff is at two o'clock." He opened the front door for Kate.

"Okay." Kate rolled her eyes. It came as no surprise that football dictated John's schedule. As she walked through the door, she looked back and saw Smudge asleep on the bottom step. "Honey, close the living room door. I don't want Smudge going in there."

* * *

The closure of the front door woke Smudge. He stretched and yawned, then uncurled and rolled on the step. His eyes slowly opened to the empty hallway. He let loose a lazy mew. When no one answered, he jumped from the bottom step and headed to the kitchen.

As he passed the living room door, he heard a squeak. He called out and tapped his paw at the door. His ears pricked, alert to every sound. From the room, came nothing. Not so much as a groan. He turned and scampered down the hallway.

Behind him, the living room door creaked open. Smudge stopped and turned back. As he neared the door, caution slowed his step. From inside, he heard the tinkle of the bell within his mouse. Smudge hurtled into the room. His head turned to the side as he searched for the source. The tinkle sounded again. It seemed to come from the wall. He crept towards the blister and raised a tentative paw.

The blister snatched hold of him. His paws skittered across the varnished floor. Little by little, he was pulled into it. Smudge's tortured cries filled the room as he was ripped open and his innards drained. Bone splintered, and then was ground into his flesh. He fell silent as the fur was stretched and torn from around his startled eyes. Smudge expelled a last, desperate whine, as his neck was snapped.

The blister sealed over him. Pulsing and moaning, it digested its catch. Then, with a cackle, it grew to a size the equal of its meal.

* * *

When Kate and John returned, it was a little after nine o'clock and the morning sunshine flooded the hallway. Kate stopped suddenly after a few steps in. The rolls of wallpaper slipped from John's hands as he bumped into her.

"What are you doing?" John asked.

"The door is open."

"If you let me in, I'll shut it," he said sardonically.

Kate moved forward. "Not that door… the living room door."

John closed the front door and, quietly cursing to himself, bent down to pick up the rolls of wallpaper. "Well don't blame me. You saw me close it. Smudge probably opened it." He struggled with the bundle into the living room.

"John, there is no way Smudge could have reached that door handle."

A steady *thump, thump—thump, thump—thump, thump*, made Kate pause in the threshold of the living room.

"Do you hear that?" she asked slowly. "It's a pounding sound. Like a heartbeat."

They stood for a moment in silence.

"I can't hear anything; it's probably Smudge up to no good somewhere," John said.

Kate remained in the doorway, trying to discern the source of the pulsing sound. It was suddenly drowned out by a booming voice. "For godly grief produces a repentance that leads to salvation without regret, whereas worldly grief produces death."

Kate's mind raced at a dizzying pace.

The voice thundered on, "Be sober-minded; be watchful. Your adversary, the devil, prowls around like a roaring lion, seeking someone to devour."

"John, what are you talking about?" Kate asked.

"That wasn't me," John laughed. "I just switched the TV on. It's some religious program. The preview for this weekend's football starts soon." John stepped towards her. "Why are you being so weird?"

"I'm... I'm not."

"You do realize you're standing in the doorway... like a weirdo? I need to get the dust sheet."

Kate stepped back into the hallway so John could get past.

"No, Milady, after you." John stepped back to clear a path for Kate into the living room.

Kate stumbled forward and threw her handbag on the sofa. She turned to assess the blister. "It's bigger," she said breathlessly to the empty room.

The heartbeat grew louder. There was no ambiguity as to the source of the sound. That thud of guilt that had once drummed in the silence between her own heartbeats was visibly throbbing in the blister before her.

The scream was caught in her throat. She turned to run, but the blister stopped her. It forced its way into her mind. This time there was no gentle leading to forgotten memories. It thrust forward the one she could never forget...

Kate was lying on her bed, trying desperately to get into King Lear. *Why did I do an A-level in English lit?* She sighed.

The door opened, and Lucy walked in. "I can't take it anymore," she sniffled as she closed the door behind her.

"What's wrong?" Kate asked.

Lucy climbed onto the bed and snuggled against Kate's shoulder. "School... I can't take it anymore. Sam Marsden stuck a sign on my back that said 'slut' in Biology. I didn't notice until Mrs. Harvey took it off in

French. Everyone knew, everyone laughed. But no one told me."

Kate put the book on her nightstand. "I know it's hard, but this is the last year of school. You won't see half those people again." Kate gently stroked Lucy's hair from her face. Tears pricked her sinuses, caused in part from seeing her sister so upset, and in part from guilt. "You're not a slut, and that's all that matters."

Lucy raised a shaking hand to her face and wiped her eyes.

In the silence that followed, Kate hoped Lucy would find solace in her words. This was all her fault. Had Kate not etched those words in the cubicle wall two years ago, the rumors would not have started. Poor Lucy would not face the scorn of the girls and lewd propositions from the boys.

"You're at college now. You don't understand. You don't see what it's like when they…" Lucy whispered.

"Come on." Kate pulled her into a hug. "It's just teasing."

In her arms, Lucy crumbled. "It's not though… Sam… he touched me," she sobbed.

The words thundered like a sonic boom in Kate's head. "What do you mean he touched you?"

"It doesn't matter… forget I said anything."

Kate released Lucy and sat up to face her. She was barely able to breathe. "No Lucy, what do you mean, 'touched you?' If you're talking about something inappropriate, we need to go downstairs and tell Mum and Dad."

"No!" Lucy's eyes went wide. "I just meant he pushed me… don't say anything to Mum or Dad. I don't want them to think those terrible things about me."

"Just tell me. What did he do to you?"

Lucy's lip quivered as she swallowed deeply.

"I'm going to get Mum," Kate said.

Lucy gripped her arm. "Please don't; I can't bear the thought of her thinking I'm a slut."

"She won't think that! Both Mum and Dad know you."

"They'll think there's no smoke without fire," Lucy looked up to the wooden beam that ran between their rooms and smiled. "Do you remember when we were little, and we used to jump on our beds and tap the beam?"

"Lucy—"

"Remember?" Lucy said. "It was our way of saying goodnight."

"Stop changing the subject."

Lucy sat up and kissed Kate on the cheek. "Tomorrow, you will know everything. Tonight, I sleep." Tears rolled over her smile.

The act was so unfamiliar that Kate chuckled. "Lucy?"

"I'm so tired." Lucy got up and walked to the door. She opened it and paused before turning to Kate. "I love you."

"I love you too." Kate stared at the space Lucy left vacant. There was more to this, but she didn't want to press her. Lucy was upset enough. Better to let her rest and talk tomorrow. Despite Lucy's protests, Kate decided she would speak to their Mum. She picked up her book and started to read.

After a few pages, there was a sudden thud from above. Kate waved away the rain of dust that fell. She smiled and jumped up. With her book in hand, she bounced on the bed and hit the beam with it. "Night!"

Thud came the response.

"I get it Lucy!" Kate began. Her voice filled the room with ghostly echoes. "Night!" She got back into bed and opened her book.

Thud.

She lowered her book and looked up to the beam. *Thud.* Freezing air shifted into the room. *Thud.* "Lucy?" *Thud.*

Sparks of concern jumped across Kate's chest. "Luce?" Kate opened her bedroom door and walked to Lucy's and knocked. "Lucy." Kate's subconscious had picked up the tempo of the noise. *Thud.*

There was no answer. Something was wrong. *Thud.* "Luce… this isn't funny." Kate's hand took the handle. "If I open this door, and you're naked. That's on you."

Kate opened the door and screamed.

Lucy's body was swaying hypnotically to the rhythm of the thudding. Her arms dangled beside her. Her head lolled to the side. Kate stopped for a moment, waiting for Lucy's still and glassy bloodshot eyes to shift and her blue lips to curl into a smile.

It was not a joke.

"Mum! Help!" Kate screamed as she ran to Lucy. Kate ducked between Lucy's legs and tried to shoulder her weight. "Dad!"

The memory left Kate in darkness. She opened her eyes. A well of tears fell as she found herself in a heap on the floor.

"It wasn't my fault. It was the boys. Sam Marsden. They pushed Lucy to suicide. Not me!" she sobbed.

For godly grief produces a repentance that leads to salvation without regret, whereas worldly grief produces death. The religious sermon had new impetus, as though it had been written and delivered just for Kate. The words finally made sense. She should have admitted etching those words into the wall of the cubicle. In doing so, her grief would have become godly. The school's scorn would have been rightly directed to her instead and Lucy would still be alive. But that had not happened. Her grief remained worldly, filled with the self-pitying fear of reprisal and punishment, producing only death.

"Just take me," Kate cried. "Just put an end to it."

But she knew that the end would not come so easy. This horror was deserved, and the torture would not end until she was broken.

Be sober-minded; be watchful. Your adversary, the devil, prowls around like a roaring lion, seeking someone to devour. Whilst busy trying to convince herself that she could not be held accountable for Lucy's suicide, she had not been watching. The guilt and regret had cultivated this thing within her. Then, unseen, it had found a more productive way to abuse her. In its endeavor to exist outside of her, it found a womb of sorts within the blister.

Kate pushed herself upwards but could not get further than all fours. She sat back on her haunches and wiped her face.

"John!" Kate screamed.

Thud. Oh... God no! *Thud.* Kate's hands were nearly at her ears before realizing the thuds were John's footfall above. The relief was short lived. There was a sudden grim belching sound in the ghastly hush of the living room. Then the blister made a noise almost like gleeful crowing.

It began to move with a sudden, rapid undulation—something was waking within the bulge, stretching and writhing, fighting for release.

It begged for blood.

Kate shrieked as a figure lurched from the doorway. It took her a moment to recognize John.

He crouched beside her. "What on earth is going on?"

Kate sobbed against his shoulder. "It's the blister... there's something inside it, trying to get me."

He turned to look at it. "What do you mean?"

"It's moving. Look!"

He frowned. "No, it's not." He pulled the scraper from his toolbox, and then moved towards the blister.

"No John, don't touch it," Kate said.

"I have to get rid of it Kate. This is insane. Look at what it's doing to you."

He raised the scraper and plunged it into the blister. It wailed—an angry resonance that filled the room. Kate cowered and then screamed.

John drew a deep ragged breath and howled. "HELP!"

The blister swallowed his hand. Shavings of skin hung loose at his wrist as something within chewed on flesh and bone. Unsatisfied, it whined for more.

As the blister hissed and suckled, it turned a horrifying deep red.

A gurgling moan rose in John's throat. The color drained from his skin as his face grimaced in pain. His mouth opened, and then contorted into an unbroken yelp.

The swollen flesh of the blister bloomed around his wrist, and then sprouted concentric circles of jagged teeth. Like the mouth of a lamprey, it flexed and plunged its fangs into John's forearm. Then it sucked.

Kate rushed to John's side and pulled his upper arm.

Torn flesh was released up to his wrist. "Oh God!" John screeched. The blister surged forward and devoured John's elbow. They were doused in a shower of blood.

There was a crunch as John's shoulder dislocated.

The smell of fresh meat turned Kate's stomach. She fought the urge to vomit and pulled again. The blister did not give an inch.

"Kate—" John's voice was strained. His head was being pushed to the side as his shoulder was consumed. "Run."

"No, I'm not leaving you."

"I… love you… go."

"I love you too. I'm not going anywhere."

"Go!"

It slurped and growled as it closed around John's head. His screams were reduced to muffled pleas.

In vain, Kate struggled against its hold. Her nails broke and her fingers bled as she tore at his clothes. "No! Please… John."

John fell silent as his upper body was sucked in. His legs flailed, kicking Kate backward.

She crashed to the floor. "Oh God!" Within seconds John's legs were gobbled to the knee. Kate raced to her feet and grabbed John's calf. She fell back using her weight to pull. Blood sprayed from the blister as it sucked again. All that remained were John's feet. Kate took hold of his ankle, but the last contraction was too strong, and his foot slipped from his shoe. There was nothing left.

The blister convulsed. Then it gagged and choked. It forced out scraps of cloth, nuggets of flesh, and fractured bone. Then it sealed.

Sobbing, Kate let go of John's shoe.

She turned, scrambled to her handbag and pulled out her phone. Kate froze.

Behind, a tearing scrape pitched to set her teeth on edge. Kate's heart thundered. She could not summon the strength to turn. The constant, grating scratch grew louder. As Kate took short, sharp breaths, the room filled with fetid air—an odor of rotting flesh that tasted like metal.

From behind, something roared, louder, furious and booming. Finally, Kate turned.

The phone slipped from her fingers.

The floor was strewn with flakes of torn paper. Her eyes rose to see all that remained of the blister were tattered shreds of wallpaper.

It was free.

THE END

Contributor's bio:

C. Bailey-Bacchus is a devotee of dark fiction. Born in the U.K to Vincentian parents, her love of all things horror started with cautionary tales of Caribbean creatures that plagued poorly behaved children. She started writing in her teens after reading Clive Barker's *Hellbound Heart*, a book that incited a genuine fear of her own damp room.

In her endeavor to recreate that heart-pounding terror in her work, she delves deep into her personal fears to express the horror that might linger at the periphery of a mundane existence.

She is a job drifter, having read Geology at university, embarking on a career in finance, before her current role in a University research office. In her heart, her career has always been—Author.

THE ONE WHO SAVED ME
Written by Varonica Chaney

Chapter 1

I imagine that the soles of her feet are too thick. I can tell by the way she hesitates before she goes down those concrete stairs beside her house. I imagine that she falls, smashes her skull, and breaks her neck. She would never tell anyone this, but I know she must be imagining this too. Or maybe I'm the only monster between us. We even see the crushed vertebrae of her neck poking out of her skin. Blood waterfalls over the remaining stairs and feeds the grass with nutrients it has never tasted before. I wonder if blood can get a plant high, and I think she wonders that too. We have come a long way, my girl and I.

* * *

We've been together ever since her information

popped up on my screen that wonderful day. The company that sent it was amazing, but not for free. I had to stall on my purchases of serrated cleavers with leather handles to keep my girl appearing on my screen. It has been worth it though. Every cent.

At first, the company was new to me. I was skeptical of the information that was organized in a nice profile not unlike the kind you can find on dating websites. My girl's picture was in the upper right-hand corner and below that was a short description and a list of her hobbies, or at least hobbies that the company could track online through shopping habits and searches. She liked horseback riding, board games, and reading, apparently.

What kind of sham is this? I asked myself. People usually jot down reading as a hobby, but it was almost always a lie. People just say it because they know how to read and it's easy to get away with. Reading makes them seem smarter. But, I reason with myself, there were only three hobbies listed. I check her picture again.

A tiny twinge in my stomach wanted to challenge the fact, and maybe that's what the company had planned all along. Like I said, this company was good. I clicked on the camera button at the bottom of her page. I checked the clock. It was eleven in the evening, primetime for a young woman of twenty-three to be online. She should be in front of her computer by then, I hoped. As the camera window loaded, I held my breath.

I can still see that first image of her now. Her face lit up by the light of her computer in a dark room. Her eyes moved from side to side across her screen. I think what really made me stay with her were her eyelashes, fluttering and following along with every move her eyes made. Her hair was an asymmetrical mess, a dark mysterious mass that was tamed in a half-hearted attempt on the top of her head. Strands fell here and there, but none obstructed her view of her computer. I heard nothing but her rhythmic breathing as she chewed her thumb. Her eyes and eyelashes kept scanning. She was reading. At the realization, a small part of me latched onto her. She was real and honest. I could get used to that, I thought.

I have been watching her ever since.

Contrary to what I first set out to do, which was to watch her like every other girl I keep for backup, I immediately made her my top priority when I came home in the evenings. Before long, I woke up and the first thing I did was bring her camera view up on my phone. I paid the company extra to give me a list of her purchases and search history so that I could study up on her while I was on breaks at work. I was not new to this game... many monsters stalk. I studied her so well that I would correctly guess which website she would visit next. *Another saddle perusal, my love? I knew it!*

I paid more to the company and I could suggest ads on all the websites she visited. There was a new game that she just had to try. I knew that she would love it! She always went for the websites I suggested. If she didn't click on any of the suggestions, her eyes hovered over my suggestion longer than the rest. It was like she was seeing me and giving me her approval.

* * *

She is consistent and I can predict her. She keeps rewarding me and I might just keep watching her the rest of my life. This is how she saves me.

My coffee tastes metallic and heavy because it's cold. I am watching her this morning very carefully. The company recently gave me access to her phone and now I can learn even more about what she does and where she does it. I don't want to compare my girl to crack, but the feeling is the same and I can hardly stay away from all the tinging notifications on my phone. It tings whenever she picks up her phone, moves to a new location, visits a new site, or purchases something.

I have had to put it on vibrate at work because the person in the cubicle next to mine has complained twice. A third time would line me up with that horrible number three and I would not be able to stomach another admonition after that. I know I am wrong, but I don't need other people to tell me about it. Besides, how am I supposed to take the man seriously with that horrible shiny blue shirt of his? I am so glad there is a wall between us.

Right now, though, I am not at work. I won't be at work for another two hours and I can let my phone ting to me as loud as I want.

My girl is going to the stables outside her family home. Ordinarily, a change of scene such as this would thrust me back into watching someone else because I just can't stand all of the variables. But, with my girl, she feels the same at home as she does at her college apartment, even without her biology classes. Plus, she'll be back at her dorm after spring break is over.

It's five a.m., and a dull light spreads across her face that isn't entirely due to her phone screen. Natural light looks even better on her in her slouchy sweatshirt and roughly pulled back hair. She is reading again. I quiz myself on what she would be reading before I check the website. There an article out about research being done on the way books and stories influence our life satisfaction. I know it must be that because her shuffling steps have stopped and she gasps. I lean in closer to my monitor as she whips up a sleeved hand to her trembling lips.

While I found the results of the research a bit of a shock, I hadn't expected that much of a reaction from her, a nod at the most. She must be reading about how most people live their lives waiting for the adventure of their dreams. The adventures they read in stories. Instead, they find that their adventures are very ordinary like losing a critical job, or a cancer diagnosis. Both instances are devastating life changes, but I know that those are not the adventures that people want to have. I know that because although I am a monster; I am a *human* monster and losing a job or cancer would not be the plot points I want in my narrative. I decide to touch the notification and cover the bottom half of my phone's screen. I'll see if I guessed the website correctly after a, not three, but a four second countdown:

Four...

Three...

Two...

One.

She slips on the wet dewy grass. I take in a sharp breath. I can feel my blood boiling to the surface of my skin. She shouldn't have taken the shortcut from the back door through the field! She should have gone out the front so that she could follow the trusted and true dirt path to the barn. She recovers and puts her phone in her pocket. I can't see her anymore but I can hear her breathe. After a few heaves she laughs at herself. Okay, she is safe.

I uncover my phone. *"Internet Spies, Are You Safe?"* I drop my phone as if it is made of a block of red-hot iron. I scrape it back off the ground. I skim across the page and only absorb every tenth word: "Privacy" "Invade" "Hackers" "Stalkers" "Criminals" I want my internal organs to fall out both my mouth and my anus to get rid of them as soon as possible. What if she employs one of these programs that claim they can protect her? The sanity that I get from watching her starts to wither away. She can't get rid of me. I would no longer feel fulfilled from her predictive ways. I wouldn't be with her on her horse or laugh with her when she beats her friends in a clever turn of a board game. It doesn't make any sense to me that she would bar herself against me when she has meant more to me than she will ever know. She is mine. She is going to save me.

It's not like this has never happened before with my girls. Sometimes they very rightly wise up and start putting tape on their cameras. But that is the extent that they take. Nothing more. I also don't need those girls as much any more. This site, though, has links to programs that could wipe me out of my girl's life forever.

My hands are still shaking as I stare at the screen. A part of me wants to reach out to the company and ask them for some security. That's the monster part, the part that needs control. Another part of me hopes that I do lose her, so that I don't kill her. The compromise between the two halves of me is to simply wait.

I listen to her walk the rest of the way to the barn because she has put her phone in her pocket. The barn door creaks open as the horse stamps the ground and whinnies at my girl. My girl giggles back. This is the worst kind of waiting. There is no way of knowing when she will decide to get rid of me until there is a swift click and my girl goes away forever.

I soak in every moment. Right now she is probably tousling the horse's hair. It's name is Sky, and blonde is about the best way to describe it. I don't know the breed. I have heard my girl say it so many times, but I still forget. I am not good with animals. They cannot validate you like another person can.

She gets up on the horse through a pattern of rustling

I am familiar with from the past two mornings. The sound is the same "huh!" as she jumps up to land in the saddle. The groan of the leather and the tinkle of little metal parts wash over me. The sound is nice and entirely different from the sound of my daily activities. I even started to think that I could be good with animals, if only for the sound my girl makes when she gets on her horse. The rest of her ride is peaceful listening. It is a YouTube video of horse riding, filmed live just for me. I get my clothes ready during this time since I know that she has at least thirty minutes until she reaches her destination. I keep an eye on the screen just in case she takes it out for a quick photo.

With my clothes all ready, I wait for when she arrives at the cliff. This makes the third morning she does this. She comes to this spot and takes a picture at exactly 6 a.m. How she gets up so early or has the initiative to keep track of a sunrise comes as no surprise to me. She somehow naturally finds habits to fall into and keep. I wish I could be like that.

The time is 5:58 a.m. I hear the hooves stop hitting the dirt and rocks of the trail. I wish that I could see the trail in its entirety. She only gives me a few photos from time to time. Somehow that only makes me like her more.

She doesn't immediately take her phone out of her pocket, which is okay. Tiny variances in her behavior are to be expected, but my stomach makes an angry lurch anyway. Is she afraid of me? That's funny because the article terrifies me. She terrifies me. I want to close out of the window, but I have to see *it* again. And she is going to take a picture. I know she will.

It is 5:59 and I haven't been able to put my stomach back down to where it belongs. My girl hasn't picked up her phone. *Calm down*, I tell myself. She has shown it to me before. I fight back the anger. Just a little longer and I'll see it again.

She sighs and all at once I can see it. She is high on a cliff holding her camera up. I can see the landscape wide open in front of us. I almost want to cry. There is a plain of grass and a pond down below that reflects the rising half crescent sun. The half of the sun is coming over a plateau in the distance, a black table of ground lifted up high above everything else. We marvel at the golden rays while standing in the plateau's shadow. Our star is brighter than it was the past two visits. I squint from all the light coming in from the sun and its reflection in the small pond. I am so happy to be seeing it. Without her, I would never have known this place existed. This is how I know she will save me.

She wakes up early and, therefore, so do I. I like the time spent watching her and the small breaks to myself. I copy what she eats. It makes me feel closer to her. Somehow I have never done this with anyone else. And the people around me are noticing. They see how I am healthier lately and more alert at work. This girl, if she ever wised up, is going to be the death of me because I can't go back to the way I was. I need her to tell me what to do and how to do it. I need her stability. But there is nothing I can do but watch and wait... unless I could find someone else. Then I could be free to punish her if she ever went away. She snaps a photo. She doesn't take a picture of herself like she usually does. What is going to happen to her project?

She now urges her horse closer and closer to the edge of the cliff. The horse halts in self-preservation and she puts her phone back in her pocket. Her breaths come in and out faster as I hear her dismount and scrape her shoes across the dirt. Her phone is back out and focused on the line between her level of ground and the other level, at least one hundred feet below. Her shoe comes into the shot and pushes a rock closer and closer to the edge. She waits a moment before finally pushing the rock over. It falls down through the air becoming a mere speck in seconds. The whole view through the camera shakes and she brings it in sharply to her chest as she steps back.

I know, I think to myself. *I know that feeling, too.*

Chapter 2

Everything is going well. My boss has promoted me to a larger cubicle next to a window. It was hard to get used to at first; I wasn't used to the space. With the window, it also feels like I have more than what I have. I feel possessive of the street below me, and the Italian restaurant on the corner. I know they are not mine, but I can see them from my spot. Most importantly, my girl is still there. She didn't use a program to wipe me from her phone. As long as I have her, I can make do with this new change in scenery.

After a few days of awkward adjustments, I am finding my new cubicle decidedly nicer than my last one. I also get more money, which is a bonus. I wonder what kind of other feature the spy company could come up with? If they do add something else, I would be able to pay for it.

I don't have anyone beside me anymore. There is a small hallway made up by the cubicle line close to the window and the cubicles in the center of the huge company floor. I wonder if my new neighbors would mind so much if I turn my notifications back on. I flip the switch on my phone and the tings scuttle along the air and tickle my ears immediately. I spend the next hour in bliss.

It is only for an hour though because, after that, I hear the wheels of a chair like mine, I want to say *gluccle*, but the sound is more hollow and made of plastic. Anyway, I hear a chair gluccle back and I see the door of the cubicle in front of me wedge open. Hollow heels hit the carpet and a knock pounds around and in between my girl's tickling tings for me. The knock is on my cubicle door.

I have never met that person in front of me, but I suspect that I have to talk to that person now. The knock raps again and I realize that I am one of the two people that can make it stop. I open the door while still sitting my chair. A woman's head pops in. I quickly glance at her and then stare at my computer screen. She has dark skin, and braids on either side of her head. Her hollow, white necklace beads click as she moves. I curl up into myself. I don't know how to handle situations like these. I am a monster and monsters are notorious for their anti-social behavior.

"Hey Ms. Popular. Turn your phone on 'vibrate' please. I'm trying to work."

I nod my head without looking at her. Through the corner of my eye, I see that she makes an attempt to smile at me before she leaves. Her perfume lingers on the carpeted walls. What is that scent? It's a calming fresh smell and I hate it. That woman's gait, voice and manner tell me that she is way more productive than me. And those hollow clicks?

Ting! I grab my phone and switch the noise off. Something tells me that I won't need a notification to look at my phone today. I'll be looking at it to keep calm.

Nothing the rest of the day serves to cheer me up or break me out of this cycle of anger except my girl fulfilling my predictions. Thank God she's back in class. I slip into narrating her life, and forgetting about the woman in front of me gets easier.

My girl gets back to her dorm room a few hours before I get off work. She watches a couple sitcoms, reads a chapter from a book her friend recommended, and then starts her homework assignments. After a page or two of her textbook, she does that cute little twist with her mouth and gets up to go to the kitchen. By this time I am putting my coat on to go home. But if she is having dinner, I should go to the grocery store.

In the kitchen, she gets out a couple tomatoes, a chicken breast, spinach, and assorted seasonings. I have most of the seasonings at home since she has made this dish before. I just have to pick up more chicken and the tomatoes. I put my phone in the holder for navigation and continue watching her as she prepares her dinner. She hums a tuneless melody. It might be a song, but it's unrecognizable. Hey, she can't be perfect, just perfect for me. *My, oh my*, I think to myself. *Look at how cheesy I have become.* She puts the vegetables on the table with a cutting board and a knife. As I pull into the parking lot, I think to myself that she should be careful. I knew she would be careful though. She's my girl.

She watches a video as she chops up the spinach and moves on to the tomatoes. I am in the fresh produce section of the store and I just so happen to pick up a tomato as she makes her first slice. *It's so right*, I think. I feel so close and connected to her. It's like I am the one actually slicing up the red, round, vegetable, oozing with cool juicy insides that slide over my fingers. I am the one using her hand to make the incision.

She plays with the edge of the knife. It's irritating. After a couple cuts, she is now running the knife's edge against her skin. It's not enough to puncture it, but just enough to push the skin down. *What is she doing?* I ask myself, while still knowing what I am seeing. *Why doesn't she move on and cut the rest of the tomato? Just dice the tomato and stop messing around with the knife. We all know what a knife can do, now use it properly.* I want to yell at her and scream, but I am in a store and that would call attention to myself. I keep watching, standing in the produce section and clutching my phone. She stops. She brings the knife up again and dices the slices she made. I breathe a sigh of relief and put the tomato into my plastic shopping basket. I look for another.

My girl screams.

I wheel back to my phone screen. She's done it! She's cut herself! I can't see her. She has ducked down below the shot of the phone. I look at the cutting board and I see it. It's the tip of her left index finger. I hear her screaming, "Someone help me! Please!"

I jump where I stand and drop my basket. I run to the restroom and bang into a stall. I wait for someone to come to her. Her screams of agony last for what feels like hours. *Please!* I willed someone to come. *Please! She can't just be left there! Someone has to help her! Anyone!*

Then it hit me.

Me.

I had to save her. I had to be the one to call 911, but I don't even know where she is. I have to explain my whole situation and let them track her from my location. I have to admit to stalking. I have to go to jail. But she is in trouble! Oh God, I will be even more so. Please, someone come save her. Am I be willing to go to jail for this? Please, someone, for both of us. I have to do something. I can't just let her go on in pain all by herself. Damn it! I have to do it! I have to make the call.

I tap the button on my phone and bring up the dial pad. *Oh God please, someone come.* 9. Her finger might not be salvageable at this point. 1. "Oh God!" she screams. She panics and her fear is injected through me. Too much adrenaline makes my eyes bulge from their sockets. 1. I press *send* and the line on the other end rings once. She cries out. The line rings again. *Come on... Come on...* "911, what's your emergency?"

"It's um."

"Ma'am, I need you to keep calm." My palms are slippery and my voice comes out what feels like sandpaper.

I hear more shuffling sounds from the spyware on my phone. A voice I don't recognize comes through my earpiece. "Come with me." Someone's back flashes blue on the screen and someone else gathers my girl's finger into a container of ice.

"Ma'am? What's your emergency? Is there someone with you?"

"I'm sorry," I say. "I am so sorry. I am one of several callers for the situation. Another person got through. I am sorry for taking your time."

"Okay, I'm hanging up now. Are you sure you're okay?"

I clear my throat. "Yes, I'm alright." And for the first time in a long time, I turn off my phone. I slide down the wall of the stall and stare at the perforated tiles of the ceiling. What the hell just happened?

Chapter 3

I am not sure how I am still working, but here I am. I can't exactly take a day off for the trauma of watching the person I am stalking cut her finger. Of course that isn't what I said when I made the call in the morning either. I tried to take off work for being sick. The boss said we were too understaffed. I tried not to yell because yelling would almost immediately give me away as having no illness whatsoever. The boss threatened me with my job after the fifth time I insisted that I was sick. No matter how convincing my sickness was, he had orders to fill and I had to help fill them. "The company is sick too," he said. "Do you want a decrease in pay?" Companies are for humans though, and I'm supposed to be the monster.

In my anger, I made sure to put some dark circles under my eyes with some dark eye shadow, and lightened my skin. I didn't take a shower and even put oil in my hair at the roots. If I lie, I have to match. That's the only way you don't get caught.

I stalked into the company with a blanket around me, sniffling to make the picture of my sickness complete. I even stuck tissues up my nose to hide the fact that I didn't have time to fill my nostrils with artificial mucus.

I sat down in my chair without a person looking up at me, and I am still sitting here staring at my screen. Papers are stacked up next to me and I imagine them yellowing in the sun as they slowly rot. And they will rot, just not soon enough for me. All things take too long to rot once they die. I should know; I have a few bodies in mind that I wish would just go away. But I can't get into it. I feel fragile enough right now.

A sudden pang in my stomach hits me. I realize that I miss her. This would probably be the twentieth time I had wandered too far away from her in my thoughts. I take my phone out, but find no notifications. My phone feels light and hollow.

"Hey."

I jolt in my chair and catch my phone before it hits

the ground. I look up and see that it's that woman again, the one who works in the cubicle in front of me. Her head has popped into my cubicle. She still has the two braids and a clean face. I feel the oil in my hair prickle with heat.

"What do you want?" I ask. I try not to show her how nervous she makes me. I know that at any moment she could use her perfectly trained body to seize me into a chokehold. I can sense she is trained anyway. No one looks that radiant in the morning unless they go to the gym.

"You look awful," she says.

"I'm sick." The tissues buzz in my nostrils and make it uncomfortable to talk, but I can't help but add, "So sorry that I am not in tip-top shape."

"I agree," she says as she crosses her arms. "I mean it's ridiculous that you should have to come in like that. Even if you weren't sick and were just…" She shrugs. "I don't know, trying to look sick. It would mean that you needed some time away."

I glare at her and don't have to fake the red in my eyes. What is this bitch getting at?

She sighs and holds her elbow. "Listen, I don't care why you wanted to be out today, but I understand the feeling. My workload has doubled in the past week and I can't keep up with all the new orders. I'm stressed all the time. I can't enjoy anything anymore." She leans in, her eyes set on mine. She holds the gaze for so long I want to scrape my skin off just to make her look away. She glances across the makeshift hall to the other employees pounding keys and shuffling papers. "There are other people who feel the same as we do. We are worked too hard and deserve a break."

I feel my head nod beyond my control. I wish for a screen to separate us. I want to run and hide in my apartment and watch my girl.

The woman from the cubicle in front of me pulls a pamphlet out of her back pocket. The tri-fold is brightly colored with bold red letters: "Make our Union Work for Us."

I take it without hesitation and slide it into the top drawer of my desk.

"There is information on a meeting we'll be having soon inside. Please consider it. Oh, and my name is Clarice." She holds out a French manicured hand to me. *Just shake her hand,* I tell myself.

"Heather," I say back, and we shake hands. Her palm is soft and warm.

"I'm glad to meet you, Heather. I hope you come." She smiles.

I nod and watch Clarice to make sure she closes my cubicle door completely. She does, and it's a quiet exit, clean-cut. It's like she was never in my cubicle at all. Only her body spray lingers on my walls again. That calm and relaxing scent.

I stare again at my screen for a moment, leaving the pamphlet in my top drawer. I wouldn't be getting that out until I leave. I look at my stack of rotting papers. I notice that my phone does not ting. Where is she?

Something else crowds my thoughts, and for once my girl does not consume me. I had never thought about my work conditions seriously before. I wanted a day off, that was all, and that bastard made me come in. It feels new and fresh and good, the rage that flickers in my body. It laps at my rib cage and I let it consume my heart and mind. It is so warm, compared to the cold disappearance of my girl. For her I would wait; but, in the meanwhile, I could use a little distraction. I don't want to kill her, and maybe this will help me resist the urge.

* * *

No, I will not go to the meeting.

I spent the rest of the day working in frenzy. I would do well even under the tyranny of the horrible boss. I showed him my best so that when I undercut him, it would be a delicious and juicy betrayal.

At quitting time, though, I find that my fervor has diminished and I miss my girl. It is now time for dinner and I haven't seen her eat, so naturally I have no way of making the decision on what to have for myself. I think about going without tonight, but I feel sick to my stomach about it. I have to match her. I just have to.

What if this betrayal at the office means that I lose my job? My income? I will have no money for seeing my girl. I would absolutely no longer see her if the money runs out. So, no, I can't risk my job like that.

I put my bag on the table as I enter my apartment when I hear it.

Ting.

My heart flies. The sound is a little different, but it's the first time my phone has been alive since last night. I rush to her, my girl.

I unlock my phone, impatiently, digging into the glass screen while scratching out my password and swiping to check my notifications. The company's app. But nothing is there. I swipe a few more times on my phone and press so hard that plasma bursts of color trace my thumbs. *Where is it! Where is the site she is on? What is she doing?*

I finally identify where the odd ting had come from. There is a number one in the upper right corner of the messages application. I touch the square. The sender is unknown, but the blurb in the preview reads, "Hey it's

Clarice. I know it's…" I raise my hand to my mouth. I think of how my girl put her hand to her mouth in shock as she read the article too, and I can't help but smile. Even that small similarity is a salve to my nerves.

A ribbon flows through my spine as I press to open the message. The screen loads and her message says, "Hey it's Clarice. I know it's late, but do you want to grab some dinner with me tonight? We could swap makeup secrets. I really want to try that hair mask you had going on today."

I have dismissed you. I no longer need you because I have decided I do not want to put my job in jeopardy. I'm sorry, but I can't be your friend.

Hair mask.

But if I were honest with myself, the offer is more than welcome. I look at my apartment, which is dark and small. The only thing of real value is my computer, which might have led someone to believe that I had a job in graphic design or some useless vocation like that. I don't want to see Clarice again, but I don't want to stop talking to her at that moment.

I text back, "How did you get my number? I don't remember giving it to you."

Three dots dance at the bottom of the screen. A new message pops up.

"I just told the boss that you were helping me with something. Just like him to promote more work instead of saying that I should respect your time."

Respect my time. I checked my long single window and see only black. When was the last time I had seen the afternoon in my apartment? This Clarice, she, she is interested in me. The interest only went so far as my being a fellow employee, but still, that is something. No, that's not all. There are at least a hundred other employees like myself. Clarice had chosen me.

What would she do? My girl? What would she do? I check my phone again, but there is still nothing but Clarice's message blaring up at me. I raise my eyebrows. I may not go to the union meeting or whatever, but maybe meeting Clarice would be a good thing. Besides, I would have my phone and could duck out at anytime if my girl came back.

I plug in my phone charger and get ready for a shower. I hit my forehead with the heel of my hand. I text Clarice back, "Where and when?"

"At the company and after you left."

I roll my eyes and force my smile down, a little sick to my stomach. I type again, "I mean, where do you want to meet for dinner? I have to wash my hair mask out before I go though, how does nine sound?"

"That sounds perfect. I'll meet you at that new Italian restaurant down the road from the company. It's called Fiorella."

"Ok."

I hurriedly take a shower, washing off my stupid attempt at looking sick and shaking my head at the absurdity. Who was I fooling with that makeup? Oil, I grimace to myself. I thought the oil would at least keep people away from me even if it didn't convince them of my sick state. But Clarice asked me to have dinner with her. I must not be that repulsive, even with crud imbedded in my hair.

I step out of the shower, wrap a towel around me and stare at the fog-covered mirror. My outline makes it through, despite the film of water. We are similar, my girl and I. We both have brown hair down to our shoulders. Mine is probably grayer than hers though. She's only twenty-three, whereas I am two decades older, at least. I don't want to wipe the fog off yet. I want to pretend I am not this old. People fear dying; but, for me, my fear was realized when I became nothing while I still draw breath. I am a nobody because I didn't get married or have kids. Is that the only way to find intimacy? Or to find people who care? Actually… no. I am not alone because I didn't follow social normative. I am alone because I am a monster.

* * *

What kind of non-monster kills her mother? I chose a pill for her because, at that time, I had decided that she had earned a peaceful death. Yes, she tried to cure me. She tried to make me a good child and a good human being. I had believed her. I had believed that she could do it! But after I dissected the family cat, I came to hate my mother. She couldn't fix me. She was the one who told me I had a problem in the first place. So, I took care of the problem. I watched her take her last breaths while stroking the side of her face. The police found all the empty sleeping pill bottles by her bed and ruled it a suicide. I positioned her body just so in her coffin. I wish I could have put it where I wanted to, but even at that age, I knew there were bigger monsters than me.

The victims' deaths only get more grisly. I think about them while staring at my shadow in the mirror. Am I hunched over? I straighten my shoulders. I only see a tousle of my hair.

My high school boyfriend, now he was difficult. It had been a typical high school romance. He stole my heart, so I stole his in my secret place surrounded by trees and the songs of sparrows. I haven't taken it out from under my bed in a while. That's what stalking can do for you. Yes, I remember how good it felt to have him finally do what I wanted, but then he wasn't around anymore. The finality hit me hard.

I recoiled from everyone, knowing that I was a monster. I decided that I was too dangerous to interact with other people, at least in the flesh where I could tear it.

Technology got better. Starved for interaction, I leapt at the chance to keep a safe distance between me and what I imagined were friends, through cameras. I didn't learn the names of the people I followed, because I would never have to refer to them to anyone. I could just watch them. Before long, I craved to have complete control and to watch their lives fall out of my hands, like a rock falling away.

The third grave in my secret place (the third because I dug up my mother and put her next to my high school boyfriend) is the first girl I followed. Blonde and morose, she wore black all the time and barely ate, except for ice cream. When I found her, I thought all of my problems had ended. I enjoyed watching her everyday and mimicked some of the things she did, like stirring my ice cream until it melted and became soft. It was great looking forward to her everyday. I had a reason to get up in the morning. I didn't need anyone else. That is until the one time where she didn't stir her ice cream before she ate it. By then my craving for killing had gotten too strong for me to stay away. I couldn't hold that disappointment all by myself. I found out where she was and I took her. I made a lot of mistakes tracking her down, missing buses and following wrong directions. I did not make those mistakes again.

I cried when I severed her head from her body. She had tried to escape. I couldn't believe it. I had to start all over again with another and it was all her fault. I had to build another relationship from the first day again. No, that wasn't fair. From my boyfriend I had learned that relationships are a two-person development. I promised myself to be more forgiving.

But that only led to watching more. I watched a couple girls at time after that so I didn't get so distraught when my one friend let me down. No, then I had two and they served to balance each other out. One was blonde and the other brunette. Both were made up of moderate builds, wore their hair parted on the side, and had comparable fashion tastes.

I cringed when the brunette experimented with the other side of her head. I gripped the table and clicked back to the blonde. Surprisingly, the steadfastness of the blonde leveled me. I kept calm and was able to stifle the need to correct the brunette for another day. The level one became my main friend and the other just a side friend that I would hang out with sometimes. I started acquiring more girls. I would be a friend to them all. Until they all disappointed me.

I never thought that would happen but it did. I went through the whole list of windows open on my computer and every one of those girls was trying something new, deviating from their normal patterns. Everything rushed inside of me. They needed to stop. It all started with that one that parted her hair on the side! She needed to pay! I tracked her down and locked her up in my basement. By then, she had dyed her hair a ridiculous purple so I bought some hair color and, after a beating, she dyed her hair back. But it just wasn't the same! She saw my rage and parted it the way she used to. I felt so much better. I hugged her and cried in her arms. She cried too.

"At least I am not killing you," I said. "You are saving so many other lives by being this way."

Her hair fell out. Was it so hard to ask to keep everything the same? Thanks to her I was able to quit watching some people by simply clicking out of their windows and deleting their files. But her hair fell out. I had no more use for her.

It took several hits with the shovel, but I freed her scalp from her head: the offending part that would not listen. I lay her nicely in her grave. I covered her and when I was done, I wiped my brow, and my body ached with satisfaction. I wondered to myself: *How much is the development of a person or a monster worth? Is it worth the life of another? How about two?* I examined the fourth life I had taken and I found progress.

I put my shovel in the back of my car and went home to wash off. Home was a few states over. Since I didn't want to risk anyone seeing me, I drove straight there. Eight hours later, I finally got home, hopped in the shower, and ran my fingers through my hair. The third finger of my left hand snagged. I stopped. I took my left hand down and stared at it. My nail was chipped. I ran to my car and searched the floor, but found nothing but crumbs. My nail wasn't there! My pulse did not stop racing. I hated my finger! I wanted to cut it off and feed it to something so that it disintegrated and no pieces were left in the same order! I wanted to scream, and did so into my hands. That nail could be anywhere from that grave to here. There was a high probability that it was sitting right on top of the freshly buried, waiting to be discovered.

* * *

"No, no, no!"

The pang of the memory courses through me and I grip the side of my sink as I look at the mirror. I am found.

My voice echoes off the walls as a theory lays itself out. I wipe the part of the mirror that is my eyes. "They found you. Why do you think they hired you? No one else would hire you without a background check. They didn't even ask for one. They just trusted you. She is in on it. Clarice. She is inviting you out to kill you tonight. There is no union meeting at the time written on the pamphlet you left at your desk, another stupid mistake. You're getting sloppy. You have to go. You have the upper hand. You know what she is going to do."

But what if she isn't set out to kill me tonight? She came up to me despite all the signs I put up to keep people away.

It was too easy for her to do that. She saw that I was discontented and took the opportunity while I was unaware. But how do I know that Clarice knows I am a murderer?

The instability feeds my craving for ultimate control. A familiar rage takes my skin for its own.

I check my phone. There is still no answer from my girl.

I sink down to the floor. That's how they know. The two companies are one. The one I work for and the one that gives me all the information on my girl. They have been setting me up. They found my fingernail. My girl will not be on my phone ever again. My eyes do not stop stinging as I remember the first time I saw her reading in her sweatshirt. My girl, she is one of them. The rage fills me again with renewed fury. The company is very good, but I am better.

Chapter 4

The nervous feeling that I had about meeting Clarice for dinner is gone. Now that she is a potential victim, I park my car easily a few blocks down the road from

Fiorella. I am on the far side of the company, of course. For a murder, Fiorella is more conspicuous than what is ideal. If it were I planning my demise, I would pick somewhere where there isn't a huge red and green neon sign. I also think this place is way too close to the company, but here we are. This was probably someone's big breakout scheme and the company thought I would be the perfect test subject. Well, company, I've already figured you out, so test me all you want. I have gotten away with all my murders. I have all the answers.

Except, is Clarice really going to kill me? I walk another block past the one that had these ridiculous new apartment buildings that feature concrete stairs. Honestly, someone will fall down those, one day, and kill themselves on them. Clarice might have to die, but no one else does.

Across the street, the restaurant faces the corner and on its side there is a set of stairs that lead down somewhere. I cross at the signal and head straight to the top of the steps. The view down includes a brick stairway fading into blackness with the faint outline of a metal door on the right. I am intrigued. Dark places are wondrous opportunities. There could be anything down there, and before I can stop myself, my feet take the first few steps and my hand grabs the railing to my left. Spider webs have collected in the corners and my shoes are careful not to disturb the tiny creatures. We monsters in the same business of killing should support each other.

"There you are!"

I catch a step with my heel and fall forward just barely catching the railing and whipping back to face the top of the stairs. Clarice stands there with her clicking necklace and this time matching earrings. Once again I bemoan the professionalism that seeps from her pores.

She starts down the stairs, saying, "I'm so sorry! Here let me help you."

"No," I say. The last thing I need is for her to find the knife against my left forearm in my sleeve. This is horrible. This is not part of the plan.

I make some swift calculations. She may trust me more this way. This is perfect. Leading her to my car will be so much easier if she trusts me.

She pulls me up and laughs. I follow her cue with some normal-sounding contractions of my diaphragm. My heart is racing too fast for anything else. She motions toward the entrance and I nod, smiling.

As we find our table, I can smell her perfume even more strongly now. I feel calmer, almost dazed. I have to find out what it is. It's disrupting my focus and if I could put a name to it, I could focus better. All of Clarice's movements are swift and purposeful. I wish I could be like that. Maybe she could teach me? What am I thinking? I either murder her or I do not.

I remember the sensation of her palm against my fingers, soft and warm. Damn, she is too perfect.

After we order, she talks excitedly about the workplace revolution and I feel myself getting swept away at the prospect. I encourage her to bring everyone together. I even propose a few solutions myself. She beams at me and I really don't want to kill her.

Then her thumb slips on the end of her fork and it plummets back down onto her plate of lasagna.

"There is one thing that I have to ask you." She doesn't look up at me.

"Yes?" I say.

"You see…" She makes a wide motion with the fork-dropping hand. "The thing is, sometimes these protests can lead to criminal records. I don't want…"

I laugh. I have never been caught. What do I have to

worry about? I lean in closer to her confused face. "It's alright. I'm not afraid."

A smile creeps onto her face. "Wow that's amazing! I didn't think..."

"You didn't think I could be so brazen? I'll pretend I don't feel that little sting. Listen, our talk earlier today and our conversation now have convinced me that something needs to change. I am not going to let the threat of a cell stop me now." Is she buying it? I wipe my mouth with my napkin and clear my throat. "Besides, I have had a brush with the opposite side of the law."

Her eyes bulge. She's good; I believe her astonishment for a moment.

"Yes," I say. "I may or may not have called in a 911 emergency without an emergency."

"Oh," she says and she picks up her fork again.

We eat in silence for a while and without much to occupy our mouths; we finish eating pretty fast. My left hand hovers over my phone, just in case, but my girl is still gone. I can hardly keep from hurling the spaghetti sitting in my stomach. I decide that Clarice has to die as I give her cash and she pays with her card. She hasn't asked any follow-up questions to my emergency call story. It's very strange. I'll let her try to kill me first, just to keep it on even playing fields.

"Hey." Clarice touches my right forearm. We are standing in front of the restaurant. Oh, thank God she didn't grab the left. "Can I walk you to your car? We can talk strikes along the way!"

"Sure!" I say. I can't believe I forgot. I needed her to come with me to my car in any case. I can't carry her body. But what if this is part of the company's plan? What if she is supposed to strike me in my own car? My muscles are stiff as we cross the street. What if she really is trying to be a friend? Should I kill her and kill any chance of having friend? One sight of a weapon, I decide, and she's finished.

We approach the ridiculous concrete stairs. Familiarity waves through me. Clarice's voice cuts through the wave.

"You sure are parked far away." Clarice's hand is in the air. Something in her palm glints in the streetlights.

Before I can think I make one long swipe with my right hand from my left forearm. Clarice stops my right hand. My knife cuts into the side of her neck. She is bleeding, but so am I. Her house key, attached to a lanyard is driven into my right wrist, and my own blood trickles down my arm into the grass. My hand goes limp and lets the knife fall. She strikes at me and I grab her other hand with my left, but she easily overpowers me and I fall backward. Her cold palms squeeze my neck. I feel around for my knife. Anger wracks her draining face.

"You will die!" Clarice says. Her blood flows everywhere, hot on my skin and into my mouth. I find the edge of the blade and grab it. It's teeth dig into my palm. I reposition it. Clarice's hands are going limp. I slam the knife into the side of her neck and twist. I hear veins pop and sinews burst. Blood boils out of her mouth and her eyes threaten to jump out of their sockets.

This is the best one yet. The mutilation is even better while they are alive! I push her off me, and the back of her head smashes on the concrete landing at the foot of the stairs. My heart races with joy. Now to just get the body to my secret place! I can't resist a little repositioning before the body goes into rigor mortis. Her arm would look so nice at her side. Oh, it feels so good again!

I hear a shuffling of footsteps above me. No! I need

to rush the body. I didn't anticipate killing her so soon. I put both of my arms underneath her armpits, my left hand grabs my right and even though it hurts to rip my wrist, it is worth it. I hardly feel the tearing in my carpals.

Ting!

I stumble back. Clarice slides from my grasp. Is my girl there? The shuffling is getting closer. It won't be too long. *Ting! Ting!* A flood of the tiny noises takes over the air. Just check. I can just check to see if it is my girl. It will only take an infinitesimal fraction of a second! I wipe my hands on my pants and pull out my phone from my back pocket. The phone glows with welcome for me. It has been so long! I open her video feed.

She's just outside her apartment! Her face lit with the light of her phone is beautiful. It's worried. She is hesitating at the top of her stairs again. Oh, I love her. The view falls away from her face. No! It circles and hits the concrete and lands. I see. I see my bloody hand wrapped around my phone. I look up. No.

At the top of the stairs, she is standing there. Her beautiful mouth hangs open and she is unconscious of how her sweatshirt slides down off her shoulder. No.

I look down. I see her phone. The case is black. *Black?* I ask myself. *Is it really black?*

"Clarice!" she shouts. I hate her scream.

"Stop!" I yell at her. "Stop! Go back inside!" This can't be happening. She cannot be disobeying me. She cannot have a black phone case. That cannot be the device through which I have been watching her all this time. Pink! Pink should have been the color!

I watch, as my girl does absolutely nothing at the top of the stairs but gape at me. I start up the stairs. Killing her would be everything. I have no reason to believe things will ever change, even if I get better.

She trembles, still planted at the top of the stairs. "No, Clarice." Tears bubble over the bottoms of her eyes and her hand comes up to her mouth. Her hand is clunky with the cast that was just put on it. "You killed her," she says.

I can hardly contain the rage inside me. How dare she disobey me? I race up now.

"You killed Clarice!" she says. "You killed her!"

I charge at her with my hand, ready to take her by the throat. She ducks and knocks me back. I fall and don't hit the ground yet. I have time in the air to gain momentum before my neck smashes into the stairs. I can't get enough air. I am telling my diaphragm to expand, but nothing happens. All my senses go, all my control. She doesn't fall. I do. I fall away like that rock on the cliff.

I knew she would save me.

THE END

Contributor's bio:

Growing up in Ohio, USA, was not particularly hard for Varonica Chaney, and so she can only attribute the stories that she writes to either boredom or the entirely natural human need for violence that is in all of us. Varonica knows which source she really thinks her stories come from. She invites you to decide that for yourself. Yep, other than those two sources, you will find nothing in her life that will explain what she writes.

But if you really want to know about her life, all right, she gets it. She is the proud wife to her husband, and parent to her dog; and they all live together in perfect harmony in South Korea. Except for the cat. The evil cat, Daisy, Varonica takes care of for fear of death.

Varonica's husband doesn't know, but the diabolical feline sneaks into their bedroom and whispers of all the nefarious, and sometimes boring, deeds she has committed in her other lives. With hot tuna breath coursing down the back of Varonica's neck, she doesn't have much choice in her life anymore. She tirelessly works to bring her cat's stories to life. For more of Daisy's deeds or Varonica's work, check out her fledging blog at: inkfeats.blogspot.kr. Please visit, for Varonica's sake.

That is uh... Currently working on her master's degree in English Literature, Varonica Chaney spends most of her days in educational bliss! There is nothing to worry about! Nothing at all!

THUNDER ROAD
Written by Marian Finch (Lady Marian)

Thunder rolls, lightning strikes
Perfect weather for me tonight
No other vehicles in my sights
But just in case, I've dimmed headlights.
About another hour's drive
Lots to do when I arrive
The car's sweet odor is now a funk
Due to my parcels in the trunk.
On my back seat lies a spade
Strong enough to dig a grave.

I came home early yesterday
And found my wife and friend at play
For better or worse, I pledged my troth
I just saw red and killed them both
I made her watch his considerable pain
As I removed his skull and exposed his brain

Removed his ears and for his guile
Gave him a permanent Joker's smile.
Next I turned to my loving wife
She begged and screamed for her life.

By then I'd really lost the plot
But she was deserving of all she got
Because she liked to share her charms
I set to work and removed her arms.
The legs she was keen on spreading wide
I detached and placed just to the side.
In refuse sacks, all nice and neat
I place mixed body parts, including feet
Filled my trunk up with the load
Now I'm traveling Thunder Road.

GAME ON
Written by Marian Finch (Lady Marian)

Shhh... Don't cry, I'll tell you why
You can spread your wings and I'll let you fly.
I'll release the ropes that tie your wrists
your tiny hands balled into fists.
I can't deny that it's been a pleasure
The memories I hope you'll treasure.
the times that you have felt my knife,
The cuts that had you pleading for your life,
the nights you spent in my embrace
face down, the pillow wet 'neath your face.
Such a feisty fun type of girl
I remember our first night really well...
You were unlocking your car
at hide and seek I raised the bar,
you didn't see me waiting there
for a girl like you with golden hair.
My approach was in no way formal
but for me, it was quite normal
though not conventional, I suppose
Chloroform over your mouth and nose.
This is a special day, you see...
our two year anniversary.
To inject some fun on our special day
I've devised a game for us to play
I'm so excited! Don't be scared...
If you complete it you will be spared...
You will head off through the wood
that I prepared because I could,
with lots of things like arrows set
to fire if you don't watch your step.
Somewhere I dug a leaf-strewn hole
With vertical knives to pierce your soul

I'll give you a five-minute start
before I join in for my part.
If you reach the end without a hitch
then you will have your freedom, bitch...
But I am coming for the kill
Happy anniversary! What a thrill!

SACRIFICE OF INNOCENCE
Written by Marian Finch (Lady Marian)

At the first sign of womanhood they gave her to the Beast...
The lust and violence of Hell then unleashed.
Held in a silent and petrified vice, chosen maiden to the blood sacrifice.
He loved his soft virgin in his own heinous way,
and her pure skin was branded in case she should stray.
Her body was used for perversion and pleasure,
euphoria and pain both in equal measure.
No respite was she granted, screaming in vain,
Her purity desecrated again and again.
The Beast had a purpose for this woman child
Gentle of nature and innocence beguiled.
The torture and vileness would never cease
until her womb accepted the damned seed of the Beast.
Oh, obsidian creature that, when it was born
would leave minds in no doubt that it was the loathsome Beast's spawn.
In time her soft flesh to its nature succumbed...
her mind was now gone, any feeling was numbed.
The Beast was victorious as her belly swelled –
He would have his base son to release on the world.

Contributor's bio:
Marian Finch lives in Essex, England, and was born in London. She started writing poetry as a child. She now writes mostly dark poetry, although sometimes writes in other genres. She is married and has two grown-up children.

Graveyard Girls

Other HellBound Books Titles
Available at: www.hellboundbookspublishing.com

The Amnesia Girl!

Filled with copious amounts of black humor, Gerri R. Gray's first published novel is an offbeat adventure story that could be described as One Flew over the Cuckoo's Nest meets Thelma and Louise.

Flashback to 1974. Farika is a lovely young woman who wakes up one day to find herself a patient in a bizarre New York City psychiatric asylum. She has no idea who she is, and possesses no memories of where she came from nor how she got there.

Fearing for her life after being attacked by a berserk girl with over one hundred personalities and a vicious nurse with sadistic intentions, the frightened amnesiac teams up with an audacious lesbian with a comically unbalanced mind, and together they attempt a daring escape.

But little do they know that a long strange journey into an even more insane world filled with a multitude of perilous predicaments and off-kilter individuals are waiting for them on the outside. Farika's weird reality crumbles when she finally discovers who, and what, she really is!

Gray Skies of Dismal Dreams

Prepare for an excursion into a gloomy world of shadows, where the days are never sunlit and blithe, and where the nights are wrapped in endless nightmares.

No happy endings or silver linings are found in the clouds that fill these gray skies.

But what you will find, gathered in one volume, are the darkest of poems and tales of horror, waiting to take your mind on a journey into realms of the uncheerful and the unholy.

An amazingly surreal collection of short stories and the darkest of poetry, all interspersed with stunning graveyard photographs taken by the multitalented author herself - an absolute must for every bookshelf!

Savages

Christina Bergling

An incredibly touching, yet unapologetically brutal trek through a post-apocalyptic wasteland of a civilization that once was.

Two strangers, reliant upon each other for survival face impossible odds, driven by little more than the primitive desire to live, are hunted by vicious hoardes of those who were once human - *savages...*

Mindless and murdering savages. Are they zombies? Are they still human? Whatever the other survivors have become, they no longer speak; they only kill and live like animals.

Parker and Marcus navigate through the ruins and battle through these lingering savages with no answers, searching for the last strain of humanity. Until one discovery changes everything...

The infant's cry shatters their already destroyed world. For Parker, the babe invokes the ghosts of her dead husband and sons. For Iraq war veteran Marcus, the child embodies his hope and gives him innocence to protect. For both, they struggle to determine if faded notions like romance can even still exist in this bleak, dying world.

In this grim post-apocalyptic portrait, the survivors face the horror of not knowing what happened to the world around them as they question whether humanity was ever human at all.

The Cabin Sessions

A confronting, hard-hitting, dark psychological thriller told with acid wit. Themes of abuse are explored through minds distorted by fear and corrupted by hatred and delusion; this is a tale in which redemption is gained in unexpected ways.

It's Christmas Eve when hapless musician Adam Banks stands on the bridge over the river that cleaves the isolated village of Burton. A storm is rolling into the narrow mountain pass. He thinks of turning back. Instead, he resolves to fulfil his obligation to perform the guest spot at The Cabin Sessions. He should be looking forward to it, but fear stirs when he opens the door on the Cabin's incense-choked air

Philip Stone is already there, brooding. He observes with a ruthless eye the regulars, from sleazy barmaid Hannah Fisher, to old crone Cynthia Morgan. Meanwhile, Philip's sister, Eva, prepares to take a bath. It¿s a ritual - she's a breath holder. At twenty-eight, Eva has returned to Burton to finish the business of her past, as memories begin to surface concerning one fateful day by the river and the innocence of her beloved brother...

No Rest For The Wicked

A modern day ghost story with its skeletons buried firmly in the past.

From beyond the grave, a murderous wife seeks to complete her revenge on those who betrayed her in life; a powerless domestic still fears for her immortal soul while trying to scare off anyone who comes too close; and the former plantation master - a sadistic doctor who puts more faith in the teachings of de Sade than the Bible When Eric and Grace McLaughlin purchase Greenbrier Plantation, their dreams are just as big as those who have tried to tame the place before them. But, the doctor has learned a thing or two over his many years in the afterlife, is putting those new skills to the test, and will go to great lengths in order to gain the upper hand. While Grace digs into the death-filled history of her new home, Eric soon becomes a pawn of the doctor's unsavory desires and rapidly growing power, and is hell-bent on stopping her.

Biddy Trott

'If Biddy knows no rest, then none shall…'

A tragedy born of malice and evil, a tortured body and soul. The townsfolk of Royal Rumney have a conscience, a secret that tears away at their sanity.

Any soul shall be offered up in place of the damned;

'And ever the church bells tell a lie, is Biddy who comes and another will die.

Set in eighteenth century England in the small market town of Royal Rumny, Biddy Trott, is a Gothic Horror novella with tragedy at its core.

A young girl, falsely blamed for a fire which destroyed the town and killed many, is hunted down, tortured and killed gruesomely, with no conscience.

Lord Abner Alexander, a member of the elite and privileged, travels to the town in search of some peace and respite from his very bawdy and raucous lifestyle.

The town seems pleasant enough and the people welcoming, although unyielding where their dark and harrowing past is concerned…

Shopping List

A simply superlative collection of spine-tingling horror from the very best minds in the business!

We decided upon the shopping list theme for this particular volume as an antithesis to those wildly successful writers (they know who they are) of whom it is often said *'we would read their damned shopping list if they published it!'*

Well, we have given twenty-one of the hottest authors in the independent horror scene the unique opportunity to have their own shopping lists read by you - along with their most terrifying tales of course!

Stories of gut-wrenching terror from:

Kathy Dinisi, Robert Over, Christopher O'Halloran, Eric W. Burgin, Russ Gartz, Mark Slada, Jeff Baker, Tim Miller, Nick Swain, JC Raye, Jovan Jones, Ben Stevens, David F. Gray, Brandon Cracraft, M.S. Swift, Kevin Holton, David Owain Hughes, Bertram Allan Mullin, Jeff C. Stevenson, Sebastian Crow and S.E. Rise

**A HellBound Books LLC
Publication**

http://www.hellboundbookspublishing.com

Printed in the United States of America